Eve's separation from Ian is amicable, her daughter Mel is a high-flier, and her son Ben, the apple of her eye, is the local charmer. She has a congenial job, good friends, and all the time in the world to improve her tennis. But passion is no respecter of plans, and Eve's chaste tranquillity, like Ben's boyhood teddy, is about to go out of the window with a vengeance. Because when sons grow up, mothers must too . . . that's when it's time for binning the bears.

THAT WAS THEN

Sarah Harrison

PARAGON

CHIVERS PRESS
BATH

First published 1998
by
Hodder & Stoughton
This Large Print edition published by
Chivers Press
by arrangement with
Hodder Headline PLC
2000

ISBN 0 7540 2243 9

British Library Cataloguing in Publication Data available

Printed and bound in Great Britain by
REDWOOD BOOKS, Trowbridge, Wiltshire

for
the Adam and Eve Muse

CHAPTER ONE

It was a tough decision.

Should I expend vital energy raising a hand to summon the waiter? Make the super-human effort to walk across the white-hot concrete to the bar? Or plunge into the tepid, sapphire water and perch on one of the submerged stools on the far side of the pool? Each had its pros and cons. The Arab waiter—whose sensitivity to minute movements was as finely tuned as any Sotheby's auctioneer—would be at my side in seconds, but the drink he brought would be warm by the time I'd raised it to my lips. If I braved—and survived—the fifty-metre endurance test to fetch it myself, the ice would remain intact for a minute or so, and I could sip it in the steamy shade of the palm thatch with the fans turning gently above my head.

But if I lolloped like a seal into that cool, crystalline, chemically enhanced water it would be no trouble whatever to glide to the bar-rail and wallow in comfort as I sipped a cocktail that was all the more luxurious for being taboo beyond the five-star confines of the Miramar Hotel.

Now *that* would be very heaven . . . if it wasn't for the sharks.

For it went without saying that the moment the seat of my chainstore one-piece hit the stool they would slide from their lounger-lairs and cut smoothly through the water towards me. And that no matter what I did in the way of studying the menu, staring reflectively at the overhead video, or tilting my face, eyes closed, to the sun, they would be there, waiting to ruin my day with their bland yet insinuating conversation, their well-kept smiles and speculative eyes.

No. I felt on the ground for my sunglasses, rested them on the oil-slick that was the bridge of my nose and caught the eye of the barman.

I don't know why the sharks bothered me so much. They weren't all that predatory—basking rather than great whites—international businessmen passing through this man-made oasis, on short contracts or en route to somewhere else. And why, I continually asked myself, would they be in the least interested in me anyway? Even twelve days of doing dignified lengths, and walking miles on the treadmill in the hotel's air-conditioned gym hadn't turned me into Jane Fonda. I still looked exactly what I was: a nice, unthreatening, not unattractive middle-aged Englishwoman with a touch of cellulite and the foreshadowing of the odd varicose vein—the sort of woman who, while looking fine *au naturelle* looks immeasurably better with eyeliner, and fully dressed. Common sense dictated that I had little to fear from the sharks. Nonetheless, I couldn't be doing with them. For one thing I no longer had the social tools to deal with the situation they presented. I wasn't part of their free-ranging, high-spending, big-talking world of work. My job at home, in a provincial English auction house, was scarcely at the cutting edge of international commerce. And my comfortable small town social life, seen from here, was like the dark side of the moon. I had nothing to say to them. I lacked confidence and conversation.

I also lacked the inclination. It was too much like work. All I wanted was to be left alone with my postcards, my factor fifteen and my freshly-squeezed lemon juice. In my newly-single, separate state, still partially protected by my obsolete wedding ring, I was content.

*   *   *

I was visiting our daughter, on my own, something that would have been unthinkable two years ago, and it was turning out to be more fun than I could possibly have imagined. I wandered the hotel like a child in a toyshop, trying this and that, ducking back to my room to watch films and make a mess of the bathroom, using the gym, braving the *soukh*, strolling on the corniche . . . Even on one occasion, when Mel had an evening meeting, booking supper on a *dhow* in the harbour—alone. The very last thing I wanted was the attention of some expense-account lothario from an oil company who was missing his wife. I'd got the T-shirt, and the long-service award. All that was behind me. Jo, my colleague at Bouviers, had attended assertiveness counselling during a post-man slump, and learned the injunction: 'Celibate? Celebrate.' I'd decided it was going to be my motto.

*   *   *

The waiter's shadow fell across my face. 'Your usual, madam?'
    'Yes—no,' I said. 'I'd like a Pimms, please.'
    'Pimms? Certainly madam.'
    'Plenty of ice.'
    'Of course.'
    'And some deep-fried potato skins.'

'Potato skins, yes madam. Salsa or sour cream?'

'Sour cream, please.'

He drifted away, dark, dry and cool in the glaring white heat. It was one o'clock, the build-up had begun. In an hour's time only the diehards would be left around the pool, and most of them would be treading water, or lying tranced beneath a carefully husbanded spinney of parasols. It was August, low season, when the fabulously wealthy locals kept to the air-conditioned shade of their houses, and the dirt poor stood like ragged storks on the corniche wielding the hosepipes which made the desert blossom as the rose. There were few holidaymakers here at this time, it was simply too hot. The temperature for the next several hours would be forty-five degrees, the pool surround unbearable to tender English feet, the effort of putting on sunblock only possible because the alternative was to roast alive.

Mind you, one thing I could always do was tan. From a child I'd had the kind of skin in which the natural pigmentation simply bloomed into a golden brown as all around me more delicate skins reddened angrily. I was more careful here, naturally, but I was still determined to return home a colour that would proclaim unequivocally: Holiday Abroad. A clear understanding of the carcinogenic properties of sunlight did not deter me. I was of a generation that grew up believing— no, *knowing*—that any age, type or quantity of flesh looked better with a tan. And as to wrinkles, well, one might wind up looking like a prune at ninety, but sunbathing produced an unbeatable appearance of health and vitality along the way.

So I would not be retiring. And neither,

unfortunately, would most of the sharks. These were men accustomed to seize the day—between meetings, on stopovers, during flight delays—they weren't going to be driven from their natural hunting grounds by a bit of old global warming.

My Pimms arrived, and with it a basket of potato skins, gleaming gold on a bed of frosty iceberg lettuce, and a glass dish of sour cream sprinkled with fresh green . . . Riches.

I yanked across another parasol to give me complete shade, and winched up the back of my lounger. Before so much as lifting my glass I put on dark glasses, the better to keep the sharks under observation.

I identified them by their reading matter. To my right, at a distance of some ten towel-widths there was a John Grisham and his chum, an *FT*. On the left, a Japanese motor magazine. Further round on the corner, near the bar, was a Bill Bryson and a *Bridges of Madison County*, who I suspected were an item. In the other direction, beyond the first two were a sprinkling of singles—a Ken Follett, a *Newsweek*, an *Alan Clarke's Diaries* and a couple of laptops. On the far side of the bar were a handful of non-readers: immaculately suited Arabs, drinking iced coffee and talking in rich, guttural tones like the bubbling-up of oil.

The music from the pool bar changed from international easy listening to the strident wailing of indigenous pop—the bar staff's happy hour.

I drank and nibbled. The half-melted lozenges of ice in my glass tinkled feebly as the burning breath of thousands of miles of desert stirred the fringes of the parasols.

Uh-oh. One of the laptops—bulging, brown and

hairy—got up, slipped his feet into thongs and began the sweltering trek to the bar. He paused at the end of my lounger.

'Hello again.'

'Good afternoon.'

'That looks nice.'

'It is.' Why was it that to have one's food commented on when eating alone was so embarrassing? I wished he would go away.

'Hot enough for you?' he asked, gazing up at the sky.

'I like the heat.'

'I can see that.' I couldn't tell whether he was commenting on my stamina or my stupidity. 'On holiday?'

This was my cue to tell him it was none of his business, but of course I didn't. Instead: 'Yes,' I said meekly. 'I'm visiting my daughter.'

'She's working over here?'

'She's with Ankatex.'

He shook his head. 'I hate to sound corny, but you don't look old enough to have a daughter working in an oil company.'

'You're right, that is corny,' I said, but spoilt it as ever by smiling.

He chuckled, his self-esteem intact. 'I'm off to get some of what you've got.'

I watched as he sashayed away, arms held away from sides, his already broad, spatulate feet like flippers in their spongey black thongs. Why did men of his age and build feel the need to wear the smallest of cozzies, barely more than a posing pouch . . . ?

I ate most of the potato skins, and reclined the lounger again. Boldly, I pushed aside one of the

6

parasols with my foot and felt the heavy smack of the early afternoon on my face. At home the only comparable sensation would have been bending too close to the open oven door when checking the joint. I felt for my glass and rested it on my chest, just above the swimsuit line. Condensation mixed with sweat and cut a trickling path through the suntan oil. Ten minutes and I'd take the plunge.

*   *   *

'You're barmy, you know that?'

I shielded my eyes against the glare. 'Hello darling.'

'How can you stand it?'

'Very easily. It'll be over all too soon.'

'Christ . . .' Mel sat in a semi-circle of shade on the lounger next to me. 'Talk about mad dogs and Englishmen.'

'I'm happy,' I assured her. 'What are you doing here? Time off for good behaviour?'

'More or less. We're not that pushed and Gerry thought I should spend time with you.'

'Did he?' Gerry was Mel's boss, a cold-eyed Cockney taskmaster. 'That was good of him.'

'He must be softening me up for something.'

He'd have his work cut out, I thought, looking fondly at my daughter. At twenty-six she was a more commanding presence than I would ever be. Even here, in this heat, she looked exactly as she had done in the Ankatex head office off Piccadilly, as she always did: cool, pale and smart. She was one of those women who are completely at ease in their good clothes, who don't suffer from the overwhelming need to remove their tights and high heels the minute they get behind closed doors. She didn't get this from me.

In spite of her observations on the heat, her pale aquamarine cap-sleeved shift with mandarin collar was uncreased, and she wore sheer tights with her low-heeled pumps. Her hair, which she wore in one of those sleek, side-parted Twiggy bobs, looked as if she'd just come out of the hairdressers, though she only went once a month. With her rather sharp features and strong jaw she was no beauty, but she knew all about presentation.

'What would you like to do this afternoon?' she asked.

'I don't know. I'd planned on just loafing around here, but now you're free ... What do you suggest?'

'I wouldn't mind a swim myself. We could go to the beach club.'

I said: 'Darling, you don't want to go yomping all the way to the beach club in this heat ...'

'You mean you don't want to. And who mentioned yomping, we'd take a taxi.'

'I know, but ...'

'Yes, yes, I know what you mean.' She gazed round restlessly. 'But I don't want you to feel bored and neglected when you've only got a couple of days left.'

'I couldn't, possibly.'

'OK. Look—' she got up, jingling her room key in one hand—'If you're happy I'm going to go to the gym for half an hour. Then I'll come down for a swim.'

'Fine. Couldn't be happier.'

She dropped a kiss and walked away in the direction of the hotel: every inch the young executive, to which the key dangling from one finger added a touch of unintentional sauciness.

I picked up the Queen of the Bonkbusters. Vicarious thrills were just about my drop these days—good clean smut, safely embalmed in print. Glancing covertly through my shades I saw the laptop taking delivery of an heroic club sandwich and fries. He chatted animatedly to the waiter—I knew the trick, it made a person alone look less of a saddo—but when the waiter had gone he shook salt, sprinkled dressing, tucked his napkin into his posing pouch and ate wth gusto. In between mouthfuls he stared unashamedly at the pool and everyone round it. When he looked my way, though he couldn't possibly have caught my eye, I could have sworn he lifted his fork in a cheery salute.

I read, then dozed—it must have been the Pimms. I awoke to find Mel next to me again, dropping her towel and other bits and pieces on the lounger next door.

'Didn't mean to disturb you. I just thought I'd leave these here in case there was an afternoon rush.'

'You're joking,' I mumbled groggily. 'In these temperatures.'

'Well quite. But some eligible hunk might come and stake his claim, you never know your luck.'

'Get away . . .'

Strangely, in view of her own fiercely independent single state, Mel persisted in the view that I needed a man. I couldn't believe I seemed such a sad and lonely creature when that certainly wasn't how I saw myself. I was quite shockingly content. I had moved into a state of placid busyness, revolving round home, work, family (well, Ben) and an enjoyably undemanding social round. I was untroubled by my lack of any sort of involvement with the opposite sex, in fact I positively welcomed it. My life felt choc-a-bloc with happy possibilities, I was like a schoolgirl once more but without the hormonal uproar.

It wasn't that there were no men in my life, but that they had their place, and it wasn't the same as mine. The jovial husbands of friends, big servers in mixed doubles, buyers and sellers at auctions—all were safely compartmentalised. I had become an expert in turning any nascent flirtation into a generally accepted joke. I'd learned that when it came to people you knew, the best way to draw seduction's sting was to seem to respond with such boisterous enthusiasm that dishonourable intentions—if there had genuinely been any in the first place—were nipped in the bud by anxiety. Not that it happened often, and scarcely at all these days, now that the message had got across.

I was grateful for that. I had a born-again dread of upheaval, of strong emotion, of all the sticky inconvenience of sex, of the disturbance of my easy-going, easy-listening existence. After the attrition of marital breakdown, even a relatively amicable one like ours, I had just about succeeded in eliminating stress from my life. I had recreated a mid-life boarding school for myself complete with chums, naughty boys, staff both kindly and curmudgeonly, outings, clubs, prep, and a bedroom as chaste and cosy as any junior dorm. As my son would have said: excellent.

Mel was fiddling about tying a bandanna round her head and putting some sort of elastic support on her knee. She wore grey cycling shorts, and an outsize blue T-shirt which could not quite conceal the fact that she was also wearing one of those crotch-slicing leotards over the shorts. She looked dismayingly fit—every bit of her seemed braced and tensile. Nothing sagged, or even trembled. For a session in the gym she had of course removed her make-up: she was far too confident to be vain.

'Back in a mo,' she said.

'Have fun.'

The gym was on the first floor of the fitness centre, its floor-to-ceiling smoked-glass windows overlooking the pool. I watched Mel's taut backview as she went in search of quite unnecessary self-improvement.

Lazily, I thought: in the days when my legs didn't rub together at the top I didn't appreciate it. Absence of flab, like youth itself, was wasted on the young. Forget job satisfaction, fulfilling relationships, the wisdom of experience—nothing, I decided happily, did so much for a woman's sense of self-worth as that precious sliver of daylight between the thighs.

*   *   *

I now faced another hard decision. Mel was coming back for a swim, and it would be nice to accompany her when she did. On the other hand I was rapidly melting and needed to cool off. So it would make sense to go into the pool now, at once, in order to have built up a good head of steam by the time she reappeared in about half an hour. I longed to be in the water, but could scarcely face the thirty seconds of physical activity involved in getting there.

I eventually managed by using a strategy

described to me by Ben when he was doing karate as a teenager: don't think of the plank/brick/concrete slab—think of the other side and move straight towards it.

So I thought hard of swimming, removed my shades, and hurtled in, taking only one stride on the red-hot tiles between lounger and pool.

And oh, the bliss of being weightless . . .! How lissom, how supple, how youthful a body felt when supported by thousands of gallons of water . . . I could almost imagine there *was* still a space between my thighs. If all social intercourse could be conducted in deep water what a grand thing that would have been . . .

Unfortunately, in deep water was where I was, in more ways than one. While talking to Mel I'd stopped tracking the sharks, but as I surfaced and started on a first length of breaststroke I heard a plop, and felt the nudging series of small waves that indicated someone else was taking a dip.

He, of course, was doing the crawl, and pretty soon lapped me going in the same direction. Determined not to be put off my stroke I swam on. It was the *Alan Clarke*, who looked the sort to regard anything under fifty lengths as a waste of time. He said 'Hi,' as he came up for air alongside, cutting through the water like a U-boat: a turbo-charged shark. The greeting was reassuringly curt, on the other hand he didn't have to give one at all—he was establishing contact between us tough early-afternoon types. Bobbing in his wake, I struck off at a tangent towards the bar. There was time, I calculated, for a quick drink before he even realised I was gone. I sat with my back to the pool nursing a second glass of Pimms, and picking at cashew nuts.

Ingrate that I was, I thought fondly of my flat on the seafront in Littelsea. Even as I sat here Ben would be embarking on the series of cosmetic measures designed to wipe out all trace of what he'd been up to during my fortnight's absence. Sheets would be changed, windows flung open, floors imperfectly mopped and lavatories scrubbed to the droning accompaniment of the washing machine and dishwasher. An inordinate number of bulging black binbags would be heaped by the front door for transportation down to the wheelie-bin, and at least one trip to the municipal tip undertaken. By the time I got back it would be perfectly possible for us to resume the usual no-questions-asked collusion which left our happy relationship undisturbed.

'Hello again.'

I'd been miles away and I jumped slightly, so that my teeth banged on the edge of my glass. It was the *Alan Clarke*. He was American, so he deserved at least a few brownie points for reading the diary of an eccentric, classbound English politician.

'Oh, hello.'

'Not many of us around, are there?'

'No, not in this . . .'

'Nice to have the pool empty though. Great for lengths.' Late forties, solidly built, hair pepper and salt and receding but cut sensibly short.

'Yes, not that I . . . I'm just a fun swimmer.'

He signalled the barman. 'Beer please.' Looked back at me. 'As opposed to a—?'

'I don't know. A fitness swimmer.'

'You look pretty fit to me.' He said it nicely, with

13

only the smallest and most acceptable hint of ingratiation, so I let it pass. 'How long are you over here for?' he added, taking delivery of the beer and taking a swig directly from the bottle.

'I go back the day after tomorrow.'

'You do? What, to England?'

'How did you guess?'

I suppose it was unwise to essay even the slightest levity, because this prompted far more of a laugh than it warranted.

'Right . . .' he chuckled. 'Right.'

I slurped on my Pimms. Where was Mel when I needed her?

'Can I buy you a bite to eat?' he asked. He pronounced it 'bite ter eat' like a character in a film or a popular song. It seemed to invite a scripted response, a 'why not?' or a 'sure', but I was now on red alert.

'No thanks, I've had lunch.' My 'lunch' sounded prim and pompous after his 'bite ter eat', but then I wasn't out to impress. Just the opposite. I drained my glass and put it down on the bar.

He nodded at it. 'Would you care for another of those?'

'No thank you. Actually—' I glanced foolishly at my empty wrist—'I must be gone.'

'Really?'

'Yes. Shopping, you know . . .' What was I saying? But he lifted a hand and turned his head aside, allowing the perfect reasonableness of my excuse.

'Those folks back home—they cast a long shadow.'

'They do. So if you don't mind—'

I slid off my stool, and he—with almost comical

14

politeness since we were both up to our armpits in water, did the same, and held out his hand. 'Charles McNally. It was nice meeting you.'

'And you.'

I left him at a disadvantage and swam off.

*   *   *

Up in our room on the twentieth floor I peeled off my swimsuit and threw it in the basin before wrapping myself in a towelling robe. Then I sat on the window seat and gazed wistfully down at the pool, which I only had a short time left to enjoy, and which I'd effectively denied myself till further notice.

I supposed it was a function of middle age that I'd had to find an excuse which removed me utterly from the scene of the perceived threat. I couldn't just say 'I won't, thanks anyway' and continue with what I was doing. I had to be away, elsewhere. Out of harm's reach.

All the same I couldn't bring myself to regret it. What if lunch had led to dinner . . . ? It was all too much of an effort, too tricky and unpredictable. I was no longer in the market for the hassle.

I could just see Charles McNally's head and shoulders at the bar. There were no more than six other people round the pool now. On the lounger next to where I'd been lay Mel's towel. I tried to remember if she'd left a purse or a handbag for me to keep an eye on.

Fortunately, at that moment I saw her come out of the fitness centre and walk round the edge of the pool. She'd changed into her severe black bikini, which was more like a crop-top and pants. On

15

reaching her towel she stopped, but not for long. She put her sports bag under the lounger, slipped out of her sandals and dived in, storming through the water to the far end with an enviably powerful freestyle action. There was no indication that she even wondered where I was.

Mildly miffed, I had a shower, got changed and tidied the room. This was something else that exasperated Mel.

'Mother,' she'd lectured me, 'you're in a five-star international hotel. There are battalions of workers paid to do that for you. Take advantage. Enjoy.'

'It's just habit.'

'Come on, you and Ben don't exactly qualify for a *Hello!* feature back home.'

I had tried to explain that there was something satisfying about re-ordering the micro-environment of a hotel room, that it responded to one's efforts in a way that the family home never could. Mel banged her fist against her brow.

'But why would you even want to try? Look at it this way, if there's not enough for the cleaners to do the hotel might decide to cut down and you'll have deprived people of their jobs and contributed to the erosion of the local economy.'

Anyway, I tidied the room.

Remembering Mel's comment about Ben and me made me realise how much I was looking forward to seeing him. This fortnight had been wonderful, a complete change, the sort of holiday I should never in a million years have arranged for myself, even had I been able to afford it. I was a little ashamed that when Mel had organised and paid for so much I'd been mildly homesick the whole time.

16

The thing was, Ben and I were pals. Mel herself had often remarked that over the past couple of years he and I had formed an unholy alliance. She also said that I ought to be a bit less accommodating or he'd never leave home, but this advice was predicated on the false assumption that I wanted him to go. Mel, with her steely ambition and self-imposed work ethic, seemed to have achieved full independence almost the moment she started sixth-form college (and two weekend jobs) at the age of sixteen. Ben was equally bright, but nothing like as motivated. 'You and Dad always said you just wanted us to be happy,' he would remind me winningly, 'well, I am.' Since Ian and I had separated he'd become an essential part of what home meant, as indispensable to my wellbeing as Radio Four and chocolate digestives.

But as my daughter clearly wasn't missing me, I went down to the Palm Court for my customary pot of Earl Grey. The air-conditioning in the lift was so intense that my bare arms broke out in goose pimples. As I got out on the ground floor there was Charles McNally in shorts and T-shirt, with a towel round his neck, waiting to get in.

'Off to hit the mall?' he enquired pleasantly.

'Pretty soon,' I replied.

He clicked his tongue in an 'Attagirl' sort of way. 'Go get 'em.'

I went over to the desk. The people who worked here were the nicest imaginable, and the receptionist greeted me as she did everyone, as if I were her favourite guest. I knew, rationally, that this was because of my connection with Ankatex, who were putting up a team of twelve, Mel included, for an indefinite period, but that didn't

17

stop it being gratifying.

'Mrs Piercy, how are you? Did you have a nice day by the pool?'

'I did thank you.'

'I see you go back to the UK the day after tomorrow. We shall miss you.'

'I shall be sorry to go,' I lied.

'You must come and see us again.'

'That depends on whether my daughter's still here.'

'Oh yes, Miss Piercy,' said the girl admiringly, 'she's always so smart.'

I didn't know whether she meant in appearance or ability—both probably, since both were deserved—but I acknowledged the compliment on Mel's behalf.

'She's having a swim,' I said. 'I wonder if you see her in the next half an hour or so, would you tell her I'm in the Palm Court?'

'Certainly.' The girl made a note and flashed me the sweet, lustrous smile that said it was her pleasure to be of service. 'Enjoy your tea.'

The Palm Court was an Arab millionaire's no-expense-spared recreation of the Ritz in Piccadilly. Sheikh Hassad—whose lizard-eyed portrait sneered down from innumerable walls—was entranced with a notional Englishness which had never existed outside the works of P G Wodehouse or Noël Coward. In the Palm Court a balding man in a tailcoat played Ivor Novello selections at a white piano. Improbably voluptuous 'nippies' in black, with starched white headdresses served tiny cakes and crustless sandwiches on platters which at the Ritz would have been Sheffield plate but here were very probably solid silver. Plants with thick, green leaves stood about in jardinières decorated with stags and pheasants. Each rose-upholstered armchair was big enough for two people, and bore pristine lace armrests and antimacassars. The tables were walnut. Only the faint stirring of the pages of two-day-old English newspapers in the air-conditioning betrayed the Palm Court's location.

I picked up a copy of the *Telegraph* and sat down in the corner—my usual corner—from which I could keep the hotel foyer under observation, and ordered tea for one. The pianist surged into 'We'll gather lilacs'. He looked unmistakably middle eastern: neither tailcoat nor music suited him, but he was earning his daily *derum* like a true pro. I sensed a Lloyd Webber medley waiting in the wings. On my first day this would have annoyed me. On my last it was strangely pleasing, like a wave from someone waiting on the quayside . . .

I was about halfway through the crossword, the Earl Grey and a slice of coffee cake when Mel sat down next to me. She was back in her plain shift, but with flat sandals, and her newly-showered hair was scraped back off her bare face. She grimaced at my teapot and ordered lime juice with ice.

'Good swim?'

'Yes thanks, just the job. What happened to you?'

'Sorry, I got unbearably hot.'

'Oh yeah? Sitting in the shade, in the water, at the pool bar?'

'Well, you know—'

She laughed silently, fiercely. 'Yes, yes, I do know Ma. I saw you scuttle for cover the moment a personable man spoke to you.'

'You were spying on me, you rotten thing!'

19

'Didn't have to, the treadmill overlooks the pool.'

'And anyway that's not how it was at all,' I protested, aggrieved at having been so thoroughly sussed. 'I suddenly felt I wanted to freshen up and get changed.'

'Yes,' she agreed, swirling her ice cubes into a green whirlpool, glaring accusingly at me over the top. 'I was amazed how suddenly. You scuttled, Mother. I saw the whole thing.'

'There was no whole thing to see.'

'Your trouble,' she went on as though I hadn't spoken, 'is that you treat every man like a potential ravisher. It dates you that, you know.'

This was really too much. 'I'm sure it does, but then I've never tried to falsify my date.'

'Not your age, no. But your attitude. Your conditioning.'

'I can't help that. You'd be the first to say I should be "comfortable" with what I do.'

'I would.' Mel put her glass down firmly and folded her arms. 'And you're not comfortable, are you? You're absolutely determined to cut off your nose to spite your face.'

'That's not true! I'm having a wonderful time.'

'Up to a point, Lord Copper—OK,' she said, suddenly bored with taking issue with me. 'OK. Anyway . . . the others were saying we should all go out to dinner together tonight. They booked the dhow for seven-thirty, on Ankatex. Are you up for that?'

'Definitely—how sweet of them. What a treat.' I gushed because in truth I was rattled. The invitation had come too close on the heels of her criticism. It was hard to show a proper appreciation

20

of the one while still rocking in the wake of the other.

'Good,' she said. 'Look, in that case. If we're going to party this evening, and you're perfectly happy I'm going to nip up and deal with a bit of paperwork. The suggestion is that we meet in the foyer at six-thirty, how does that sound?'

'Fine by me.'

'Oh, and by the way . . .' Mel opened her bag. 'This came for you earlier, I've been carrying it about all day.'

She handed me a postcard and rose, pointing at my half-eaten cake. 'Leave some space for dinner.'

*   *   *

The postcard was from Ben. Who else? Only Ben would think of sending a postcard from England to the United Arab Emirates saying: *Riotous parties every night, case comes up next month. Hope you're having a good one, give my love to the Melon and see you and the Sheikh at Terminal Four Friday a.m. Ben XX*

The picture was one of the Ernest Shepard illustrations from *The House at Pooh Corner*— Pooh, of course, accompanied by Kanga and Rabbit. I was sure no parody was intended.

I hoped Mel hadn't read the postcard and so hadn't seen that 'Melon'. As an adolescent she had for a short while been plump. The nickname, whose origins were not in her weight problem, had been immediately banned. Its occasional use these days was regarded by her father and brother as a kind of oblique compliment to her slimness, but I knew Mel didn't see it that way.

I re-read the few words a couple of times and put the card in my bag. Knowing how long mail—even airletters—took to get here from the UK, he must have posted it on the day I left. Bless him.

*   *   *

By nine p.m. the dhow was furthest from the shore, way out by the harbour wall. We'd finished eating: a mediocre meal for which the Ankatex crowd had picked up an extortionate tab, but the food wasn't what we were paying for. A huge paper lantern of a moon, casting an endless net of stars, hung over a sea smooth as silk. The dhow didn't seem to move so much as simply to breathe, and that so gently that it was barely perceptible. The crew had lit sandalwood burners, but the sweet warm smell was edged with something sharper where sand and salt met. To our left, at the end of the pale, curving arm of the harbour wall was this city's only remaining ancient building, a turreted fort whose crumbling towers and minarets were like something from Edmund Dulac. Even the rebarbative skyscrapers of the city itself were transformed by the hour and the distance into twinkling piles of lights like fallen stars on the shoreline.

We'd all gone a bit quiet. The younger ones sat around in that relaxed, touch-happy way that the young had these days—touch without commitment, closeness without the taint of intimacy: an enviable ease.

I'd moved my chair slightly apart, and facing out across the bay. Mel threw down a tasselled cushion on the deck and sat cross-legged next to me. After a moment she said: 'You know who he is, don't you?'

'Who . . . ?'

'Charles McNally. The great white shark?'

How did she know that's how I thought of them? 'No.'

'He's a troubleshooter. Not office politics. Disasters—like Red Adair.'

'I'd never have guessed.'

I had an idea she gave me one of her despairing, sidelong smiles. 'No,' she said. 'I don't suppose you would, he doesn't go swimming in a yellow crash-hat and a flak jacket.'

Back at the hotel they were all going for more drinks in the American Bar, but I cried off for an early night. Mel came with me as far as my room and outside the door I gave her a big hug. Though her arms went round me and her hands patted my shoulders, her body felt stiff and unyielding.

'It's been so lovely, darling,' I said. 'I can never thank you enough.'

She stood back. 'You already have.'

'I can't wait to get all my photos developed and show Ben.'

'Oh yes,' she said, and I knew at once that had been the wrong thing to say. 'Ben will be pleased to see you.'

*   *   *

Drifting into sleep on the great, smooth wastes of the hotel's king-size bed I allowed myself the luxury of unashamedly looking forward to home.

And yes, Ben.

Child of my heart. Apple of my eye.

23

CHAPTER TWO

The following night at the airport we were both a little emotional. In my case it was the usual embarrassing routine—tears, snuffles, the odd audible sob. In Mel's it was the merest blurring of the edges, something only a mother would recognise. And I almost wished I didn't, for my own tears sprang partly from remorse—that I didn't care more, that no matter how grateful I was, I was glad to be going and she knew it. The glint of sadness in my daughter's eye—its restraint the more poignant for being surrounded by the jabbering and ululation of departing locals—was a devastating reproach to my shortcomings.

'Give my regards to our kid,' she said. 'And to Dad when you see him.'

'I will.'

'*If* you see him,' she added pointedly.

'You know us,' I said, 'we keep in touch.'

I noticed the slight tightening of the mouth which meant she was buttoning her lip. If we hadn't been about to say goodbye she'd have had a comment to offer on this particular aspect of my domestic arrangements. Instead, she said:

'Hope the flight's OK. It usually settles down after Bahrain.'

'I'm sure it will be fine.'

'Off you go then.' She gave me a peck on the cheek, turned, and walked briskly away from me without looking back.

For two hours afterwards in the hot departure lounge, I felt that kiss like a cool full stop on my

24

face.

*   *   *

We were delayed in Bahrain for reasons that were not vouchsafed to us. After we had all sat obediently—the Brits more obediently than some others—in serried rows in the take-off area for an hour, we were told we'd be at least another hour and that we were therefore allowed to go and amuse ourselves in the transit lounge.

I had my phone credit card number with me and decided to ring Ben and tell him about the delay, since he certainly wouldn't think to make enquiries before leaving home. I wasn't the only person with this idea, and had to wait for about twenty minutes before taking my place in the small plastic head-stall that reminded me of a commercial hairdrier.

After a couple of botched jobs I got through, only to hear Ben's recorded voice announcing that we couldn't come to the phone right now. As the beeps went I glanced at my watch—it was one thirty in the morning here, about ten p.m. in England.

'Ben,' I said, 'it's Mum. I expect you're still out somewhere. This is just to tell you that we're held up in Bahrain. They say we should get going in an hour but I'll believe it when it happens. So it looks as if we'll be at least a couple of hours late, and you'd be advised to give Heathrow a ring and check, either first thing or tonight before going to bed. OK? Ring and check. Thanks for your postcard love. See you soon. Bye.'

*   *   *

An hour and three quarters later we took off. It was the small hours, but time had ceased to mean anything. We were given a late-night snack of cold, dense cake, layered in pink and white, with tea or coffee. The film was the latest Mob movie, starring De Niro, Pacino, or Garcia—possibly all three. I didn't put the headphones on—I couldn't face that much casual brutality. But I wasn't sleepy either, and although I opened my book my eye kept being drawn up to the ghastly goings-on on the screen. Men in suits garrotted other men in suits, or drilled them full of holes in restaurants, so that soup and spaghetti sauce mixed colourfully with the blood and guts. One fat man had a fork poked into his eye. A glamorous woman dabbed at the gore on her dress with a paper napkin. The lack of sound contributed to the gruesome humour of it all. It was the sort of film that Ben and his friends loved: total gross-out.

I had a window seat. On my right, between me and the aisle, were two young Arab women in long black coats, like soutanes, and white headscarves. They watched the film with avid attention, headsets over the scarves. They didn't speak, they didn't flinch, they certainly didn't laugh. It was impossible to tell what they made of it. Were they horrified? Disapproving? Turned on? I began to get a stiff neck glancing from my unturned pages, to the screen, to these two grave, sallow profiles.

The cabin staff came round with thin grey blankets and eye masks, and I decided to make a determined effort to sleep. It was as wretchedly uncomfortable as ever, but I must have dozed a bit, because time passed. At some point the flashing

26

screens went quiet and the lights were dimmed. Every time I turned over I saw the two Arab women still impassive, still wide awake, still listening to something on their headsets. Their calmness was comforting.

Booming along, several miles up over southern Europe I felt curiously close to both my children, as though I were the apex of a huge triangle: Mel, just beginning to wake behind the white curtains and tinted glass of the Hotel Miramar ... Ben, profoundly asleep, wherever he was ... and me, up above the clouds, the fragile and inadequate link between the two.

But as the window-blinds began to be rimmed in light and the clatterings of a northern dawn sounded from the galley, Mel's image was already fading.

*   *   *

Looking forward as I was to meeting Ben, I'd prepared the right kind of face to wear when emerging from customs—relaxed and unassuming, not the face of a parent who was going to be either embarrassingly emotional or wracked with neurotic suspicion. I came round the partition with my stride steady and head high. I tried not to scan the rows of faces, I was going to let him spot me first.

But he didn't, because he wasn't there. I stood just past the exit, being jostled, an annoying obstacle to other people's greetings and reunions. Outside it was grey—we'd seen the wet tarmac and shreds of dingy cloud as we landed—and I felt suddenly exhausted, and let down. Please God, I thought, don't let anything awful have happened.

27

As I made my way to the information desk I saw the two Arab women who'd been next to me on the flight. They were with a hawk-faced elderly man in a dark suit, wearing a white cotton pillbox hat. The women pushed their trolleys, he walked alongside, a fiercely proprietary presence. They looked as calm as ever. And why wouldn't they? They were well met.

Harrassed and neglected, I queued for assistance. The girl behind the desk was maddeningly bright.

'We've received no message.'

'Well look, I'll go and have a cup of coffee, can you let me know if . . . ?'

'I've made a note of your name, we'll page you if anything comes through.'

I trundled to the coffee-and-baguette bar, parked alongside a free seat, and fetched a large espresso with two sugars.

Even a much needed caffeine hit couldn't replace the adrenalin that was ebbing away. I was horribly disappointed. And there was that foolish, wriggling worm of worry. Had Ben taken off somewhere? Was that why he'd sent me a postcard on day one—not because of a fond impulse but because he planned to disappear? I could picture his cronies going to work on him, telling him it was time he cut the cord and flew the nest. 'Do it while the old dot's away, and she'll hardly notice the difference, bottle of wine when she gets back and bob's your uncle . . .' My familiarity with the way they thought was frightening. And hadn't I often done the same thing myself, taking advantage of Ben's absence to clear out his drawers and his wardrobe, consigning old clothes and grotty

28

paperbacks to outer darkness without his even knowing?

He'd moved out twice already. Once, in order to put a somewhat ragged girdle round the earth with his best pal Nozz; the second time to university, but his positively epic failure to do any work at Newcastle (club heaven, as other parents had warned me) coincided with the break-up of our marriage, so what was expedient was nicely linked to what seemed at least to be filial. He came back and took a job behind the counter at HMV. Since his return, his sure instinct for self-preservation and natural sympathy towards me had ensured a happy and serene household. But now that I was quite clearly over the trauma of separation I knew he was under pressure from Nozz and co. to quit the nest. Perhaps, with me out of the way, that pressure had finally born fruit—

'Mum?'

I don't know when the seat opposite had been vacated, but it had been, because Ben was now sitting in it, red-eyed, unshaven and grinning, like a fairground gypsy.

'I was, like, you'd be shitting yourself, having my name given out on the public address system, but here you are sat down with a nice cup of coffee, you don't care do you?'

I didn't any more. 'I knew you'd show up. How are you, love?'

He leaned across and kissed me, stubbing out a cigarette in the ashtray at the same time. He exuded the unkempt, feral smell of youth. His dark, curling hair was slightly greasy. There was a single zit among the stubble.

'Look at the state of you,' he commented

29

admiringly. 'Tan or what?'

'Not bad is it?' I agreed.

'How's the Melon?'

'You really mustn't call her that—'

'Why, you didn't bring her back, did you?'

'No, but you put it on your postcard.'

He beamed with obvious self-satisfaction. 'You got that, then?'

From this I inferred that he hadn't received my message and therefore had probably not spent last night at home.

'Yesterday,' I said, 'what timing.'

'I aim to please.'

He lit another Marlboro like a man with all the time in the world. At twenty-one, one does.

'Shall we make a move?' I suggested.

'Two minutes—' he held up two fingers, then added a third—'three. Pearl's gone to the bog.'

'Pearl?'

'A friend.' He flicked ash, grinned. 'Trust me.'

I didn't, of course, and I was right not to. When Pearl showed up she was no friend, but a white-faced, yellow-haired, damson-lipped houri, with a figure to stop traffic, kitted out in denim cutoffs that revealed the lower curve of her buttocks and an angora crop-top which threatened to do the same for her breasts. She had a small silver ring through her eyebrow—or through where her eyebrow would have been if she hadn't plucked it out and repositioned it with kohl pencil. The whole voluptuous, undulating structure was balanced on black chunky high heels with fetishistic ankle straps.

Sex, in other words, on a stick.

'Here she is,' said Ben. 'What are we waiting

for? This way girls.'

He set off with the trolley, Pearl and I followed. She seemed preoccupied, but I was used to that.

'Did you have a ghastly journey?' I enquired.

'It wasn't too good.'

'I am sorry,' I said. 'The M25 can be absolute hell in the early mornings.'

'Yeah.'

'Is it all still coned off near the junction with the M40?'

'Sorry?'

'There are so many contraflows,' I explained.

'Yeah—Ben!'

We were approaching the automatic doors when Pearl darted past both of us and out into the set-down area with astonishing speed and agility considering the shoes. Fortunately she just made the edge of the pavement before creating her very own contraflow right there and then, and pebble-dashing the area with the contents of her stomach.

'Go Pearl,' urged Ben unnecessarily. He sent me an amused 'what-can-you-do?' glance. 'Sorry about this. Should've brought a bag of sawdust, she's been at it since four.'

It was clear now why they'd been late. Ben explained that he and Pearl had spent the night at the house of a mutual acquaintance in Ealing, host of the event which had given rise to Pearl's indisposition. Since she'd scarcely slept anyway, Pearl had plumped for a lift home via Heathrow, in Ben's company, rather than face the challenges of the journey back on her own.

We had to stop twice on the M25. We pulled over at speed, hazard lights flashing, with Pearl already opening the rear passenger door as we

31

shuddered on to the hard shoulder.

'Poor girl,' I said, as we waited for her somewhere near Junction 12. 'What have you been doing to her?'

Ben raised his hands from the steering wheel. 'Not guilty. She did it all on her own.'

We dropped Pearl off on the outskirts of town. She managed a 'Bye' to me, and a slightly more forceful 'Ring me' to Ben.

'Where did you meet her?' I asked.

'Can't remember . . . Pub I think.'

'What does she do?'

He sent me a sly look. 'Parties. Puts out.'

'I mean in the hours of daylight.'

'She's doing retakes at college.'

We turned off the motorway. 'And are you going to ring her?'

'Could do.' He let this sink in, and then reached out and patted my arm. 'Cheer up, Ma, you weren't seeing her at her best.'

*   *   *

Littelsea was a stolid seaside town, big enough to support an out-of-town superstore, several smaller supermarkets, a two-screen cinema, three persuasions of church and half a dozen ethnic restaurants, but too refined to harbour anything as louche as a nightclub. That kind of thing, reasoned the Littelsea elders, was best left to Brighton, a safe distance along the coast. The result was that at least half the town's pubs, knowing where their most profitable customer-base lay, had reinvented themselves as happening venues for the young. So instead of the feared goings-on being driven,

32

literally, underground, they now occupied many thousands of square feet at street-level and spilled out on to the pavements, where they frightened the horses and provoked letters of dignified discontent to the local paper.

Today the offshore breeze was keeping the clouds away from Littelsea, and the sun sparkled on the white plaster work of Cliff Mansions as we approached along the seafront. I'd bought Number Fourteen with my half of the proceeds from our marital home. I loved it to bits. After the thumping great country rectory with its rampant acre and a half, its five cavernous bedrooms and its bank-busting fuel habit, this flat in a Victorian mansion block was very heaven. One front door, one large living room, two good-sized bedrooms and a small one; main hall, staircase and windows the province of the residents' association; and a balcony from which you could see the Channel—testy, sullen, or indolent according to the prevailing wind. From the Mansions you could walk to the long sweep of shingly beach with its stubby black breakwaters in less than five minutes. Far from having come down in the world, I felt I'd gone up, up and away— loosed from my moorings like a helium balloon.

The front door of the Mansions was at the back. From habit, I glanced down into the black hole which housed the wheelie-bins but could make out nothing untoward. Ben went ahead with the key, and my big case.

In the big central hall with its still grand staircase I went to look in our pigeonhole, but he jerked his head. 'They're all up there.'

There was no lift in the Mansions which for the moment we considered to be a good thing—it discouraged the elderly and retired who might have been oversensitive to noise, and it also precluded young families at the pram and pushchair stage. Our less fit visitors tended to arrive on the fourth floor completely out of breath, but we were used to it.

Ben flung the door wide and stood aside for me to enter. 'Welcome!'

Apart from being a little stuffy and filmed with dust, the flat was fine. I realised as soon as I went in that he'd kept it respectable by spending almost no time there. If there had been a party just after I left (a circumstance which might have prompted the postcard) there had been plenty of time to erase the evidence in the days immediately afterwards.

Ben put down my case, and indicated a pile of letters on the table by the phone. 'I wrote down your messages,' he said, adding: 'I'll open up,' and strolling into the living room with an air of complete assurance.

When I joined him he had opened the balcony door. A gush of seaweed-salty air bustled through the room, bringing it to life. Ben's hands were in the back pockets of his jeans but he made a gesture with his thumbs which offered up the whole area for my inspection.

'So what do you reckon?'

'Not bad at all,' I said, glancing round. There was one of those mixed bunches of flowers you can buy at filling stations, still in its cellophane, stuck in a lager glass on the mantelpiece. 'In fact very good.'

'Thought you'd be impressed.'

'I am.'

'To be honest I haven't been around that much, but I've been looking in, you know, keeping an eye on things.'

'Well thanks for doing such a good job.'

'You're welcome. Want to see the rest?'

'Sure.'

Dutifully I went to the kitchen and took in the empty draining board, the wiped surfaces and the two pints of semi-skimmed in the fridge. The top half of the sash window was down about six inches.

'Brilliant.'

'Bathroom?'

'I'll take your word for it, love.'

'Fancy a cup of tea?'

'I wouldn't mind another coffee.'

'Coming up.' I went to take my flight bag along the corridor, and he called after me: 'Leave the big one, I'll do that.'

I liked my bedroom. It was tranquil, comfortable—a haven. After years of feeling that if I wasn't actually asleep I should be up and about, making a difference, I had rediscovered the indulgent pleasures of eating, reading, watching TV, listening to the radio and making phone calls, in bed. I had even, since coming to Cliff Mansions, moved my pillows into the centre of the bedhead, a step from which I had shrunk before, because it seemed to consitute a painful admission of my solitary state. Now I took a clean nightshirt out of the drawer and dropped it on the pile of pillows that was all for me: I'd sleep well tonight.

Ben bumped in with my case in one hand and my coffee in the other. I took the mug off him before he slopped any more.

'Lovely, thanks.'

'So ...' he flopped down on the bed, hands behind his head, ankles crossed. 'Was it a good holiday?'

'It was a wonderful holiday. Mel was absolutely great, considering she was working most of the time.' I put the coffee down and unzipped the case.

'She's a workaholic.'

'I wouldn't say that, but she's got a responsible job and she's very conscientious.'

'Workaholic. Has she got a bloke?'

'No one special. Plenty of men friends, though.'

'No bloke. What about you?'

'Me?' I stuffed underwear into a drawer.

'Any dinners under the desert stars?'

'Yes, but not the way you mean.'

'Thank God for that,' said Ben. 'I'm not sure I'm ready to be kicked out yet.'

*   *   *

At eleven, Ben went into HMV. Having unpacked and put the washing in I sat down on the sofa with the telephone, the mail and the list of messages.

Everyone had been in touch. Ben, though he had quite understandably wiped my phone messages along with his own potentially embarrassing ones, had been scrupulous in capturing their exact flavour. Sabine was desperate for tennis on Saturday. Desma ditto. Helen, who described herself as an emotional wreck, said she didn't know where I was, but if I could see my way to giving her a ring that might well be the only thing to stand between her and a messy end. Ronnie had sent a welcome home card. Even the presence amongst my mail of several bills and a hefty parking fine

36

incurred by Ben (he must have been in my car) couldn't tarnish the glow of happiness I felt to be back. People had occasionally said that friends were the most important thing in life, and I now knew this to be true. Love and marriage, even passion and romance, were all very fine in their way and in their place, but friends were indispensable.

It was Friday, and I wasn't due back in the office till Monday, but I decided to give Jo a ring. Her voice rose heartwarmingly.

'You're back!'

'Yes, early this morning.'

'And you couldn't wait to call work.'

'Well, I thought I'd just check that I still had a job.'

'You're joking, the place has practically fallen apart without you. Did you have a great time?'

'Yes. I'll bore you with my photos, don't worry.'

'You must—why don't we go out for a drink after work on Monday?'

'You're on,' I said. 'See you Monday.'

I called Sabine and Desma, who were both out, and left messages saying yes to tennis. Then I tried Helen who was, naturally, at home.

'Sorry to be a pain and a drag,' she said in her flat, drawling voice.

'Oh, come on,' I said, 'you're not a drag.'

'I know you're all burnished and bucked up from your holiday, but do you have any entrenched objection to mixing with someone who isn't?'

'Of course not.'

'You don't have to do anything but sit there.'

'Sounds fine, why don't you come round?'

'Oh—' she sighed wearily—'car's in dock. I can't possibly ask you to come out here on the very morning you get back, can I.'

It wasn't a question, but I answered it anyway. 'Certainly you can, and of course I will.'

'Be a dear,' said Helen, not one to demur once an offer had been made, 'and pick up a bottle of something restorative on the way and I'll settle up when you get here.'

I was just about to walk out of the door when the phone rang. I picked it up, interrupting the message.

'So you're there.'

'Mel! Yes, we were a bit delayed, but no serious problems.' I wasn't going to enlarge on Pearl at this stage. 'And thank you for everything darling—'I'll be writing.'

'My pleasure,' she said, getting that out of the way. 'Cliff Mansions still standing?'

'Rather more than, actually. I suspect he hasn't been here much.'

'No signs of last-minute plastering or re-glazing?'

'None whatever.'

'Well hush my mouth, what a suspicious cow I am.'

'Not at all, I was fairly trepidatious myself.'

'OK, look, I'm calling from the office so I'd better go. Catch you later.'

'I'll write—and thanks again, for everything—'bye love.'

As I left I wondered whether I'd been correct in detecting the tiniest hint of disappointment in my daughter's voice at the lack of domestic disasters this end. Sibling rivalry simmered away, it seemed, even where there was no obvious reason for it. What a good thing it was that my offsprings' paths were so divergent: that Mel was several thousand miles away earning a small fortune in the desert, and Ben was here where I could keep an eye on him.

*   *   *

I went into the supermarket and picked up a couple of bagfuls of necessities as well as the restorative suggested by Helen—a Clancey Creek sauvignon. I chose it mainly because it was on special, and in spite of Helen's promise to reimburse me I knew she'd forget and I wouldn't dream of reminding her. My watch, though not my well-travelled stomach, told me it was lunchtime, so I added a bag of tortilla chips and some salsa dip. Then I drove the five miles inland to the village of Hawley End, thanking my lucky stars that I didn't live there any more.

Helen opened the door of her rented tied cottage—kept at just-habitable level by the local landowner—and at once retreated into the dusky interior, apologising half-heartedly for the mess. Come to Helen for an effusive welcome and you'd be disappointed. I closed the door and went with her into the kitchen, clearing a space on the table and putting down my offerings.

'This is quite incredibly sporting of you,' she said vaguely. 'Corkscrew's in the drawer. I just need to bore the pants off someone with my gloom, and you're so good at being bored without looking it.'

'I shan't be bored,' I assured her.

It was true. Whatever Helen's shortcomings, she was never dull. And one would have to have been born on another planet not to recognise that her life was a mess. That the mess was largely of her own making didn't stop it being pretty frightening. They say it's a mistake to give advice to friends, in case they take it. In Helen's case there was no temptation to do so: you were lost for words.

I uncorked the Clancey Creek, opened the tortilla chips and popped off the lid of the salsa dip. Helen got two tumblers off the draining board.

'Fire away,' I said, 'I'm all yours.'

Most of what she told me amounted to a rerun of events leading up to her present situation. What it boiled down to was this. Helen and Clive Robinson were academics who'd met at Cambridge, stayed together, and enjoyed a long, cultured, child-free marriage. Clive, who was the younger by two years, had risen to become Professor of Middle English at Sussex, and Helen was a freelance editor for an academic publisher. In happier times they lived in what Ian used to refer to as The House That Time Forgot. It wasn't especially old—the same age as Cliff Mansions probably—its development had been arrested at some point in the twenties. The porch contained old-fashioned wooden tennis racquets, mostly warped, an iron boot-scraper, a threadbare brown leather football, though no one had seen either Clive or Helen engage in any sport other than croquet, the equipment for which lived in a wooden shack in the garden, known as the summer house. The Robinsons' long canvas capes and strange hats hung on branching hooks, with galoshes, of all things, beneath. A Morris Traveller leaked oil on to the drive, but its owners preferred to cycle wherever possible on their sit-up-and-beg bikes, both with capacious baskets.

40

Inside were thousands of books, many dusty plants, a G-plan radiogram passed on to them by a student, and the same carpets and curtains they'd bought with the house in the late sixties. There was neither television, computer nor microwave—no form of domestic technology, in fact, other than the cooker and fridge.

In spite of their elective fogeydom, they were a likeable couple. They gave good parties, which consisted in them simply stating a date and time, buying whatever was cheap at the off-licence, and opening their doors. If you wanted anything other than the plonk and ploughmans liberally on offer you brought it yourself and were never made to feel the least embarrassed about doing so.

Helen was tall with a peculiarly English type of drab, unadorned good looks. She was pale, with eyes as grey as Channel fog, a long nose, and chiselled colourless lips. Her hair was straight and reddish and had for as long as I could remember been chopped off just above shoulder length, and hooked back behind her ears. Her complete lack of any sense of personal style had, with middle age, turned into a style all its own. It was impossible to imagine her in anything but her trademark droopy kilts and felted handknits in funny colours. She didn't even have a sense of herself as a mildly eccentric bluestocking. She had, we considered, no sense of herself at all.

Clive was as fat and florid as his wife was thin and pale, but no more worldly. He favoured bow ties, but we always felt that was because some of his more sophisticated colleagues did. He was like a happy, Bunterish child, doing exactly as he liked and being paid for it. His contentment amounted almost to hubris, and he was destined to pay for it. He thought Helen was the most beautiful woman in the world and seemed to imagine that everywhere she went she inflamed passions and unleashed a riot of almost ungovernable priapism. The rest of us thought 'How sweet'.

Until it really happened.

It was simple and corny, almost a cliché if it hadn't been so agonising. The House That Time Forgot began to leak to the point where even Clive and Helen noticed it. A new roof was needed, and the boss of a local building contractor came along to give them a quote. Well, not strictly speaking 'them', since only Helen was there that day. The builder drove up in a Mercedes sports. He was brown-eyed, and well set up, and thirty-six years old. Somewhere between the cup of instant and the final estimate, something happened. Ten days later Helen left Clive for John Kerridge who, she claimed (with a telltale hint of colour in those pale, hollow cheeks), had made her realise what it could be like . . .

The trouble was that John Kerridge was married, with a nice house outside Brighton and two kids at private school. He was happy to accept the attentions of this belatedly awakened academic, but not to make any adjustments to his life to accommodate her. Helen didn't care. All she knew was that now she had tasted the best she could settle for nothing less. It would be not just dishonest, but unfair to both Clive and herself, to continue in a marriage which fell so far short of her new, exacting standards. The rest of us looked on in astonishment as this hugely intelligent woman took the brave, mad, pathetic step of becoming

42

John Kerridge's bit on the side.

And the result was everyone was wretched. Kerridge, his bluff well and truly called, didn't know what to do with this unwanted grand gesture. Clive was like an orphaned child, pitiful in his grief. Helen was miserable on account of having made so many people unhappy when she felt she'd done the only decent thing.

Sometimes she cheered up. John was still 'a revelation'. But she was not a woman who blossomed with independence: she was lonely and bereft in the cultural desert of Hawley End. Much of the time, unsurprisingly, she could not imagine what the future held. And neither could the rest of us.

So the nature of her emotional troughs didn't really alter. You just sat there in the hope that as she talked she would suddenly see the light and return to Clive, and The House That Time Forgot, and sanity.

' . . . I wish the clouds would part and a bearded deity, to whom all things are known, would make them all clear to me,' she said now, between glum gulps of Clancey Creek. 'If he would only oblige I should believe in him from this time forward for evermore.'

'But that's not going to happen,' I reminded her gently, 'so perhaps it's time to be pragmatic.'

'By which you mean go back.'

'Either that or go forward. You, Helen, go forward, with or without John. Do what you want to do.'

'But I don't know what that is,' she said. 'I only know what I can't do.'

'I know.' We'd been through all this so often,

43

and to no avail.

'Have you seen Clive at all ...?' she asked, staring set-faced out of the smeary window.

'No. But then I've been away for two weeks.'

'Yes, you said, how egocentric I'm getting.' She glanced at me. 'Have got.'

'Not at all,' I said sturdily, refilling her glass. 'But it would be nice to see you happy again.'

'You mean content. Not the same thing.'

'Well, not in despair, as you seem to be— whatever you like to call it.'

'Eve ...' She lit a cigarette with big, bony, trembling hands. 'I didn't know what happiness was until I met John. And now I've experienced ecstasy.' It was the oldest, corniest scenario in the history of human relations but she imbued it with the grandeur of Greek tragedy.

'Are you hungry?' I asked, giving the tortilla chips a push.

She ate her way through them. While her mouth was full I told her about my holiday.

'What fun,' she said, who would have hated every moment of it. 'How does it feel to be back?'

'Very nice. Home's best.'

'You know,' she said, staring at me as though seeing me for the first time, 'it's remarkable how you've come out of all your difficulties. I can't tell you how I admire you, Eve.'

*   *   *

It was four o'clock when I got back and Pearl was sitting on the steps outside Cliff Mansions, with her back against the railings.

'I got a lift with a friend,' she explained as

though I might have been worried about her.

'Ben's not here,' I told her. 'He's gone to HMV.'

'He told me he had the day off.'

'Did he? I don't know.' I opened the door. 'That's where he told me he was going.'

'Do you mind if I wait for him?' she asked, coming into the hall and closing the door after her.

I set off up the stairs. 'No—no, of course not, if you don't mind me getting on with a few things.'

'I'll go and sit in his room.'

'You don't have to do that,' I said over my shoulder. 'Would you like a cup of tea?'

'No thanks.'

She did go to Ben's room to begin with, but as I began putting the shopping away she came and stood around in the kitchen. I didn't mean to keep saying 'Excuse me' but that was how it worked out—she was always in the way. It didn't seem to bother her. She had obviously recovered, and was in a mood to talk.

'So do you like having Ben here?' she asked.

'Yes I do as a matter of fact.'

'You should talk to my Mum,' said Pearl, 'she'd kill to get me out the house.'

I could believe it. 'We get on fine,' I said. 'Ben's very easy.'

'That's what I hear.' There was a glitter of sarcasm in her voice which I chose to ignore. She was fishing, but she'd get nothing from me.

'He tells me you're doing retakes,' I said, putting her in her place. 'What subjects?'

'English and Art. But I don't know if I'll go back in September, I'd rather get some money together, go backpacking.'

'Time spent travelling's never wasted.'

45

'Yeah, and I need to meet some new people,' she said.

I devoutly wished her out of my kitchen and off my back, and she must have read my mind, for shortly after that she went back to Ben's room and put on his cherished reggae album. 'No woman, no cry . . .' I didn't somehow think that Pearl was easily reduced to tears.

*   *   *

When Ben got in he came into the kitchen, jerking his head in the direction of his room.

'Who's here?'

'Pearl.'

'Shit,' he said. 'For how long?'

'An hour? Something like that.'

'Shit,' he said again, 'better go and lick backside.'

I couldn't make out from his tone whether he was pleased or horrified at her presence. But some twenty minutes later their voices began to rise, and ten minutes after that a full-scale row was in progress.

She came out first, belatedly lowering her voice to a hiss to tell my son to fuck off as she crossed the hall. The front door crashed shut behind her. The music continued steadily. When Ben emerged I called:

'Everything all right?'

'Yup,' he said. 'No big deal. Going out, OK?'

'OK.'

I'd made lasagne, so he could heat some up when he got in. Looking in my handbag for a biro I came across the A A Milne postcard. It had now crossed the world twice, and in recognition of this fact I pinned it to the top right-hand corner of the kitchen noticeboard.

CHAPTER THREE

If success with the opposite sex was to be calculated in numbers, Ben was phenomenally successful. He'd been going out with girls since he was fourteen, usually more than one concurrently. The passage of arms with Pearl notwithstanding, he had the unusual talent in one so young of being able to free himself from liaisons that were becoming irksome without acrimony. Girls I remembered from two or three years ago would still from time to time turn up on the doorstep asking for him.

As a very small child, still in his pushchair, he'd been admired for his looks and winning smile. When women said 'Look at those eyelashes—he'll be a heartbreaker', it did my own heart good. I didn't pause to consider whether the breaking of hearts was something desirable, and if I had I suspect that the question wouldn't have detained me for long. I quite liked the idea of my son being a bit of a romeo. Better that one's son should be fancied and faithless, than nice, nerdy and forever overlooked. I had to admit that his girlfriends weren't picked for the size of their intellects. From first to last they were stunners with attitude, to whom the things of the mind were a dusty irrelevance.

I'd read somewhere that boys tended to be attracted to girls who reminded them of their mothers, but if that were so Ben was the exception that proved the rule. Even (perhaps especially) my most devoted friends would not have described me as beautiful. I was interesting-looking, and now, in my late forties, I was perfectly happy with that.

But Ben liked babes. They never seemed to me to be quite good enough for him, and he accepted this traditional mother's point of view with equanimity. 'So whaddya think?' he'd ask sometimes when the teen-angel of the moment had just left the house.

'She's very pretty.' I always tried to be positive.

'Naturally.'

'No, she's fine—I liked her.'

'But.'

'No buts. And anyway, it's none of my business.'

This was usually his cue to give me a squeeze round the shoulders and say something like: 'Take it easy, Ma, if I want my mind expanded I'll read a good book.'

I wasn't bothered. Not one girl so far had had enough about her to seduce Ben permanently from the comforts of home. I knew serious competition when I saw it, and it had not yet broken the horizon. While the babes ruled, he'd stay.

Ian, my estranged husband—we were still married, though drifting quietly towards a permanent dissolution—took a dimmer view. He lived in London, and tended only to meet the babe of the moment when visiting.

'What on earth's he doing with her?' he would ask, baffled.

'I'd have thought it was obvious.'

'Yes, but she's not in his league.'

'Perhaps that's the way he likes it.'

48

'What does Mel think?'

Ian had a great respect for Mel's opinion, probably because it tended in most matters to coincide more directly with his own. In the circumstances I was usually able to report that she couldn't see the attraction, but then we wouldn't expect her to.

This comforted Ian. He was a painstaking achiever, without his daughter's buccaneering streak, who suffered from the perfectionist's complaints of migraine and, from time to time, peptic ulcers. Muddle and make-do made him feel physically ill. But he had always been an adoring father, more idealistic in many ways than I, who considered that his offspring, even at their least promising moments, were simply gathering themselves before sprinting towards their goals. When Ben had dropped out of his degree course, Ian choked back his disappointment and rationalised the failure to his own satisfaction.

'I suspect he was bored.'

'Bored?' I gaped. 'Don't make me laugh. He's been turning night into day for two solid years.'

'Yes, and I'm going to have a word with him about that. But there simply isn't the rigour and quality to the teaching in these places that there was even in our day. All these people want to do is be on television, or write contentious lightweight books that will make them a mint. There's no real desire to engage the interest of the students. Ben's bright, and they failed him.'

It was useless to argue. And anyway, Ben was undeniably bright. But my husband could never accept how different his son was from himself: that for Ben, the pleasure principle was not ancillary,

49

but pivotal. I once had the misfortune to come across Ben's diary. Misfortune, because once happened upon I could not resist a peek, and those who peek see only what is unwelcome. On the Saturday in question were scrawled, in red biro, as if deliberately to shock the unwary snooper, the words: 'GOT TROLLIED—GOT LUCKY—GOT LAID.'

The entry made me laugh, a trifle nervously, but it would have shocked Ian to the core.

*   *   *

Predictably, Pearl showed up again at the weekend with an aggressive 'Just-don't-ask' air.

'He's still in bed,' I told her over the intercom. It was eleven-thirty a.m. on Saturday, and Ben didn't have to be at HMV till two.

'Ri-ight . . .' she said sarkily, 'mind if I come up?'

When she arrived in the flat I said, 'I'll go and stick my head round the door.'

She stood in the middle of the hall lighting a cigarette. As I went along to Ben's room I was aware of her shaking the match and wondered, pickily, what she'd do with it.

I knocked. 'Ben . . .?' There was some sort of grunt, so I went in and addressed the mound of purple duvet. 'Ben, it's after half past eleven and Pearl's here.'

'What?'

'It's twenty-five to twelve. Pearl's in the hall.'

'OK,' he said, quite placidly, and threw off the duvet. I flinched, but he had on boxer shorts.

I withdrew discreetly and went back to Pearl. 'He's on his way.'

That, it appeared, was her cue to join him. The dead match, I noticed, was in the bowl with my Christmas cactus.

I turned the radio on in the kitchen as a cover, and after a few minutes ventured with shameful stealth out into the hall. The reggae was still jogging away in there, but there was no accompanying sound of voices, so I assumed they were using the music for the same reason I was using mine—disguise.

Half an hour later I went as noisily as possible up to my room and got changed into shorts and a polo shirt, with much thumping of drawers and cupboards. On the landing I called: 'I'm going to play tennis!'

'Have a good one,' replied Ben in that bright, we're-not-up-to-anything-in-here voice which didn't fool me for a second. The voice was slightly over-projected, to compensate for coming from the horizontal.

*　　　*　　　*

Sabine, Desma, Ronnie and I played on the municipal courts down near the prom, twice a week, winter and summer. This time of year was easy street, but our winter games had become a point of honour with us. Like Christian martyrs we endured the exigencies of the snarling coastal weather, the vulture-like wheeling and crying of the storm-tossed gulls and the jibes of the local yobbery as we played the best of three short sets in several layers of clothing. We told each other we were completely mad, but if we were mad we were also smug. Our reward, if not in heaven, came in the spring of the following year when we astounded fairweather players on neighbouring courts with our accuracy, consistency, and fitness.

These things are all relative, of course. Three of the four of us weren't that good, and by mid-June of any given year the really flash players had long since drawn level and were beginning to pull away, leaving us middle-rankers still struggling with our unsound service grips and dodgy backhands.

Still, we were addicted to tennis, that most psychologically testing of games. We played for fun, but also to win. Our cries of 'Sorree!', 'Shot!' and 'Bad luck!' were a thin veneer covering both our determination to grind each other into the dust and our fury when we failed to do so, either through their superior skill or our own unforced errors.

The only one of our number who didn't care about winning was Ronnie, who was also, unsurprisingly, the best player. As Veronica Toozey she had been tennis captain of one of the biggest, smartest girls' boarding schools in the home counties. As Ronnie Chatsworth, married to local solicitor Dennis, she was still the woman to beat, not least because she was so maddeningly impervious to the ignoble pleasures of victory. A tall, square-shouldered, fresh-faced natural athlete, she had all the strokes, including a serve so venomous that she could actually come in on it, and the speed to do so. But she played with a smile and a shrug—Desma and I would speculate as to whether she laughed when having sex with the dry and serious Dennis, and concluded that she must, because if she didn't she might cry. The Chatsworths' was one of Littelsea's more curious unions, but it had lasted twenty-seven years and

52

given them two grown-up sons, so we allowed fair play to them.

Sabine was the one who most wanted to win, which was unfortunate because she was never going to be quite as good as Ronnie. Sabine was French, and married to a rich, likeable landowner, Martin Drage. A state-of-the-art astro-turf court was at that moment being built to accompany the heated pool with retractable cover in the garden of their splendid house, Headlands. She made no bones about the fact that Martin's bank balance was a major part of his charm. Martin had a daughter by his first marriage, but he and Sabine enjoyed a brisk, affable, child-free accommodation. I suspected that, Sabine's svelte femininity notwithstanding, theirs was a low-level sex-life held together by a fidelity based on indifference rather than conviction.

Sabine had a franchise for a home-sales clothing company, Chic. She was one of their least active but most successful agents, motivated not by the need to make money—Martin made more than even she could spend—but by a steely Gallic urge to impose her will on her customers. Sabine didn't so much sell you a garment as imply that you would be untouchable if you failed to buy it. Unlike the rest of us, she had private coaching, read books on tactics, and adopted an unusual stance to receive— racquet held out to one side, and aloft, the other arm outstretched, like a lion tamer approaching his charge with a whip and a chair. She alone belonged to the local posh club, protected from the hoi polloi by extortionate fees and impregnable green canvas windbreaks. I think that, but for the presence of Ronnie, she would have judged our game quite beyond the pale.

Desma was a relative latecomer to the game. Short and stocky, she was a natural ball player who had taken up tennis when age halted her involvement with the local women's hockey team. She had the convert's zeal and what she lacked in technique she made up for in strength and an alarmingly high work rate which resulted in her getting almost everything back. She was about ten years younger than the rest of us, but had married late, so although she was in her mid-thirties she had a two-year-old daughter. Richard 'Rick' Shaw was a couple of years younger than her, shy, handsome and devoted. Our theory concerning the Shaws—and you'll have gathered that we had theories on everyone—was that Rick was one of those men who couldn't handle being gorgeous, so jolly, unthreatening, tomboyish Desma represented a safe haven. Blissfully happy with his lot, he was not only adorable but a new man and a treasure, who happily toted Bryony around the shops in a backpack while his wife worked up a sweat on the courts.

And that left me. Like my French, my tennis was what I'd learned at school, good and bad habits more or less unchanged, but rendered passable with practice. In the pecking order I came below Ronnie and Sabine, and officially above Desma, though here my temperament let me down. My strokes were superior to hers—they should have been, I'd been playing since I was twelve—but I lacked her bull-dog qualities, her never-say-die perseverance and gnat-in-a-paper bag agility about the court. If I was having an off day, my head, as they say, went down. I got cross and frustrated and defeatist. I lacked self-belief.

We four of us played at midday on a Saturday because everyone else seemed to be at superstores, garden centres and DIY emporia, or perhaps just eating lunch. Not to be left out on this score we always went to the Esplanade Hotel afterwards, for wine and the special in the Cutter Bar.

On this occasion Desma and Sabine were already there, knocking up with Sabine's fluorescent pink balls. Sabine wore a tiny, scarlet pleated skirt and a red-and-white striped singlet. Desma's chunky thighs were encased in the usual grey marl cycling shorts, topped with a Littelsea LHC sweatshirt.

'Hi there!' she cried, swiping at a penetrating Drage forehand in such a way that the swipe effectively became a lob and sent Sabine (who had charged the net) scampering back to the baseline. 'How are you? You look terrific!'

'Thanks.' I let myself in and unzipped my racquet cover as Desma and Sabine came over to join me.

'What a tan,' said Desma admiringly. 'I wish I went brown.'

Preferring hypocrisy to Sabine's lecture on skincare, I said quickly: 'You won't in ten years' time when you're a peach and I'm a prune.'

Sabine gave both of my cheeks an approving air kiss. 'How was your daughter?'

'Very well. Working hard but being well paid for it.'

'Did you manage to play at all?'

I didn't tell her I hadn't even taken my racquet. 'It was a bit hot for tennis.'

'So,' said Sabine, giving her own racquet—which

had a newfangled triangular head—a threatening twiddle, 'you need the practice. We'll let you go on your own till Ronnie gets here.'

'She rang me to say she might be late,' explained Desma. 'They were driving back from London this morning.'

I managed about five minutes knock-up on my own before making way for Desma. When Ronnie arrived she joined Desma, and called:

'It's so good to have you back, Eve! News over lunch, right? Sorry to hold things up, I don't need a knock-up.'

She didn't, either. Their skill and our combined temperament problem ensured that she and Desma made hay with us. It had to be said that I didn't play well, and Sabine's wasn't a forgiving nature. As we approached the net to shake hands I could sense, if not actually see, the gritted teeth behind the smile. She let down the net in a manner that suggested she was trying to ease her own tension.

'Sorry everyone,' I said as we returned to the bench. 'Not one of my better efforts. That's holidays for you.'

Ronnie laughed. 'Don't apologise, we won.'

Sabine opened the gate to usher us out. 'Did you have a good evening in town?'

'Yes,' said Ronnie. 'Do you know I was dreading it but it was actually rather fun.'

'What was it?' asked Desma.

'Dennis's old boys do. Every other summer they include wives and girlfriends.'

The thought of Dennis and his fellow old boys silenced Sabine and me, but fortunately Desma was up to the job.

'Was it a dance?'

'No, a dinner, but they had music—a little combo sort of thing, twiddling away in the background.'

'Lloyd Webber?' enquired Sabine, nostrils flaring superciliously.

'Not that I recollect. Gershwin, Berlin, that sort of thing, it was nice.' Ronnie opened the boot of her car, which was closest, and we dumped our racquets and balls before walking on in the direction of the Esplanade.

'What did you wear?' I asked.

'That purple dress—the one I've had for ages. The one I wore to your last thing.'

'Good choice, you look smashing in that.'

'You know,' said Sabine, 'you should try something short, Ronnie. You have the figure for it.'

'If I had your legs I would.'

'You have good legs.'

'I only display the bits that are good. And that means below the knee.'

'Fifty per cent more than I can manage,' said Desma, glancing ruefully down at her rounded knees and sturdy calves.

'It's all a question of proportion,' explained Sabine.

'Telling me.'

'No, the proportions of what you wear,' went on Sabine, addressing herself to Ronnie. 'Some kinds of short clothes look like mutton dressed as lamb, other kinds are superbly elegant.'

'I have an idea,' replied Ronnie, pasing the rest of us a look, 'that the other kinds are also wickedly expensive.'

'Not necessarily!' said Sabine. 'The new Chic

57

range, for instance . . .'

We jeered affectionately as we went through the hotel's revolving door.

The Esplanade was a once grand Edwardian seafront hotel which had fallen on hard times since the war, and been rescued ten years ago by a chain with the money—and the good sense—to restore its fortunes in a way which did not alter its essential character. The Cutter Bar was the only real innovation, and one which we applauded. It was a pleasant, long bar with a conservatory overlooking the sea. Anywhere else in the hotel our tennis clothes would have been in violation of an unspoken, rigorously maintained dress code, but the Cutter was a meeting place, more comfortable than a pub but with a pub's relaxed, democratic atmosphere. Also, the Esplanade's management had hired a chef who was a disciple of Rick Stein, so the fish and seafood were wonderful.

Clay, the barman, greeted us in his usual way.

'How was it this morning, ladies?'

'Well up to our usual standard,' said Ronnie.

'Speak for yourself,' said Sabine.

Clay—whom nature had intended for precisely this job—clicked his teeth as he poured our usuals. 'Who won then?'

'They did,' I told him.

It was a measure of Clay's interpersonal skills that he gave the impression of knowing exactly what I meant.

'I see. The game's the thing, though, isn't it?'

Ronnie said 'Absolutely' and the rest of us 'You're joking'—or something like it, all at the same time.

We retired with our drinks to the corner table in

the conservatory upon which Clay had thoughtfully placed a 'Reserved' sign. Littlesea having preserved its reputation as a resort of the old school, there was nothing on the promenade opposite to interrupt our view of the sea, except one or two people walking dogs. In the gardens of the Esplanade a Union Jack stirred flaccidly atop a tall flagpole. The Channel swell gleamed in the early afternoon sun.

I took that first tinkling, sparkling sip of gin and tonic than which there are few more intense pleasures. There was a special charm about this drink, on this occasion, in this company. In the sun-baked luxury of the UAE I had consciously missed it, and it was good to be back. I often wondered if the others, with husbands, so to speak, still in place, set as much store by it as I did. Probably not, though instinct told me that only Desma always rushed back to her family with unalloyed delight.

Ronnie lifted her glass. 'Welcome back, Eve!'

We clinked, the four musketeers. Sabine lit a cigarette. 'You're never going to believe this, but I am going to be a parent.' We gaped, and she fluttered manicured fingers to dispel our misapprehension. 'No, no—please! How could you think such a thing of me? No, Martin's daughter is coming to live with us for a while.'

'I'd forgotten Martin even had a daughter,' said Ronnie.

'Had *you*, Sabine, that's the question,' said Desma.

'No, I have been fully aware of her, always. Martin has paid for her education. But since for nineteen years she has been perfectly happy with her mother in Yorkshire I've not given her a great deal of thought.'

'And how,' I enquired, 'do you feel about that?'

'You want the truth?' We indicated fervently that we did. 'I am not looking forward to it in the least.'

'It might be fun,' suggested Ronnie. 'I always wished I had a daughter. Someone to talk girl-talk to.'

I thought about Mel, whom I loved dearly but who did not somehow fit Ronnie's picture. 'Have you met her?' I asked Sabine.

'Once or twice when she was at Bedales. A sweet, shy, plump little English dumpling,' said Sabine, causing Desma to tweak at the legs of her cycling shorts. 'And I'm sure she is still sweet, but that doesn't mean I want to have her around the house for months on end.'

'It'll be fine,' said Ronnie. 'Nineteen-year-olds aren't around the house. They're either out, or in bed.'

Sabine lifted a cynical eyebrow. 'Why am I not able to take comfort from that?'

'Why's she coming, anyway?' asked Desma. 'You need to know that.'

'She's going to work on Martin's farm out at Hawley before going to vet school.'

Ronnie and I exchanged a look. This, at least, was familiar territory. The English dumpling ceased to be the overstated product of Sabine's waspish tongue and became instead a distinct probability.

'What's her name?' I asked.

'Sophie,' said Sabine, adding graciously: 'Pretty name.'

As our pasta-seafood bakes hove in view I thought: poor Sophie . . . poor little vet.

                    *   *   *

On the way back through town I had to pick up
some cleaning, left before I went away, and
dropped in at HMV. It was chock-a-block with the
usual Saturday mob of teens and twenty-
somethings with wads to spend, and a sprinkling of
harassed older people in search of birthday
presents ('Have you got—er—hang on, I've got it
written down—have you got Get It On by Mona
and the Plastic Mac Company? Oh thank God . . .
what? Oh, tape I should think—or no, has he got
CD on that thing of his? Golly, I don't know . . .
Sorry, you're busy, how much is the CD? Dear
God, I'll take the tape . . .') and so on.

The reason I knew I'd be able to grab a word
with Ben was that he was on videos at the moment,
and that counter was never as busy. He and Nozz
were sharing a joke by the till. I feared the joke was
at the expense of a neat couple in Dannimacs—
pale blue and beige respectively—who were
walking away empty-handed, their quest for the
Vince Hill Songbook, or perhaps James Galway
Live at the Point, redirected to the gulag of Easy
Listening.

'Hiya,' said Ben. 'What can I do for you?'

'Nothing, just a social call. Hello Nozz.'

'How you doing.'

It was a greeting, not a question. 'She doesn't
always dress like this,' explained Ben, 'she's been
playing tennis.'

'Did you win?' asked Nozz.

'No, but it was a good game.'

'A very sporting attitude,' he told me kindly.

61

Nozz was an art school graduate who had got the job at HMV on Ben's recommendation, having so far failed to secure any commissions in his chosen field of ceramics. Privately I thought this state of affairs suited him down to the ground, allowing him to feel that he was only slumming, while waiting for something more suited to his gifts, and making a very adequate buck while doing so. Ben had given me one of Nozz's pots (doubtless purchased at an advantageous price) for my birthday the previous year, and it was actually rather pleasing: I kept foreign coins in it.

'Dissatisfied customers?' I asked, nodding in the direction of the Dannimac couple.

'They wanted Glass.'

'Did they ever come to the wrong place!'

'No,' said Ben. 'The composer.'

'She was joking,' said Nozz kindly. They slipped in and out of this third-person mode with unsettling ease, as if I wouldn't notice.

'I know that,' replied Ben. 'I just decided not to give her the benefit.' He now addressed me directly. 'So Mum, what's occurring? There's no such thing as a social call.'

'I was passing anyway. I wondered if everything was—you know—OK.'

'What can she mean?' Nozz asked.

'Girlfriend trouble,' explained Ben.

'Pearly put-out?'

'The same. Don't worry,' he added soothingly, 'I sent her on her way with a smile on her lips and a song in her heart.'

'If you did it'll be a first,' said Nozz.

'Give over.'

'I mean for her. That has to be one of the most

congenitally disconnected mares it's ever been my misfortune to come across.'

'Actually you're right,' agreed Ben with the greatest good humour. 'I think you may just have put your finger on the source of our problems.'

*   *   *

I was also sure Nozz was right, but I knew from experience that this consensus on Pearl's character deficiencies wouldn't make a blind bit of difference to the status quo. Ben rather liked a hard time.

Walking back to where I'd parked the car I saw Pearl across the street, talking to a girlfriend outside New Look. Both were smoking in the manner of women dishing serious dirt. They were very much on display, standing in the middle of the pavement, tapping out their ash in such a way that passers-by had to take evasive action. Most of the male ones, I noted, gave Pearl not just a wide berth but a phwoah look.

Pearl looked round and caught my eye. I knew she'd not just seen but identified me, the beam of mutual recognition hummed unmistakably between us. But she looked away at once, and went on talking to her friend. I had seen her moment of weakness, and now she was cutting me dead.

In spite of this I felt, as I returned to the car, that this small victory had been all mine.

CHAPTER FOUR

There was always that sense when I returned from having been away, that everything to do with my life back home crowded round me crying pitifully 'Me, me, me!', reproaching me for my heartlessness in having bunked off for a couple of weeks. And, to be honest, that was how I preferred it. I liked to hit the ground running; to feel that even if I wasn't exactly indispensable, that I had been missed. I found the recognisable rhythms and restrictions of life in Littlesea a comforting security blanket after the heady and unsettling freedom of abroad . . .

All the same I was a bit taken aback, when settling down to *omelette fines herbes* and a well-known Cop on the Edge on Sunday night (Ben was out), to answer the doorbell and hear Ian's voice over the intercom.

'It's me!'

'Good heavens.'

'Can I come up? I've got Clive with me.'

'Well—yes, all right.' I stabbed the button. The buzz of the downstairs door opening went nicely with the grinding of my teeth. I put my own front door on the latch and stalked back into the living room. The ravaged features of the Cop on the Edge wore an expression nearly as grim as my own. I zapped the TV, picked up my plate and carried it back to the kitchen, shovelling down omelette as I went—there was something wince-making about being found eating on one's own, even more so when one had made a bit of an effort, chopping fresh herbs, sprinkling Parmesan and so on.

Back in the living room I stared irritably at the view from my window—the wide sweep of the shingly Littelsea bay, the sturdy lines of breakwater, the battered shelter with its attendant group of bored, trouble-ripe teenagers, the distant dignity of the Martello tower. It had been a fine day and there were still some people on the beach, one or two were even breasting the gentle swell. A tanker rode at anchor in the bay. And I could hear Ian's and Clive's voices on the stairs.

'Shop!'

'In here.'

The front door closed and Ian came in, followed by Clive. Ian came over and we exchanged a chaste, respectful salute. In an attempt to blast my own grumpiness out of the water I embraced Clive, who held his arms away from his sides to keep contact to a minimum. He was panting, as the more ample were prone to do after an assault on the Cliff Mansions stairs, and his cheek felt hot.

'Good holiday?' asked Ian. 'I bumped into this chap and he was asking after you, so I said I knew you'd like to see him.'

I couldn't imagine where my husband had got that idea from, at eight-thirty on a Sunday evening, but it was too late now.

'Of course,' I said. 'Who'd like a drink?'

'Are you sure it's no trouble?' asked Clive with a look that was both anguished and, as Ben would have said, gagging for it.

'None at all—whisky? Ian?'

'No thanks, I've got to get back to town in the car—do you have some fizzy water?'

'Sure. Take a seat.'

Clive muttered something about not wanting to disturb me, and the quality of the view, and sat down in the red, wing-backed chair which I had come to think of (I was getting set in my ways) as mine.

Ian followed me into the kitchen. 'Is Ben about?'

'He's not actually.'

'Any idea when . . . ?'

'Not really. He's at the pub.'

'Fair enough,' said Ian. As I got out the glasses and poured he stood near the fridge, absentmindedly brushing the worktop with his hand and then staring at his fingers. To stop him I handed him his tumbler of Highland Spring.

'Help yourself to ice.'

As he did so, splashing and banging cackhandedly in the sink and dislodging all the cubes at once, he said: 'If I'm gone when he comes back, will you tell him I was here? I'll call during the week.'

Ian was a conscientious father, but it was wasted on Ben, who was too indolent to award brownie points for good behaviour. Ian was also the source of the lady-killing looks, though the genes had found a subtly different expression in father and son. My husband's dark hair was regularly subjected to an expensive Jermyn Street haircut and gold spectacles lent a hint of severity to his even, serious features. His chin was never less than baby smooth and he almost always changed his shirt in the late afternoon—a habit which I was delighted not to have to service any more. Ben had taken the raw material and made it his own— stubble, greasy gypsy curls, sunken cheeks and all. The one feature that put the tin hat on it was the

66

eyes. Ian's eyes were grey, but Ben's were a wicked, roving, merry brown.

'How was Mel?' he asked.

'In good form.'

'I may get over there myself some time. Business, if I can wangle it.'

'She'd like that.'

'You're disgustingly brown.'

'Is that good at my age?'

'Now, now, don't come the old soldier, you suit a tan. Always have.'

We returned to Clive, who at once pointed at the oil tanker to show he hadn't been bored in our absence.

'A veritable behemoth. One careless seaman and we'll all be plunged into eco-hell.'

I gave him his Scotch. 'True.'

'But not very likely,' said Ian. 'Those things are safe as houses.'

'We'll have to take your word for it,' I said, sitting down opposite Clive.

Clive took a big slurp. 'Cheers.'

'So what on earth brought you two into the middle of Littelsea on a Sunday evening?' I asked. It was odd, the three of us sitting there, old friends, separate but connected, unable quite to gauge the mood and the weight of the meeting, unsure of what to say to one another.

'Oh, I've been at a thing in Brighton and thought I'd drop in on the off chance . . . as I drove through the centre of the town by Memorial Gardens there, I happened to see Clive at the autobank.'

I got the picture instantly—it was easier to turn up with someone else in tow, and gave evasion the appearance of a kind deed. Clive's presence meant that if, as was the case, Ben wasn't around, Ian wouldn't have to engage in too much heavy talk with me, and also had an excellent pretext for leaving in good time.

'It's always nice to see you, Clive,' I said politely.

He chortled nervously. 'Ian hailed me from the car. Made me jump. One feels so furtive about getting money out of the hole in the wall—I've come to the conclusion that's because the posture one adopts is exactly the same as using a urinal.'

'Speak for yourself,' said Ian.

'No, I notice it in others as well—the backview with the slightly hunched shoulders—a striking similarity.'

'So—how are you Clive?' I asked, with what I hoped was the correct mixture of casualness and concern.

'Top-hole, thank you for asking.'

I pulled a reproving face, and Ian said: 'He's shot to hell.'

'No, no, no . . .' Clive shook his head vigorously. 'OK, not wonderful, but not hellish either. I'm afraid I've no experience of this, so I've no idea how I should be under the circumstances.'

'Of course not.' I was sorry to have asked such a crass question, and was debating whether to mention Helen, when Clive leaned forward, his Bunterish features contorted, and blurted out:

'I don't suppose you've seen Helen?'

'I have as a matter of fact.'

'And how is *she*?'

This, like 'How old do you think I am?' was a catch question. Would it be good if she were happy, or good if she were sad? Neither, clearly. But I decided that on balance sad was probably better, and had the advantage of being true.

I felt the eyes of both of them upon me as I answered, 'She was absolutely wretched.'

Caught in a storm of conflicting emotions, Clive snatched at his drink again. It was something no actor, however brilliant, could have reproduced, this complex, stifled mix of anguish and gratification. I felt quite awestruck to have been the cause of it.

'She's terribly confused,' I went on. 'She's not comfortable where she's living and she can't see the way forward.'

'Any more than I can,' muttered Clive, his face bulging with emotion. 'I mean, Eve, for God's sake what is going on? What are we doing to one another? We were so happy, we had such a lovely life together until she took up with this fellow. Can she have forgotten so completely about all that?'

I was stumped for an answer. He just didn't get it. His misery was painful to witness, but there were no comfortable words. Fortunately Ian stepped in. He didn't really get it either, but there were certain bland, formulaic responses which for some reason seemed perfectly appropriate between men.

'She'll come round,' said Ian. 'She's gone off the rails for a bit, but left well alone she'll be back. Especially if she's not happy.'

'You think so?' Clive's brow furrowed. He turned to me. 'Eve?'

'I don't know.'

'God . . .'

Ian gave me a reproving look. 'You said she was unhappy. I wish Helen nothing but good, but that has to be a sign of returning sanity.'

'Absolutely,' I agreed. He was right. What was

69

the point of striving after honesty? Clive wanted warm cuddly towels, not a brisk scrub down with wire wool.

Ian looked relieved. 'Brave and calm's the thing,' he said. 'She'll be back.'

Clive rolled his tumbler between his plump, cushiony palms. 'I'd like to go and see her ...' He screwed his face up. 'Should I do that? What do you think?'

I said 'No', and Ian said 'I wouldn't', both at the same time. My turn now to look relieved: I could think of nothing more likely to prevent Helen's return than the presence on her doorstep of her painfully needy and rotund spouse. In his present state everything about him would remind her of why she had fallen so heavily for the mean, lean Kerridge.

'But,' went on Clive, 'she may think I simply don't care, that I'm indifferent, when—' he wavered, got a grip, and wobbled on—'when the opposite is true.'

'She won't think any such thing!' This was one point on which I felt fully confident. 'She absolutely knows that you adore her, and miss her, and want her back. But there's nothing more you can do for the present. You're better off keeping your distance and giving her plenty of time to reflect.'

'Being cruel to be kind,' Ian weighed in with another cliché, and a wildly inapposite one.

'Maybe you're right ...' sighed Clive tremulously.

We both declared heartily that we knew we were, and I got Clive and me more drinks.

It was ten o'clock when they left, and Ben still wasn't back. As we waited in the hall for Clive to

70

emerge from the bathroom, Ian suddenly said:

'And you—you're all right?'

'I'm fine.'

'I think about you a lot, you know.'

'Do you?'

'Don't sound so surprised.'

I wondered what he would have said if I'd told him I hardly thought about him at all.

'There's no need to worry,' I reassured him. 'I'm enjoying life.'

Was it my imagination or did he look a touch crestfallen? Clive emerged, to the flushing of the cistern. He'd combed his hair, and he smelt of soap.

'This has been nice, Eve,' he said. 'You create such a tranquil atmosphere.'

'Thank you.' I kissed him warmly to prevent myself from catching Ian's eye. 'You must come over properly next time—have dinner and stuff.'

'Oh, I don't know about that . . .' He shuffled towards the door, a lost cause, who couldn't contemplate a social engagement without the help and support of the woman he loved.

'How are you getting back?' I asked him.

'If Ian will very kindly drop me off at Town Centre P, I shall make my way . . .'

'No problem,' said Ian. '*Au revoir* then.'

I opened the door. 'Bye.'

'Give the prodigal my best.'

'I will.'

They trotted down the stairs. On the bend, Ian raised a hand without looking up. How did he know I was still standing there I wondered, as I went back in and closed the door. Collecting up the glasses, I decided it was just the pre-programmed

71

response of more than two decades of marriage.

I had no idea whether there was another permanent woman in Ian's life, but I assumed not, firstly because I was sure he would tell me if there was and, secondly—perhaps arrogantly—because I reckoned I would know anyway. No third party had been the cause of our separation, and at the time we had characterised it as an experiment, a trial period. One of the reasons I was so comfortable with my semi-detached status was that I had the best of both worlds: I enjoyed a greater financial security than my job at Bouvier's alone could have provided, the emotional support of a man who was nothing if not loyal and responsible, plus the freedom to live my own life without fear of censure or resentment. I had never been to his London flat, but I pictured it as orderly and comfortable, the home of a middle-aged man happy, as I was, to be a free agent once more.

*   *   *

The weather had changed slightly. In the gathering darkness a brisk offshore breeze grated the smooth surface of the seas and handfuls of rain pattered on my window. I put on my mac and boots and went out, leaving the living room light on so Ben would know I wasn't going to be long.

I ran across the road and turned right on the promenade, to where the first long flight of steps tumbled down the side of the wall to the shingle. Since living at Cliff Mansions I'd become an ozone junkie. The first hit of damp, salty air went to my head like strong drink. The restless rush and suck of the sea was music to my ears. I couldn't imagine how I'd survived all those years hugger-mugger in the man-made English countryside, hemmed in by cushiony hills and cabbagy trees, where even if you couldn't see another house you knew there was one just over the rise or round the bend.

I reached the steps and went down them, leaving the pallid glow of the promenade lights behind. This was what I liked, this swift transition from concrete to the noisy tumble of the beach. From being a background presence, unfurling its long, sullen waves, the sea's growl became thrillingly close, and its fine spray joined the rain on my face.

I trudged down the sliding shingle banks to the water's edge. The pale foam scudded round my feet and then hissed away, dragging the small pebbles with it, exposing shining muscles of sand. When the tide was really low, small children tried to make sandcastles down here, but their efforts were always unsuccessful. This wasn't old, quiet powdery sand that had settled down into a comfortable accommodation with people. This sand still belonged to the sea. It was thick, and wet, and granular, full of minute, scuttling marine life, constantly on the move, not susceptible to patting and piling by small hands.

A bigger wave bounced at me, testing, and I jumped back, feeling a cold trickle of water over the top of my boot. I began to walk at a rather more respectful distance, away from Cliff Mansions towards the western headland. I made myself walk fast, my calf muscles ached with the effort of hauling my feet in and out of the shifting stones. Slimey black rags of weed and bladderwrack marked the tideline, along with the usual marine debris of plastic, fish bones and splintered wood.

73

This wasn't a beach on which to meander barefoot, looking for shells, it was a piece of the British coast still locked in an attritional embrace with the Channel, giving nothing away, taking nothing much, hanging on like grim death. Periodically, when there were fierce winter storms, the sea wall would be breached and the buildings on the promenade, Cliff Mansions included, would have their foundations shaken by maddened waves suddenly let slip. In the old days the Esplanade Hotel had taken some pride in the tilt of a massive oil painting in the residents' lounge: when first-time guests pointed out, as they invariably did, that the painting was at an angle the staff would explain that it was not the picture, but the building, which was crooked.

I walked for about half a mile, clambering over the sodden breakwaters. People sitting indoors would have thought it dark, but it was quite easy to see one's way down here. There was a bit of moon, the shape of an orange segment in the patchy sky, and the racing sea caught and dispersed its small glow. In the distance the oil tanker was now no more than a compact constellation of lights. The gulls who yelped and screeched overhead all day long were gone to roost.

When I reached that part of the beach where the fishermen kept their boats I turned back. I was deterred not so much by the thick hawsers stretched up the slope like trip wires and the slippery logs sunk into the shingle, but by the ubiquitous smears of tar. Distant memories of my furious mother battling the tar menace with Thorpit and a kitchen knife made me wary.

I trudged back up the ledges to the promenade

for the walk home. At this end of the bay the authorities had run out of goodwill and cash—there were none of the little civic niceties that marked the stretch from Cliff Mansions to the Martello Tower, no concrete tubs of windproof annuals, no heritage lamp-posts, or seats dedicated to the deceased. On the landward side of the road the ground fell away sharply to the bleak expanse of the sports ground. The ground was below sea level, which meant that in the winter, and even from time to time in inclement summers, it was easily flooded. Tonight, a glimmer of light in the cricket pavilion indicated a home win.

I was almost back at the flats when I heard soft footfalls behind me, first walking, then breaking into a padding, lupine trot. I stiffened with pre-programmed anxiety and turned towards the road. HORRIFIC SEX ATTACK IN SEASIDE TOWN, NO ONE HEARS LOCAL WOMAN SCREAM—

'Hi.'

'Ben—for goodness' sake!'

'Think I was the Beast of Littelsea? Dream on.'

He fell into step beside me and my nervously pattering heart quietened.

'So what's occurring?' he asked. 'Just out for a bit of a walk?'

'Yes . . . Your father came round.'

'Oh yeah?'

'He was hoping to see you, he stayed for quite a while. Sent his love, says he hopes he catches you next time.'

'I was only along at the pub.'

I refrained from pointing out that the Rat and Ferret might have been Ayers Rock for all its

75

accessibility to the rest of us.

'Give him a ring,' I suggested.

'I might well do.'

We walked down the side of the Mansions, leaving the sound of the sea behind.

'How's Pearl?' I asked.

'Search me, I haven't seen her.'

'Right.'

I felt his amused look first, then his indulgent pat on the shoulder. 'Pleased?'

'Not at all, I was only asking—'

'You're chuffed to little bits.'

'That's not true,' I protested, though I was beginning to laugh, 'Pearl was fine—in her way—'

We were both paralytic by the time I'd unlocked the door.

*   *   *

Bouvier's was a provincial auctioneers with big ideas. Ours was a small satellite branch—the head office was in Hove, and the smartest in Brighton. The owner, Piers Bouvier, claimed he could trace his lineage back to the Huguenots, and his grand house named (pretentiously, we thought) La Falaise, had a walled and terraced garden which he said was a classic French design for growing grapes in the English climate. It had not escaped our attention, however, that Piers had bought the house some ten years ago, and not inherited it as he might have liked us to believe.

Still, we weren't complaining: Bouvier's was our meal ticket whatever its provenance. Its success was probably due to the lack of local competition, and also the fact that Littelsea was a retirement area, with plenty of well-heeled senior citizens moving house, and passing on.

My job had originally been solely clerical but the bit I'd picked up about the trade, plus a penchant for dealing with the public, meant that these days I occasionally got sent out to do the less-demanding valuations.

In the Littelsea branch of Bouvier's we were only four—Geoffrey, the manager; Emma, the Sotheby's-trained second-in-command; Jo, the administrator; and me. And a very happy little ship we were. Geoffrey was a smartly independent widower in his early sixties. Emma was the sort of thirty-something single woman who, if she had not been studying Georgian whatnots for Bouvier's would have been doing research—and the rest— for some smooth home-counties MP. Jo was a jolly local girl who lived with her parents, went clubbing at weekends and holidaying with girlfriends— 'never take a bloke on holiday' being her watchword. Our harmonious working relationship depended on our differences. If our lives outside the office had begun to resemble each other or, heaven forfend, to overlap in any way we should certainly have fallen out irreparably.

Bouvier's was situated in a side street running off the Memorial Gardens—not the Lanes, exactly, but quite a pleasant little backwater with an Italian restaurant and a bearable pub, the Magnet, at the non-gardens end.

On the Wednesday of my first week back, Geoffrey came into our office to ask if I'd do a valuation in Hawley End.

'It should be Emma, but she's had to go to the sale in Brighton—they've slipped in that oak dining table and chairs she thinks so highly of and she wants to keep her eye on things.'

'Fine,' I said, 'I'd like to.'

'Jammy thing,' said Jo, not seriously.

Geoffrey looked at her. 'Do you want to go?'

'You're joking!'

'What's the score?' I asked.

'As I understand it it's a modest house with a few nice pieces—the old lady's gone into a nursing home and the family are dealing with the contents. To be candid I think it's more your sort of job than Emma's anyway, because dealing with the people will be at least as important as putting a price on the items.'

When he'd gone out of the room Jo made a get-you face. 'You and your soft skills—I should be so lucky!'

*   *   *

Because I was due at the client's house at two-fifteen I left the office at lunchtime and went to call on Helen. She was in, attending to some page proofs at a gate-leg table in the living room.

'No, no,' she murmured in response to my demurs, 'come on in, it must be time for a break of some sort.'

Having no expectations on the refreshment front I'd bought a prepacked sandwich at a petrol station on the dual carriageway, but to my surprise Helen got out a loaf of solid, greyish bread, heavily barnacled with seeds, some low-fat spread and a nice chunk of farmhouse cheddar with proper rind.

'This is it, I'm afraid, but you're quite welcome . . .'

'It looks great, thanks.'

'I believe I've got some cider as well.'

'Even better.'

The cider, bought from the village shop, was flat, cloudy and ferociously strong. It seemed to have no effect on Helen, but after half a glass I could feel my face overheating and my voice working slightly ahead of my brain. Perhaps this was what prompted me to mention Clive's visit.

'He was asking after you,' I told her. 'I said I'd seen you.'

'And how did you say I was?' enquired Helen in that languid way which would have sounded sarcastic to someone who didn't know her as well as I did.

'I told the truth but not the whole truth. I said you weren't epecially happy with your lot.'

'Hmm . . .' mused Helen, chipping at the cheese, 'I wonder if that was wise . . .'

'What would you rather I did?'

She sighed. 'Heavens, I don't know. I just truly couldn't bear Clive to turn up on the doorstep. I should embarrass myself and everyone else and absolutely no useful purpose would be served.'

'He won't do that,' I assured her.

Something in my tone or manner caught Helen's attention, because she said, with rather more asperity: 'Why are you so sure?'

'He doesn't feel sufficiently confident to attempt anything so bold.'

'Thank God.' She looked at me, blinking as if seeing me properly for the first time. 'So tell me how everything is with you?'

I told her. It didn't take long, I was versed in the art of the breezy summing up. Helen lit a cigarette and waved a hand at the smoke.

'Perhaps I should take up tennis,' she said, coughing languidly, in response to some reference of mine about having plenty to do. 'What do you think?'

'Why not? Have you ever played?'

'At school. I wasn't completely palsied, but I never made a team or anything.'

'If you're interested you should invest in a bit of coaching,' I suggested.

She pulled a face. 'That smacks of trying altogether too hard ... I've never made my veins stand out yet, and I'm convinced it would be unwise to start now.'

'How are things with John?' I asked.

'Sublime and ridiculous,' she replied, regarding her slightly trembling cigarette. 'But what can I do?'

It wasn't a question, or if it was it was only a rhetorical one, so I said nothing, and she added almost dazedly: 'I'm not myself.'

I thought of poor devoted, distracted Clive, and concluded that whatever clumsy attempts I had made to promote his cause, he was on a hiding to nothing.

*   *   *

The client's house was actually a neat semi-detched bungalow in a small close off the village high street. A Volvo estate occupied the paved parking bay to the full, so I parked in the road. The front door opened as I approached and an exhausted-looking middle-aged woman in big shorts greeted me.

'Hello—Bouvier's?'

80

I introduced myself. 'How do you do, Jane Rymer,' she said. 'You're such a welcome sight. One more thing I can cross off my list, does that sound terrible?'

'Not in the least.'

'This is such a trying job, and rather a depressing one, and it tends to fall to the womenfolk, doesn't it?'

'I suppose it does.'

She led me into the living room. 'This is actually my mother-in-law's place, but Julian is an only, and has to be in the States this week, so muggins here is well and truly lumbered.'

'Poor you,' I agreed. 'I sympathise. I moved house myself not so long ago and even sorting out one's own possessions is a headache, let alone someone else's.'

'Well, I don't know ...' she was a coping type and didn't want to seem to be whingeing. 'Actually I mustn't make too much of it. It's only a small house, and Mother has chosen what she wants to keep.'

'Where is she?'

'Whitegates.' She named a converted Georgian pile between Hawley End and Littlesea. 'Do you know it?'

'I know of it. It's got a good reputation.'

'Yes, we had very reliable recommendations and the staff are perfectly sweet ... I'm sorry, how rude of me, would you like a coffee or something? Teabag?'

'No thanks, I'd better get on.'

'Are you sure? It's being in someone else's house, it throws one.'

'Of course.'

81

'So how do you like to do this, do I just point you at the relevant bits?'

'If you would.'

Old Mrs Rymer's bits were nice—an eclectic assortment of Georgian and Jacobean pieces, far too big for the bungalow, some oriental porcelain, quantities of silver, half a dozen pleasing Victorian watercolours and a hideous but fashionable clock of the same period, its face peeping out like a shy bride from the surrounding squadron of cherubs.

It didn't take long to get round. Jane Rymer accompanied me with exclamations of surprise and gratification, sometimes genuine, sometimes merely polite, making her own notes. In spite of her rather distracted manner, she was the right stuff, and nobody's fool. When we'd finished, I explained that I would send her a printed copy of my estimates by the end of the week.

'Excellent,' she said. 'I must say it really is astonishing what one accumulates in a lifetime. I dread to think what our offspring will have to contend with when Julian and I pop our clogs. Do you want that coffee now, because I'm going to.'

This time I accepted. While she was in the kitchen I studied the collection of photographs on Mrs Rymer's cherrywood piecrust table. I recognised Jane and the absent Julian on their wedding day, their faces alight with absolute confidence, and another of them a few years later with three children, two boys with shiny fringes and ties, and a little girl in an alice band and a smocked dress. Julian was a little shorter than his wife, sleek and thin-lipped.

At the back, half-hidden behind other assorted family groups, was an oval-framed black-and-white

82

photograph of a young man in uniform whom I took to be Mr Rymer. Even the ancient mount spotted with damp, and the dusty glass could not dim his heroically Saxon good looks.

When my hostess came back in with the coffee I pointed to the photo.

'What a wonderful looking man.'

'Isn't he just? One's tempted to say they don't make them like that any more.'

'Is he—I mean I assume he's your father-in-law . . . ?'

'No. But for history he might have been.'

Her expression invited enquiry. 'How do you mean?'

'He was a close friend, a very close friend, of Mother's before the war.'

'And she kept a photo of him all this time.'

'Oh yes. It was no secret that he was the love of her life.'

'She sounds quite an unconventional woman.'

'Indeed she is.' She picked up the photo and rubbed the glass on her shorts before replacing it.

'He was German.'

*   *   *

After I'd printed out the valuations I wrote a standard letter to Jane Rymer and posted the whole lot off to her at her home address in Beaconsfield, as directed. Then I left the office and went home, stopping off at the supermarket en route. By the Indian goodies I encountered Rick Shaw, still in his work suit—he worked in the council planning department. He gave me his shy, warm smile—Desma was a lucky woman.

'I said I'd take back something that requires no cooking,' he said. 'What do you think?'

'You can't go wrong with tikka masala,' I agreed. 'Some pilau rice, a couple of bhajees and you're home and dry. The nation's favourite dish.'

'Just what I thought.' He popped a positive feast in his basket with admirable lack of caution. As we parted company a girl in tight jeans gave him a scaldingly appreciative look, which Littelsea's favourite dish was far too nice and modest to notice.

*   *   *

Ben was out again. I took the opportunity to dive into his room and take out the past week's quota of cereal bowls and rubbish. With regard to my forays into what the papers would have called 'his space' we adopted a policy of discreet openness. I went in and out on these occasional clean-up forays with impunity: on the other hand he made not the slightest attempt to conceal anything, on the grounds that if I went in uninvited I got everything I deserved. Whatever I saw, I made no comment.

It was the usual story this evening. There were plenty of fag ends and beer bottles, a couple of questionable magazines and an unopened condom on the bedside table. I took it all in my stride, stacking the crockery on a tray and dropping the rubbish in a binbag, both of which I put outside the door. When I went back in to open the window I noticed, scrunched between the pillows and the bedhead, the ageing stuffed bear with alopoecia, last vestige of a bygone innocence.

Touched, I retrieved the bear—Algy—and sat

84

him up on top of the pillows. Then I went into the kitchen and put my spinach cannelloni in the microwave.

CHAPTER FIVE

'She's here!' hissed Sabine, who was ringing me at work.

'And how many heads does she have?' I asked.

'You make a joke of it, Eve,' she said reproachfully, her voice still lowered, 'but it is very alarming to have a strange young woman in the house when one is not used to it.'

'You'll soon shake down,' I suggested. 'What's she doing at the moment?'

'Nothing until Monday—*merde*!'

'No, I mean at this exact moment. As we speak.'

'Calling her mother.' The last word faded slightly as though Sabine were looking over her shoulder. 'I still can't believe she's going to be living here.'

'She's not that bad though, is she?'

'Oh, who can say,' said Sabine, as though this was actually the last thing to concern anyone. 'Round-face, brown hair, plummy voice, your typical English schoolgirl.'

Visualising some of the schoolgirls I knew I took leave to doubt that Martin's daughter was typical.

'But she's not a schoolgirl, she's a student,' I said.

'No, no—this one is a schoolgirl, believe me.' Sabine was clearly undecided whether to represent her charge as being nothing but trouble or too boring to be trouble. 'I use it as a generic term.'

85

'At least she doesn't sound the sort to give you a hard time.'

'She is here. That is all.'

'Poor Sabine.'

'Don't laugh at me, Eve.'

'I wasn't. I'm not.'

'Yes, you are. You don't understand.'

She was serious, so I tried to be. 'Maybe not, but I do have an imagination. I think you're winding yourself up unnecessarily. Everything will be fine.'

'What I find so unreasonable,' went on Sabine as though I hadn't spoken, 'is that this is Martin's daughter, but it is I who will have to make all the effort.'

'Why?'

'Because he goes out and I am here!'

'Isn't she going to work on the farm?'

'*Eventually*. Until then *I* shall have to talk to her, to keep her amused, to eat lunch with her for as far as the eye can see—Hell, she's coming! Bye—!'

It was just as well she hung up because by this time I was laughing out loud.

*   *   *

It was, as Sabine had not said but might well have done, easy for me to laugh. It was the lunch hour and as soon as I'd put the phone down I switched off the VDU and went out into the breezy sunshine to eat my sandwich on the prom. I was awfully glad I didn't have a strange nineteen-year-old to entertain at this moment, let alone back at Cliff Mansions for the next several months. My sympathy for Sabine was more heartfelt than she could possibly realise. I took no pleasure in her

86

discomfort, if you didn't count my relief that it wasn't me. I had come to the single life late, and like all converts I was more passionate about my cause than those who had known no other. Sabine's house was so empty, so immaculate, so perfect and pristine, and her existence (Martin notwithstanding) so flawlessly self-centred, that I could all too clearly imagine her dismay at this invasion. Martin's blameless, expensively-educated daughter must appear to her like a noxious incubus, sucking away her freedom and leaving a ring round the bath. Whatever Sophie Drage was, she'd never be right. The girl didn't exist who would have suited Sabine. If she were a crisp sophisticate she'd be competition. If she were pretty and fluttery she'd be dismissed as vacuous. As it was, she was a chubby trainee vet. But none of that was the point. Her chief and unforgivable crime was that she was *there*.

*   *   *

Yes, as I returned to my flat at the end of the day I could find it in my heart to feel some sympathy for Sabine. I had my space to myself, except for Ben, who as my own flesh and blood didn't count. I remembered longing, along with everyone else, for the children to be old enough to leave home, but since Ben's return I'd discovered the comfort to be derived from having another adult about the place, one who expected little, demanded nothing, and was too happily self-absorbed to make judgements. There was also something touching in the fact that he was here because he chose to be. He could have given in to Nozz's blandishments or shacked up—

heaven forfend—with Pearl or any one of her smitten predecessors, but he had chosen to live here, with me, where he could keep Algy on his bed without fear of mockery. I wasn't entirely naïve, I acknowledged that this state of affairs had much to do with the presence of a washing machine, tumble drier, and well-stocked freezer, but just the same . . .

Sabine rang again at about ten, and launched straight back into her diatribe as though she'd never hung up.

'She's gone to bed! Can you imagine? It's barely ten and she's gone upstairs!'

'I'd have thought you'd have been pleased.'

'But what sort of nineteen-year-old goes to bed at this hour? It's not natural.'

I ignored the comment and answered the question: 'A clean-living one?'

'Eve—would you care for a nightcap?'

'Well, I don't know, really—'

'Please, I need some adult company.'

'Where's Martin?'

'He's around somewhere, but that doesn't matter.'

No point in explaining that wasn't what I meant. 'It's a bit late, Sabine.'

'Don't you start!'

'I mean I couldn't even be with you before about half past—'

'Horror upon horror!'

'I'll see you shortly.'

*   *   *

Sabine had her own separate drawing room, full of

pretty and elegant French things, and it was here that she poured two huge Armagnacs and announced:

'I have reached a decision.'

'Oh?'

'I am going to give a party for her.'

'Good idea,' I said carefully, wondering what had brought this on. 'Who will you invite?'

'Everyone. *Le tout* Littelsea. I need to wrest back the intitiative.'

'You feel that Sophie's taken it then . . . ?'

'By default—default? Is that what I mean?'

'Possibly.'

'It's Martin's birthday at the end of next week, so I thought I might combine the two.' She sipped her Armagnac and flashed me a quick look. 'What do you think?'

'A party never does any harm. As long as you—'

'What?' She was imperious, impatient.

'As long as you invite some people her own age.'

'I do not wish to preside over an orgy, for heaven's sake. The idea is to have a civilised gathering, Pimms on the terrace I thought, to enable her to meet some of her father's friends and colleagues. And her stepmother's, of course.' She drooped one perfectly manicured hand, wrist uppermost, in my direction. 'To make her feel more at home.'

And to put the poor girl firmly in her place, I thought. My face must have betrayed something because Sabine said sharply: 'You are not convinced.'

'Of course I am. Anyway, it doesn't matter what I think. It's not up to me. It's Martin's birthday, and she'll like that.'

'Quite.' We sipped in silence for a moment. 'Oh! This is something I shall miss—a quiet drink with a friend.'

She was determined still to represent herself as the condemned woman, but the party idea had cheered her up.

'Would you like to come and see the court?'

'I'd love to.'

Sabine dipped the brandy bottle over our glasses for a second time and led me out through the French window. There was a clear sky, with the midsummer stars still coming out, and a half moon, but we'd have been able to see in any event because the Drage acres were equipped with cunningly concealed uplighters which bloomed into life at our approach and died in our wake. From the terrace we went across a lawn, and followed a winding path through a tall shrubbery, where occasional statuary flexed pale muscles among the foliage. We were up on the bluff over-looking Littelsea, and about half a mile from the cliff edge. On this still night we could hear the soft surge of the sea.

At the court, which was shielded on the seaward side by trees, Sabine flicked a switch and we were in full daylight. The work was more or less complete except for the surrounding patio and summerhouse. We walked to the service line and Sabine tapped her *ne ultima* wedge-soled trainer on the ground. It was smooth as a billiard table.

'This is the best surface in the world,' she told me. 'We shan't know ourselves.'

I suggested mischievously: 'Maybe Sophie plays.'

'Maybe.'

'Private schools are usually hot on tennis. She

could even be rather good.'

'We shall see,' said Sabine forbiddingly. 'But who would she play with?'

It was no good. On this subject Sabine was operating in a parallel universe, from which she would have to return of her own volition and under her own steam.

We strolled in silence round the court, sipping our brandies. We paused by the plastic-shrouded structure that would be the summerhouse.

'It's going to be fully equipped,' she explained to me. 'There will be a fridge, a sound system ... With this climate of yours one needs a bolthole.' It was Sabine's habit to play off her adopted country against her natural one. So bad weather was always ours, sunshine always hers; apalling restaurants were typical of us, excellent ones just like home; any kind of elegance or good living was something the poor benighted British had learned from her countrymen, but any display of drunkenness and sloth was—*naturellement*—all their own.

'It's going to be quite wonderful,' I assured her. 'Perhaps Martin will start to take an interest?'

She pulled a face. 'I do hope not. If there is one thing I cannot stand it's those terrible mixed doubles with a lot of middle-aged men soft-balling the women, and desperate wives with their cellulite on show flirting with other people's husbands.'

You had to love her. 'Well, if you put it like that ...'

'I do, Eve, I do! Shall we move on?'

Sabine switched off the floodlights and we left the tennis court. I followed submissively where she led. We went back through the shrubbery, between the stony gazes of the statues, and then round the

91

lawn to the south side of the house. Here, on a terrace all of its own, the Drages' asymmetrical rounded pool, the shape of an artist's palette, lay smooth as glass in its setting of terra-cotta tiles, lavender and tumbling pelargoniums. On the far side was the Victorian gazebo, the remains of which had already been here, and which Sabine and Martin had had moved and restored to considerably more than its former glory.

We walked down shallow rustic steps towards the pool. I glanced up at the house, with its many gables and splendid conservatory, and wondered where the others were. The odd light burned, but that meant nothing, because the Drages had assorted lamps on a time switch to dissuade the hapless burglars who would otherwise be caught bang to rights by their fiendishly sensitive and centrally-connected security system. It was odd to think that Martin and his daughter were around somewhere, and might even, separately or together, be watching us as we discussed them.

The possibility of invisible spectators clearly didn't bother Sabine, because when we reached the bottom of the steps, she suddenly said: 'Would you like to swim?'

'I don't know . . . I don't have a cozzie.'

She gave me the look she was undoubtedly going to bestow on Sophie. 'Eve—you are in a large private garden in the middle of the night.'

'Of course, how silly.'

'I'm going to.'

Smartening her pace and swallowing her brandy she set off round the pool to the gazebo. She put her glass down on the table, heeled off her shoes and began peeling off her trousers, shirt and halter top, revealing the fact that she wore no underwear and was the same even colour all over. I watched enviously, and in some alarm as she dived in, her smooth, slender, long-limbed body making only the smallest splash as it cut the water.

She surfaced just as people do in films, shaking silver arcs of drops from her head and face, slicking her hair back with long, tanned fingers. the transformation in her mood was now complete.

'Come on in, it's beautiful!' she called, her smile brilliant in her shiny wet face. 'Don't be shy,' she added, 'you're looking wonderful at the moment.'

If Sabine genuinely wished me to overcome my shyness, she should never have made that last remark, which indicated all too clearly that she had been sizing me up not just recently but for some months, or even years.

She flicked water at me playfully. 'Get those clothes off, Eve.'

I retired to the gazebo to undress. At least I had a tan, though my bikini areas were humiliatingly white. I knew I should have strode forth tall and proud, but it was no good—I scuttled, doubled up from the gazebo and belly-flopped into the water with Sabine's laugh ringing in my ears.

She was still laughing when I came up for air.

'Really Eve—are you glad you came now?'

'Yes . . . !'

Now that I was doing a leisurely breast stroke towards the end of the pool, I was glad. The last time I'd swum was on holiday, when the water had been blissfully cool. In the freshening English evening Sabine's pool was as tepid and comforting as amniotic fluid.

She waited for me to draw level and then began

to swim alongside me.

'Did you meet anyone interesting when you were away?' she asked.

'Lots of people.'

'Eve!'

I sighed. 'You mean a man.'

'Of course.'

'There were plenty about—an embarrassment of riches, I suppose. But no one interesting in the way that you mean.'

'What a shame.'

'Not really. I couldn't have been bothered with it anyway.'

She sucked her teeth. 'What sort of attitude is that?'

'A lazy one.'

She chuckled as we turned and headed back. 'At least you're honest about it. But you mustn't close your mind to opportunities, Eve.'

Gosh, but she was arrogant. If I'd been at all xenophobic I might have put it down to the natural *hauteur* of the French, but she was just Sabine, who had life and its mysteries sewn up.

'Hello there! Is this a private thing or can anyone join in?'

It was Martin, coming down the steps from the house with a towel over his shoulder.

'It's a private thing, my darling,' replied Sabine, not joking.

Martin leaned over the side peering exaggeratedly. 'Is that Eve in there?'

'Hello Martin.'

'She got you swimming in the buff, I see.'

'Under protest, I might say.' I began moving away from him again, though the remark had been not in the least salacious.

'You won't catch me doing it—there are some things better kept covered. In my case, anyway.' He sat down on a bench outside the gazebo, and dropped his towel on the ground. 'So are you saying I'm not allowed to come in?'

'Yes. Eve and I are having a nice peaceful ladies swim,' replied Sabine.

'In that case I shouldn't dream of disturbing you.' He really was the most genial and tolerant of husbands—big, balding, confident: an immensely reassuring presence. On the other hand he didn't move, but folded his arms and gazed up at the heavens.

'What a night. Astonishing stars ... Did you go out in the desert while you were there?'

'We did, yes.'

'That's the place to see the stars, don't you agree? Quite wonderful.'

I came to the side and rested there, a little ashamed of my earlier prim reaction.

'I never believed people who said endless sand could be beautiful. And you're right about the sky—you feel you could touch it, or bring the stars closer just by breathing in.'

'What are you two talking about?' called Sabine from the other side.

'Inhaling the desert stars, darling,' replied Martin. 'Do you remember that feeling? In Marrakesh?'

'*Superbe*,' she agreed. 'It was only a pity Eve didn't find someone to gaze at the stars with.'

'That's her business,' said Martin. 'If she chooses to turn down offers, then . . .' He let the remark tail off flatteringly. What a nice man he was.

95

'How's your daughter?' I asked.

'Sophie is tucked up in bed so far as I know.' Sabine made a watery sound of disbelief, but he went on: 'I'm pleased to have this opportunity to do something useful for her, that isn't just a case of writing a cheque.'

'What exactly will she be doing at the farm?'

'General dogsbody, how her father started out.' Martin was justly proud of his self-made-man status. 'Help with the stock, learn about the accounting, fetch and carry, grumble about Brussels—you name it.'

'It will probably put her off animals for life,' said Sabine, joining me at the side.

'If it does,' said Martin, 'then that's a useful lesson learned, and a damn sight better now than when she's halfway through vet school.'

'Ugh ...' Sabine shuddered fastidiously. 'It's beyond me why a girl would want to do such a job anyway, we have seen those terrible programmes on television.'

'Sabine my cherry, she'll probably wind up in Solihull or Frinton putting cats on diets and giving placebos to poodles. Anyway, she's a good girl, she'll turn her hand to anything.'

'I look forward to meeting her,' I said, 'at the party.'

'What party's that?'

'The one I am going to give for Sophie,' said Sabine, 'in a couple of weeks time. Your birthday.'

'I see! So what's going to be on the menu then— heavy metal, hot-and-cold-running sex and lashings and lashings of happy pills?' Martin had been at the back of the queue for political correctness, it was one of his greatest charms.

96

'Martin! No, I thought a pleasant, congenial Sunday drinks party to meet some of our friends.'

'What the devil would she want to meet them for?' asked Martin robustly, putting the question I'd been too timid to ask myself.

'It will be a start, Martin,' said Sabine, a frosty warning note in her voice. 'A few introductions, and who knows what else may come her way.'

'I bow as always to your superior judgement, cherry.' He rose, picked up his towel and lobbed it carelessly into the gazebo. 'I'm for bed. Tell you what though Eve—you know a few of the younger generation, why don't you bring them along?'

I tried, wildly, to imagine the likes of Pearl and Nozz sipping Pimms *chez* Drage at an hour on a Sunday they would scarcely recognise as day. 'I don't actually know all that many.'

'But you've got a spy in the camp. Get Ben to bring a few along.'

'I'll see what I can do.'

'And haven't the Chatsworths got a couple of boys?'

'They have—yes, I'll ask.'

'Not your job, Eve—Sabine, you'll be inviting the Chatsworths, won't you? Get them to bring their two along.'

Sabine ducked under water without deigning a reply, but Martin didn't seem to expect one, and departed with a wave.

I decided against returning to the subject by any route whatever, and set off to do a few more lengths. I was conscious as I did so of Sabine darting past in the opposite direction, a pale, silent form beneath the surface.

When we'd swum enough, and got dressed I would have gone straight to the car, but I'd left my bag with my car keys in Sabine's drawing room. She waited in the drive while I went in to fetch them.

As I walked back across the hall I heard light footsteps behind me and glanced over my shoulder to come face to face with Helena Bonham-Carter, wearing a Nike T-shirt and holding a chunk of baguette fringed with lettuce and dripping with salad cream.

'Sorry,' said the vision, 'night starvation.'

'That's OK,' I replied, 'I know the feeling.'

She flashed me a quirky, conspiratorial smile and trotted up the stairs. Her backview displayed dark hair worn in a fat, untidy plait, and good legs, not of the never-ending, up-to-the-armpits variety, but trim and shapely. I retained an impression of large, dark, intelligent eyes, a humorous cupid's-bow mouth and a heart-shaped face as unlike a pudding as any I'd seen.

As I went out to the car I thought it was no wonder Sabine was unsettled. And decided, without even trying, to bring Ben to the aid of the party.

*   *   *

'I don't mind,' he said when I asked him. 'I'll give it a go.'

'Thanks, you're a sport.'

'An absolute jolly old brick, aren't I.'

It was Saturday morning, and we were in the kitchen. He was smoking a cigarette and drinking

98

chocolate milk out of a plastic bottle prior to going in to HMV, I was sitting at the table in my dressing gown with a mug of tea and the Weekend section of the *Telegraph*. In the background Cliff Morgan cast his amiable spell over heroes and villains alike in *Sport on Four*. On the other side of the passage a dazzle of sunlight streamed into the sitting room. I had plans to go on the beach early, until tennis time, and then after lunch to take myself for a long walk along the cliffs. Simple pleasures, but I was a slave to them.

'You met her then, did you?' Ben asked without much interest, dropping the empty chocolate milk bottle in the bin.

'Only fleetingly, not to talk to.'

'Nice?'

I knew what he meant. 'I thought so. Unusual.'

'Not sure I like the sound of that.'

'But you will come anyway—imagine the poor girl immured up there with no one but Sabine for company.'

'She'll probably be shagging sheep by the time the party comes round, you know what these farming folk are.'

'No. Do you?'

The cigarette end followed the bottle into the bin. 'I read about them in the papers.'

As I returned to the Hatches, Matches and Despatches, I thought, with great satisfaction, was he ever barking up the wrong tree.

*   *   *

Tennis wise, as I saw it, there were two possibilities for Sabine. Her perturbation would either fire her

99

up to play the game of her life, or it would prove her undoing.

On Saturday the latter prevailed. She fluffed, she over-hit, she double-faulted, and her simmering temper, always a fellow traveller on the tennis court, boiled over with some regularity. Desma was as dogged as ever, but with Sabine on self-destruct nothing could save their partnership from complete annihilation.

Ronnie was at her most breezy and good-humoured. 'Of course I'll bring them along,' she called, as she whacked the balls up to our end after another love service game. 'Or at least I'll definitely bring Philip, he's around that weekend. I don't know about Simon, but I'm not sure you'd want him anyway . . . !'

'It's Martin's idea to invite young people,' said Sabine frostily. 'I'm sure they will be bored to death.'

'Why should they be?' asked Desma. 'It's a nice idea to mix up the generations, and your stepdaughter will appreciate it.'

I was about to agree with this, but caught Sabine's expression as she strode to the baseline to serve and decided against further encouraging remarks.

'Do you want any more?' asked Ronnie, 'because I'm sure we could rustle up a few.'

'Whatever,' replied Sabine, lifting racquet and ball together in preparation. 'Are you ready?'

'Ready as I'll ever be,' said Ronnie. 'Fault! But not by much.'

*   *   *

For one reason or another we didn't go on to lunch that day. The Chatsworths were going to visit Dennis's mother, Desma had to see her sister in hospital, and Sabine pleaded extreme domestic pressure.

As I opened my front door, my legs trembling slightly from running up the stairs immediately after tennis, I experienced one of those sudden and entirely unexpected frissons of melancholy: I was the only one of the four of us returning to an empty flat—no one waiting, no calls on my time, nothing to do but my own thing. It was what I most liked about my life, and yet it still, occasionally and from out of the blue, had the power to rattle me.

As if I had exercised some telekinetic power, the phone rang.

'Hello there.' It was Ian. 'I was expecting the machine.'

'No.'

'I thought you'd be having lunch with the girls.'

It annoyed me sometimes that he knew so much about my life and I so little about his. My routines were in his memory bank, but I was far too proud to ask how he spent his weekends.

'No,' I said, 'not today.'

'Well look,' he said, 'I wondered if you'd like to come up to town one evening this week—we could have some dinner or something.'

'Why?' I asked baldly. I realised that sounded unnecessarily rude, and added: 'I mean, any particular reason?'

'Oh, just an opportunity to talk . . . I could come down there if you like.'

'We're not exactly overburdened with four-star restaurants in Littelsea. As you know.'

'No, but we could drive out somewhere. It's up to you.'

I really didn't know why I was hesitating. Dinner in town with Ian was not something to be sniffed at, and it wasn't as if my diary were black with invitations.

With an unsettling flash of insight, he said, quite without sarcasm: 'I don't want to disturb the peaceful tenor of your life.'

'You're not,' I replied, 'I'd like to come.'

'Good—Thursday? I'll meet you at Victoria.'

'Fine.'

'How's Ben?'

'He's fine, at work at the moment.'

'Well give him my love. Tell him there's a good chance for tickets for the Oval Test.'

As I dumped my tennis kit in the washing basket and changed into jeans, I had to concede how fortunate it was that Ian and I were on good terms. Our separation was nothing if not amicable, and our dealings with one another always friendly and harmonious. His call had cheered me up. I was not a sad person, deserving of sympathy: I had a life.

In this benign frame of mind I gave Helen a ring before leaving to see if she fancied a walk. The phone rang several times before it was picked up and a man's voice answered.

'Yup?'

I realised with a shock that I was speaking to John Kerridge, but there was no backing out now.

'May I speak to Helen?'

'Can I say who's calling?'

'It's Eve.'

'Oh hi, Eve, I'll pass you over.' He assumed a familiarity with me which I should never have dreamed of returning. We had met once, and fleetingly, but my name had obviously been bandied about in some context or other.

He'd put his hand over the mouthpiece for a moment, but as he removed it I heard the unmistakable rustle of bedding. Oh God, they were indulging in afternoon delight and I was—

'Eve.'

'Look Helen I'm sorry, I didn't realise you had company, I'll call another time.'

'That's OK, I'm here now.'

'But it's irrelevant anyway, because I was going to ask you if you wanted to do something this afternoon.'

'You're right, I can't.'

'Not to worry—'

'Another time perhaps . . .'

'Yes, yes, see you soon.'

I was sweating as I put the phone down.

*   *   *

I walked right up the cliff path, over the bluff and down into the next bay which was accessible only on foot. On the way I passed within a few hundred yards of the Drages' boundary, and wondered what they were doing this fine Saturday afternoon. There would certainly have been no point in inviting Sabine to accompany me—she considered walking a mindless pursuit fit only for the British and their dogs. And what about Sophie? Were she, her father and stepmother enjoying a swim together? Or stretched out on parallel loungers on the sunny stones outside the gazebo? Or perhaps they'd all gone out somewhere *en famille*?

Somehow I couldn't picture this. Family outings were another activity sure to be well beyond Sabine's pale.

My question was answered when I paused at the point where the footpath crossed the lane, and the Drages' runaround, a grey Range Rover, hummed past with Martin at the wheel and Sophie sitting next to him. They were smiling and talking happily, and didn't see me. Of course—Martin was taking her out and relieving his wife of her onerous responsibilities for the afternoon. Whatever Sabine might imply, this snapshot left me with the impression that Martin and his daughter were on excellent terms.

*   *   *

The path began to drop down into the next bay. Ancient geography lessons told me that this was a hanging valley, scored by a river of ice a million years ago, now just a smooth grassy cleft in the chalky headland. The path met the foot of the valley about fifty metres above the beach, but there was a narrow shelving scramble down the cliff between crouching clusters of broom and gorse, and wind-shrivelled brambles that yielded only the smallest, sourest berries.

Knowing the track like the back of my hand, I went down at a canter, trying not to think of the long trudge back up in the evening sun. In a minute I was on the beach. At least, I thought of it as a beach but you couldn't possibly have done beachy things on it—no cricket, volleyball, sandcastles, dabbling idly in rock pools or dashing headlong into the surf. This was an obdurate tumble of great smooth stones like Henry Moore rejects, lying as they'd fallen any old how, God knows how many millennia ago. After the calf-crunching scuttle down the cliff I now had to swarm and clamber and teeter and leap for several more minutes until quite suddenly the boulders went quiet and flat beneath me, as though performing a massed, petrified salaam before the might of the sea.

This was where I got my reward. Now I could sit with the pale rocks prostrate before me, and the smooth silver-green hills rising on either side, and feel like Britannia, ruling the waves.

The tide was on the turn when I reached my usual vantage point. The surf poured in, sighing, over the rocks and retreated, muttering, between them, leaving a gradually widening dark band to show where it had been. With each retreat, legions of tiny crabs scuttled and sank in the gulleys of granular sand. Overhead to the west a flock of herring gulls wheeled watchfully, not so interested in this deserted beach as the man-made pickings of Littelsea.

It was another cloudless afternoon. I sat on one rock with my back against another, my arms resting on my knees, my closed eyelids red against the sun, revelling in the privacy.

In spite of the hardness of the rocks I think I dozed off, because when a voice called my name it penetrated my consciousness like the crack of doom and I was badly disorientated, my neck stiff and my backside gone to sleep.

'Eve, sorry to disturb you—it's me.'

'Who . . .?' I looked up, dazzled by the sudden glare of the sun. 'Rick?'

He was bare-chested, in shorts and desert boots,

and carrying Bryony in her backpack.

'Don't often see anyone down here,' he said, 'so thought I should at least greet a kindred spirit. Desma's gone to visit her sister in hospital in Dorking,' he explained.

'Yes, she did say. Nothing serious I hope.'

He blushed. 'Routine plumbing so I'm told.'

I scrambled to my feet and smiled at Bryony's round, pink face looking over her father's shoulder. 'Hello sweetie.' She turned her head away and clutched at Rick like a koala.

'Going through a shy stage,' he explained. 'Part of growing up, I suppose.'

'Of course.'

'Anyway—we didn't mean to disturb you, we always come down here to look at the waves. We'll be on our way now.'

'It was lovely to see you. Do give my best to Desma, and I hope her sister's OK.'

'I will. Thanks. Bye ... Give Eve a wave, Bryony.'

But she still averted her face, so he waved for her. I sat back down on my rock and watched them go back up the track to the cliff path. He made astonishingly light work of the gradient, considering he'd got a toddler strapped to his back. At the top I noted with further admiration that he did not turn in the Littlesea direction, but the other way, where the path rose steeply to a series of rolling bluffs: a fair hike by any standards.

I waited till the sea had retreated another twenty metres or so, and the rocks in front of me were pale and dry in the sun. Then I clambered to my feet, tottered, stretched and began the long scramble up the cliff.

*   *   *

By the time I began the descent to Littelsea I was sweating and my legs were heavy, but I was experiencing the anticipatory glow of a well-earned g and t and something tasty in the pasta line for supper.

As I headed down the shallow steps towards the long curve of the promenade, I reflected fondly on my home town, and the many friends who made my life there so thoroughly agreeable, and my reflections gave the expression 'to know one's place' a fresh meaning. I knew this place, and my place in it, and the knowledge was a sure source of comfort and of peace.

CHAPTER SIX

I always liked the hour's train journey to London. In fact, I liked train journeys full stop. Provided, that is, I didn't meet someone I knew on the platform and had in consequence to be sociable instead of slipping into auto-pilot. Driving was all right, but one had to remain alert. That 'Let the train take the strain' was an astute piece of advertising.

On Thursday evening, travelling up to have dinner with Ian, I furnished myself with a copy of the *Brighton Evening Argus* which I would leave on the seat at Victoria, and a very slim, very torrid, designer novel, also purchased at the station, which would fit easily into my bag. I wore a long chainstore dress in shades of blue, light at the top and fading into indigo at the hem. It wasn't new—I'd bought it before going to stay with Mel—but Ian wouldn't have seen it before, and it was cool and comfortable. Also, I liked myself in it. It was kind to my figure and displayed my holiday tan to advantage. I wore a pair of silver dolphin earrings Ben had given me and flat silver-grey sandals.

I was entirely relaxed about my evening with Ian. Now that the burden of marriage had been removed from our friendship, it flourished. He would be, as he always had been, a perfect dinner companion—attentive, thoughtful, amusing and generous. I wouldn't even notice those aspects of his character—his slight fussiness, a tendency to pontificate, a way of sniffing when he laughed—which used to grate on my nerves. Why should I pay them no never mind these days, when they were no longer my problem? At the same time there remained enough regard for our old relationship for me to value his good opinion. I wanted him to say I looked nice, and, less worthily, for his admiration to be tinged with regret. There was no going back, but I wished the past to be accorded the rosy glow that was its due.

In the event, I didn't read my paper or my book on the way up, but leaned my head back on the seat and gazed out of the window, watching my reflection skim over the warm, dusty, great southeastern countryside. The train was almost empty, since most people at this time of day were heading in the opposite direction. I'd seen very little of my friends so far this week, and it had been busy at work. But with Sabine's party on Sunday I anticipated all that would change. She had even invited Desma and Rick, who were not normally (in common with other parents of young children) on her entertaining A-list, so it was clear this was an all-hands-to-the-pump job. Sensible of the honour, and knowing where their duty lay, the Shaws had prevailed on friends to look after Bryony. Ronnie had exceeded all reasonable expectation by getting hold of both her boys for the occasion and Ben was going to bring Nozz. At first I'd been doubtful about this, but Ben pointed out that Nozz scrubbed up quite well, and would bring a Bohemian touch to the party which Sabine—even while keeping one eyebrow caustically raised—would appreciate in retrospect.

'Besides,' he added, 'we have to think of the girl. There's going to be enough suits there without us adding to them.'

Thinking of the girl, I concluded that he might be right. So Nozz it was. Though what the Drages' seriously well-heeled friends would make of him was hard to imagine.

At Bouvier's I'd spent most of the past few days organising the transportation, accurate labelling and future sale of Mrs Rymer's pieces. I found that I thought of her a good deal as I went about this task, not as she now must surely be—old, shapeless, increasingly androgynous, perhaps confused, eking out her days in the nursing home—but as she must have been when she won the heart of the handsome enemy. I wondered how many of the other people at the home had the smallest inkling of her reckless secret past. Did she have a photograph on her dressing table, or was that the only one that she'd left behind in the bungalow? And where was that photograph now? Had her son and daughter-in-law returned it to her when they sold the house? Or had they, either having regard to her wishes or in spite of them, taken it with them? And if the latter, was it proudly and openly displayed, or lying face down in some box room? As I carried out a more detailed examination of the old lady's possessions, and made my notes and contacted salerooms I'd been accompanied by a shadow of sadness—a glimpse of something just out of view which, if I attempted to catch it, melted and dispersed and refused to make itself known. Old Mrs Rymer, whom I had never met and about whom I knew scarcely anything, had all unwittingly become a player in my life.

*   *   *

When Ian said he would be somewhere, he was always there, a few minutes before the appointed time and focused on the imminent arrival of whoever he was due to meet. Not for him the casual, disengaged pose—reading the paper, talking on the mobile, gazing into space. When Ian met you, you knew you had been met. In the very early days of our relationship I had found this charming, with its implication that I alone mattered most in the world. A little later I began to suspect that it was not I that mattered, but the sacred principle of good time-keeping. In any case I hadn't the slightest doubt that Ian would be there, just a few metres beyond the barrier, looking out for me when I arrived.

It was therefore a bit of a surprise when my eye didn't alight on him at once. I'd scanned the dozen or so people obviously waiting, and was making the return scan, more slowly, when a hand appeared, scything up and down before my face, and his voice said:

'Here I am.'

'Oh—hello. Why didn't I spot you?'

'I've no idea.' He kissed my cheek. 'You looked right through me about twice.'

'Did I? Sorry.'

'Think nothing of it.' Before I could take evasive action, he grasped my elbow and began steering me through the early evening crowds towards the forecourt. Fortunately a weaving derelict near the news-stand caused us to separate, and by transferring my bag from one shoulder to the other I managed tactfully to elude the return of the guiding hand. It was another habit which had once made my heart leap and now caused it to wince.

As we emerged he said. 'I brought the car—I'm over there.'

'You shouldn't have bothered.'

'Nonsense. Now that I'm a fully paid-up Londoner I frankly begrudge a cab, and we don't want to be racketing around on public transport at our age.'

'No ...' I knew Ian well enough not to be put out by the unconscious, companionable ageism— but for some reason I was piqued by that 'fully paid-up Londoner'. Oh, he was, was he? So soon? And what did that make me—a provincial lady?

'Anyway,' he went on, unlocking the black Toyota. 'I thought we'd head out, in this weather. I booked a table at the Boathouse.'

'Fine.'

The Boathouse was, as its name suggested, on the river at Chiswick—a perfectly OK restaurant rendered more desirable by its location. But its choice as the venue for dinner left me slightly disgruntled. Instead of the smart, hot, buzzy metropolitan eaterie I'd looked forward to, the fully paid-up Londoner was taking his provincial ex somewhere touristy.

It took us about half an hour to get there, and after a little general conversation Ian put on some music. It wasn't until we were crossing the bridge that I realised why I hadn't recognised him at Victoria. It was the shirt.

I'd noticed it, of course, but had not till now got my mind round it. By any standards it was a darn nice shirt: heavy, soft, silky cotton in a deep bottle green, loosely cut with dropped shoulders. It was the kind of luxurious casual garment that the old Ian would never have bought. He paid a lot for formal and work clothes, in which he never looked less than immaculate, and regarded the rest as make-weights which it wasn't worth forking out for. His wardrobe at home had had a shelf full of inexpensive felted sweatshirts, unflattering shorts and comfort-cut jeans. This was a whole different thing.

He was also wearing it right, with the sleeves loosely rolled to halfway up the forearm and plenty of slack at the waist—he was usually a rather over-assiduous tucker-in. Cream trousers and shirt were held in place by a nice, narrow plaited leather belt.

'By the way,' he said, glancing at me as we rolled down the other side of the bridge. 'I forgot to say— you look nice.'

'Thank you,' I replied. 'So do you.'

*   *   *

You could sit outside at the Boathouse. There was a wide wooden verandah with a painted balustrade, and a jetty sticking out into the river beyond that, where you could stroll with a drink, or just lean on the rail and watch the Thames slip by. Ian had thoughtfully booked a table in the covered part of the verandah where we would have the best of both worlds. Wandering up the jetty after we'd ordered, furnished with a large, tinkling g and t, I began to unwind and to feel once again perfectly ready to enjoy myself. Ian was right—who needed the sweat and swank of a West End brasserie on an evening like this?

'This is nice,' I conceded. 'Good choice.'

'I'm glad you think so. I wanted us to go somewhere special. It's a touch cheesy, I know, but I've always liked it.'

'I spoke to Ben about the cricket. He would like to go.'

'Great. In that case I'll snap up the tickets. We'll be much better off at the Oval, there are fewer braying blazer types than at Lords.'

'I can believe it.'

He took a swig of his beer. 'Eve, I've been meaning to say—sorry I inflicted Clive on you the other evening.'

'That's OK,' I lied, 'I didn't mind.'

'No, but he and his broken heart are becoming a bit of a bore. I'm afraid I just selfishly sought to spread the load.'

'I know, but that's all right. I'd have done the same.'

'It's such a pity he can't meet some nice sympathetic woman to draw the fire a bit,' Ian said.

'I don't mean to sound patronising.'

'No, I agree with you, but it's not going to happen. Clive's is a classic case of absence making the heart grow fonder.'

'It's all so dismal!' exclaimed Ian, quite impatiently. 'The thought of Clive, at his age, moping about ad infinitum. Besides which, if he upped and took up with someone, Helen might see him in a different light.'

I shook my head. 'She'd breathe a huge sigh of relief.'

'Do you really think so?'

The waiter came and told us our starters were ready. As we walked back to the table I entertained the wild surmise that Ian had envisaged me as the nice sympathetic woman with whom Clive might take up . . . But I dismissed it as utterly ridiculous.

We ate with gusto and discussed the food. It had always been our contention, Ian's and mine, that much restaurant eating was emperor's-new-clothes stuff, and that it was the duty of the diner-out to scrape away the extras and see how much and of what temperature was left, before even thinking of moving on to flavour. But we didn't do that tonight because this was a date, of sorts, and it would have been ungallant of both of us. Just the same I waited for him to open the batting on his chargrilled goat's cheese (yummy and plentiful) and was able honestly to counter with my polenta and black olive sauce (parts excellent, whole a bit confusing). This, and a lovely South African sauvignon, got us laughing and I would have said it was quite like old times, only it was rather better than that.

With the lamb cutlets—pinker than Ian liked them, but perfect for me, so that was all right—I became mellow. We were after all in the course of rediscovering one another in a new, gentler light, a process not vouchsafed to many estranged couples.

'So how's life?' I asked. 'You look awfully well.'

'I am, thanks for asking.'

'And business?' Ian was co-director of Inline, a small, but smart and expanding information technology outfit, specialising in systems for business in Europe. He was by far the oldest person there, but I had no doubt that not a day went by without the rest of the Inliners thanking their lucky stars they had him on the team.

'It's good. We've just pulled off rather a pleasing deal with a Dutch return-to-work scheme. We beat off some quite impressive competition. Malcolm's even thinking of getting some new premises on the strength of it. And even though I'm usually the voice of caution as you know, on this occasion I think he may be right. King's Cross isn't doing us any favours, it's probably adding ten per cent effort to every sale we make.'

'As much as that?'

'Oh, for sure. It's not a measurable effect, but I'd be prepared to bet on it. Presentation's not everything, but it is something, and I believe we've reached the point where we owe ourselves something a bit smarter.'

'So where will you be looking?'

'Further in. I rather favour somewhere like Bloomsbury—casting against the role if you like. But Malcolm will probaby want the full monty, you know him, West End or bust.'

We laughed. Malcolm at forty-five was a hot-headed youth compared to Ian and they both played up the differences for all they were worth.

'Do you—'

'Eve, I—'

We had both spoken at once. 'Go on,' I said. 'You first.'

'Um—' he frowned, and then paused as the waiter removed our plates and refilled my glass. 'Shall we get another of those? Same again please.'

If it had been anyone but Ian I'd have suspected him of trying to get me squiffy. 'Yes?'

'I don't want to make too much of this—be portentous about it or anything—'

'Heaven forbid.' I was teasing but he didn't smile. 'Spit it out, then.'

'It's just that I wanted to tell you I've formed an attachment.'

Considering how much forethought he must have given to this announcement, he'd picked a curious form of words. So much so that it took a minute or two for his meaning to become clear. It still hadn't, quite, when I answered automatically:

'Have you?'

'Yes.'

'I see.' His expression begged me to cotton on. 'I see.'

'In spite of our changed circumstances I wanted you to know from me rather than find out via some other means.'

'Right.'

He twiddled the stem of his glass before looking at me with the sort of directness that is the clearest possible indication of the longing to look elsewhere. 'Also, of course, I wanted you to know before Mel or Ben.'

'Of course.'

'You agree that's right.'

116

'I suppose so.'

'Good.' He sat back, placing his hands on the edge of the table as if about to get up, then leaned forward again. 'So—that's it really. I don't want to burden you with far more than you could possibly want to know.'

'Thank you, how kind.' There was no need for that particular little grace note, but I threw it in anyway. Ian looked pained.

'I'm sorry, Eve, I don't seem to be handling this very well.'

'You're doing fine.'

'It need not alter our relationship in the least. I very much hope it won't. Maybe I'm being complacent, but I really believe we've managed this whole thing exceptionally well, with the minimum of upheaval and no bloodletting. Speaking for myself I feel we have a pretty unshakeable bond . . .'

In so far as my husband could ever be said to babble, he was babbling.

'So that's what all this is about,' I said acidly.

'All this—? No, not at all. Not in the least. I wanted to see you, I always want to see you, and it was high time we had a pleasant evening together.'

'Ah, pleasant.' I kept opening my mouth and hearing these sad, sarcastic little comments coming out. 'That's the thing.'

'I'm sorry,' he said, dropping his head.

'Why?'

'I've upset you.'

'We're separated, you can do what you like.'

'Essentially that's true, but—'

'But what?'

'But it still changes things, I realise that.'

117

'You said it wouldn't,' I crowed, bitterly. 'That you hoped it wouldn't.'

'Not change our relationship, no. I meant that. But it is nonetheless a change, if only of perspective.'

'Oh, please.'

I was shocked at the nastiness of my reaction. Whatever he said was not going to be right. In fact the more careful his wording the angrier it made me.

'Eve—' The waiter advanced with the pudding menus, but Ian's distracted, unseeing stare caused him to retreat almost at once. 'Eve, what's the matter?'

It might have seemed a silly question, but in fact its simplicity was its strength. For what exactly was the matter? After all, I'd said it, we were separated so we could both do as we liked.

I hid behind bluster. 'I'd have thought that was obvious.'

'It's not actually.' He sounded humble, and his bloody humility brought out the beast in me.

'You're patronising me, Ian! You invite me up to London, set up this dinner, make out it's something we owe ourselves for being such wonderful people, and then hit me with this!'

'That wasn't how it was intended, I assure you.'

'That's how it feels.'

'Perhaps,' he ventured, 'it was going to feel like that anyway . . . ?'

I sensed he was approaching, all unawares, the truth of the matter, and rushed to head him off.

'I don't think so. I'm perfectly reasonable, I'm not a complete idiot!'

'Very far from it.'

'What did you think I would do, throw a vase at

118

your head?'

'No.' He didn't have to say more, because it was obvious to both of us that given the way I was behaving in a busy restaurant, vase-throwing in another context was entirely on the cards.

'This,' I went on, gesturing at our surroundings, 'is obviously an announcement.'

'Do you want to go?'

'I should think so, wouldn't you.'

'I'll get the bill.'

He gazed over his shoulder and lifted chin and eyebrow at our waiter. I thought: damn. Because I didn't want to go. I was cutting off my nose to spite my face, and far too proud to acknowledge it. What I wanted—what I *needed*—was to sit here quietly until the urge to self-destruct had passed, and then to try and talk calmly and *amicably* for God's sake about this latest development. As Ian had intended.

But no, the bill was now approaching, and Ian was taking out his pen and his plastic, and all I could do was say 'Excuse me' and sweep off to the Ladies.

When I got back he rose at my approach.

'Right then,' he said, his voice lighter as though he'd effected the necessary emotional gear change. 'Let's go.'

In the car, I asked: 'So who is she?' It was intended to be emollient, a friendly enquiry, but it sounded sullen and hostile.

'Oh—I met her at a party.'

'What does she do?'

'Her name's Julia Kendal. She writes for the *Nursing Times.*'

I thought I detected a note of pride, which I was

quick to squash. 'I've never seen it.'

'Well no, you wouldn't have.'

It was obvious that as far as Ian was concerned, caution was now to be the keynote—any further information was going to have to be wrung out of him. I lasted for about another two minutes before muttering between gritted teeth:

'What sort of age is she then?'

'Um—fortyish, I believe.'

Gimme a break. 'Ish?'

'Forty-one.'

'Right. Thank you.'

Another silence. At one point Ian took his left hand off the wheel and made a jerky little unfinished movement before replacing it. I think he wanted to put on some music, but thought better of it. Meanwhile I burned with wretched, malign curiosity. I wanted to know everything—to bathe in the scalding water of my ridiculous, irrelevant jealousy.

'I take it she's single.'

'Yes.'

'What, divorced?'

'Never married.' Ian paid careful attention to the oncoming traffic at a T-junction, and added: 'She was in a long-term relationship until about two years ago, but that ended, so . . .'

'What happened?' I asked.

'To be honest, I don't know all the details. She didn't want children and I understand that was something of an issue . . . but I don't know.'

He was talking about her, this other woman, as though she were a candidate for a job. Which I suppose in a sense she was.

'And you bumped into each other at this party.'

'Yes.'

'What, your eyes met across a crowded room.'

'I suppose so—yes.'

'So just how stunningly beautiful is she? On a scale of one to ten?'

'I don't think you'd put her on the scale of stunning beauty at all,' Ian said gently. 'That's got nothing to do with it.'

Those few words put me in my place, and brought me to my senses. My choleric heat was doused by the cool, restrained touch of truth. As I stared ahead through a stinging veil of tears, Ian stretched out his hand again, this time without hesitation, and laid it over both of mine where they lay locked together on my lap.

*   *   *

At the station I declined his offer to accompany me to the train. I'd recovered just enough to swallow my pride and say: 'By the way, that's a nice shirt.'

He looked down at himself. 'Do you like it? I bought it in Bath.'

*   *   *

Bath? I thought, as the train rattled through the snaggle-toothed streets south of Victoria. In a reasonably well-travelled life I had never been to Bath. But the new-look Ian and his better-than-beautiful Julia had been. And while they were there she'd bought him a shirt. For one thing I knew—his might have been the cash but hers, for sure, the taste.

Ben was lying on the sofa, reading *Marie Claire* with the TV on when I came in.

'Hi there, good time?'

'Yes thanks.'

'Good grub? Where did you go?'

'Oh, Hammersmith—on the river. Yes, it was nice.'

I went into the kitchen. 'Kettle's boiled,' he called.

'Why, do you want one?'

'Wouldn't say no.'

I made a couple of mugs of tea. He zapped the TV as I walked in.

'Cheers. How was Dad?'

'Fine.'

Ben gave me a bright, sceptical look. 'Fine as all that, huh?'

'No, I meant it. He was in good form. He'll get those Test tickets.'

'Cool.' He picked up *Marie Claire* and gave it a waggle. 'I was reading this article about more women wanting to live alone.'

'Interesting?'

'So-so.'

This was one of those exchanges, not uncommon with Ben, where a statement had seemed to herald an observation, which was then withheld.

I sat down and took off my sandals. 'So what conclusions do they reach about this phenomenon?'

'Nothing very startling. They reckon women don't want to wash socks any more. So far so plausible. There you go—' he tossed the magazine in my direction. 'You can read it yourself.'

'I probably will.'

He stretched and yawned mightily, rotating his feet at the ankle and pushing his linked fingers towards the ceiling.

'Anyway,' he gaped round the yawn, 'it's not going to tell you anything you don't already know—is it?' On the last two words he relaxed, brought his face to order and grinned expansively in my direction.

'Probably not ...' I picked up the magazine. 'Why?'

'You're one of them, aren't you?'

'One of what?'

'Women who choose to live alone.'

I was uncomfortable. 'I don't live alone. You're here.'

He yawned again and rubbed his face. 'You know what I mean.'

'No. Ian and I are separated. It's not something I chose.'

'Take it easy, Mum, suit yourself.'

'It's just that I don't understand what you're getting at,' I insisted. I kept my voice down and smiled but even I could feel it was an anxious, angry smile.

'Nothing, Mum, settle down—'

'Don't tell me to settle down!'

'Who rattled your cage?' he asked, laughing. 'Dad forget his wallet or something?' He dropped a glancing kiss on my temple. 'Chill.'

*   *   *

I was unable to 'chill' as he put it. I stayed up far

too late in an effort to distract myself with television, and when I did finally go to bed I couldn't sleep. Ben's question was apposite—who, exactly, *had* rattled my cage?

*   *   *

Ian and I had met at the wedding of mutual friends in 1970. He knew the bridegroom, James Palmer, I the bride, Linda Price. We first saw each other across the aisle of a soulless church in Birmingham, as we turned to watch Linda make her entrance on the arm of her father. These nuptials were a lavish, hard-edged, no-expense-spared affair, a big bash thrown by Mr Price with an eye to future business for his industrial cleaning company. It was difficult to make the connection between Linda, the shy secretary I shared an office with in the Rover showrooms in St Johns Wood, and this congregation of full-to-bursting morning dress, high complexions, sugar-almond bouclé suits and lethally chic hats on spun-glass coiffures.

Linda was a plumpish girl with difficult hair. I had the uneasy suspicion that her mother, in a cerise costume with gold buttons and a hemline that revealed (as they all did that year) a pair of best-kept-hidden knees, had knowingly allowed her daughter to select a spectacularly unflattering wedding dress. With hindsight, the vast nimbus of flounces and frills prefigured the choice of Lady Diana Spencer a decade or so later, but at a time when frocks were either sculpturally spare or whimsically girlish it appeared gross. Linda's rosy skin looked florid, her hair—scraped up into the style, popular at the time, which looked as though

124

several giant rollers had been left in on the crown—was too fine for what was being asked of it, and her beam had never been broader.

I cringed on her behalf, but I caught sight of Ian just after she passed between us, and was shamed. For his expression betrayed not a hint of censure, but was serious and benign, almost tender.

In those days, as now, Ian had the reassuring, conservative good looks of a young TV intern. Never one to alter where he alteration found, his style, give or take an inch on the hairline, had remained the same over the years. This meant that he was now enviably free of those embarrassing photos featuring elephant loons, pop-art tanktops, mutton-chop sideburns and highwayman jackets which haunted other men who had considered themselves the dog's bollocks at the time.

The wedding reception was at Mr Price's Country Club deep in the expense account belt of Solihull. The modern all-day event, culminating in dancing, had yet to come in, but this was a four-course lunch with a combo of the Royal Marines playing hits from the Broadway shows, a river of champers and a free bar serving everything else including fancy cocktails.

It would be true to say that Ian swept me off my feet. He had the sort of manner that I'd always found particularly charming—focused, generous, enquiring. He wasn't just a good listener, he was an inspired one. He made me feel like the only girl in the room, and (I discovered this later, it wasn't his style to mention such things) he had an ice-blue Lotus Elan in the carpark.

I got sloshed, but his chivalrous attention never faltered. We both of us laughed immoderately at my jokes, and when I asked about the groom he said he didn't know him all that well but that in his opinion he was lucky to have netted such an obviously sweet girl as Linda. This perception of her, in the face of the Frock from Hell, endeared him to me still further. If he could somehow see the real Linda beneath all those frills and flounces, then it must be the real me he was attracted to, too.

She was a creature quite hard to find, the real me. I was wearing a pink gingham mini dress from Ginger Group, with cutaway armholes and a zip up the front, pale tights and pink chunky shoes, and a floppy white hat with a pink rose stuck on the side. In the photos which Linda sent us afterwards, and which I still had in the desk drawer, it was the same old story. Ian looked the same but younger, I was the sort of freak show that made my children howl with disrespectful mirth. The Rocky Horror, they called me in those photographs, whereas Linda looked no worse than a thousand later Di-wannabees. An object lesson in the perils of being a fashion victim.

'I'd have you know,' Ian would say to the children, loyal, but laughing in spite of himself, 'that your mother was the undisputed belle of the ball.'

'There's no need to overdo it,' I growled.

'I'm not. You were. You were probably too pie-eyed to notice, but I was fighting off the competition.'

'You're having a laugh, Dad.'

'Certainly not. And she hasn't changed a bit.'

Ah, palmy days, when we were the happiest married couple that anyone knew. Too happy, it now transpired, or at least too content. Too content to notice when love first began to slip

126

through our fingers and then, when we'd lost it, so separately and secretly shocked that we nearly let our friendship go too.

And we might have done, if not for Ian. We had reached the point where we were no more than carefully co-operative room-mates, leading separate (and, it must be said, sadly blameless lives), avoiding one another's eyes, leaving a space in the bed, embarrassed by love songs. We were living through a grinding daily attrition of suppressed suffering, but to everyone we knew (and who knew us so much less than they believed) we were Ian and Eve, the redoubtable Piercys.

Ian was the brave one. 'Don't you think,' he said one Sunday morning when the sun shone and the children were still in bed, 'don't you think we should stop this marriage spoiling our relationship?'

For a week, I did nothing but weep. I thought my world would implode and my heart would shatter, simply because he was right.

My husband had uttered the unthinkable, and set us free.

*   *   *

But now this had happened. No longer was it just Ian and I, amicably separated but essentially unchanged, the thread of our relationship still stretched even and unbroken between us. We were suddenly and alarmingly sundered by this offstage presence who went to Bath and bought clothes.

Discreet, *Nursing Times* Julia, with her inner beauty and her good taste in shirts ... She it was who'd rattled my cage.

CHAPTER SEVEN

Sabine and Martin were party-givers of note. As Ronnie said, they had both cash and dash, and Sabine in particular was a natural show-off. She also had a keen sense of the hierarchy of social events, and those who were reasonably regular attenders had learned to appreciate the finer points of the Drage scale of entertaining.

For instance, Sabine's fortieth had been the top-of-the-range do, a Georgian extravaganza awash with fresh-fruit sculptures, tinkling spinnets, and an apparently endless procession of crystal flutes brimming with Bolli borne on silver salvers by flunkies liveried in green and white. The marquee alone, with its real doors and spindly gold furniture must have cost more than several average weddings, and the rock band which followed the spinnets was one that had actually featured in the charts, even if Ben, on being told their name, dismissed them as sad bastards. And as for the guests—we were transformed. Never had *le tout* Littelsea looked so alluring. Powdered *embonpoints*, fluttering fans, fetchingly rumpled stocks and smoothly sculpted breeches transformed every couple, if only in their own imaginations, into Elizabeth and Darcy.

Their wedding anniversary was a lunchtime affair—jazz band, American food, tables on the terrace. Very nice too, but the message was that whereas growing old glamorously was a triumph, staying married to one man for fifteen years was something like a perfect school attendance record, to be celebrated with a touch of irony.

Sophie's drinks (Martin's birthday had become somewhat eclipsed) was a mere *bonne bouche*—the sort of little something that Sabine could knock up in her sleep with one hand tied behind her. That wasn't to say that it wasn't good of its kind: all Sabine's entertaining was pre-eminent in its field. But there was a certain studied insouciance in its delivery which flagged that it had been thrown together for the dear child on the spur of the moment.

There was Pimms, champagne and passionfruit juice, and an array of fancy bottled beers for the young ones (I took credit for suggesting this, Sabine cared not a fig for beer). The caterer's girls, under the fearsome auspices of Sabine's Maltese housekeeper, Clea, moved tirelessly among us in the conservatory and on the terrace, bearing trays of artfully prepared seafood bites, devils on horseback and hot cheese straws.

The only wrong note—in the sense that it was a touch *too* tasteful—was the harpist, a young woman in a flowing terra-cotta robe. She was tiny, which made you wonder not so much that the harping was done well, but that it was done at all. Every ripple of notes caused her to lean forward stressfully as if using a rowing machine, and in the more passionate passages her small feet left the ground altogether.

'She's piloting that harp,' observed Ben. 'Lift off is imminent.'

That was about the only remark he addressed to me, because 'the young', as they were wont to do, and as Sabine had intended, gravitated to one another outdoors, leaving the rest of us covering

129

the usual ground inside.

I left my amusing card for Martin on the mantelpiece, and washed up near the french windows with Dennis Chatsworth.

'Well done you,' I said. 'Getting the whole team out.'

He shrugged. 'They both just happened to be at home this weekend with nothing better to do. Can't really take any credit.'

'Where's Ronnie?' I asked.

'Not too jolly as a matter of fact. Putting her feet up at home.'

'That's not like her.'

'No it's not, but maybe that's what people mean by saying one isn't oneself.'

'Good point.'

'It's not serious, anyway. Would it be terribly incorrect of me to say she's at a funny age?'

'It would,' I smiled. 'But we all are, there's no getting away from it.'

'She sent her regards, so let it be minuted that I passed it on.'

'Do you think she'll be on for tennis next Saturday?'

'Good heavens, yes.'

Out on the terrace, the Drages' stone balustrade was already adorned with clusters of beer bottles and glasses, and the flagstones were acquiring a scattering of cigarette ends and bits of canapé. At first I couldn't see Sophie, but then I spotted her on the far side of the room talking earnestly to a tall, toothy woman in a smock. Why on earth didn't Sabine usher her outside with the rest of them? What was the point, when the flower of Littelsea's youth had been pressed into service to make the girl feel at home, in leaving her beached with what looked like rather dull female company? Especially since, on this second meeting, Sophie did not disappoint. The dark, humorous good looks, the mop of what in a more formal age would certainly have been ringlets, the carelessly voluptuous figure ... all were still much in evidence, today arrestingly presented in some sort of floppy dark red sundress with an uneven hem, which might have been from a jumble sale or Bond Street, it was impossible to tell. In spite of my misgivings I had to concede that she looked perfectly content to be talking to the smock. But that might just have been good manners.

Dennis and Ronnie's older son, Philip, came over. Of those offspring here present the Chatsworths' were—at least outwardly—the sort you could take anywhere. Philip was the image of his mother, tall and fair and open-faced, king of the wet bobs at Radley, and now a hopeful for the Cambridge eight.

'How you doing Eve—so where is she?' he asked.

'Don't ask me,' replied his father, 'I wouldn't know her from Adam, and Sabine's omitted to introduce us.'

'Well, by a process of elimination we've reached the conclusion she's not out there.'

'That's her—' I nodded—'by the door.'

Attuned as I was, I caught the micro-flicker of assessment. 'OK ...'

'Not the tall one,' I said. 'The dark one.'

An infinitesimal reappraisal. 'OK.'

'Pretty girl,' said Dennis, glancing over without much interest. 'Why don't you go and do the honours?'

'I think I will.'

We watched as Philip made his way in Sophie's direction. I couldn't help wishing that it was Ben making this first, gallant approach. Where was he, for heaven's sake? Leaning on the terrace wall, legs crossed, gassing to Nozz, was the answer.

Martin joined us. He acknowledged our birthday wishes and then tilted his head in Philip's direction and leered amiably at Dennis.

'Sent in the crack troops, I see . . .'

'Don't know about that,' muttered Dennis.

'How are you getting on?' I enquired. 'It must be quite a change for all three of you.'

'Fine, fine, tremendous!' declared Martin. 'I'm a completely proud and doting father.'

'She looks a lovely girl.'

'Want to meet her?' He grabbed my arm. 'Come on—'

'No, no, leave her be. Let her talk to the others of her own age. I have met her anyway,' I assured him, 'that night when I came over.'

'A great girl,' declared Martin, 'and no slouch with cattle, either.'

'What can he mean?' asked Dennis as Martin moved on.

'She's going to train as a vet—working on one of Martin's farms for the summer.'

'Gosh. Impressive. Like some of these round-the-world yachts-women, look as if a puff of wind would blow them over, but they're tough as old boots underneath . . .' I smiled and waited, because he seemed to be about to add something, but all he did was peer again at Sophie and say: 'Extraordinary.'

132

The Shaws arrived, and Desma towed Rick over to talk to us. Perhaps because of their relative youth they were not one of those married couples who felt it was their duty to separate the moment they entered the room.

'Hey, Eve,' she cried, 'Rick says he met you on the cliff path—talk about a double life, I had no idea he yomped that far with Bryony on board.'

'Well he does,' I said, 'I can vouch for it. Springing up the slopes like a chamois, he was.'

Not many men blush, but it was the second time I'd seen Rick colour up. 'I like it up there.'

'I tell you what,' went on Desma, 'it isn't half nice to be child-free of a Sunday lunchtime. I love Bryony to bits, but you need to be away from them sometimes, don't you?' Dennis and I agreed that you did. 'Of course I'm a late starter,' she added, 'you can probably hardly remember this stage.'

'I can,' I said, 'all too clearly. Especially Mel. She screamed blue murder for six months.'

'God . . .' breathed Desma, 'how awful.'

'You're lucky,' observed Dennis. 'We couldn't leave ours at home today, could we Eve? We were instructed to shoehorn them from their pits and drag them along.'

'For Sophie, of course,' said Rick. 'So what's she like?'

'She's standing right next to you, before you answer that.'

Rick jumped. Sophie was indeed standing next to him, glass in hand and looking, disconcertingly, not at Rick but at the rest of us, with a cool, quizzical smile. It was poor Rick, however, on whom the blush rose for the third time.

'Oh God, I'm so sorry, how terribly rude that

must have sounded, what can I say . . . ?'

'It didn't sound rude at all,' she said. 'But someone else's answer might have, so I thought I'd better declare an interest at once.'

We laughed—a nervous laugh tinged with relief at the thought of how close we'd been to being caught bang to rights. I introduced the others.

'I hear you're a horse doctor, Sophie,' said Dennis. 'Or going to be.'

'Hope to be—the horse among others.'

'You look far too pretty.'

'Thank you.' Ten out of ten to Sophie, I thought, for accepting that gently sexist compliment in the right spirit.

'Do you play tennis?' asked Desma.

'I do, but I'm a complete rabbit.'

'Now,' I said, 'we have to decide whether that's false modesty or the real thing.'

'It's the real thing—I've got lots to be modest about, believe me.'

Philip, who'd been hovering at her shoulder, said: 'I find that hard to believe.' He was working well.

'And you're enjoying life on the farm?' I asked.

'It's no doss, but it's good, yes.' She looked round at us. 'Do I know everyone?'

'I'm so sorry,' I said. 'You and I have actually met before and I—'

'Yes, you went skinny dipping with Sabine.' I joined in with the general laughter, pulling my stomach in as I did so. 'You are brave,' she added generously.

'Not really, it was a warm night—'

'I don't mean doing it, I mean doing it with Sabine.'

She didn't need to enlarge, we all knew what she meant. The men chuckled and looked at their feet, Desma and I exchanged a look.

'Anyway,' I said, 'let me introduce us.'

I did, and she shook hands firmly with everyone, looking into each face as she did so as if memorising it. She exuded, as well as charm, common sense.

'OK,' said Philip. 'I'm going to drag you outside.'

'Fine.' She smiled at us. 'Looks as though I'm off.'

We chorused our farewells.

'Impressive young lady,' commented Dennis. 'Bet she's got Martin round her little finger.'

I watched Sophie's small figure being swallowed up by a group which included Ben. Then, knowing that if I stayed there I'd be tempted to watch her progress, I detached myself from the others and headed back into the room. A steely clutching hand on my arm announced Sabine before I heard the equally metallic tinkle of her voice.

'Eve, where are you off to?'

'I'm circulating.'

'What a good guest—so perfectly trained—let me find you some nice people to talk to.'

I knew what she meant—she meant she wanted a quiet word. The next thing was that I found myself near the door with Sabine's face twelve inches away, still wearing its ironed-on hostess smile, but emitting a steaming hiss of pent-up curiosity.

'So what do you think?'

I didn't need to ask what she meant. 'She's lovely.'

'A cool customer?'

'Certainly. But you'd rather have that, wouldn't you, than a shrinking violet? It's a lot less bother.'

'I never know what's going on in her head,' protested Sabine.

'Much better not to.'

'What do you mean?'

I could see nothing was going to allay her groundless and amorphous fears. 'Well, what you don't know can't cause you to lose sleep.'

'So—you think it would? If I did?'

'Sabine!' I was exasperated. 'No. I think she's a nice, pretty, self-possessed modern girl and you should have no worries whatever on her account.'

'I do hope you're right . . .' She shook her head, then broke once more into an animated smile as she caught someone's eye. 'She is certainly more attractive than I remembered, but I find her curiously unsympathetic.'

I didn't find this curious at all, but I knew better than to say so. 'Just get on with your life, Sabine, and let her get on with hers. You're devoting far too much head space to the whole thing. Let Martin do whatever needs doing. He's like a dog with two tails anyway.'

Sabine's brow darkened jealously at this, but at that moment Martin himself approached from the hall, accompanied by another guest.

'Darling—look who just bowled up.'

'Chuckie!' The storm clouds were dispersed by a ray of genuine sunshine. The late arrival opened wide his arms and engulfed his hostess in a thoroughly disrespectful bear hug such as only a broad-shouldered all-American male could carry off successfully.

'Put her down man,' said Martin. 'And shake

136

hands nicely with Eve Piercy.'

'It'd be my pleasure,' said Charles McNally. 'Especially since we have already met.'

* * *

'But when?' Sabine asked breathlessly as Charles was being introduced elsewhere. 'Where?'

'When I was visiting Mel. He was staying at the hotel.'

'You never said!' She was quite put out by what she clearly perceived as my treacherous evasions, but at least it had drawn the fire away from Sophie.

'There was nothing to say. It was nothing more than an encounter.'

'Encounter?'

I laughed and shook my head. 'Stop trying to make something of it, Sabine. We met. We exchanged a few pleasantries, that's all. I'm surprised he even remembers.'

'Ah, but he does. And so—' Sabine tapped my shoulder with a crimson nail—'do you.'

I think I may have appeared a little discomforted, for she laughed knowingly before cruising away, secure once more in her position as woman of the world. Not that I presented even the smallest challenge to that position. It was an area, I reflected wistfully, where I gave ground to almost every other woman of my acquaintance.

I talked for a while to two other couples, part of the Drages' freemasonry of money. New or old was of no consequence, it was the cash that counted. At their parties one could clearly see that being wealthy was a far more bonding experience than poverty. All that we-lived-in-a-two-up-and-two-

137

down-but-we-never-thought-to-lock-our-doors stuff was so much rose-tinted guff. It was the rich who needed each other in order to be able to talk about money without embarrassment. And what's more they seemed to be able to sniff out comparable levels of income for a radius of fifty miles. The appearance of some palatial residence on the market got the antennae waving, and its subsequent sale sent the message that the local chapter had new members. These were people with never less than three cars and as many homes; people with live-in domestics and a driver; people who were Friends of the Royal Opera and Ballet, and a couple of hand-picked charities; whose children's engagements were in *The Times* and whose family weddings (five-pole marquee on the lawn, four-course dinner, three wines, two bands and a cabaret) cost more than most people's houses. People who, despite their life of conspicuous consumption stayed fit because they owned their own court, pool or gym—or all three. People who very understandably found it a great relief to get together with the similarly loaded to discuss the best and most profitable way to spend it.

The couples I spoke to were perfectly congenial. The uncharitable might have asked, Why wouldn't they be? But no, they were charming people, habitual party-goers and givers who knew instinctively that I was not as they were and stuck accordingly to safe, non-cash-driven topics. Of which there were surprisingly few when you got right down to it. In a Basil Fawltyish don't-mention-the-war sort of way the more disparate incomes were a factor the more they reared their ugly heads.

Anyway, we managed for fifteen minutes or so— the equivalent of a week in politics at a cocktail party—and then I said something about wanting to make sure my son was behaving himself (they laughed, but I was being perfectly serious) and I escaped.

I had a nasty moment on first going out on to the terrace: there was no one there. I had visions of a mass exodus to the Ferret, instigated by Ben. But they were down on the lawn, lying indolently about on the grass like lions at a kill. Unlike us clean-living oldies they all smoked, and had created their own micro-environment, a haze of pollution that hung over them and separated them still further from their elders. I tried and failed to pick out Ben. Some mysterious generational juju made them all look alike at this distance.

'Jealous?'

It was Charles McNally, hands on the wall on either side of his Scotch, arms braced as if about to push a pick-up truck out of a ditch.

'How do you mean?'

'Wish you were young again?'

'You're joking.'

He gave a small, slow shake of the head. 'Not me.'

'Do you? Wish you were?'

'Sure.' He turned round and leaned against the wall with his arms folded. 'I'd go back, given half a chance.'

'And would you do things differently?'

'Now then would I ...?' He had an easy, unhurried way of moving, and had scarcely glanced at my face. I remembered something about eye-contact being threatening to children and animals—he must have read the same article. 'I don't know,' he concluded, 'but I'd certainly make sure I had more fun.'

'Anyhow,' he added, after a pause. 'I'm making up for it now. Swell party.'

'Absolutely.' I couldn't be sure whether he was being serious, but now he gave himself away by breaking into a grin and mimicking me:

'Absolutely!'

I laughed. 'No, it is.'

'You know our hosts well?'

'Pretty well. I play tennis regularly with Sabine—a group of us do—and I got to know Martin later.'

'Martin's one of the good guys. And all this is in aid of his daughter—whom I haven't yet met.'

'She's down there—' I nodded in the direction of the lawn beneath us—'mixing with her own kind.'

'Yeah, well, that's as it should be I guess.'

We gazed down for a while, the young people on the grass providing a shared focus.

'One of those gilded young things belongs to you?' he asked.

'My son's there somewhere.'

'And you have that smart cookie of a daughter in the UAE.'

I was surprised by this. 'You know Mel?'

'I met her. Ankatex gave a reception last time I was over.'

'Ah. Yes—she certainly knew who you were.'

As soon as I'd said this I regretted it. Had I sounded in some way insinuating? But he seemed not to have noticed.

'That's one clever girl.'

'She is, isn't she?' I agreed. 'I don't know where

140

she gets it from.'

'Her mother, perhaps?' He turned his head and gave me a steady, civil look.

'Oh God, hardly! I'm almost totally disorganised, and what brain I have is scarcely ever in gear, I just muddle along.'

He didn't bother taking issue with me, but gave a little laugh and drained his drink, gesturing with his empty glass at mine.

'Can I get you another?'

'Umm, it's OK, I've got a drop left,' I waffled. He was bored by me and my gauche need to run myself down. Why embarrass myself any further by forcing him to come back with a drink?

'Right. OK, if you'll excuse me.'

It was a relief to watch his backview—high, wide and handsome—disappear into the crowd. The sort of men I liked about me these days were safe, pleasant, companionable men; men who were happily married (I realised I had no idea whether he was or not); men who knew me enough to set us both at ease, but not so well as to get under my skin; men who flirted with me, if they did so at all, in a spirit of friendly mutual regard. Charles McNally was in every respect an unknown quantity. His calm questioning had exposed in me a dismaying lack of savoir-faire, which I was afraid might have been his intention. He was, I reminded myself, one of the sharks.

I turned back to the garden, just in time to see Sophie, with Ben, returning from the direction of the new tennis court and the trees that shielded it from the cliff. They were in animated conversation. When they rejoined the others Sophie lay down flat on her back with her hands behind her head. Ben,

141

laughing, sat next to her with his arms resting on his upbent knees. But in less than a minute he too lay down, and I could no longer see their faces.

'I brought one anyway.'

A full glass appeared before me on the wall.

'Oh—thank you.'

'My pleasure.'

He'd come back—why? For something to say I blurted out: 'I just saw my son with Martin's daughter.'

'All right . . . And—excuse me—that's good? Or not so good?'

'I'm not sure. Good, I think. Because he's a bit of a loose cannon and she seems like a really nice girl.'

'And your ambition for him is to consort with a nice girl.' This was presented as something between a question and a statement. I got the impression that he'd already decided, but he was sufficiently polite to couch it as a query. Nettled, I adjusted my words.

'I didn't mean nice as in nice. I don't know what sort of girl she is, but she certainly seems bright and she's undoubtedly attractive.'

'Sounds good to me.'

I took a huge gulp of my new drink, which somewhat undermined my earlier insistence that I didn't need one.

Charles McNally said: 'I don't have kids, but I can imagine you want them to have what we want for ourselves.'

'Yes. Health, happiness . . .'

'Love and lots of it?' he suggested.

'Love, certainly.'

He gave another of his little laughs, a barely

audible grunting exhalation.

'What does your husband think?'

This threw me. Because Ian and I weren't yet divorced I still wore my wedding ring and, on this occasion, my eternity ring as well. But I was not used to being with someone who didn't understand, who didn't know me—someone who might have glanced at my left hand on purpose to ascertain my marital status. I found it difficult, even now, to admit to not being fully married.

'Well—we're separated.'

'So what does he think?' The question was repeated unblinkingly, with an almost dismissive lack of reaction.

'He wants the best for his children, naturally.'

'Naturally. Including the nice girl.' Another of those left-to-hang query statements, which I could pluck down or ignore as I chose. I decided it was my turn to set the agenda.

'We aren't heavy parents,' I declared. 'We never have been. I've never dreamed of white weddings and grandchildren, and I don't mind who my children go to bed with provided it's safe and legal.'

'Good for you,' said Charles McNally. He ducked his head in the direction of the young people. 'Judging by the body language down there your son is in the process of making another conquest.'

At the same moment that he piqued my maternal pride and curiosity into looking, he prevented me from doing so by thrusting out a huge hand.

'I'll be saying good-bye. I have to talk to Martin before I go.'

'Oh . . . good-bye.'

'It was nice meeting you again.'

My hand was clasped and released in such a way that it felt small and cold afterwards. I felt I'd been subjected to some kind of test, but I had no idea whether or not I had passed.

The young, with one of their instinctive, herdlike impulses began one by one to get up and head back towards the terrace. I saw that Ben rose first, but that Sophie, still languorously prostrate, held up a hand, and he grasped it and pulled her to her feet. The group collected up the glasses and the bottles, and someone with a conscience—one of the Chatsworth boys—picked up cigarette ends and dropped them in a glass.

They arrived on the terrace, and infiltrated the room beyond. Ben and Sophie were last to arrive.

'We're going to wander down to the beach,' said Ben.

'Now?' I asked stupidly.

'Sure.'

'All this time I've been here and I've never clapped eyes on the sea,' said Sophie by way of explanation. 'I'm always headed in the opposite direction.'

'Well don't expect too much,' I said. 'It's not exactly the *Promenade des Anglais* down there.'

'I like grim seaside towns,' she asserted, a touch backhandedly.

'So that's OK,' said Ben. They disappeared into the throng of drinkers. It was impossible to tell from their demeanour whether the flame of a true passion had been lit in either of their breasts— Charles McNally was a better reader of body language than I. I caught myself wondering if Ben would remember to thank Sabine and Martin, and whether Sabine had planned one of her inimitable cold collations for a chosen few, and if she had what would be her attitude to the guest of honour buggering off to the beach with a bloke? My motives were entirely selfish—I did not wish to be sucked into Sabine's vortex of agitation about her stepdaughter.

It turned out I needn't have worried. No sooner had I re-entered the drawing room and gravitated once again towards the pleasant and undemanding company of Dennis, than Sabine cut me off at the pass, cornered me and fixed me with her glittering eye.

'The young people are going down to the beach,' she informed me.

'I thought I heard something being discussed ... I do hope that isn't fouling up any arrangements ... they tend not to think of anyone but themselves ...' I wittered feebly.

'It is just as it should be,' declared Sabine. 'I had organised a little lunch, but so much better that she should be off with people of her own age.'

'Are you sure?' I asked guardedly, preparing myself for the whiplash sting in the tail.

'Of course! Your son is such a charmer,' she added, touching my arm with what almost amounted to affection, 'and now you can take Sophie's place at the table.'

I was too relieved to worry about Sabine's quite open designation of myself as first reserve, or her blithe assumption that I would accept both this role and a place at her lunch table.

'Thank you,' I said.

When she'd moved on I caught up with Dennis and asked if he was staying for lunch.

'They were kind enough to invite us,' he said, 'but with poor Ronnie laid up I really want to get back, so I've made my excuses.'

'Do give her my love,' I said. 'I hope she feels better soon.'

'Oh yes, I'm sure she will. I hope so,' he added with an anxious smile, he was a nice man. 'It's rotten for her, especially when she's never ill.'

I recalled his earlier remark about a 'funny age' and it didn't seem to accord with this evidence of genuine concern.

'I'll call in on her,' I said, 'during the week.'

'She'd appreciate that, I'm sure, poorly or not.' He glanced around. 'I'd better round up my team before they drink the bar dry.'

'I think they've all gone off somewhere—the beach or something.'

'Oh well, never mind. If you hear my name being blackened for not having given them a lift home perhaps you'd step in on my behalf.'

The room was beginning to empty. Sabine had Charles McNally by the elbow and beckoned me over, which was the very last thing I wanted.

'Eve, it turns out Dennis has to go and I am trying to persuade Charles to alter his plans to include lunch.'

'What a good idea,' I said hoping and probably failing to sound appropriately enthusiastic.

'A great idea, Sabine, but out of the question,' he said. 'I'm already late, so sadly it has to be no.'

'Won't you keep Eve company?' Sabine cast me a sparkling, woman-to-woman look which I did not return.

'No I won't,' said Charles McNally. 'Not because I don't want to, but because I can't. G'bye Sabine, and thanks for including me, it was fun.' He raised a hand to me, as one who had already been said good-bye to, and was gone, assertiveness on wheels. Martin accompanied him into the hall. Beyond the open front door I caught sight of a forest green Daimler with a dark-suited driver at the wheel.

Sabine gave one of her expressive Gallic shrugs. 'I'm sorry, Eve.'

She could not know with how much heartfelt sincerity I replied: 'Don't be.'

CHAPTER EIGHT

When I left the Drages' lunch party it was a quarter to four. The skies had clouded over and the offshore wind had turned the surface of the sea into a grey cheese-grater.

I felt for once at a loose end, not content to return to Cliff Mansions on my own (for I knew Ben wouldn't be back) and put my feet up with the Sunday papers. I'd only had two units—and possibly a top-up, but random breath-testing was unheard-of in the Littlesea area—so I put The Best of Dolly on the tape deck and drove inland. I headed in the general direction of Hawley End, but that meant nothing, because short of taking the London or coast roads, that was the only way to go. The fact that Helen Robinson would almost certainly be languishing in her cottage without the company of either husband or lover had, of course, nothing to do with it.

On the way I passed the entrance to Whitegates

and was reminded of old Mrs Rymer. I wondered if she had any visitors this Sunday afternoon. It must have been the two and a half units, because I made a spur of the moment decision and turned up the drive.

The house was a handsome Georgian pile, with some not too offensive practical additions—fire-escapes, a back kitchen extension, a satellite dish and so on. The solid outer wooden front doors were open, but there was a round brass bell below a sign advising visitors to Ring and Enter. The hall was like a dentist's waiting room with a table on which was a pot full of ferns and a slew of magazines, mostly *The Lady* and the organ of the Countrydwellers' Association. A great fluffy tortoiseshell cat was dozing in a puddle of sunshine on the Turkish rug, unimpressed by my arrival.

A girl in a green uniform appeared. 'Can I help you?'

'Well, I don't know—I wondered if I might visit Mrs Rymer?'

'Oh, lovely,' said the girl, so that I experienced a small glow of virtue. 'Hang on a moment, I'll be right with you.'

She crossed the hall and opened a door into what appeared to be an office, currently empty. She returned carrying a large book which she laid on the table.

'Now then, Mrs Rymer ...' she ran her forefinger down a page. 'Oh, what a pity, she's out for the day.'

'Never mind. It was a long shot anyway, I was passing so I called in.'

'Yes, but it's a shame,' said the girl. 'She doesn't get all that many visitors, but she's gone out to lunch with her son. Shall I tell her who called?'

'Well the only thing is, she won't have any idea who I am. I work for the auctioneers who are dealing with some of her things, and I met her daughter-in-law recently. I thought I might just introduce myself and, you know, assure her that her property is receiving our best attention.'

'Of course, what a nice idea, and your name is?'

'Mrs Piercy, Eve Piercy. And my company's called Bouvier's.'

'Oh yes, I've heard of them, they've got a very good reputation.' She wrote down Bouviers alongside my name in the big book before closing it.

'We like to think so.'

'Do call in again, won't you?'

I promised I would, and left. As I drove back down towards the road I felt pleased that Mrs Rymer had gone out to lunch with her family.

*   *   *

When I got to Helen's house, John Kerridge was just coming out of the gate, aiming an electronic key like a six-shooter at his silver Mercedes. Which all went to show how wrong you could be. I wondered what excuse he had offered to his wife and children for skipping the Sunday roast and visiting Helen in her rural slum. Or (a disloyal thought but a recurring one), why he would want to. I was the first to accord my friend respect—as a clever, interesting woman—but it was terribly hard to cast her in the role of the *femme fatale*, and her present circumstances offered little in the way of creature comforts. Kerridge was not, so far as I

149

could see, a soda bread and cider man. I was forced to the conclusion that absolute availability had a lot going for it.

I didn't wish to exchange pleasantries with him, so I drove straight past, intending to gain some time by turning round at the crossroads. But he glanced up and our eyes met fleetingly. Something passed between us in that split second, a flash of acknowledgement and recognition which left my cheeks burning with embarrassment. Though why *I* should have been embarrassed was a mystery.

I turned the car, paused, composed myself and drove back. To my intense relief the Merc had gone.

Helen answered the door in her brown chenille dressing gown, a garment of many years' service for which the tie had long since been lost and replaced by a red-and-grey striped cord, presumably from one of Clive's. She didn't appear to have anything on underneath and her long, bony feet were bare.

'Hello,' she said, 'did you bump into John?'

'Nearly. I avoided it.'

'You sound awfully stern,' she said in her uninterested way, flapping ahead of me into the kitchen. 'Are you telling me off?'

'Of course not,' I replied, realising at once that I had been.

'Not that it makes the slightest difference ...' She moved the clutter about vaguely and produced a crumpled packet of Camels, dispelling any notion I might have had of being offered refreshment. My last visit was obviously not to be seen as a precedent.

'Take a pew.'

She sat down on one of the bentwood chairs and

crossed her legs, revealing momentarily a whisp of auburn pubic hair—she must have been Titian-haired in her youth. She had good legs, with long, lean thighs, a high calf muscle (quite undeserved since she never took any exercise) and shapely ankles.

'Cupboard's bare,' she remarked. 'John ate the last of the cheese.'

For this, I thought, he gave up the perfect executive roast and all the trimmings . . . ? 'I could do Marmite toast,' she offered. 'And vodka, I've got a bottle of Smirnoff.'

The vodka sounded tempting, but I realised it would be most unwise to add any more units to those already totted up, and since Helen was clearly going to have one I needed something to keep me occupied.

'OK,' I said, 'thanks, I'll have some toast.'

She took a couple of slices from the packet in the bread bin and examined them before slamming them into the toaster. I told myself that whatever lifeforms they harboured would be killed by the heat.

'You're looking very smart,' she said, lighting her cigarette with a match.

'I've been to a party.'

'God. Parties . . . I've forgotten what they are.'

I saw an opening. 'You've cut yourself off, that's the trouble.'

'I know.'

'If I had a party, would you come?' It was the two and a half units speaking, I knew that a few hours from now the very last thing I'd want was a party in my nice, orderly flat.

Helen coughed, long and wheezily. When she'd

recovered, she said: 'Could I bring John?'

'Honestly?'

'You mean no.'

'Anyway, I'm not planning a party so it's academic.'

'An academic party,' she mused, 'that's me. An ageing academic party.'

She wasn't inviting any emollient remarks so I didn't venture any. Tendrils of smoke began to rise from the toaster to join those coming from her cigarette, and a pungent smell filled the air.

'Damn thing,' she said, switching the machine off at the plug and turning it upside down, tweaking the smouldering toast out amid a hail of carbonised crumbs. 'I'm perfectly happy using the grill but John insisted on giving me one of these, so I feel obliged . . .' She put the slices on a plate in front of me and provided me with a knife, a tub of sunflower spread and a jar of Marmite.

'Bit overdone,' she conceded, 'but charcoal prevents flatulence.'

This observation was matter of fact. I started on the toast as best I could, gumming the blackened shrapnel together with spread. Helen poured herself a vodka and gazed at me vacantly through her cigarette smoke.

'How's Ben?' she asked, out of the blue. It was so unusual for her to take any particular interest in someone else's life, especially their children, that I was quite taken aback.

'Ben?'

'Your son?' She furrowed her brow. 'He is called Ben, isn't he?'

'Yes. He's fine, thanks.'

'What's he doing with himself?'

'Earning a few quid at HMV.'

'Going out with girls?' This phrase, usually associated with a teenager's first tentative encounters with the opposite sex, seemed scarcely apposite when applied to Ben's social life, but then Helen lived in a parallel universe.

'All the time,' I replied.

'Good for him. Is he still rather handsome?'

'I think so, but then I would say that wouldn't I?'

'No, he was handsome when I last saw him, anyone would have said so.'

I glowed maternally, but she didn't take the subject any further. She didn't know my other friends—she and Clive had encountered them in the old days, but she never remembered names or faces—so it was pointless to enlarge on the Sophie business.

I munched as much as I could and then dusted my palms together. 'Thanks, I needed something to soak up the alcohol.'

'Yes,' she agreed, 'you can't beat good old toast. What about you?' she asked. 'Are you getting on all right?'

'Yes,' I said firmly. 'I'm enjoying my life. I'm very happy and content. Surprisingly so.'

'Without Ian.'

'I think that's all turned out for the best.'

'Aren't you lucky . . .' murmured Helen, leaning over to tap ash into my toast crumbs. 'Ian feels the same, does he?'

'As far as I can tell.' She was getting a bit too close for comfort, and I tried to steer her away. 'We don't see that much of each other any more.'

'Has he got someone else?'

I wondered what on earth had brought on this

unwelcome surge of interest. Her manner was, as usual, laconic to a degree, but this was still an uncomfortably straight question.

Ashamed of my duplicity, I said: 'Not that I know of.'

'But he will have, won't he? Bound to,' she drawled vaguely, 'I resist the idea of it being different for men, but I suspect it's true.'

'What?'

'My appalling mother used to say that women put up with the sex to get the love, and men offer love to get the sex.'

I laughed, relieved to have got things back into a more general arena. 'Sounds about right. Is that what you think about you and—John?' I still found it difficult to confer upon her lover the acceptance implied by the use of his Christian name.

She coughed at some length—while fishing out the last Camel—before replying: 'John doesn't love me. I mean look at me—' she spread her big hands at shoulder level. 'I'm not exactly a siren. But I do it for him, he says.'

'Obviously,' I agreed.

'And of course I adore him which makes the sex astonishing . . .'

I remembered what she'd said to me before about not being herself. 'But you love Clive,' I reminded her.

'No I don't.' She shook her head slowly, gazing at the ceiling. 'Not like this.'

*   *   *

On the way back I drove past the Chatsworths' house, Shandford, a large Edwardian villa in the

154

professional hinterland of Littelsea. I slowed down, in the hope of seeing Ronnie and offering the verbal equivalent of a bunch of seedless grapes. There was no sign of her, but the house presented a quiet, relaxed aspect, with windows and even the front door standing open and one of the boys—I couldn't see which—lying under a campervan in the driveway. I experienced another Sunday-afternoonish pang for the more ample life of the long and still happily married. But when Dennis appeared in the front doorway I at once moved on, embarrassed by my behaviour. It was a curious fact that had I been with Ian we wouldn't have hesitated for a moment. On the contrary, Dennis's appearance would have been our cue to get out of the car and go over. In my single state I feared that would seem, on a Sunday afternoon, too bustling and intrusive: too needy.

As I drove down the road I hoped Dennis hadn't seen me.

* * *

Ben came in at eight and went straight into the kitchen where I heard cupboards and the fridge opening and shutting and water being run into a saucepan.

'Good time?' I called from where I was sitting on the balcony.

'Sure,' he replied as though I'd made a suggestion—that generation seemed to have a whole range of inflexions designed to confuse the issue. 'I'll be through in a moment.'

'Putting on some pasta,' he explained. He came and leaned on the balcony rail, his back to the view, smoking. 'How about you?'

'Sabine had organised a wonderful lunch, I enjoyed myself. And then I went out to see Helen Robinson.'

'Ah, the Hellcat.' He hadn't a clue who I meant.

'So what did you make of Sophie?' I asked. I stood no chance of an unsolicited opinion on this subject, so there was nothing for it but a direct question.

'Yeah, she's OK,' he said, as though surprised to hear himself saying it. 'Not what I expected.'

Praise indeed. Now it was time for the more oblique approach. 'She must feel rather isolated up there with Martin and Sabine, working on the farm all week and—'

'I'm going to see her again, don't worry.'

'Are you?'

'Come on, Mum, don't give me the wide-eyed number. She's nice—nice eyes, nice tits, nice voice, functioning brain. I wouldn't push her out.'

'I wasn't trying to imply anything.'

'No, no, no—as if.'

'Oh all right,' I admitted. He was teasing me and it was disarming to be teased. 'I won't pretend I didn't notice how different she was from Pearl.'

'Now don't you go laying the harsh word on Pearl. She's no rocket scientist, but with that body she doesn't need to be.'

In this age of political correctness it was extraordinary how little the young cared about it. 'You can bring Pearl, she's a darn nice girl,' I murmured, but the allusion was lost on him.

'How's Sophie getting on with Sabine?' I asked. 'Did she say?'

'She mentioned that it was a bit sticky to begin

with, but improving.'

'I wonder if she realises how nervous Sabine was about the whole thing.'

'I doubt it.' Ben pulled a face as he shied his fag end on to the promenade. 'Sabine? Nervous? That'll be the day.'

'No, she was,' I pressed on, feeling that I was performing a useful social service. 'Still is, a little. After all it's unknown territory for her, having a girl in the house, and the fact that it's Martin's daughter makes the whole thing still more complicated, because she's not sure what her role is or how she should play it.'

'She seems to be doing fine. As a matter of fact Sophie quite likes her.'

'That's a relief.'

'I don't see what either of them have got to worry about,' he added. 'They're both pretty cool in their separate ways.' A buzzer sounded from the kitchen. 'There's my twists, do you want some?'

I declined. As I sat there thinking fond thoughts about possible youthful romance (something one could only do or even admit to in the privacy of one's own home) the phone rang.

'It's Sabine.'

'Hello! That was such a lovely—'

'Are you alone?'

'Yes—no, kind of.'

'I'll call tomorrow.'

'Sabine—' But she'd rung off.

Ben came in, carrying a Pyrex dish heaped with pasta twists, liberally covered with tomato ketchup and grated cheddar cheese.

'Who was that?'

'Oh, it was just Sabine, but she got called away.'

157

'As you do,' said Ben. 'Mind if I watch *Cracker*?'

*   *   *

It was quiet at Bouvier's during August, with no big sales due to take place until the beginning of the following month. Our days were taken up with valuation and assessment visits (not as many as usual because people were on holiday), stock-taking, and establishing reserves on those items scheduled for sale in September. Emma and I spent the best part of a couple of days poring over old Mrs Rymer's possessions.

'She should realise a tidy sum on these things,' remarked Emma respectfully, running her fingers over a walnut and marquetry bureau. 'But how sad she's got to part with it all.'

'I think she took quite a bit into Whitegates with her,' I said. 'And selling the rest will help her to stay there.'

'This is so pretty.' Emma lowered the flap of the bureau, and the supports glided out of their cavities with silken smoothness. 'Beautifully crafted.'

She began opening the compartments, pulling the tiny handles of doll-size cupboards and drawers between her finger and thumb. 'Isn't it darling? Oh look, there's always something . . .'

Her questing fingers had found a key, one of those old-fashioned black ones with a broad oval handle.

'What fun,' said Emma, 'like a children's story.'

'Is it for the lid of this?'

She shook her head. 'Too big, but I'll try it—nope, too big. I think we'd better send it to her.'

'It's all right,' I said, 'I was going to drop in on

158

her, I'll take it.'

I think if it had been any of the other things we commonly found in drawers—a pen, say, or coins, or even a bunch of common or garden Yale keys—it wouldn't have exercised such a spell. But a key such as this seemed to be inviting and perhaps even promising something, throwing down a challenge like the whistle in the M R James story: use me if you dare.

Emma gave me the key and I zipped it in the inside pocket of my handbag, a hostage to fortune.

*   *   *

On Saturday it turned out that Ronnie, though recovered, was still feeling a bit washed out, and not up to tennis. Desma said that in that case, rather than play American which was never awfully satisfactory, she'd drop out too so she and Rick could make a start on decorating the bathroom—which left Sabine and me to play singles.

I had no expectations whatever, but on this occasion Sabine played poorly by her standards, with an unprecedented number of unforced errors and double faults, and I actually snatched the second set. This rattled her sufficiently for me to take her to seven-five in the third, so although I emerged the loser yet again, it was with greater honour than usual.

As we shook hands over the net she didn't go so far as to congratulate me but said: 'I'm sorry, I simply was not seeing the ball today.'

'That's all right. Your loss was my gain.'

'Drink?'

'Of course.'

In the Cutter Bar she lit up a king-size and ordered a bottle of sauvignon.

'Do you mind? I'm in a drinking mood.'

'Be my guest.'

'No, you be mine, Eve.'

'Thank you.'

I knew better than to argue, even though both of us had cars parked out on the prom. It was understood that I would stay within the limit (a phrase, I thought, which might have been my motto) and nervously pass at least one panda car on the way home, while Sabine would quaff as much as she wanted, jump straight into her four-by-four and belt back up to her clifftop hideaway completely unremarked.

She sighed impatiently like a steam train in a siding as the waiter poured us both a glass. The moment he'd gone she took a generous draught and announced:

'So—these young people seem to have formed a *liaison.*' She gave the word its full French pronunciation, resonant with erotic possibilities.

'Have they?'

'Of course—Ben is almost living at our house!'

'Really?' My first question had been rhetorical, the second was prompted by genuine surprise.

'Oh yes! Surely you knew—you must have noticed.'

'Well, I knew he liked Sophie, but he's out such a lot . . . to be honest I don't keep a very close track of his movements.' I heard how this might sound, and added: 'I do hope he's not making a nuisance of himself.'

'Not to me!' answered Sabine gaily. 'I can't speak for Sophie.'

160

'Just so long as he's not.'

It was ridiculous, really, that I should be affecting all this concern for Sabine, the absolute tranquillity of whose life was beyond dispute. She had the space, the time, the money and the marriage to ensure that she need never be bothered by anyone. On the other hand the thought of Ben prowling in and out of Château Drage at all hours of the day and night in hot pursuit of the lovely Sophie embarrassed me slightly. Unlike me, Sabine wasn't used to the brutally open way in which the amorous intrigues of the young were conducted. Sophisticate though she undoubtedly was, I had a nasty feeling that she cherished notions of courtship which bore little relation to the pungently hormonal reality.

But no, she was all smiles. 'Far from it, Eve, it's a pleasure to have him around. And anyway, as you know, he's doing me a favour. If Sophie is happy, then I am happy. Ben has relieved me of the burden of responsibility.'

I was pleased, even if I was surprised. 'Good. I'm delighted.'

'Who knows,' mused Sabine happily, 'where it may lead?'

'I don't think we should get too carried away,' I said, adding with a certain shy pride: 'I'm afraid Ben has a bit of a reputation.'

'I'm not surprised, with his looks, and his air—' she twirled a slender hand in the air, suggesting much that was alluring but indefinable. 'I think this is the perfect way for Sophie to learn about romance. A young girl should have an affair with someone more experienced. And if it's someone close to her own age, then so much the better.'

'What makes you think Sophie is inexperienced?' I was genuinely intrigued. 'Nineteen isn't the same as it was in our day.'

Sabine laughed benignly. 'I admit she is not as naïve as I at first thought, but Eve, she has led a very sheltered life. Martin is an old-fashioned father.'

'She hasn't spent much time with him,' I pointed out. 'What's her mother like?'

'A country lady with a big bottom,' said Sabine. 'Please. I don't care to think about it.' Bottoms were a key criterion with her, a kind of fleshy barometer of acceptibility, and I shifted my own self-consciously on the seat. Unaware of any discomfort she might have caused she raised her glass. 'Here's to young love!'

'Why not?' I agreed, and we clinked glasses.

* * *

After I'd done my shopping I had to go to the library, and my route from the multi-storey took me past HMV. Though in the face of Sabine's untypical enthusiasm I'd presented a cool façade, I was actually aglow with the possibilities of a relationship between Ben and Sophie, and I couldn't resist glancing into the shop to catch a glimpse of my lady-killing son. It just so happened he was on the till by the door, swiping somebody's credit card through the machine.

'Hi there,' he said to me, and then, 'Sign here please,' to the customer.

I went in and hovered. When the customer had gone, I said: 'I wasn't actually going to come in, I was on my way to the library.'

'You need to cut out all this wild self-indulgence, Mum.'

'As a matter of fact I've been playing tennis and drinking with Sabine.'

'Frenchie—how was she?'

'She won, but less convincingly than usual.'

'Glad to hear it.'

On duty as he was I had him on the spot, so I dared to add: 'She said you've been up at their place a lot recently.'

'Did she? Well if she said that it must be true.'

'I didn't mean to be nosey.'

'Yes you did.' He flashed me a look that was, for him, almost angry. 'It's in your job description.'

It was in his job description to tell me to butt out, and I did.

*　　　*　　　*

'Well, well,' said Mel on the phone a couple of nights later. 'So you bumped into Mr McNally again.'

'Heavens, news travels fast!'

'It does in the business community. We're worse than any curtain-twitching suburb.'

'Who told you?'

'I'm friendly with the PA in his office here, and she told me the great man had met my mother at a bash in the UK.'

'It was one of those silly coincidences,' I said lightly. 'I was at a drinks party given by the Drages and it turned out he was a friend of theirs, or Martin's anyway.'

'Did he recognise you immediately?'

'He seemed to.'

163

'And you?'

'Well obviously he rang a bell . . .'

'How fortuitous.'

'But the *real* news is that Ben's seeing Martin's daughter.'

Mel's rather harsh laugh came snapping over the line. 'Poor girl!'

'I can assure you she's well up to the challenge from what I can see.'

'I'll believe you.'

'I think it's quite serious for once. I got my head bitten off the other day just for mentioning it.'

'OK. And what about Charles McNally, are there plans afoot?'

'Of course not!' Even I realised how ridiculously emphatic I sounded, and it certainly wasn't lost on Mel.

'It's not such a silly question.'

'I mean we don't know each other, it simply doesn't arise, we just happened to bump into one another at a drinks party. Plus he's over there.'

'Fine,' said Mel. But as she went on to tell me about her trip to Dubai both she and I knew that she had had the last word, and that 'fine' wasn't really it.

I went to call on Ronnie after work one day. It was, of course, a friendly gesture, but also a selfish one—I needed to know she was fully recovered. It was a quirk of mine: I hated losing things, and that included the company of my friends. It put me off my stroke. So I was checking up on Ronnie for my own sake as well as hers. I made it appear as casual as possible, turning up on her doorstep in my Bouvier's suit and leaving the car door open as though I anticipated jumping straight back in.

164

She looked the picture of health and was delighted to see me.

'Eve, come in! Tea? Drink? Sun's over the yard arm.'

'Just the one, Mrs Bridges.' I went and closed the car door.

'This is so nice,' she said, leading the way to the large, well-appointed kitchen. 'I'm not used to being ill, I've missed everyone.'

'Are you tennis-fit again now?'

'Good grief, yes, can't wait. But I'll be sadly out of practice.'

'Your loss is our gain, we'll get to look better.' I took a glass of wine and we went out into the garden and sat down on the bleached swing seat. Shandford, though not a fraction as lavish as Headlands, was middle-class and mellow, with contents that appeared to have been there for ever. In Sabine's house you marvelled at how impeccably thought-through were the design, the decor, the furnishings: in Ronnie's nothing seemed thought about at all.

'Where are the boys?' I asked.

'Philip's just gone to Turkey and Simon's in Cornwall, so all is peace, perfect peace. But speaking of tennis, Dennis and I are withdrawing to the Auvergne in ten days' time, for two weeks, so it would be good to get a game in before then.'

'We will, definitely. I'll ring round the others and fix it.'

We sipped and swung idly. Ours was not an especially close, but a pleasantly relaxed and undemanding friendship. Ronnie was a contented woman, and her contentment cast a glow on those in her company.

'Your roses are lovely,' I remarked.

'It's been a good year. The old-fashioned ones have been amazing . . . the scent . . . would you like to take some with you?'

'They're nicer here.'

We swung a bit more, and then Ronnie said: 'Sabine rang me up. She was in a matchmaking mood.'

'You don't say.'

'She's been on to you as well, then. What am I saying, of course she has!'

'About Ben and Sophie, oh yes.' I smiled tolerantly. 'It wouldn't surprise me to find she's booked the marquee already.'

'Young love has certainly found approval in the Drage household, she's absolutely full of it.'

'Heaven knows why, it wouldn't exactly be a glittering match for Sophie. In fact knowing Sabine I'm amazed she doesn't suspect Ben of gold-digging. But she seems to think he's the answer to a maiden's prayer.'

'Which is all rather sweet when you come to think of it,' observed Ronnie, reaching for the bottle and topping us up.

'Just as long as it doesn't end in tears.'

'Eve!' Ronnie sighed humorously, shaking her head. She tapped the bottle. 'It's half full, not half empty.'

'A third full.'

Ronnie ignored this. 'I tell you what, she seems to cherish some hopes concerning you as well.'

'What?'

'Somebody called Chuck? McDonald? McAlpine?'

'Charles McNally.'

'That's the one.'

'She's barking up completely the wrong tree.'

'Oh well, it's all keeping her happy. I've never known Sabine so sweet-tempered.'

I was suddenly restless. I put my glass down and said: 'I ought to be going.'

Ronnie continued to move the swing gently, with one foot, just enough to detain me. 'How's Ian?'

'Fine.'

'Do you see anything of each other these days?'

'A little. We're still friends, after all.'

'I do admire you for that.'

I felt a flush of embarrassment at my hypocrisy. 'It's not very admirable. I'm not even sure it's true any more.'

'Why's that?'

'He has someone else.'

Ronnie's expression of friendly interest didn't alter. 'Only to be expected, I suppose.'

'Yes—yes of course.'

'It sets you free in a way, doesn't it,' she suggested.

'I hadn't looked at it like that.'

'I mean you were free anyway, but this sort of gives you permission to go for it.'

I grimaced. 'I can't exactly see myself going to singles bars or joining a dating agency.'

'No, no, that wouldn't be you, Eve. But at least you can move on.'

'Yes.' I knew she was right, but I wanted to cry. Unexpectedly she stopped rocking the seat and pressed my hand.

'It must be difficult, though.'

*　　*　　*

167

The minute I turned out of the drive the tears began to course down my cheeks. Sniffing and choking I trundled along, swiping unprettily at my nose and cheeks with my sleeve and praying no one else I knew would spot me. I hadn't really got a clue what I was crying about, or who for, but it hurt so much that I could only conclude it was for myself.

I'd just about got a grip by the time I reached Cliff Mansions, and was sufficiently in command to plan a stiff walk along the cliffs. I'd been brought up to believe in the restorative properties of fresh air and exercise which, while resolving nothing, made one so much more philosophical about the problems.

As I opened the door of the flat I felt a waft of sea air, and realised I must have gone out and left the balcony door open. It wasn't until I walked into the sitting room that I saw Ben and Sophie sitting on the floor of the balcony, drinking bottled beer. They were both looking my way, alerted by the sound of front door.

'Hello!' I cried, painfully aware of my mascara- and emotion-blotched appearance. 'Hang on, must dash.'

I went into the bathroom, splashed my face, touched up my eyes, and flushed the loo before coming out. They were still sitting there, but no longer looking in my direction. I went out to join them. Sophie was in her farm overalls, like a fetching *ingénue* in some musical production of *Li'l Abner*. Now that I had, literally, regained face, I was cheered to see them.

'This is nice,' I said. 'Are you staying for supper?'

168

'That's really kind of you, Eve, but I think we're going out,' replied Sophie, casting a quizzical look at Ben for his confirmation of the arrangement.

'Well in that case I'll get myself a drink . . .'

'I'll do it,' said Ben. He pulled himself up in one long movement, ankles crossed, arms stretched forward, and went past me towards the kitchen, giving my arm a confiding and affectionate squeeze on the way. My inconsolable wretchedness of a few minutes ago was transformed by this small gesture into quite unjustified happiness.

I sat down on one of my two black wrought-iron chairs. Sophie moved her finger round and round on the mouth of her beer bottle. I sensed she was looking at me through her lashes.

'How's work?' I asked. 'How's the farm?'

'Big business,' she replied. 'To be honest I'd be better off on some smallholding in the sticks, but Father's intent on doing his bit—which I appreciate,' she added with a rueful look. 'So I'll see it out.'

'He obviously loves having you around,' I said, and then added boldly, 'and it's nice for Sabine, too—having another woman about the place.'

Now the eyelashes lifted and that dark, remorselessly candid gaze levelled itself at me.

'Hm . . . Maybe.'

I was prevented from taking her up on this by the arrival of my glass of wine. When Ben had placed the glass in my hand he laid his hand on my shoulder and exerted a slight, meaningful pressure. He had always been an affectionate son, far more demonstrative than his older sister, but this second touch convinced me that there was another agenda here, a message struggling to find a medium.

He sat down, in the other chair this time, and Sophie hitched herself backwards so that her back rested against his leg. He stroked her hair, and rubbed the side of her face with his finger in a way which warmed my heart. Let them have their fun, I thought, let them have it all and to the full, and not worry about the future. I felt calm and beneficent, set apart from the schemings of Sabine, and even the good-natured speculations of Ronnie. Beyond the prom the sea, at low tide, twinkled lazily in the early evening sun, and a couple walked along the shingle, the man with a toddler on his shoulders.

'I called in on Ronnie Chatsworth on the way home,' I said. 'She's fully recovered now.'

'I didn't know she'd been ill,' said Ben. In the far off world of the olds someone had literally to die before he realised anything was amiss.

'No reason why you should, really. Philip's in Turkey, she said.'

'Yeah? Nursing a broken heart, is he? Gone away to forget?' They both cracked a smile.

'I really couldn't say, why?'

'He fancied me,' said Sophie. 'But it was not to be.'

'Of course . . .' I remembered the party, Philip's swift moving in, and Sophie's subsequent change of direction. It was wholly improper of me, but I was delighted. Faint shouts from down below didn't register with me until Ben said:

'I take it you know those people.'

'Sorry?'

'They seem to know you.'

It was the couple with the toddler, now back up on the prom and recognisable as Desma and Rick.

'Hi!' I shouted expansively, 'do you want to

come up for a drink?'

'Are you sure?' called Desma. 'We're with child.'

'I know—lovely—I've got some Ribena.'

'OK, you twisted our arm.'

They began to cross the road and Ben and Sophie got up.

'There's no need to go,' I said. 'They're awfully nice.'

'It's not that,' said Sophie. 'But we are going out anyway and I have to go home and change.'

I saw them out and watched them go down the staircase, encountering the Shaws coming the other way. There was a brief exchange—laughter, Sophie being charming, Bryony's piping petitions—and then they were gone and Desma lifted her face and spotted me.

'God, Eve, when are you going to get something with a lift?'

I laughed, I was pleased to see them, but unfinished business hung tantalisingly in the air like the scent of a fascinating, unknown woman.

CHAPTER NINE

'I'm coming over for a meeting,' said Mel. 'End of next week. I'll be down to see you on Sunday.'

'Good—great!' I said, with slightly more enthusiasm than I felt. My daughter was so crisp and commanding. In her family life as at work, she took no prisoners. There was no question of my being asked, I was placed firmly in an opt-out situation. If I absolutely could not manage to have her to stay, I would have to say so—otherwise I would have to make shift.

'What are you doing on Saturday?' I asked.

'Going to the theatre with some pals in the evening. Having lunch with Dad and his new woman.'

It was a shock, realising that she knew. 'Who told you?'

'Dad wrote. He said he'd seen you, and how well you'd taken it considering. Did you take it well, or was that my father being diplomatic?'

'I really don't know. I took it, that's all. I didn't have much option.'

'Have you met her?'

'No!' I said rather snappishly, and then modified my tone. 'What on earth would be the point?'

'None, granted. But since you and Dad have remained such chums I rule nothing out.'

'Well, I have.'

'I'll give you a detailed report, Mother,' said Mel. 'Never fear.'

*   *   *

I told myself that details were the last thing I needed, but of course I was eaten up with curiosity. From about eleven a.m. on Saturday I kept picturing Mel, and Ian, and Julia Kendal. Sometimes they were in a smart restaurant, sometimes in a pub, sometimes in a discreet hotel. Depending on the setting Julia was a vamp in a tight black suit and vermilion lipstick, attractively casual in faded denim, or all country elegance with pearls. Whatever her get-up the three of them were having a wonderful time, talking up a storm and breaking into great bursts of warm, spontaneous

172

laughter. Mel was more relaxed than I'd ever seen her—

'Fore!' yelled Ronnie as her topspin serve kicked up off the line and hummed past my right ear.

'Sorry!'

'I take it you weren't ready?'

'Of course she wasn't ready!' shouted Desma, who had the misfortune to partner me on this, the morning when my concentration was at an all-time low.

'I'll take two.' Ronnie sportingly heeled up another ball. Even out of practice she could afford to be generous. 'OK?'

'Yes,' I said. She served and the same thing happened, except that this time I took a wild swing, the ball just nicked the frame, and sailed high over the wire netting.

'Ace!' cried Sabine. 'Great serve.'

It had been, but I'd dealt more efficiently with greater. I mumbled an apology to Desma, who told me to think nothing of it. The score stood at forty-thirty. Desma returned the next serve towards the tramlines, generally a good move with Sabine, whose forehand volley was a weakness, but on this occasion she saw it like a football and smacked it back at my feet. The game, and the set, was lost, and it was undoubtedly I who had lost it.

We shook hands at the net and I apologised again to Desma who patted me forgivingly on the shoulder.

'No worries old thing, it happens to the best of us.'

'We mustn't patronise you,' said Sabine, radiating the victor's magnanimous glow. 'You were having a nightmare, Eve, you let us off very lightly this morning.'

I bared my teeth in acknowledgement. Ronnie headed to the bench and began zipping up her racquet.

'Sorry, I'll have to pass on lunch today—packing to do.'

'Have a terrific time,' said Desma. 'Will you be playing any tennis?'

'*Au contraire*,' replied Ronnie, 'I shall be sitting about on my backside researching the local gastronomy and viticulture. Cheerio *mes braves*.'

'Thank God for that,' I said as we walked along the prom to the Cutter Bar. 'If she spent her holiday honing her game I'd be obliged to drop out.'

'Though I have to say,' put in Sabine, 'that she may be expecting too much of the food and wine in that particular area.'

'She was playing well,' conceded Desma, 'but we made it easy for them. Is anything wrong?'

I told her while Sabine vamped Clay at the bar.

'Don't torture yourself,' was Desma's advice. 'Why should you care? Ian is your ex-husband—'

'We're not actually—'

'Divorced? Then maybe it's time you were. I mean to put it brutally you don't want him back, so let him go.'

'That's pretty much what Ronnie said.'

'Good for Ronnie.'

Sabine joined us with the drinks. '*Salut*. Are we still on tennis or something juicier?'

'Ian's got a new woman in his life,' I said, 'and Mel's meeting her—' I glanced at my watch—'as we speak. I can't stop thinking about it.'

'Perfectly natural my dear,' remarked Sabine,

174

who was full of surprises these days. 'Get mad, then get over it.'

'I will, of course I will,' I mumbled doubtfully. Sabine gave me her most worldly look.

'Get someone yourself.'

'Easier said than done.'

'Well of course you have to be *ready* to do it,' said Desma. 'The light bulb has to really want to change. But maybe this is the moment.'

'Actually it makes me feel less ready than ever.'

'You are very change-averse, Eve,' declared Sabine, taking delivery of the menu. 'It is a female failing, and one to which you are especially prone.'

I really couldn't take all this wise-woman stuff from Sabine. 'Steady on,' I said, 'I got out of my marriage, didn't I?'

'*Exactement!*' Sabine gloried in having proved her point. 'You got out of it—now walk away from it.'

'But not on an empty stomach.' Desma tweaked the menu away from Sabine and placed it in front of me. 'Make-your-mind-up time.'

*   *   *

They made it sound so easy. And they spoke only the truth. My torture was not only self-inflicted but irrational and immature. But knowing this made it no easier to bear. Julia of the *Nursing Times* haunted my attempts to clean the flat that afternoon, and even a background of Ute Lemper seeing to Kurt Weill could not drown out that imagined warm conversation, that infernally carefree laughter . . .

In the end I conceded defeat, and telephoned

Whitegates. Mrs Rymer was in, they said, and not expecting visitors, so I told them to expect me. The key was still in my handbag.

I realised I was quite unprepared for what I might find. Mrs Rymer might be in her dotage and completely gaga, or a tyrannical old boiler, which in either case would bode ill for my intrusion. But I badly needed a diversion and this afternoon she was it.

The matron, immaculately coiffed *à la* Thatcher and dressed in a striped silk frock, greeted me effusively.

'Mrs Piercy, how lovely to meet you. Mrs Rymer's going to be so pleased, her family are all away at the moment.'

'How is she?' I asked. 'I mean, she doesn't know me from Adam, and she might be a bit startled.'

'Mrs Rymer? No.' Matron gave me a roguish look. 'It would take a lot more than a strange visitor to startle her.'

She took me out into the garden, where residents were parked here and there under parasols or beneath a shady tree. There were three little groups, and one on her own—Mrs Rymer, who was reading *The Times* with the aid of a magnifying glass.

'I'll leave you to it,' said Matron. 'We told her you were coming.'

The moment I'd introduced myself I realised how ageist had been my assumptions about the woman I was visiting. For a start, she was handsome in that way which can only improve with the years—I suspected that the tall, awkward goose of seventy-odd years ago had become this wonderful eagle of a woman through a life lived to

176

the full. The Roman nose, sweeping brows, broad mouth and strong jaw which must have been hell at seventeen were at their most striking now. Looking into her fiercely intelligent grey eyes, feeling the strength of her handshake, and hearing the steady resonance of her voice I knew that this was first and foremost and most emphatically an individual whom age stood no chance of wearying and the years had condemned to nothing more than an increase of natural authority.

'I hope I'm not disturbing you,' I said, indicating the newspaper on her lap.

'I live to be disturbed, Mrs Piercy,' she replied. 'What can I do for you?'

That put me in my place. She was civil and attentive, but I was doing her no favours: I was the petitioner.

'When we were checking the drawers in your bureau, we found a key,' I explained. 'It didn't fit any of the pieces we have, so I thought you might like it back.'

'Let me see.' She held out a hand as big as a man's. I laid the key in her palm and she picked up the magnifying glass and examined it. She wore glasses, and her hair—thick, wavy and dark, barely streaked with iron grey—was cut short and brushed back off her face.

'No,' she said shortly, handing me back the key. 'No idea. Sorry.'

'It's yours, though, don't you want to keep it— just in case?'

This made her laugh. 'I don't think so! I have very few things here, and none of them lock.'

'Very well, if you're sure . . .' I put the key back in my handbag. 'We'll double check that it doesn't fit anything at Bouvier's.'

'Then throw it in the sea. Make a wish. Do something symbolic,' she suggested.

Now it was my turn to laugh. She understood how I felt about the key.

'I probably will,' I said.

'Sit down.' She felt behind her for a cushion and tossed it down on the grass. I noticed that her long legs were bandaged from knee to ankle. 'Sorry to disappoint.'

'There's something about keys, isn't there.'

'Deep dungeons, tall towers, sealed caskets— fairy tales, yes.' She glanced at her watch—a large, practical timepiece with bold Roman numerals as a concession to her failing eyesight. 'Would you like some tea?'

I made a quick assessment of the distance from here to the house, the state of her legs, the time of day.

'Oh, no thank you, I'm really not—'

'I can whistle it up.' She produced, like a conjurer, a mobile phone from the side of the chair. 'I have the technology.'

'OK then, if you're sure. I'd love one.'

With great deliberation, holding the phone close to her face, she pressed several digits. As she waited for an answer she bestowed on me a broad, straight-faced wink.

'Ah—is that Arlette? Arlette it's Mrs Rymer— fine thank you. Look I'm out to grass this afternoon and my visitor and I would simply love a pot of your best—are you sure? Thank you so much. Good-bye.'

She switched off the phone with a flourish. 'My legs are such a damn nuisance these days, I've

178

realised if you don't ask, you don't get. And most of the girls here are perfectly fine if treated nicely. So—tea is on its way.'

'You seem to have the system sussed—sorted out.'

'I do have it sussed. You have to. I'm thinking of starting a gambling school.' She was perfectly serious. 'Do you play cards at all?'

'I'm afraid not. I have friends who are tigers at bridge, but I stopped at happy families.'

The strangeness of what I'd just said struck me, and she must have noticed, because she said: 'You're lucky to have got that far, my dear! So you work at Bouvier's—do you think my odds and sods will fetch much?'

'They're very desirable pieces, actually. We expect them to do well.'

'You make them sound like bright young graduates going out into the world, instead of a few fusty bits of furniture.'

'You don't miss them?'

'It's only clutter,' she said, 'only things. I miss having a home of my own, but the bungalow was no great shakes and I couldn't manage on my own any more so I'm better off here. And look at all this—' she waved a hand at the garden—'it really would be churlish to complain ...' She took in her surroundings appreciatively for a moment. 'And when you're not working at Bouvier's, what do you do?'

Confronted with such a question I suddenly felt extraordinarily dull, and defensive about my tidy flat, my single state, my ordered womanly life.

'I play a lot of tennis,' I told her. 'I was playing this morning, but I seemed to be having an off day.'

'Singles?'

'Doubles.'

'I used to play a lot,' she said, 'with my gentleman friend between the wars.'

She put a subtle, ironic spin on the phrase 'gentleman friend' so that instead of sounding archaic it implied a host of decadent possibilities. I realised I'd been handed my opening on a plate. Perhaps the key had worked after all.

'You partnered each other?' I asked.

'In very many senses we did. But on the court we played singles, to the death.'

I was impressed. 'Did you beat him?'

'Sometimes. But he was a very, very good player. Later on when I played club tennis with my husband we won no end of cups and it was really all down to Gerry.' She caught my look. 'His name was Gerhardt. Not very helpful when hostilities broke out, as you may imagine. Now then tell me, what does your husband do?'

'He's in information technology. But we're separated.'

She made no comment other than to muse. 'As a great many of us are, for one reason or another. Do you have a family?'

'A son and a daughter—both grown up.'

'You've met my son?'

'No, only your daughter-in-law, she was at your house the first time I went.'

'She's a very nice woman,' said Mrs Rymer, 'extraordinarily energetic, and I'm lucky to have her. I always feel I want to say to her, Jane, calm down, don't get into a flat spin, the sky won't fall if you draw breath for ten seconds.'

'There's a lot of pressure these days to be busy.'

180

Mrs Rymer ignored this. 'She must be about your age. Perhaps a bit older, or doesn't look after herself so well. At any rate she's running herself into the ground . . . Now *she* ought to separate.'

My astonishment at this opinion in a mother-in-law was thankfully covered by the arrival of the tea. It was on one of those trays with legs, which Arlette set up on the grass.

'Thank you Arlette,' said Mrs Rymer, and then to me: 'You pour, or we'll be all night.'

'My son reckons his children are monsters,' she continued, 'which I think is an awful pity. They seem perfectly normal to me by the standards of the day, and since they're both over twenty-one now he should stop feeling embarrassed by them. What are your two like?'

I summed up Mel and Ben as succinctly as I could.

'So your daughter is going to be a captain of industry and your son is in training to be a rich woman's plaything,' summarised my hostess breezily.

'Something like that.'

'And they have lovers?'

I was beginning to adjust to Mrs Rymer's conversational style, but even so this was a facer, coming from an elderly party whom I scarcely knew.

'My son definitely does, my daughter keeps her own counsel.'

'Wise woman,' commented Mrs Rymer.

I knew that on a sauce-for-the-goose basis I should be able to pose an equally direct question to her about Gerhardt, but because I wanted to know everything, I couldn't formulate the question

181

quickly enough.

'My son,' she went on, 'has never been able to accept the fact that his offspring have biological urges. On those occasions when the subject's reared its head in my presence I've told him he should be jolly glad that they do, but he seems to regard it as a hanging offence.'

'I expect he feels protective,' I suggested.

'Hm . . . the jury is out. However, we'll give him the benefit of the doubt for the time being. Tell me, do you enjoy your work?'

I talked to her about Bouvier's and we drank our tea. She was an extremely attentive audience with, I was sure, excellent recall. She had a way of listening with downcast eyes, as though to cut out all extraneous visual distractions. Then when she spoke she'd look up and startle you with the intense, unblinking brightness of her gaze.

When I got up to go, she said: 'Excuse me if I don't come with you to the door, I have to hobble and clutch, and I prefer it to be with someone who's paid to be clutched. Old age is a grim business.'

'Yes,' I agreed. 'I'm sure.'

She laughed drily and said: 'Perhaps you'd like to come again?'

'I would.' Something occurred to me. 'Or would you like to come out? My flat has a million stairs, but we could have lunch somewhere, a pub or a—'

'What a good idea, I'd like to,' she said firmly, and once again held out that commanding hand. 'So it's farewell and not good-bye.'

I left Whitegates with a lighter heart, not because I had done a good deed, but because I had made a friend.

*   *   *

Ben came with me to meet Mel at the station the following morning. I wasn't planning on waking him, but on hearing me in the kitchen he must have pitched out of bed straight into his jeans and boots, and now appeared, heavily shadowed from a late night, in the doorway.

'I'll come.'

'OK.'

'Is that tea?'

He held the mug in both hands and drank in long gulps, eyes closed the greater to experience the relief. 'Thanks.'

It was a cool, damp morning with the high tide making irritable little rushes at the sea wall. The car was slow to start, but Ben sat placidly in the passenger seat, still half asleep while the engine whinnied abortively a few times before lurching into life.

After a couple of minutes he cleared his throat and asked: 'So what's the Melon been up to in town, then?'

'Don't call her that. Some meeting or other, she didn't go into details.'

'So what's she been doing for fun?'

'I know she met her father for lunch yesterday. Him and his new lady friend.'

'OK,' said Ben. 'But no bloke in her life—that she's admitting to?'

'Not that I know of.'

He shook his head. 'I don't get it.'

It was becoming increasingly obvious that no one shared my feelings about Julia of the *Nursing*

183

Times, or what Mel thought of her. To everyone else it was just a simple, inevitable, humdrum next-step sort of thing which should not concern anyone much, least of all me. But as we pulled up in the station car park, Ben remarked:

'I wonder if he's likely to bring her to the cricket.'

'Oh, I wouldn't have thought—' I began, but he'd got out of the car to pay into the machine. I backed into a space and watched him return with a great feeling of tenderness. He did understand.

Mel's train was fifteen minutes late, and almost empty. She hopped down from it with characteristic briskness, somehow conveying the impression that BR's inefficiency would have been even greater had it not been for her personal intervention. She wore jeans, elastic-sided boots, a crisp white shirt and a blue blazer, and carried no case except for a small black rucksack on her back. She was nothing if not casual but next to her I felt rumpled and unkempt. As her cool lips brushed my cheek I smelt some light, fresh, girl-about-town scent.

'Good God,' she said, looking Ben up and down. 'What brought this on?'

'I thought I would. Nothing else to do. Good trip?'

'Yes, I played a blinder.' It was typical of each of them that he'd been enquiring about the travel, and she'd replied concerning her work.

We began walking back towards the exit. Ben laid a hand on the strap of the rucksack. 'Shall I take that?'

'No thank you. It was one of the best day's work I ever did, buying this, it makes overnighting a doddle.'

Ben paused to light a cigarette and she glanced over her shoulder. 'He's not still doing that.'

'I'm afraid so.'

'I hope you ban it in your flat.' She never called it 'home'.

'I can't say I do.'

'Mother—honestly.'

Ben caught up with us. 'What are you two griping about?'

'This.' She tweaked the cigarette out of his hand, dropped it on the ground and trod on it.

'Hey, Mel, fuck off . . .' He was gently plaintive rather than angry.

'I'm not sitting in a car inhaling your filthy smoke,' she said calmly.

He took out another. 'I'll have one before I get in then.'

'Suit yourself. But if you want to do away with yourself there are cheaper and less antisocial ways of doing it.'

By the time we got into the car I was almost in tears. Why, when we only had twenty-four hours together, when Ben had got out of bed to come and meet her, why did she have to be like this, so censorious, so contentious? I told myself she was an adult, too old to reprimand, but in my craven heart I knew that much as I admired my daughter, I was also a little afraid of her. Ben wasn't, and what I feared more than anything was his capacity, not used since childhood, to wound his sister. I knew in my heart that her formidable competence was a carapace developed against the world—but it was a brittle carapace, and I dreaded what might be revealed if it was shattered.

185

For now, however, the bad moment blew over, along with Ben's smoke.

'Did you enjoy the show?' I asked.

'The play itself was rubbish,' she declared, 'but the production and the acting were so good that you could enjoy it anyway. It must have been reasonably entertaining because I stayed awake through the whole thing.' This was no affectation, she was one of those preternaturally busy people to whom sitting still and watching is simply an opportunity to recharge the batteries.

'How was Dad?' asked Ben from the back.

I stared tensely, smilingly at the road ahead.

'Good,' she said. 'We only went to a wine bar off the Gloucester Road, but they had some historic Australian whites and the food was a lot better than I feared.'

'Well,' I commented with awful brightness, 'they do say London's the best city in the world now for eating out.'

'But has the metropolitan influence spread to Littelsea, that's what I want to know,' said Mel. 'Is there anywhere I can take you people which won't be death by gravy?'

'Now don't you go patronising us,' I began, but Ben chimed in again.

'What about the woman?'

'Darling,' I said, 'don't let's—'

'Oh, fine,' replied Mel. 'Perfectly normal and nice, size sixteen, all her own teeth.'

I ground the gears.

Ben leaned forward so that his head was by my shoulder, but he was facing Mel. There was something in his manner that suggested he was interrogating his sister on my behalf. Which in a sense he was, because although my knuckles were white on the wheel I didn't tell him to shut up.

'How old?' asked Ben

'God, I don't know, no one looks their age these days, fortyish?'

'Forty-one,' I said.

'Blonde, brunette?'

'Mid brown. Smart but not drop-dead. Neat but not gaudy. On the quiet side—'

'Don't suppose she had much choice there,' said Ben, leaning back sharply to avoid his sister's swiping hand.

So Julia was nice, neat, quiet, mid brown and size sixteen, was she? Damn her eyes, I might have known. Her unexceptionable ordinariness, which Mel, to be fair, had subtly presented as slightly dull, was gall and wormwood to my soul. What could it all mean? That beneath that spotless, well-pressed exterior there seethed a volcano of ungovernable lust and sexual know-how, that was what.

'Does she wear glasses?' I asked.

'Not all the time, but she put them on to read the menu, like you.'

'Oh.'

My worst fears were confirmed. *Take off your glasses, Miss X, and here, let me unpin your hair. My God, but you're beautiful and I never saw it . . .*

'Glasses apart, she was nothing like you,' added Mel. 'And she didn't look to me like someone good at the net.'

* * *

Back at the flat Mel watched me put my popular boned and stuffed shoulder of lamb in the oven and said in that case a) she wouldn't bother about taking us out in the evening and b) she was going to go for a brisk walk by the sea and pick up a couple of bottles of something amusing at the off-licence on the way back. She changed out of the blazer and cowboy boots into Nikes and a Ralph Lauren sweatshirt, and leaned in passing into the kitchen.

'Are you happy, Mother? Or am I a rat leaving the proverbial . . . ?' She hated cooking, and was no good at it.

'Quite happy, darling. I've done the complicated bit.'

'Would it be impertinent to ask if it's bread and butter pud for afters?'

'It wouldn't and it is.'

'Tops. And by the way—' she came and laid a hand on my back as I sliced courgettes—'*after* the feast you and I are going to sit down and have a proper talk.'

'A threat or a promise?'

She ignored this. 'I'm going to take Ben with me, he looks as if he could use some fresh air and exercise.'

'Good luck.'

He was on the phone talking to Sophie, but in less than a minute the receiver went down and I heard him say 'All right already, but only if I can smoke . . .' Then from the kitchen doorway: 'Would it be OK if Sophie came to lunch?'

'Sure, liberty hall.'

'Cheers, because as a matter of fact I already asked her.'

They left and I made myself coffee—aromatic blended grounds in the cafetière, not instant, because I'd taken to heart all the written advice

188

about indulging oneself. It was good that Sophie was coming because it would ease any possible friction between brother and sister, and I suspected she would be perfectly capable of fighting her corner should the need arise.

About an hour later I was laying the table, and thinking how nice it was to be doing that, and for four people, when the bell rang.

I pressed the button in the hall but all I could hear was heavy breathing. Sexual harassment was thin on the ground in Littelsea (more's the pity as Sabine would have said), especially on a Sunday morning, but at Cliff Mansions we did occasionally get kids mucking about with the doorbells, so after a token 'hello' I released it. At once the bell sounded again.

'Yes? Who is it?'

There followed a series of accelerating gasps culminating in 'Eve—!'

'Who is that?'

More gasps. 'It's Clive—!'

'Clive, for goodness sake, are you all right?'

The gasping turned into a coughing fit, which diminuendoed as Clive stepped back, or bent over, and then crescendoed once more before he croaked: 'Can you come down?'

'I'm on my way!'

'Eve—' a huge intake of breath—'water!'

I put the front door on the latch, rushed into the kitchen, filled a beer tankard from the cold tap and ran down the stairs, carrying the slopping glass out in front of me.

I opened the front door on a strange little tableau. Clive, wearing a pale blue, sweat-soaked singlet and shorts, was standing bent over with his hands on his knees, in some physical distress; his legs were trembling and his shoulders and neck were mottled. On either side of him, in the role of comforters, were Peggy Whiteley, one of the ground-floor residents, returning from the Methodist Chapel, and Sophie.

'Poor man,' said Peggy, busily chafing Clive's back with her gloved hand. 'He has got himself in a state.'

Sophie spoke to Clive slowly and clearly: 'Eve's here with some water. Why don't you sit down?'

He allowed himself to be manoeuvred so that his back was to the step, and Peggy and Sophie bravely placed their hands beneath his armpits to take the strain as he went down.

'Here,' I said, like someone in a soap opera. 'Drink this.'

He took a few gulps, and then thrust his hand into the tankard and splashed water on top of his head.

'Poor man,' murmured Peggy again. 'Should I call a doctor do you think?'

I stared helplessly at Clive, who looked no better physically, but did seem to be regaining his composure. 'I don't know.'

Sophie sat down next to Clive and put her arm across his shoulders. She looked up at me and mouthed: 'What's his name?'

'Clive Robinson.'

'Clive,' she said firmly, 'have you got any pains?'

He drew a long breath and then shook his head, sending drops of sweat flying on to Peggy's showerproof.

'Are you sure? Arms and legs all working?'

'Yes . . .' He made a few awkward, jerky running

movements.

'Are you cold?'

'Yes.'

In a trice the showerproof was off and draped about him and Peggy pointed into the hall where her husband Bernard now stood with a copy of the *Sunday Express* and a baffled expression.

'Bernard dear,' she said threateningly, 'put the kettle on, we're coming in.'

Bernard shuffled off.

'This is very kind of you,' I said, 'I'd take him up to my place, but he'd never make it up the stairs in this condition.'

'We're going inside,' said Sophie to Clive. Peggy bustled past us, probably glad of an excuse not to reacquaint herself with the patient's armpit, and we hauled him to the vertical. His colour drained for a moment, and he swayed groggily before rallying, and announcing.

'It's not a heart attack . . . but I am a stupid sod.'

We were saved from having to agree with him by the arrival of Mel and Ben, carrying respectively two bottles of red and a slab of 4X. Their faces reflected the strangeness of finding me in my gorilla pinny, Sophie in black bell-bottoms and a bare midriff, and Clive in baby-blue briefs and a lady's showerproof, posed like the three graces on the front doorstep.

'Mother!' said Mel. 'And I thought you led a quiet life . . .'

191

CHAPTER TEN

Eventually, we had lunch, the five of us. The shoulder of lamb turned out Peking-style, as Mel remarked, falling apart into thin, dry strips, the stuffing—which contained sultanas—reduced to something that looked like sheep droppings. But the vegetables, produced at speed in the microwave, could have done useful service in a six-gun. Only the bread and butter pudding, thrown together at the last minute and cooked as we ate our first course, was perfect—light, creamy, and crisp on the top.

Whatever its shortcomings, all the food was extremely welcome after the vicissitudes of the previous hour. We had remained *chez* Whiteley while Clive recovered. Peggy had insisted we all have a glass of amontillado ('Sorry you young ones, no beer') and Clive sipped at a large Bovril. Bernard, a big, pear-shaped man had produced a diamond-patterned sweater in turquoise and lemon and some Sta-prest beige slacks in which Clive looked completely out of place but seemed happy enough. I thought he'd want a lift home, but the casual mention of staying for lunch caused him to perk up no end and declare that he could manage the stairs if helped by two attractive young ladies. I fully expected him to get a rap over the knuckles from Mel for this flirtatious sally, but none was forthcoming and since it was already two-thirty I left them to it and went to parboil the veg and lay another place.

Actually, Clive was just what we needed. He was

a strange shape and colour for a lightning conductor, but he fulfilled the role to a T. We all sat round with eyes and ears for no one but him, and listened as he explained himself. It was a story in which, like all the best stories, tragedy and comedy were inextricably mingled.

'There's a girl in Social Sciences with whom I've struck up a friendship,' he told us, adding: 'No more than a friendship, mind, but she's a great believer in the links between physical and mental health—she does yoga, Alexander technique, more things than are dreamt of in our philosophy . . . As you know we—Helen and I—are—were—' he blushed—'not in the least interested in exercise for exercise's sake, but Catherine does radiate this air of wellbeing and I began to wonder if it wasn't a sort of arrogance on my part to ignore the obvious benefits. I mean my dear wife has always been blessed with whatever it is that keeps you thin, but I arrived too late when it was being handed out . . . In short I took a look at myself and decided that I represented a rather dismaying sight, a man in late middle age, losing his hair, gaining in girth, unable to run for the hypothetical bus, or even to go upstairs without needing something medicinal at the top. By the way, Eve, this is perfectly delicious—'

Everyone endorsed this remark without taking their eyes off him. In spite of his monologue he was getting through his food twice as fast as the rest of us. I'd scarcely begun mine, but two glasses of chianti on top of the Whiteleys' amontillado was having a deleterious effect on my self-control. I kept on having to haul my jaw back into place and refocus my gaze.

193

'So anyway,' went on Clive, 'I suppose I underwent a Damascene conversion, of which Catherine was the unwitting agent, and decided to make some moves in the direction of cardiovascular fitness. Sports revolt me—sorry, Eve—and I've never been able to swim. I couldn't countenance anything involving equipment. I looked at a gym and it resembled nothing so much as a mediaeval torture chamber run by a terrifying harpie with more muscles than I could ever aspire to . . . jogging, as it is misleadingly called, seemed the answer. I bought the clothes and a pair of shoes, and here I am.'

He popped in his last mouthful and patted his mouth with his napkin while we gaped.

'Is that it?' asked Mel, speaking for all of us. 'Because if so, I have several supplementaries that I'd like to put to you.'

Clive swallowed and patted some more. 'Fire away.'

'For a start,' said Mel, fixing him with her almost-rude unblinking look, 'you were having a seizure down there.'

'I may have overdone it slightly.'

'How long have you been running for?' asked Sophie.

'About an hour, I should think.'

'No, I don't mean today, I mean since you started.'

'I understood the nature of the query.'

'Hang on.' Ben tilted his fork at Clive and looked at him through narrowed eyes. 'This was your first time?'

'Yes.'

'And you *ran*—for an *hour*?'

194

'Well . . .' Clive chortled nervously. 'I use the term loosely. I walked up most of the hills.'

'Most. Of the hills.' echoed Mel. The conversation was turning into a kind of ensemble piece for four voices, with an audience of one.

'That's right. There are several fairly daunting inclines between here and Brighton.'

Sophie clapped her hands to her cheeks. 'Did you say *Brighton*?'

'Um—yes.' Clive's eyes flicked round the other faces gauging whether to be vaunting or modest. But vaunting was never his style, and he began folding his napkin fussily. 'I was probably being over-ambitious.'

Mel put her knife and fork together and slid her glass towards me to be refreshed.

'No you weren't.'

'You think not?'

She shook her head. 'Not ambitious, Clive. You were out of your tiny mind.'

I had to bite my tongue not to check her. But Clive, bless him, was the least self-important person on the planet, and merely gazed round anxiously at us all.

'Yes, I believe you're right.'

'But how did you do it?' exclaimed Ben, rocking his chair back from the table. He turned to the rest of us, eyes wide. 'How did he do it?'

Sophie leaned across to Clive. 'We want to know how you did it.'

He knitted his brows apologetically. 'You may well ask,' he said. 'And the answer is, with the greatest possible difficulty.'

*   *   *

195

By the end of lunch we had persuaded him of the advisability of taking things in easy stages. While the others stacked the machine he and I sat on the balcony, and I asked him what I hadn't liked to ask in front of them.

'Clive—what exactly brought this on?'

'Well as I said, Catherine—'

'No, but why, really? I mean, are you and Catherine—is there something between you? I only ask,' I added gently, 'because it would be so lovely if there were.'

He shook his head so vigorously his spectacles nearly came off.

'Absolutely not, Eve! A thousand times no.'

'But you like each other,' I said hopefully. 'Something could develop.'

'There isn't even the remotest possibility, I do assure you. For one thing she's probably twenty years younger than me—'

I brightened. 'That's no barrier these days.'

'It is to me. Or would be. But the thing of it is, I love my wife.' He gave his empty little laugh. 'Sadly.'

Mel came to the door. 'Coffee, people?'

We declined. 'It is sad, but not in the way that I think you mean,' I said when she'd gone. 'Helen has someone else, but you're a lovely, intelligent man, Clive, don't go looking gift happiness in the mouth.'

He gave me a wistful look. 'Are you telling me to learn to live again?'

'Something like that.'

'Strange as it may seem, that is what I'm trying to do. Catherine has this thing that she says: "it

196

doesn't have to be like this". At first I thought it simply jejune, but the other day I suddenly felt the force of it. I don't have to be this repellent, prematurely-aged fat person.'

'Clive, you are *not* repellent.'

He hadn't heard me. 'I can do something about it, Eve! I intend to. I feel sorry for Helen, all these years, putting up with me. My wife is a tall, beautiful woman and I—I'm a troll.'

'*Clive* ...' I wanted to cry. I held out my hand but he waved it away. His self-loathing was terrible to see.

'Physical appearance isn't everything,' I said lamely. 'Especially when it comes to women's feelings for men.'

He plucked at the knee of Bernard's beige slacks. 'You've seen Kerridge, have you?'

'Well, I've glimpsed—'

'I rest my case.'

I should certainly have cried then, had not Ben and Sophie announced that they were going over to Brighton.

'Can we give you a lift?' asked Ben.

'That would be terribly kind. Are you sure it's no trouble?'

'Of course not.'

'What nice children you have,' Clive said as he picked up the plastic carrier into which I'd packed his ill-fated running gear. 'And good neighbours. I shall return these things as soon as I can.'

I nodded, not trusting my voice. Then Ben and Sophie were upon us, Ben took the bag and they were gone, happily ignorant of this small tragedy. On the bend in the stairs Sophie looked up and gave me a little wave. For a nanosecond I relived the earlier sensation that there was a disclosure waiting in the wings, and my heart lifted.

As I closed the door Mel called from the balcony: 'Come on out, the water's lovely!'

The muffling Channel dampness of the morning had given way to sunshine. The prom still gleamed with puddles and the sea, on its way out, was playful with small, bounding waves. A golden retriever ran in and out fetching a stick. Some boys were dragging a dinghy down the shingle. The air, that rang with gulls' cries, smelt salty and clean. Above the Martello Tower a bright orange kite swooped and strained against the white cliffs.

'Proper sea,' observed Mel as I sat down. 'Not like that warm soup we have to make do with over there.'

'Yes,' I said, 'I'm very lucky.'

'We had such a nice walk this morning. He enjoyed it once he got going.'

'Good.'

She put her feet up on the rail and said, without looking at me. 'I wouldn't set too much store by this Sophie thing if I were you.'

'I don't set anything by it,' I lied.

'That's all right then. Because it's my belief they're nothing more than chums.'

'Really?' I couldn't conceal my scepticism. 'That's not how it looks to the rest of us.'

'Rose-coloured specs, Mother.'

'Don't take my word for it, you should hear Sabine.'

'Should I?'

'She says he practically lives up there. And rather to my surprise she seems thrilled with the whole thing.'

Mel ignored this remark so completely that I was left wondering whether I'd just imagined making it. When she next spoke it was to change the subject completely.

'So what's the story with Clive?'

'Oh, I can hardly bear to . . . He wants to turn himself into a sex god like Helen's inamoratus, John Kerridge.'

'Is Kerridge a sex god?'

'Of a certain type. Dapper, well-presented. Almost certainly goes to a gym and plays squash, or possibly soccer.'

'He sounds ghastly.'

'But Helen doesn't know or care how he gets his muscles, she only knows he has them.'

Mel snorted dismissively. 'A schoolgirl crush.'

'Mel! She's my age! She left home for it!'

'Mother! QED.'

'But Clive's so lovely—so intelligent and generous and thoroughly honourable.'

'That's his problem, then.'

'What?'

Mel put down her coffee mug and addressed me with an air of studied patience. 'No danger. The attraction of Kerridge isn't his washboard stomach, it's his complete lack of generosity and honour.'

I shook my head. 'That's much too simplistic—'

'And Clive's solution isn't?' I opened my mouth. 'Look. I'm all for the poor soul smartening himself up a bit, getting the flab under control—there are far too many middle-aged Englishmen wandering about with their paunches wobbling over their waistbands, but if he thinks it's going to bring the lady wife home he's barking up the wrong rowing machine.'

199

I agreed with her, but not for quite the same reasons. 'He needs to do something,' I said, 'and this at least will make him feel better.'

'Yes.' Mel laughed shortly. 'I could see that, down there on the doorstep.'

'You know what I mean. In the long term. If he goes about it the right way.'

Mel didn't reply. She didn't need to—the expression on her face said it all.

After an interval, she swung her feet down and said: 'Shall we go down on the beach? I've got an uncontrollable urge to divebomb that floating branch.'

*   *   *

It was nice to be on the shingle. I took the director's chair that Ben had given me, with SHE WHO MUST BE OBEYED on the back and sat like a politically-correct Canute while Mel stood barefoot at the edge of the water, shying stones at the bobbing piece of driftwood. After a bit she gave up, and hobbled back to sit by me, rummaging with one hand for interesting stones.

'Did you sink it?' I asked.

'I would have done, but the tide's still going out. Now then, Mother, what about you?'

'What about me.'

'Well, Dad's got himself fixed up, Ben has plenty to occupy him. Isn't it time you had someone in your life?'

'I'm not looking,' I replied, weary of this subject and of Mel's obsessive worrying of it. 'It's the last thing on my mind.'

'I don't believe you—' she held up a carnelian—

'that's pretty.'

'Yes it is.'

'Did I tell you,' she said, pocketing the stone and continuing to rummage, 'that Charles McNally's in London at the moment?'

'No you didn't.'

'Well he is. And he asked after you.'

'That was civil of him.'

'No it wasn't! He wasn't being civil Mother, he was being interested. He's *interested* in you. I'm tempted to add God knows why since you're such a spoilsport about the whole thing, but unfortunately there's no escaping the fact that you're a good-looking, educated, sympathetic sort of woman of the right age and he finds himself thinking about you!'

Even as I smarted I realised I'd been given a compliment.

'Thanks.'

'My pleasure. And he, in case you hadn't noticed, is rugged, savvy, loaded and has all his own hair. And single, Mother. Watch my lips. Single. No dependants. Not even a previous marriage and no stains on the character that I know of.'

From an ingrained habit of doubt, I said: 'That in itself is a bit suspicious.'

She lowered her head despairingly on to her knees, and said from there: 'Well I dare say if it makes you happy there may be some blighted teenage romance in the dim and distant. I'll see what I can come up with.'

'So what's he doing in London?' I asked with what I hoped was the right degree of sophisticated detachment.

'Looking for a flat, *inter alia*.'

201

'Oh? I thought he was based in the States.'

'He hasn't been based anywhere much. I told you, he troubleshoots, so it's wherever he lays his hat. But now he's coming up to fifty they're taking him out of the front line and from January he'll be in London for a couple of years.'

'I see.'

Mel gazed up at me. 'He asked if you ever got up to town.'

'And what did you say?'

'I said yes.'

'Mel!'

'Straight question, straight answer. I didn't tell him your bra measurement or anything. Gosh, I wish I'd brought my bimmer.'

Wearily, I told her she could borrow mine.

* * *

She went back to the flat and came back over with my M&S purple interlock under her jeans. I watched as she waded, dived, and swam furiously out to sea. If the shock of the bracing English sea had made her gasp she would never let me know it. When she was a couple of hundred yards out, no more than a bobbing speck on the glittering swell, she lifted an arm, and I waved back.

But when she eventually returned she was shivering, and dragged her clothes back on with impressive sleight of hand for one used to the luxurious changing facilities of a five-star hotel. Then she lay back with her hands behind her head and closed her eyes.

I almost believed her to be asleep when she suddenly said, loud and clear:

202

'Clive. Can you credit it? It never ceases to amaze me what people will do for love.'

*   *   *

That evening she got restless, as I knew she would. My daughter was not one of those who, when cooped up in luxury, dreamed only of a boiled egg, Marmite soldiers and the *Antiques Roadshow*. So in spite of the large lunch we'd eaten in the middle of the afternoon, we left a note for Ben and went out.

She drove, with one elbow on the door and three fingers on the wheel, the other hand resting lightly on the gear lever. I had tender feelings for my little car and to begin with my foot was pumping up and down on an invisible brake pedal. But Mel was an accomplished driver and got us to the Saxon Mill without a moment's anxiety.

'Darling,' I said, 'this place is horrifically expensive and I'm not even that hungry.'

'Well, we can just have a starter then, my treat. But it's more fun to watch the world go by.'

I wasn't sure whether the Saxon Mill was the sort of place where two women eating only starters would be especially welcome but told myself that Mel was figuratively as well as literally in the driving seat, so that would be her problem.

We were sitting in the *faux* drawing room, whose bay windows overlooked the garden and the millstream, when a waft of familiar scent reached me just ahead of the voice:

'Eve! And can that possibly be Mel?'

'Hello Sabine.'

'May we join you?'

'Do.'

203

'Perhaps,' suggested Martin in her wake, 'you'd rather talk amongst yourselves.'

I suppose I would have said no—what else can one do—but Mel's reply was far more emphatic than mine would have been.

'You're joking, Martin, this is exactly what we were hoping for, isn't it Mother?'

I agreed weakly that it was, and they sat down. Martin ordered drinks for them, another gin and tonic for me and a diet Coke for Mel.

'Well!' he said, slapping his big hands together in obvious delight. 'Sorry to bandy a cliché, but do you come here often?'

'Virtually never,' I said. 'This is courtesy of Mel.'

'And we thought you were out in the desert,' said Sabine, 'and not back for another year.'

'They gave me time off for good behaviour,' explained Mel.

Martin chortled. 'We'll believe you.'

'Did you know Chuck McNally was in London?' Sabine's insinuating glance slid over me for a microsecond. 'He's posted here for a while.'

'I had heard,' said Mel, 'on the bush telegraph. He and I aren't exactly in the same stratum, but the oil community's worse than an English seaside town when it comes to gossip.'

Martin laughed heartily. 'Sabine's hoping that Eve will really give them something to gossip about!'

'Martin!' Sabine was reproving, but coquettishly so. Mel raised a laconic eyebrow: she didn't have to say anything. And I was damned if I was going to.

Martin, entirely unrepentant, moved swiftly from one contentious subject to another. 'If you're wondering where your son's got to, he's up at our place.'

'*Comme toujours*,' said Sabine.

'Yes, I guessed.'

Mel was studying the menu. 'This looks quite good . . . But we're only here for the movement and colour, you know. Mother killed the fatted calf at lunchtime.'

'Actually,' I said, 'it was three o'clock.'

'Don't worry,' said Martin, 'we're meeting some oppos so you're not going to be stuck with us—in fact, darling, there they are. Bill! Hey!'

Sabine unfurled from her seat, willowy in a buttermilk shift. Her movement caused another flutter of expensive scent to settle over us like rose petals. As she dropped delicate kisses on our cheeks I realised what was different about her. She had always been elegant, but tonight she was pretty.

Unusually, Mel commented on this too as we ate our *assiettes de campagne*. 'She's looking good, don't you think?'

'She always does.'

'Smart, yes, but whence this glow?'

'Maybe their marriage is enjoying a renaissance.'

With one accord we looked across the dining room to where the Drages and their glossy pals were taking delivery of a dizzying array of starters.

'Maybe,' said Mel.

*   *   *

Her flight the next day was at one, but she needed to get back to town to pack up and check out of the hotel, so it was seven a.m. when we stood together on the station platform. She was itching to be gone now, to have the farewells over with and return to her other more exhilarating life, but I wasn't about to let her off so easily. At this time of day there was a distinctly autumnal feel to the air, and she shivered and stamped, peering up the line with ostentatious impatience.

'You're still enjoying it over there, are you darling?' I asked.

'Sure. And anyway, let's not be mealy-mouthed, you don't take a UAE placement for the spiritual enrichment, you take it for the bunce.'

'I suppose so. But we miss you, you know. It'll be nice when you're back properly.'

'Don't bank on it Mother. Jesus—!' She blew her cheeks out and chafed her upper arms—'Right now I can't wait to get back to some reliable sunshine.'

'But you'll be home for Christmas, will you?'

'I should think so.'

'I *hope* so.'

'I shall certainly try, Mother. Thank God, here it is. Bye.' She gave me a quick, I'm-outta-here sort of kiss. 'And remember, Barkis is willing.'

My early-morning brain was still catching up with this allusion as the train pulled out, and it was rounding the London-bound bend when I realised she had been referring to Charles McNally. And so had had, as always, the last word.

*   *   *

That Wednesday saw the first of the sales containing Mrs Rymer's things. All bar one exceeded expectation, and the Ruskin vase which only barely made its reserve was one of a divided

206

pair, so it was hardly surprising. As well as the usual formal documentation for Mrs Rymer junior I wrote a note to her mother-in-law telling her the good news, and promising that after the second sale we would go out to lunch.

On Thursday Clive brought Bernard Whiteley's clothes back and came up to see me. It was a stormy evening and we drank Scotch in the sitting room with the rain lashing the windows and the white horses tossing their wild manes furiously in the unseasonal, whistling dark.

'How's the exercise going?' I asked. The understanding smile in my voice anticipated a very different answer from the one I got.

'Making progress,' he said, 'thank you for asking. I have seen the error of my ways and begun using the students' track.'

'Good for you!'

'As you know I dread the proximity of others more athletic than myself—whose numbers are legion—but no one spares me a second glance. All too dedicated I suppose. And at least I am someone whom even the weakest can overtake, so I am serving a useful social purpose.'

'I'm very impressed,' I said. 'I thought your earlier experience would put you off completely.'

'No, no, I'm quite determined.'

'You will feel much better for it, I'm sure.'

'I couldn't feel much worse, Eve.' He pulled a rueful face. 'Vanity, vanity, all is . . . Catherine, the dear girl, is giving me every encouragement.'

'It does help to have moral support,' I agreed.

He sighed gustily. 'I bumped into Helen at a performance of *The Trojan Woman* . . .'

I waited. His lips were pressed together, but his

cheek was working slightly.

'How was she?'

'Startled. Couldn't wait to get away, really.'

'You're not surprised, surely.'

I saw, too late, that this remark, intended as consoling, could be taken in two ways.

'No,' said Clive, in a voice heavy with gloomy irony. 'I am not.'

'I didn't mean—'

'I know you didn't Eve, you are a true friend. But I did.'

*   *   *

'Do you fancy getting in a Chinese?' asked Ben on Saturday night.

'Why not?' I replied, though his suggestion struck me as one of those verbal forms that would have been open to the wildest misconstruction as little as forty years ago.

'I'll get an assortment, yeah? My treat.'

'Yeah—yes. Great. When are you going out?'

'I'm not.'

'Good lord!'

He ruffled my hair. 'Thought I'd stay in and keep the old dot company.'

'And the rest . . . !'

'No,' he said, shrugging into his magnificently dilapidated leather jacket. 'Sophie's gone to see her mum for the weekend, so I reckon why shouldn't I see mine.'

Can you wonder I loved him?

He came back from the Lotus Palace three-quarters of an hour later with enough food for about half a dozen people. The weather was still wild, and he staggered in through the door like some latter day Paul Revere, hair slicked to brow, drops streaming from his jacket, boots muddied, the prize in his arms.

I was all ready, with plates heated, hotplate switched on, cold beers and chopsticks to hand.

'Right,' said Ben. 'Let's get stuck in.'

We ate for the first ten minutes or so in a silence punctuated only by grunts and lip-smackings of appreciation. This, I thought, was a way you could only eat with family. Forget mealtimes being occasions of social intercourse and bonding, when parents and children could talk through their feelings and the events of the day. This was open-it-up, dollop-it-out and shovel-it-down time. Instead of napkins we had a roll of kitchen towel on the table, and we drank the beer out of the cans.

We both slowed at about the same time.

'Good old Palace,' I said, 'hits the spot every time.'

In endorsement of this encomium, Ben belched. Since childhood he'd had the ability to adjust the volume, pitch and duration of his burps to form a kind of primitive musical sequence. I both admired and deplored this small talent.

'Ben . . .' I reproved, when he'd finished.

'What? You can't beat it. And Sophie doesn't like Chinese, so I was in danger of getting withdrawal systems.'

This was the first comment that came within hailing distance of the topic I most wanted to discuss, so I swiftly latched on to it.

'How is she?' I asked.

'OK.'

'I like Sophie.' I snapped open another can. I felt
209

freed by the atmosphere of cosy contentment that prevailed in here, with the elements snarling and swooping ineffectually outside the window. 'She's a sweetie.'

'Yeah.' He pushed his plate aside. 'Mum—'

The phone rang and I got up. 'Don't go away.'

He lit a cigarette as I picked up the receiver. 'Hello?'

'Eve, it's Sabine.' Her voice was warm and bustlingly vivacious. I pictured a fragrant dinner party in full swing in a neighbouring room. 'You're going to think this is the most peculiar question on a Saturday evening, but is Ben with you?'

I looked across at where he sat, elbows on the table, tapping ash into the remains of the Sechuan Chicken with Cashews. It was rather pleasing to be talking about him in his presence without his knowing.

'Yes as a matter of fact.'

'Oh good. I gambled on him being there—with Sophie away. I expect he's going out, is he?'

'Not that I know of.'

'Eve, do you think I might have a word? Only I have a message for him from his beloved!' She gave a rippling, throaty laugh. Her good humour was infectious and I smiled at Ben who was paying no attention.

'Hang on.' I held out the receiver, facing him. 'It's for you.'

'Who?'

'One of your many women.'

He hitched his chair along and took the receiver. I helped myself to some more food.

'Oh ... right. OK ... Well, thanks for that, Sabine. Sure ...' He turned to me, eyebrows

210

raised, listening to the other end. 'Do you want another word with Eve? Yeah, I'll do that . . . Bye.'

He put the phone down and stubbed out his half-smoked cigarette. 'Seconds, nice one. It's true what they say about Chinese—ten minutes later you can eat it all over again.' He began shovelling egg fu yung on to his plate.

'So how is she?'

'You know Sabine—all gush and garters.'

'No, no—Sophie.'

'Oh, she's in a flap about some notes or other that she can't locate at her mum's, and thinks she may have brought down after all. She needs her mind putting at rest, I may go over to their place and conduct a search.'

'Can't they do it?'

'What, Sabine and Martin, poking around in Sophie's room? I don't think so.'

I took his point. 'So, what—you'll pop over tomorrow? It's a disgusting night.'

'My thinking exactly.'

Heroically, we managed to eat most of the food and I surprised myself by having a third beer while Ben had scarcely breached his second.

'I really enjoyed that,' I said. 'Thanks, love.'

'Fancy a coffee? A cuppa?'

'Coffee would be nice.'

'Stay right there—' he put out a restraining hand—'I've started so I'll finish.'

I curled up in an armchair near the window, comfortably between the storm and the mellow warmth of the flat, listening to Ben stalk back and forth doing what I knew would be an adequate, if not a brilliant job. I told myself, as I'd told Mel, that I was pretty lucky.

211

Ben's hand, holding a mug of coffee, appeared in front of my face. 'There you go.'

'Thanks—aren't you having one?'

'No, I'll pass.'

'Take a look in the paper, I think they've got that film on, the Robert de Niro one none of us got to see at the flicks . . .'

Ben picked up the paper and passed it to me. I suddenly knew what he was going to say.

'Look, I think I'm going to pop up there and see if I can find Sophie's notes.'

'Of course you are,' I said indulgently, and shamelessly echoed Mel's comment: 'It never ceases to amaze me what people will do for love.'

*   *   *

I watched the de Niro film, and it was fair to middling: I only fell asleep once, and missed very little that was germaine to the plot. At eleven p.m. I switched everything off except the hall light (an ingrained habit) and took my teacup out to the kitchen. The swing-bin bulged with tin foil, greasy styrofoam and beer cans—the chopsticks were in the sink. It looked like the postscript to England v Holland on Sky: I liked the less-orderly picture of myself that it showed, even if it wasn't typical.

I went to bed, read half a page of a riveting new novel about incest and fell soundly asleep with my glasses beneath my face.

When I woke up, the sense of cosy wellbeing had gone. The light was still on, my glasses had made a deep furrow in my face and my bladder was bursting with all that beer.

I staggered out into the passage and down to the

loo. As I emerged, Ben came in through the front door. He closed it very softly behind him, turned and started visibly when he saw me.

'Mum—! Sorry, did I disturb you?'

'No, beer and Chinese disturbed me.'

'Oh, OK . . . night then.'

He turned the hall light out. We passed each other as we went to our rooms. There was still a breath of cold air hanging around him, it made me shiver when his jacket brushed my sleeve. I got into bed and turned the lamp out. In the sudden black the numerals on the alarm clock showed bright and clear: it was three a.m.

I turned away from it and closed my eyes. Inside my little flat there was no sound. Ben's arrival might have been an hallucination, so completely had he been reabsorbed. But in the thick, sea-brushed darkness a host of unformed questions flittered and dived like bats.

CHAPTER ELEVEN

Until, in the ensuing days and weeks, I came to look back on that night, I'd never understood the expression 'a sea change'. At the time I was conscious of no great shift or alteration, just an unease, as though somewhere in the back of my head a door had been left open to admit a cold, disturbing draught, and those pestering bats.

It was only with hindsight that I came to recognise the defining moment after which nothing was to be the same. Some of this had to do with a change in perception, a different way of seeing

213

things that was forced on me by events. And yet, I kept remembering the words of Clive's new friend: 'It doesn't have to be like this'. She of course meant that he had it in his power to change what he didn't like. In my case the words had a more sinister ring, a grim warning against complacency.

*   *   *

For I was complacent, I see that now. I was virtually anaesthetised by complacency, blinded by it. The very next morning I closed my mind, and that banging door at the back of it, on the unsettling sensations of the night and carried on regardless.

I got up, had my bath, and knocked on Ben's door on my way back to my room. Pushing it open I saw Algy the bear lying amongst the debris on the floor, his stubby arms and legs pointing at the ceiling. A sweet, silly pang of nostalgia swept over me, and I went over and picked him up.

'Hey,' I said, 'sleeping beauty—time to get up.' I pushed Algy down into the crook of Ben's shoulder, but he shrugged him off and burrowed his face into the pillow with a groan. Smiling, I pulled back the curtains and dropped Algy at the foot of the bed.

It was the usual routine. During the fifteen minutes it took me to get dressed and made up I called Ben another half a dozen times without effect. Then when I went to get breakfast he would suddenly be there—clothed, washed and (sometimes) shaved. We moved about the kitchen in a kind of silent dance, passing and repassing each other on our familiar routes to the kettle, the fridge, the sink, the cupboard, after which Ben sat on the edge of the sofa with his black coffee, banana and cigarette watching *The Big Breakfast*, while I consumed tea and bran flakes to the accompaniment of *Today* on Radio Four. Ten minutes after that we were ready to leave. On the pavement at the back of Cliff Mansions we parted company—Ben usually walked, there was no point in taking the beetle into the town centre—and I drove to Bouvier's.

This morning he waited till I was behind the wheel and then leaned both hands on the roof, and said: 'May not see you tonight, Sophie's picking me up from work.'

'She's back today then?' I asked stupidly.

'Looks like it.' He stood up, raised a hand. 'Don't wait up.'

*   *   *

I hadn't, for years. He didn't have to say that.

*   *   *

I called Helen from work in the late afternoon and asked if she'd like to come out for a drink. She said why not, nothing else in the diary—big enthusiasm by her standards—so I arranged to pick her up.

When I got there I was amazed to find that she must have been looking out for me, for she came out of the door when I hadn't even switched the engine off and was in the passenger seat before you could say knife.

We went to the least rebarbative of the village pubs and I bought her a large malt, and myself a

215

ginger beer shandy. She, as usual, had omitted to bring any money. In spite of being so eager to get out her silence was positively Trappist, and I found myself telling her, slightly desperately, about the de Niro film I'd watched the previous evening. As I did so she gazed at me through her smoke as though I was speaking a foreign language of which she understood just barely enough. But I must have engaged her interest a little, for when I'd finished she broke with all known precedent.

'I don't suppose you could stand going to the pictures now, could you?' she asked, with such an air of utter exhaustion that it took me a moment to take the idea on board.

I regrouped. 'Good idea—was there something in particular you wanted to see?'

'What is there?'

'I mean—Woody Allen? Tarantino? Disney?'

'Something amusing . . . ?'

It turned out she hadn't been to the cinema for something like thirty years. She was quite fazed by the Warner Multiplex and kept murmuring 'Oh my God' as though we were amid the brothels of Bangkok.

I chose Steve Martin, whom I'd always thought funny, and who had also been on for a couple of weeks already so it was easy to get tickets. Determined that Helen should have the full experience I also bought popcorn and Coke.

She sat in the dark with the casket of popcorn unopened on her knee and the Coke with its still-wrapped straw clutched in one hand like a talisman. She never took her eyes off the screen, but neither did she display the smallest flicker of amusement. Rather embarrassed by my own bursts

216

of laughter—I was a herd animal who laughed more when others did so—I toned them down to slightly superior muted chuckles. But at the end she said: 'That was quite good' and I felt I'd scored a major hit.

As we shuffled out of the auditorium she was still carrying the popcorn and Coke, and I said 'You can leave those here, you know.'

'Nonsense,' she replied. 'I've paid for them.'

I forbore to remind her that this wasn't true. She placed them carefully in the footwell of the car while we went into the King James for another drink and a sandwich. The whole thing had turned into what by Helen's standards was definitely a Big Night Out.

There didn't seem much point in not diving straight in, so over the prawn in marie rose on brown, I did.

'I gather you bumped into Clive the other day.'

'That's right.'

'He's hellbent on self-improvement, did he tell you?'

'No.'

'He's taken up—'

'Self-improvement? That doesn't sound like Clive.'

'Well I can assure you he has,' I went on, encouraged by this show of interest. 'He's really going for the *corpore sano*.'

'There was never anything the matter with his mind,' Helen reminded me.

'No indeed.' I made a quick decision, and went on: 'It appears he's met this woman who's a great believer in the links between the two, and it's persuaded him that taking a little exercise might

217

change his life.'

'That'll be Catherine,' said Helen, holding a match to her cigarette with a trembling hand.

I was taken aback. 'Do you know her then?'

'I know who she is. Don't particularly want to know any more, but I'm sure she's just what Clive needs.'

'They're only friends,' I assured her, perhaps a little too quickly.

'I don't doubt it.'

She tipped her head back as she exhaled, studying the ceiling. Her neck looked long and white and vulnerable.

'Kerridge is cooling, by the way.'

This was like Mel's 'Barkis is willing'—coming as it did without build-up or preamble it took a second to sink in. When it did I tried to keep the delight out of my voice.

'Oh, Helen . . .'

'It was never case of if, only when.'

'You're wonderfully philosophical.'

'I wouldn't say that.'

She seemed almost to be laughing, but when I looked at her face her eyes had a treacherous shine.

'I'm so sorry.'

'I doubt that, Eve. Anyway, it hasn't happened yet. It's just a train in the distance, but I can hear it, and I know it's for me.'

This was like poetry, beautiful and sad. 'I meant it,' I said, 'about being sorry. It must be so bloody painful.'

'Not yet. But it will be.'

'Can't you take matters into your own hands?'

She looked at me steadily as I sought a form of

words. 'Head the train off at the pass?'

'I'm not going to end it, if that's what you mean.'

'I'm only thinking of you, Helen, that it might be less painful to seize the initiative.'

She shook her head. 'I want him for as long as I can have him.'

I tried a different tack. 'But what about your pride?'

She gave a little half-smile. 'That isn't a concept with which I'm familiar.'

'Then maybe it's time you familiarised yourself. I don't know how you can bear simply to sit out there in Hawley End waiting to be ditched by a man who, if I may make so bold, simply isn't worth it.'

There was a pause, during which she gazed about the room. I found that I was holding my breath. When she spoke, it was so quietly and offhandedly she might have been talking to herself.

'Nevertheless, it's what I intend to do.'

She enraged me, she really did. After I'd dropped her back at the cottage I found myself praying, through gritted teeth, that if Kerridge was cooling, Catherine would come good.

*   *   *

There was a message on the answering machine. I perched on the edge of a chair and played it through more than once.

'Er ... hello, this is a message for Mrs Eve Piercy ... I guess that must be your son on the machine. This is Charles McNally calling from London, I wondered if you're ever up in town whether you'd care to have dinner, or do a show. Anything that takes your fancy, I'm the new kid in

219

town. Give me a call if you feel like it, I'm at Troughtons in Vane Street.'

He ended with the number. When I'd finished listening for the third time I switched the machine back to receive, and stood staring out at the sea. The wind had dropped today, but the sky was still overcast and the sunset was a sullen affair, skulking behind dirty hedges of cloud.

The ball had been put well and truly in my court. Thank goodness, I thought, that I hadn't been here when he called. On the other hand, I had been given time to think, which increased the need to make a sensible and considered decision. My responsibility weighed heavy on me.

I was all at sea. Following our conversations at the weekend I might have suspected my daughter's hand in this new development, except that that was clearly ridiculous—why would a man of McNally's age and stature be even remotely influenced by a twenty-something upstart like Mel, even assuming she had the brass neck to approach him on the subject? It was unthinkable.

I poured myself a whisky and tried to be rational. I was out of practice. I couldn't deny that a small part of me was flattered, but a far greater part just wished to be left alone. I had no need of all this and I was damn sure he didn't either. He must spend most of his waking hours in contact with clever, sophisticated, independent-minded women who shared a similar kind of life.

I tried first to think what I would have said if I had picked up the phone in the first place.

'Charles—what a surprise. How are you? Excellent. My daughter told me you were in London for a while. Yes, I do get up very occasionally. But it's not really my cup of tea, I like to be down here by the sea. How sweet of you, what a very happy thought. Can I bear it in mind? As I say I'm only rarely in town, but if I do come up in the foreseeable future I shall certainly bear that in mind. Good luck with the househunting, Charles, I don't envy you. Bye.'

In my dreams.

I cudgelled my brain for another helpful template. What, I wondered, would Sabine have said in these circumstances?

'Chuck, *mon cheri*, when are you coming to see us—'

Stop right there, I told myself. That 'us' put the kibosh on Sabine as a role model. She might be the queen of savoir faire, but she was still wed wealthily, and as far as I knew happily, to Martin.

There was nothing else for it, I was going to have to make my own excuses. Or not call back at all. But that might prompt him to call again, to check that I'd received the message . . . There again that was a terrifically un-cool thing to do, so perhaps he wouldn't . . .

I was dithering for Britain. The Scotch went down without touching the sides. How, I asked myself, had I had the nerve to think disparagingly of Helen, who next to me was a positive virago of determination and self-esteem? Her affair might be dead in the water, but I was too frightened to get my feet wet!

If I was going to call him one thing was for sure—I needed a prepared line, one which presented me in the best possible light (I was vain enough not to wish to lose his good opinion) but still achieve the desired outcome: no dice.

221

As I sat there Ben came in and stood in the hall, looking in at me, his hands in his pockets.

'Who died?'

'No one.'

'That's OK then. Mind if I go to bed, I'm knackered.'

'No, you carry on.' I got up and went into the hall. We were both dragging our footsteps a little. I felt the same bat's-wing of unease, that had nothing to do with my own dilemma.

'Ben—'

He was almost at his bedroom door and even now he only half-turned—he was still heading away from me.

'Yeah.'

I realised that I didn't know what I was going to say, only that I wanted to detain him for a moment.

'How was Sophie?'

'Sophie?'

'Yes—you've been out with her, have you?'

'Oh, right—yes, earlier on. But she went back, she had to do some work.'

'But everything's all right, is it?'

'Fine.'

'Good.'

He still stood there in his slightly awkward attitude, neither with me nor gone from me. His natural ease of manner seemed for the moment to have deserted him and it made me unhappy so that I went over and kissed him impulsively.

'Night love.' I stroked his cheek. 'You smell nice.'

Did I imagine it, or did he without moving draw slightly away, just perceptibly shrink inside his skin . . . ?

'Night, Mum.'

*   *   *

After I was in bed I heard him in the bathroom. Usually there was a flurry of tooth-cleaning, the loo being flushed, and then the click of the light pull as he emerged. This time there was an additional sound, that of water being run into the basin, and vigorous, prolonged washing. Only a few days ago this determined purging of a girl's scent would have struck me as rather sweet. But tonight, staring blankly at my book, it failed to make me smile.

*   *   *

The next morning we went through our usual routine. On the way out I picked up the post, which included a postcard from Ronnie and Dennis in the Auvergne.

'So much for a single Europe,' remarked Ben laconically. 'Even from France the postcards still arrive after the people get back.'

'How do you mean?' I asked, closing the door behind us.

'The Chatsworth olds are home. Couple of days ago.'

'Are you sure? Ronnie said they were going for a fortnight.'

'Dead sure. Simon's back from Newquay, he told me in the pub . . .' His voice faded as he headed in the direction of town.

I climbed into the car and pondered the postcard. It held no clues. The picture was of smooth, green, flower-scattered hills. The message,

223

written by Ronnie in her large flowing hand, was perfectly standard: 'We're sleeping, walking, eating and drinking. Glorious sunshine which they say is going to last. Not a tennis court in sight so I'll have some catching up to do when I get back, but you won't find me complaining, Love, R and D.'

I decided not to go round. Whatever domestic disaster had brought the Chatsworths back from France early, it would be kinder to leave them to report it. On the drive to work I also shoved my vague concerns about Ben to the back of my mind. Ian—a worrier in the professional but not the personal arena—had always maintained that there was no use in fretting over those things you could do nothing about, a theory which displayed a total lack of understanding of the true worrier's pysche. I might have closed the door on those worries for the moment, but I knew they would rattle the latch persistently till readmitted.

Fortunate for me, perhaps, that I had something more immediate about which a decision had to be made—Charles McNally's invitation. On the principle that disinterest provides the best advice, I invited Jo to have lunch with me at Roots, a health-food bar, and laid the situation before her.

'Sounds like you've netted him,' was her first comment. 'Let me be the first to say congratulations.'

'Thanks Jo, but no thanks.'

'Oh, I see. You don't want to get involved.'

'No.'

She mopped up salad dressing with a heel of stone-ground bread. 'So what exactly's the difficulty?'

'I don't know what to say.'

224

'Just say no.' She delivered the formula on a sing-song note.

'But I don't want to seem rude.'

'You don't have to be rude. But you do have to be firm. There's no point in making an excuse, because excuses run out. And if you're never going to see him again, what does it matter what he thinks of you?'

There was no answer to that—it was a good point, which did nothing to improve my state of mind.

When we left Roots we went our separate ways back to the office, because Jo needed to go to the post office to re-licence her car. Crossing Memorial Gardens I was astonished to see Pearl and Nozz sitting on the grass near the fountain. I pretended not to see them, because I was sure that Pearl would rather die than acknowledge me.

But I'd reckoned without the amiable Nozz.

'How y'doing?'

'Oh, hello ...!' I feigned pleased surprise and walked over to them. Pearl gave me a lowering look over the bottle of Hooch she held in heavily beringed, green-nailed fingers. 'Hi Pearl.'

'OK?'

I turned my attention back to Nozz. 'Taking a long lunch hour? It's a nice day for it.'

'You can't work all the time,' he agreed.

Pearl jerked her head in his direction. 'He's taking a leaf out of Ben's book.'

'Ben's?'

'All work and no play,' explained Nozz. 'Nothing we can teach Ben about long lunch hours. Quality of life's the important thing.'

This was incontrovertible, if a bit surprising

coming from Nozz, who had never struck me as a grey wage-slave sort of guy. His next remark was even more surprising.

'How's the new relationship?'

'Sorry?'

'Ben's new woman.'

'Fine. She seems nice.'

I just caught the expression of sheer vitriol on Pearl's face.

'No,' said Nozz, as if he'd seen it too. 'Fair play to them. Looks like the real thing.'

'Do you think so?' I said, pathetically grateful for this unlooked-for boost to my hopes.

'Only my opinion.'

Pearl made no comment, but slid her plump lips off the end of the bottle with a moist plop. Cheered by Nozz's observations I chose not to think of this as rude. After all, the girl had been dumped by Ben, why would she want to extol his latest love?

I was back in the office first. When Jo came in she came straight over to my desk.

'Look,' she said, 'I've had some time to think, in the queue from hell. I do realise these things are a lot easier in theory than in practice. First up, you do need to be dead sure you want to say no.'

'Of course I'm sure.'

'In that case, say it.'

*   *   *

The next day, the day the rest of Mrs Rymer's things were being sold, I told Ben during our shared three minutes in the kitchen that I had seen Pearl.

'And how was she?' he asked with a downward,

226

let's-get-this-over-with inflection.

'She was taking the sun with Nozz, in the gardens.'

'Pearl out of doors? She must be pushed.'

'They said they were taking a leaf out of your book.'

'Of course I'm never out of Memorial Gardens.'

He was in a foul temper, it wasn't like him. 'No,' I said. 'Nozz said you'd been having long lunch hours. He put it down to love.'

'He did, did he?' Ben picked up his coffee. 'What a simple soul he is.'

*   *   *

The sale left Mrs Rymer two thousand richer. As promised, after I'd done the paperwork for her son and daughter-in-law I sent a handwritten note suggesting we go out for lunch on Sunday. As I wrote it, I thought how surprised she would be if she knew just how much I was looking forward to seeing her. I said that unless I heard to the contrary, I'd pick her up at half past twelve.

Desma called in the evening, about tennis.

'Are you on for a singles?'

'I would be,' I said, 'but did you know Ronnie had to come home early, so she might be available?'

'I did know, because Rick bumped into her at the doctor's when he went about Bryony's grommets. The poor thing's got a recurrence of that wretched virus, apparently. There was no question of her having a good time, so it seemed more sensible to both of them to come back and put the doctor back on the case.'

227

'Have you spoken to her?'

'Yes, she was very pissed off, but they've put her on a course of something, so we'll just have to see . . .'

'What about Sabine?'

'Yes, well that's the thing, Sabine can't play either. Martin's taking Sophie to some agricultural show or other and she's got to stay in for the men doing maintenance on the pool. Must be tough being loaded. So anyway, it looks like singles or bust.' I hesitated, she waited. 'Please, Eve.'

'I'm not playing very well at the moment.'

'Sounds good to me. Look, I'd like to see you, I'm not like everyone else, tennis is the highlight of my week. We could just play the best of seven and then go to the Cutter.'

I laughed. 'If you put it like that.'

'Great! See you there.'

I sent some flowers to Ronnie with a card expressing commiserations about the curtailment of their holiday, and telling her to get in touch as soon as she felt up to it. On Saturday morning there was a note from Mrs Rymer accepting my invitation. Ben was still in bed when I left for tennis, having responded tersely to my wake-up call that he was having this Saturday off. Could he, I wondered, be going to the agricultural show with Martin and Sophie? That would certainly be proof, if proof were needed, of an undying passion.

Desma and I called it a day—and an honourable draw—after two short sets. Our game scored low on both technical merit and artistic impression, but high on hard graft—we both dug in on the base line and scurried back and forth making a lot of uncultured, labour intensive shots. By the end of it

228

we had worked up a virtuous sweat.

Over beer and sandwiches in the Cutter Bar (without the other two we went cheap and cheerful) we agreed that it had definitely been worth the effort.

'And anyway,' added Desma, 'I need to keep up my Saturday outings, because they keep Rick off the streets.'

'That's important, is it?' I asked carefully, betraying no anticipation of the anwer.

'At the moment. I think he's being tempted, Eve, so this is one small thing I can do to keep him out of temptation's way. There's nothing like a lively toddler to nip illicit romance in the bud.'

I was flabbergasted. 'Desma! You're not serious?'

'Pretty serious.' Her cheeks were pink as she took a pull at her beer.

'But that's awful.'

'It is a bit of a bummer, but I'm surprised at how practical I feel about it. After all, come on, he is gorgeous.'

'Yes, he is.'

'Remember that song, "When You're In Love With a Beautiful Woman"—well it's the same but the other way round.'

'There's a line "You watch your friends",' I said. 'I hope you don't feel you have to do that.'

'Of course not! Eve!' She was reproachful. 'But I know everyone wonders how on earth I snared him, and the answer is I haven't a clue, but snare him I did and there was always a chance someone was going to come along and test the rope.'

I shook my head in disbelief. 'Do you have any idea—'

'No, and I don't want to. I don't care about her, only about us. It may not even have got very far, but any distance is far enough.'

'Have you talked to Rick about it?'

'Not yet. It sounds silly, but I don't want to hear him squirm, or have to lie about it. I want the whole thing to stop before it comes to that.'

'Isn't that a bit optimistic?' I asked gently. 'I mean, if he thinks you don't know, or perhaps don't care, human nature being what it is . . .'

'Ah, but I know my husband. He's not very brave,' she said bluntly. 'If I ever get clear evidence of anything I shall deliver an ultimatum, never fear. But till then, you know, I love him, and—' she took a short, deep breath—'and I want him to do the right thing off his own bat.'

'Absolutely,' I said. I wanted to hug her. 'Good luck, Desma.'

*   *   *

It was one of those curious coincidences that when I set out for a walk that afternoon (Ben had left a BIZZY BACKSUN note on the kitchen table) I actually saw the Shaws down on the beach, a little further along from Cliff Mansions on the more deserted stretch opposite the cricket club. Bryony was tottering, bending, falling, tottering on again in her small red wellies. Her parents, in close attendance, were nonetheless absorbed in their own conversation. Rick's hands were in his pockets, Desma's arm was tucked through his. Heads bowed, they walked in unison, their feet swinging forward together in a slow, trudging march along the shifting stones.

230

I, on the other hand, walked briskly, happy to be on my own on this clear, bright afternoon, and to be looking forward to my lunch with Mrs Rymer tomorrow. Perhaps, I reflected, one was never too old to need a wise older woman in one's life. I had the feeling, not yet tested, that I could say anything to her and that she would be neither shocked nor judgmental. Which was foolish, considering her age. I was secretly, selfishly glad that she was at Whitegates and in effect always available. Had her legs still been able to carry her, and she still able to manage at home, I should not have been able to hide behind this presumption of kindness, of brightening the life of a lonely old person.

This was the tail-end of the season in Littelsea. Not that we were a resort to which people flocked in their thousands, but the locals made good use of the beach during the summer, especially in the school holidays. I got used to the August high-tide of humanity below my balcony, but there was a special pleasure for we sea-front dwellers in the ebbing of that tide, first when the children returned to school and then with the almost-imperceptible drawing-in of the days and the change in the light that presaged autumn. In Cliff Mansions we weren't just fair-weather promenaders, but people who knew 'our' sea in all her moods. I looked at her now, twinkling benignly in the pale sun and told myself she'd have to do a lot to disaffect us, her true friends.

There were quite a few other walkers out on this sunny weekend afternoon, but as I climbed higher their numbers dwindled—there were various strategically placed viewpoints, with benches, which the less determined used as staging posts from which they never moved on.

When I reached the top of the cliff I left the path and scrambled up to the edge of the headland where I sat down on the grass. A sign in huge, black letters warned 'Ramblers' that the cliff-edge was subject to erosion, but I took a childish delight in being where I could see in all directions.

To my left was Littelsea, made almost pretty by distance and the glow of the westering sun; ahead, the sea, with a Channel ferry in the far distance, cutting diagonally towards the horizon and France. Steeply down to the right was the little bay with the overlapping flat rocks where I'd sat that earlier afternoon and met Rick and Bryony. With hindsight, I wondered whether he'd had some scandalous personal reason of his own for walking so far with his daughter on his back ... an assignation, perhaps? But Desma was surely right when she said a toddler was a deterrent to such things. Perhaps, as she hoped, he was still only tempted, and hadn't strayed at all.

Considered options for the second stage of my walk, I realised there was one I couldn't see and hadn't taken into account. Behind me, on the other side of the cliff path and behind its carefully-managed belt of woodland, the Drages' house.

Considering it now, it seemed more and more an attractive proposition. At Headlands there would be Sabine stuck in on her own, always pleased to have company and especially good value when enraged by workmen. And where there was Sabine there, too, would be a long cold, possibly alcoholic

232

drink and something delicious to eat in luxurious surroundings . . .

Having made my decision I was happy to defer these pleasures for a few minutes, and lie back with my eyes closed. The short, springy grass under my back was like the pelt of an animal, an animal that seemed to breathe with the sound of the sea below, and to stir occasionally when the ever-present Channel breeze nudged it. What with the sun, my contented solitude, and the imminent prospect of congenial company, there was nowhere else on earth I would rather have been at that moment.

I fell asleep. What woke me up was the first of a small flotilla of clouds sailing across the sun. The sudden shade allowed the breeze to whip up goose-bumps on my hot arms and legs, and I opened my eyes with one of those disobliging jolts of disorientation. I'd fallen asleep like a carefree child on the grass: I woke up a middle-aged woman, stiff, chilly and self-conscious.

Fortunately there was no one about to witness me staggering creakily to my feet and picking the bits of grass off my clothes and out of my hair. Knowing how I was going to appear next to Sabine I experienced a moment's pause about visiting her, but only a moment's—no one ever looked as elegant as Sabine, and she was hardly going to notice or care if I had dropped a little further below her impossible standards.

I walked away from the sea and over the main cliff path, and up the narrow track that threaded between the rowans and conifers to the back gate of Headlands. The breeze was continuing to get up, and as I moved in amongst the trees the sound of the waves was replaced by the sibilant whisper of

233

the high branches. My footsteps, down here, were silent on the springy mulch of leaves and pine needles. It was quite cold.

I paused at the gate. From here I had a view of the side of the house, the descending planes of well-manicured lawn, tumbling rockeries and luxuriant bursts of herbaceous border and shrubbery, the corner of the terrace where I had stood with Charles McNally. The swimming pool where the maintenance men were working—I could hear faint music—was out of sight.

A little to my left, and further up was the brand new tennis court in all its sharp-edged, pristine magnificence. It would be nice, I thought, to play up here on crisp, bright days during the autumn and winter, in perfect privacy and with the promise of Martin's well-stocked drinks trolley to follow.

I opened the gate quietly, conscious of being an intruder, and closed it carefully behind me. Walking across the grass it occurred to me that the entire floor area of my flat could comfortably have fitted inside the Drages' tennis court. What must it be like, I wondered, to own so much, to be the rulers of this small, perfect clifftop kingdom? I admired it, but I was genuinely glad that such a kingdom, with all its attendant responsibilities, wasn't mine. This thought cheered me up— perhaps I was after all the carefree soul who'd fallen asleep on the grass, who cared nothing for possessions or appearances.

As I got nearer the house so I could hear more clearly the music being played down at the pool. Surprisingly, it was Puccini, the overture to *Madame Butterfly*. Trust Sabine to employ workmen with refined tastes, or to make it her business to refine them.

The pool came into view. The music swelled. There was no sign of any work being done—on the contrary the water was a clear sapphire blue, the tiled surround immaculate, and someone was swimming. Or at least there was someone in the water, in the farthest corner, perhaps taking a break between lengths. I walked down the slope, not wanting to advertise myself until I was sure it was Sabine.

When I was about fifty yards away I caught a glint of her favourite lime-green swimsuit. But at the very moment that I smiled, raised my hand, opened my mouth to call her name, another head rose from the water between her body and the side of the pool, dark and sleek as an otter between her guiding hands.

*   *   *

I ran back the way I'd come, my heart beating so violently that I felt blood might suddenly burst in a hot spray from my nose and mouth. I didn't look where I was going. I didn't even know if they had seen me. My flight was not just from this place, but from knowledge and discovery and change. I wanted to run until I dissolved the picture that was in my head.

My own panic shocked me. Nothing could have prepared me for what I'd just witnessed, nor for the violence of my reaction.

The tide had turned. The sea change was complete.

CHAPTER TWELVE

Looking back, it seems unbelievable that I said nothing to Ben for over twenty-four hours. And yet I can all too easily recreate the sensations which prevented me from doing do.

For one thing, when he returned that evening at about nine it was obvious that he did not know I'd been there, and had seen the two of them. He was in buoyant form, at his chattiest and most charming. He'd gone up to Headlands this evening, he told me, and Sophie and Martin were back from the show, so he'd stayed for supper. He didn't seem to notice my quietness, and he made no mention of Sabine beyond the invitation to supper.

I don't mind admitting that this behaviour threw me. Not only was there no visible mark of Cain, but no evasions, no lowered eyes, nor any of the elusive strangeness of several recent occasions. On the contrary, this was a return to the old Ben, who could make me feel that he and I had a special relationship, a shared way of looking at things.

I began to doubt myself and the evidence of my own eyes and instincts. After all, I didn't want this to be true—so maybe, *maybe* it wasn't. After all, what had I actually seen? Only Sabine, a naturally flirtatious character, taking a dip in her own pool with my son who was a regular visitor to the house, her stepdaughter's boyfriend, for heaven's sake. People did lark about in swimming pools, it meant nothing, and anyway I had been an interloper and interlopers, like eavesdroppers, get what they deserve.

I understood now why women did not always scream when they were attacked. Because along with the dread and fear there was the ludicrous, programmed response—is this real, or a joke? Surely it can't be happening? In the same way I was reluctant to make a scene in case there turned out to be a perfectly, blessedly, reasonable explanation.

So, in the face of every natural impulse the fear—and hope—that I might be mistaken closed my throat.

*   *   *

All the pleasure had gone from my lunch date with Mrs Rymer. In fact if I'd remembered in time I would have selfishly cancelled no matter what the disappointment to her. But it was eleven the next morning when her note, still lying on the dining table, reminded me, and by then it was too late. I suppose I could have invented some sudden, violent indisposition but on balance I wanted to be out of the flat before Ben got up—away from him, away from the doorbell and the telephone and anyone that I knew.

I got changed and made up hurriedly, dreading the least sound from Ben's room. My hand shook as I applied eyeliner and lipstick and when I'd finished I felt not enhanced, but grotesquely disguised. At one point I wept from sheer tension and the bleak sadness of it all. As I closed the door of the flat behind me I was sure I heard his bedroom door open, and I fled down the stairs with the skin on the back of my neck prickling. Fled, for the second time in twenty-four hours, from my own son.

Mrs Rymer was waiting for me in the hall at Whitegates. She was elegant in a lovat-green dress with a long red-and-green scarf draped round her shoulders and caught with a large, Celtic-looking brooch. Ribbed burgundy tights covered the bandages on her legs. One of the nurses hovered, but she had her stick with her and managed the short walk to the car very well, only leaning on my arm slightly to negotiate the two shallow steps from the front door to the drive. Once in the car I noticed that she had on some wonderful, poignant scent—not the sort of thing one buys in an atomiser at the high street chemist. In my vulnerable state the scent made my eyes sting with tears.

I cleared my throat. 'I haven't booked anywhere,' I said. 'But if you're sure you're happy with a pub . . .'

'My dear I shall be in seventh heaven even if all we do is drive about and admire the view,' she said.

I took her to the Fore and Aft (known locally as the Up and Under) on the seafront near the Martello Tower, and we sat at a table with a view of the promenade and the beach.

'How clever of you,' she said. 'This is just the ticket.'

She had a glass of white wine, and I a glass of red and we ordered sea bass. As I came back from the bar with our drinks I caught her looking at me in her intuitive way, but she came of a generation which would have regarded personal questions as impertinent. If I wished her to be anything more

238

than a charming, appreciative guest, that would be up to me.

We talked about the sale, and about Littelsea, and Whitegates, and her family. Or at least she talked, which was how I wanted it. I didn't trust myself to remain composed on any subject relating to myself. Since she had mentioned him so freely at our last meeting I asked her about Gerhardt.

'What happened when war broke out?'

She flicked a hand. 'Over. *Kaput.*'

'That must have been devastating.'

'The whole thing was no picnic, which perhaps put the personal side of it into perspective. One just got on with it.'

'Did you try to keep in touch?'

'He wrote me some letters. I didn't reply.'

She paused. It wasn't a hesitation, but a quite deliberate pause, which made me wonder if I'd overstepped the mark. It was my turn now to wait. Our food arrived and made the wait even longer. Then she spread her big hands on either side of her plate, adjusting the alignment of her knife and fork with her fingertips, like piano keys. When she did reply her voice was matter of fact.

'He was a Nazi, my dear. I couldn't be doing with that.'

She made it sound so crystal clear, so perfectly practical and simple. And yet I knew it couldn't have been. My admiration for her was boundless, but when I said so she waved it aside.

'This looks absolutely delicious,' she exclaimed cheerfully. 'Do you mind if I tuck in?'

It was good, and we both cleared our plates, she with gusto and relish, I more from habit than anything else. She declared herself not a coffee drinker, so I had a double espresso while she put away sticky toffee pudding and a second glass of wine. I realised that this pleasant interlude was drawing to a close and that when I got home everything would still be there, waiting for me. The really bad stuff I could not possibly mention, but I sensed that like Jo she might have a clear perspective on my dilemma with Charles McNally.

'I wonder if I might ask your advice—it's only a small thing.'

'In the unlikely eventuality that I can be of the least help, I will.'

'I think I know what you'll say.'

'Of course.' She sat back, hands folded round her wine glass. 'We only ask for advice to have our own opinion confirmed, don't you think?'

'Perhaps. But I'm not sure I have an opinion.'

'As soon as I open my mouth, you will have. Go ahead and tell me.'

I sketched out the problem, sounding as casual as I could. 'I did say,' I concluded sheepishly, 'that it was trivial.'

'On the surface it is,' she agreed. 'But the fact that it's exercising you so much proves that it isn't, at least as far as you are concerned.'

'Well—no.'

'I don't want to ask you another thing, but perhaps I could suggest something. If you do nothing, or say no, to this man, you will certainly be relieved of the problem, but you will never know why it was important. And if at some later time you do see why, that might prove bothersome.'

I waited again, sure she was going to add something, the other side of the argument. But she didn't.

When we left the Up and Under I took her for a short drive. As we cruised slowly along the prom we passed The Esplanade and I saw the Chatsworths—Ronnie, Dennis, and the boys—sitting over lunch at a window table in the restaurant. Of course they didn't see me, I was just another car, but I was cut through by a pang of envy for their happy, sociable family outing.

I went along the Brighton road, and then described a curve for a few miles inland, and came back through Hawley End, forgetting that this might have poignant associations. But if it did, she didn't let them show. Instead, she stared thoughtfully out of the window and remarked:

'You know, I don't miss this place.'

'No?'

'No, it was never my home in the way that our married houses were. And latterly it was rather less amusing than where I am now.'

At Whitegates, I saw her to her room.

'That was so lovely, I can't tell you,' she said, giving me her firm handshake. 'I wish I could say I shan't eat for the rest of the day, but it would be an empty promise. Meals mark out the day here.'

'We must do it again.'

As I drove off, I could still feel the bracing touch of a tougher, no less passionate but more pragmatic generation. She doubtless did think my problem trivial—I almost wished I'd mentioned Ben, to really shake her—and though she was prepared to take it seriously, she wasn't going to indulge me for a second longer than the situation merited.

I was on my own.

On the way home I decided that I would walk straight into the flat and dial Charles McNally's number. Now, while my life was overshadowed by something so much greater, would be the right moment to Just Say No.

Ben, of course, was not there.

In spite of my resolve it was still a shock to hear Charles's voice only seconds after I'd spoken to the reception desk.

'McNally.' He sounded curt and peremptory, not at all Sunday-afternoonish.

'Oh—hello. This is Eve Piercy.'

'Eve, hi.'

There was a just perceptible warming of his tone, but he didn't exactly express unbridled delight. Then again I didn't want him to, so that was alright.

'Thank you for your message, by the way.' *By the way?*

'You're coming up to town?'

'I don't know.' He had skipped an entire stage of the exchange, assuming that it was not a question of if, but simply when.

'OK.' I recognised that moving-right-along intonation from Ben and his peers. 'So how do you want to play this?'

'I'll call you, shall I, if I'm coming?'

'I'd really like that. I want to go to Ronnie Scott's—do you like jazz?'

'I don't know enough about it. I started and stopped with Acker Bilk.'

'Who?'

'"Stranger on the Shore"? Early sixties? And
242

Kenny Ball—' I was stumbling into a quicksand of inconsequential conversation from which it would be horribly difficult to escape.

'Never heard of the guys. It would be my privilege, Eve, to convert you.'

'You can try,' I said, fatuously.

I think he laughed. He had one of those almost voiceless laughs in the back of the throat, infectious to witness but disconcerting over the phone.

'Right . . . I'll look forward to hearing from you, I really will.'

'Bye.'

I put the receiver down and sat there. It had all been perfectly simple, perfectly friendly and I was committed to nothing. Why then, was my heart racing? And why could I not tell whether I was elated or disappointed? Mrs Rymer's cryptic words came back to me: ' . . . you'll never know why it was important.' I still didn't.

That night Ben called to say he was going to spend the night at Nozz's. I could have dialled to see where he was calling from, but I chose not to.

*   *   *

On Monday I called in sick, something I never did. My integrity at work was legendary, I never appropriated so much as a paperclip from Bouvier's, let alone their time. But this morning integrity had rather lost its lustre.

Trying not to think too far ahead, I drove up the hill to Headlands. In this encounter, unlike my recent exchange with Charles McNally, I intended to rely on instinct. My face, hands and feet were cold; I kept yawning with anxiety. If I had ever

243

wished to bring Sabine down a peg or two, to shake her famous composure and rattle her cage, this was not the means I had envisaged. I actually dreaded what I was about to do, because I was doing it to all of us—to Ben, Sabine, me, her family and mine, and all our friends. It felt as though I were about to bring about the end of the world as we knew it.

It came as a shock to encounter Sophie, of all people, in the drive, getting into her Mini. As soon as she saw me she came over, smiling broadly.

'Hello, how are you?'

'Not so bad.' How could she not tell? How could she not know?

'She's in there—it is Sabine you're after?—yes, she's in there, handing out grief to the indoor plants people. I'd better rock off, I'm late.'

'Bye Sophie.'

'Tell Ben I'll call . . . !'

She executed a rasping three-point turn on the gravel and was gone, the Mini accelerating alarmingly as it went down the hill.

The front door wasn't quite closed, and I could hear Sabine's voice in the hall. I pushed it open and went in: an interloper again, but this time she saw me, and widened her eyes in a smile of greeting while still pouring contumely on the hapless plants man. Clea, watering flowers halfway up the stairs, gave me a politely anxious smile.

' . . . no I'm sorry I am *not* satisfied, because what you have sent is not what I ordered. I should like those plants that I did not order taken away this morning, please, and replacements here by the end of the day, otherwise I shall be demanding my money back and it is very doubtful that I shall be using you again.' She waggled her fingers at me,

244

left her hand in the air as she listened with bored impatience to the excuses on the other end. 'No, no, you are not paying attention. It is very simple. I want the matter put right. I want two standard bay trees and a weeping fig here this afternoon and the rest of this clutter removed. Otherwise I want it all to go, and my money refunded. Good morning.'

She put the phone down and beamed at me. She was positively sparkling—nothing improved her humour like a spat with the trades people. Or almost nothing, I reflected bitterly.

'What a lovely surprise—are you on holiday?'

'No, I called in sick.'

'Come and have a cup of coffee.'

'Not for me thanks.'

'Do you mind if I do, I need it after dealing with those idiots . . .' She walked away from me towards the kitchen and I followed, unable from habit to break into her self-absorbed prattle. 'Would you prefer tea, Eve, I have some Lapsang and some Jasmine . . .?' I shook my head. 'You know Mrs Moss, don't you?'

'Oh yes,' said Mrs Moss, the occasional help, who was cleaning silver, 'we've met before.'

Mrs Moss was one of those women who, though certainly younger than either of us, seemed old at heart. The wording of her greeting was ominous, as though she had something on me which she would reveal when the time was right. It flashed across my mind that perhaps she knew—but no, if there was one thing Sabine would consider absolutely sacrosanct it was the separateness of the lower orders. Nothing would ever have taken place while any *domestique* was within snooping distance.

'Mrs Moss,' said Sabine. 'Are you ready for a cup

of tea?'

'If you're making one.'

Any fears I had that we were going to have to sit here making small talk with Mrs Moss until she returned to her Silvo were shortlived. The idea would never have crossed Sabine's mind.

'Come along, let's go and be comfortable,' she said.

Mrs Moss got out her cigarettes. 'Cheerio.'

On the way Sabine called up the stairs, 'Kettle's on, Clea!' and gave me a woman-to-woman smile that said her responsibilities were unending.

We went into the conservatory. Everything in here was white, cream, and blonde wood, and I was about to spray filth all over it.

Sabine, too, was in white—loose trousers and a sleeveless shirt tied on the waist.

'So what is the matter with you?' she asked, smiling.

It was only much later that I realised she'd been enquiring about my health.

'I want to ask you about Ben,' I said.

'What about him?' Her smile was unchanged. She took a sip of her coffee.

'About him—and you.'

'I'm sorry?' Now the smile was still in place, but it was tissue-thin.

'I don't think I'm wrong.' My voice was coming from a million miles away.

'About what, Eve?'

She used my Christian name as she'd used that 'please' to the men on the phone—as a weapon. That one word told me irrefutably that I was right.

'About what is going on.'

'I beg your pardon?' She turned to put her cup

246

down. There was the suggestion of a flush on her cheekbone.

'I believe there is something going on between you and my son.'

'That's ridiculous!' She flicked at the immaculate trousers. 'Ridiculous!'

'Yes it is. But that doesn't mean it isn't true.'

She sat with her head turned away from me. The silence was only intensified by the hoover starting up in some distant area. I had absolutely no idea what Sabine was thinking, or feeling, or what expression might be on her face.

'Sabine?'

'Yes, it's true.'

It was a relief, in a way, to hear it. A relief from tension, but a giddying, plunge into the greater unknown.

I tried, without success, to say something, but I had lost not only the words—what words could express this tumult of confusion and despair—but the voice with which to utter them.

To make matters worse, when Sabine turned towards me her look was one of coldly burning defiance.

'It is true.'

I think, now, that we believe our family and friends only exist in the spotlight of our experience—that is what we choose to believe. Life would be hell if we knew who they were, how they behaved and all that they said for the much greater part of time when they are away from us. Sabine's words did not simply confirm what I already knew, but made shockingly real her other, proper, life. And, by implication, my son's. In other words, I knew next to nothing about either of them.

It was I who lowered my eyes first. 'I don't know what to say.'

'There is nothing.'

'Or too much,' I said. 'I don't know where to start.'

'Before you make any accusations,' said Sabine, 'remember that Ben is an adult.'

'What?'

She spread her hands. 'If he were not living at home you would know nothing of his life.'

'What are you trying to say?'

'He has not been led astray or corrupted or anything of that sort. He entered willingly into our relationship.'

She was being grand with me. It was unconscionable.

'Sabine! You are one of my best friends. You are a married woman. Does Martin know? And what about Sophie? I thought Ben and Sophie were—' I fumbled—'going out together?'

'They are.'

'But you and he—' Again, words failed me.

'It is not the same thing.'

'You're telling me it's not! What about Martin?'

'He knows nothing.'

'Then he should do! I hope you don't expect me to keep your sordid little secret, Sabine, because I see no reason why I should.'

Her left eyebrow rose, infinitesimally. 'It is not only my secret, surely.'

'Ben's half your age—less than half your age—the responsibility rests with you.'

'Responsibility for what?'

'For your adultery with someone young enough to be your son—your stepdaughter's boyfriend.'

248

'He wanted me, Eve.' She couldn't keep the purr of satisfaction out of her voice. 'He pursued me.'

'And that's all it takes, is it?'

'Not all, no. Your son is adorable.'

I couldn't ignore it, the treacherous caress of flattery. And that made me even angrier.

'But Sabine, it's *wrong*. Didn't you ever say to him—this is wrong? Didn't you think of anyone else—your husband, Sophie, me? Well?'

'Often. But never at the right moment.'

She was rubbing my nose in it, the smug French bitch.

'Don't dare take that line with me,' I snarled.

Mrs Moss appeared in the drawing room behind us. 'That's it, all done.'

'Oh thank you, Mrs Moss.'

'I'll see you tomorrow then.'

'*A demain. Au revoir.*'

'Bye Mrs Piercy.'

I wondered how much she'd heard as she padded across the hall in her trainers. Sabine's ability to adapt her face and voice to circumstances was frightening. What a fool I'd been.

We waited until the front door closed behind Mrs Moss, and then Sabine said:

'Have you spoken to Ben about this?'

'Not yet.'

'Why not? I should have thought you would have talked to him before coming up here.'

'I wanted to hear it from you first.'

The eyebrow again. 'Were you afraid he might lie to you?'

'I didn't want to accuse him of anything that I wasn't certain of.'

'Eve—you have no right to accuse him of

249

anything.'

Her arrogance was breathtaking. 'Don't tell me what rights I do and do not have. Ben is my son.'

'But he is also a grown man.'

'A *young* man, of twenty-one, having a relationship with a married woman twice his age who happens to be—who was—my friend.'

'All of that is true, but it is not your place to make accusations.'

'I shall do whatever I want!' Why, when I was so sure I was in the right, did I sound like an hysterical child? And why, when she was so patently in the wrong, was Sabine contriving to emerge with her dignity intact?

I got up to leave. She followed more slowly. When I reached the front door she was standing in the drawing-room doorway, her arms folded.

'You are going to tell Martin?' I asked.

'That need not concern you,' she replied, almost gently. 'But you must speak to Ben.'

'Stop giving me advice.'

She gave a one-shouldered shrug. 'I cannot speak for him.'

'Did I ask you to?'

She looked down at her shoes. I left and closed the door.

*   *   *

Nothing had been as I expected. I had, I realised, been spoiling for a scene, and been denied it. The messy explosion of guilt, remorse and self-justification that I'd dreaded was actually what I'd been looking forward to. It would have cleared the air. Instead, the atmosphere was more stifling than before. Was she really not going to tell Martin? And had she really meant it when she said Ben and Sophie were still together? Could those things be separated out?

By Sabine perhaps, but not by me.

*　　　*　　　*

It was a long day. I spent it prowling about, lying on the bed in despair, and writing a letter to Sabine, setting out more cogently and in vastly greater detail what my feelings were about her and Ben. At six-thirty, Jo rang up to ask how I was. Without thinking, I told her fine.

'Ah—diplomatic illness, then.'

'God, I'd forgotten all about it. Yes.'

'My silence doesn't come cheap, you know ... Eve? You OK?'

I got a grip. 'A bit depressed, that's all.'

'Want to come out for a drink?'

'That's sweet of you but no thanks, I'd be rotten company.'

'Let me be the judge of that.'

'No thanks.'

'OK. See you—when I see you.'

'I'll be back in tomorrow.'

The other person to ring was Sophie. 'Is he back yet?'

'No.'

'Can you get him to call me?'

'I'll tell him you rang,' I said, knowing it wasn't the same thing, and putting the phone down.

I was sitting on the sofa surrounded by the scribbled pages of the letter when I heard Ben's key in the lock. I shuffled the paper together and

251

he walked in as I was closing the desk.

'Aha!' he said, in a mad professor's voice. 'The secret journal, at last I know where you keep it! Mum . . . ?'

I had dissolved into tears.

'Hey, take it easy, what's occurring? Come on . . .' He put his arms round me. It was a rite of passage—him comforting me like this—and it did not make what I had to say any easier.

'I'm OK—please—' I disengaged myself and went to the kitchen to fetch a tissue. When I came back, mopped and blown, he was sitting on the sofa, still in his leather jacket, gazing expectantly towards me.

'Sorry,' I said.

'Don't mention it.' He patted the cushion next to him. 'Come and sit down and tell me all about it, I could do with hearing someone else's problems.'

I didn't sit down by him but on the chair opposite.

'Body language is a touch ominous here,' he said, smiling, still trying to tease me out of my depression.

'Ben,' I said. 'I want to tell you that I know about you and Sabine.'

'Oh.' He didn't move at all, but the smile died, leaving his face drawn and curiously exposed, like a woman's with the make-up scrubbed off.

'How did you find out?'

'I saw you—in the pool on Saturday.'

'I see.'

'And then I went round to Sabine's this morning. She didn't deny it.'

He whitened. 'You went to talk to Sabine? Before you talked to me?'

252

'I was angry, Ben. More angry than I've ever been, and I still am.'

'Yeah, I know just how you feel . . .'

'What's that?'

'For God's sake!' He bounced to his feet and towered over me. 'And I thought we had a pretty good relationship! How could you go up there and talk to her as though I were a child?'

It struck me that this was pretty much the same thing Sabine had said.

'You are my child!' I shouted back, 'And she was my friend!'

'Shit! I don't believe this!' He was furious and it frightened me. His reaction, like Sabine's, was not what I'd been expecting. I'd anticipated high emotion but not this blast of withering rage. 'So what the fuck did you say to her?'

'Don't swear at me Ben!'

'What?'

'That I was sure the two of you were having— whatever you want to call it—a thing, an affair, a *relationship*, and—'

'And? And?'

'And I took exception to it! I was outraged! Ben, how could you do this to me, both of you but especially you!'

'Christ!' He banged his fist so violently on his forehead that it left a red wheal on the white skin. 'Why does everything have to revolve round you? Neither of us have done anything to you.'

'How can you say that?' Although we weren't touching I felt that we were engaged in a physical battle; that I was clinging to him, trying to hold him still so I could look into his eyes as I had when he was little, but now he was too strong for me and

253

simply shrugged off my attempt to grasp him. The roughness with which he did so shocked me.

It had, I suppose, been a rhetorical question, but when he didn't respond to it I still felt impelled to repeat myself.

'How you can say that, Ben? You've both of you lied, and cheated, not just me but other people—'

'When did I lie to you?' He leaned over me, cold and fierce, his finger pointing rigidly at my face like a knife threatening to mark me. 'Go on. When did I tell you a single lie?'

I managed a bitter little laugh. 'You didn't need to tell a single lie, Ben, you were living one.'

He stepped back and pushed his hands into his jacket pockets in a bruising gesture of self-restraint. 'I see. You want to know everything, do you?'

It was a trick question, and we both knew it. I hesitated, and he gave me a quick scornful look. I felt it scorch me just before he left the room, and the flat, and slammed the door after him.

CHAPTER THIRTEEN

I stayed up into the small hours, hoping to talk to him again when—if—he came back. The silent emptiness of the flat was agony. I realised how used I had become to anticipating his return, to knowing that the two separate wheels of our lives, while turning at different speeds and in different rhythms, still interlocked smoothly where they touched. How much, I now wondered, was that smoothness due to blind ignorance?

I fell asleep on the sofa and woke to find him standing in the doorway as though he'd been there all the time. He wore the same clothes, but his face was darkly unshaven and he carried an old sports bag with a broken zip, from which bits of clothing protruded.

'I'm off then,' he said dully.

'Where to?'

'Nozz has got a spare mattress.'

'Ben—' I got up stiffly, scraping my fingers through my hair—'Ben, please don't go—*please*.'

'You just don't get it, do you Mum?' His voice was no more than a whisper.

I wanted to hug him, to implore him to stay, but the bad stuff was beginning to seep like black ink into my system.

'No Ben, *you* don't get it. If you don't understand why I was so upset, why I was so devastated, then I can't explain it to you.'

'Oh, but I do understand.' He patted my arm lightly—it was worse than nothing. 'That's the trouble. I know where you're coming from the minute you walk into the room. We've been around each other for too long.'

'But you can't just take off like this!'

'Watch me.' He began heading for the door. I followed, almost running.

'What are you going to do—about Sabine?'

'Mum—' He'd opened the door and stood there, effectively barring my way. 'Please—cut it out.'

He closed the door very quietly after him, but the shock was as great as if he'd slammed it. I stood stock still, listening to his footsteps going down the stairs.

I made tea. I washed and changed. I called Jo and said I was really ill this time, and was taking to my bed. She believed me.

I was wronged, injured, mortified. It would not have been too much to say my world was in tatters. And yet Ben and Sabine, the guilty parties, the wrongdoers, had between them contrived to make me look like an hysteric.

I rang Ian at the office.

'I need to talk to you urgently, it's about Ben.'

'Fire away.'

'No—not over the phone.'

'I could make lunch.'

'All right, shall I come there?'

'Yes. Eve—'

'What?'

'I've got to go into a meeting, now. But I'd like to be prepared. On a scale of one to ten, just how bad is it?'

'Nine point nine nine recurring.'

'All right. I'll see you later—get them to call up when you arrive.'

*   *   *

I drove up to London this time, because I needed something to do. And besides, the car afforded privacy. I could play music to suit my mood, on a day when every sad song seemed written for me. I could weep, wail and gnash my teeth and other road users would see nothing but a metallic grey Toyota travelling a shade too fast in the outside lane.

Of course all this changed as I came into town.

256

Every junction and traffic light had its attendant array of bored drivers with nothing better to do than stare. I turned the music off and effected repairs with a tissue in the driving mirror.

Ian's office had some limited staff parking at the back, in which he always used to wangle me a space. In spite of everything I was touched to discover that he had done so again—his obliging PA, Anthea, must have moved her own car on to a meter at his expense.

The receptionist said he'd be down right away. Full marks to her, she greeted me as charmingly as always, blotchy face and all, and I had to accept that this was in no small part due to Ian's own popularity in the company. Whatever the vicissitudes of his private life, everyone at Inline thought the world of him.

He came out of the lift looking pale and preoccupied, kissed me on both cheeks (how odd that two kisses are more formal than one), and took my arm as we left the building.

'I told Anthea to hold my calls,' he said. 'Let's just go to Joe's shall we?'

If I had been more myself I would have found the choice of Joe's Place quite unbearably nostalgic. It was where we used to go when we couldn't afford the time or the money to go anywhere else. The menu, of a moussaka-and-chips kind, hadn't changed in twenty years: the smell as we entered was pure time travel.

'OK,' said Ian as we sat down in a cracked-leather booth, 'We're going to have a stiffener, we'll order, and then you can go ahead and wreck my day.'

He was as good as his word. Within ten minutes

I was filling up with an emotional Bulgarian red, my Cumberland sausages in cider lying neglected and cooling on the plate, as I told Ian the whole sad story.

He listened attentively, closing his eyes and shaking his head from time to time, but managing, I noticed, to consume all of his risotto.

'So there it is,' I concluded. 'A nightmare. I feel as if everything's just blown up in my face.'

'It's not good, I grant you.'

'Not good? Ian, what are we going to do?'

He laid his knife and fork together. 'Do?'

'Yes—I don't know where to turn. I don't know how to behave, how to arrange my face—I'm going to pieces over this—' My voice broke and he took my hand firmly.

'No one's suggesting it's your fault, are they?'

'No one's suggesting anything, I don't suppose anyone even knows yet. But obviously they're going to—'

'Why?'

'Because Littelsea's a small town, and these things get around! I think that gruesome ex-girlfriend of his knows already, something she said to me the other day . . .'

'I have to say,' said Ian, withdrawing his hand and laying his crumpled napkin by his plate, 'that the opinions of Ben's former molls will not be causing me to lose any sleep.'

'Will you talk to him?' I heard the pleading note in my voice and despised myself for it. 'Maybe if you talked, you know, man to man.'

'I will, of course, if that's what he wants.'

'I'm not bothered about what he wants, it's a case of what he should be doing!'

258

'Eve ...' The tilt of his head told me Ian was embarrassed by my loudness. 'Eve, don't get me wrong ...' My heart sank. 'I don't condone what Ben's done, but I don't condemn it either. I can't honestly say that I condemn Sabine, either, which is more to the point.'

'*What?*'

The angle of his head grew more acute. 'Would you like to go back to the office we'd have a bit more privacy?'

'No!'

'How about some coffee?'

'No. Thank you.'

'Look.' Ian cleared his throat to herald a fresh start. 'It's a bit of a shocker I grant you, but I do think we need to keep a sense of proportion about it. I mean God knows, these things happen. The fact that it's our son and someone we know brings it a bit closer to home, but it doesn't make it any worse, per se. I for one am not about to put on a hair shirt because of it, and neither should you.'

I felt as if the walls of Joe's Place, with their cheerful Picasso prints, were beginning to tilt inwards.

'So you're saying you're not going to do anything?'

'I don't think either of us should "do" anything in the way that you mean, no.'

'And you won't talk to your son about this?'

He closed his eyes, exercising patience. 'On the contrary, Eve, I'm quite sure he and I will talk about it. It's hardly the sort of thing, once known, that one can ignore. Apart from anything else I should think he's pretty unhappy with the state of play himself just now.'

259

'Jesus wept!'

'But if—but if you mean will I play the heavy father, the answer is absolutely not. It's never been my style, or yours come to that, and this is hardly the time to change.'

Everything he said, now, was making me more furious. 'Who said anything about being heavy? You're deliberately misinterpreting me.'

'I was venturing my opinion.'

'I will *not* allow you to simply sit up here with your lady friend and be benign and liberal and forgiving while I take all the flack and do all the dirty work down in Sussex's answer to Peyton Place!'

His face closed down on me. I'd gone too far and we both knew it. 'I'd be very sorry if I really believed that's the way it was, Eve.'

'Me too,' I mumbled with a poor grace. 'And I don't want it to happen.'

We sat there in silence for a moment while the waiter took our plates.

'Will you change your mind about the coffee?'

'OK. I'll have a cappuccino.'

'And a double espresso, thanks.'

Ian watched as I filled my glass, but covered his own with his hand.

'Let's be practical for a moment,' he said. 'Does Martin know what's been going on?'

'Sabine said not.'

'We shouldn't set too much store by that. He's pretty astute.'

'So you're saying—what?'

'I'm just trying to work out where any potential difficulties may lie.'

'The potential difficulty is how I'm going to

conduct my life down there with all this happening.'

'Yes.' Ian cleared his throat. 'If you want to put it like that.'

Under the influence of the blushful Bulgar, rage was beginning to give way once more to self-pity. 'I'm not putting it like anything, Ian. Am I the only person on the planet who can see that this is an appalling situation and likely to get a lot worse before it gets better?'

The coffee arrived.

'I refuse,' said Ian tensely when the waiter had gone, 'to make a drama out of a crisis.'

'So you admit it's a crisis?'

'It's a form of words. I'm not going to engage in histrionics.'

'You're saying that's what I'm doing?'

'Eve—for goodness' sake.'

'I can see I'm wasting my time,' I said, and got up to go.

'Eve!'

I stormed between the tables quite effectively, but the fresh air stopped my grand departure in its tracks. I was still hovering giddily in the doorway when Ian caught up with me, having no doubt tipped lavishly to compensate for the untouched coffee.

'Come and have a coffee in comfort in my office why don't you?' he suggested. I allowed myself to be escorted back there. Anthea, good as gold, simply said 'Hello Mrs Piercy!' and began loading the cafetière.

The little walk had caused us both to change gear. My physical symptoms were now far outweighing the emotional ones, and I began eating Ian's tasteful bowl of mint creams as though they were the last food on earth.

'Poor love,' said Ian sympathetically. 'You're right, it's a bummer. Shall I send Anthea out for a sandwich?'

'No thanks.'

'I'm bound to say I don't know how happily those will mix with the plonko rosso ...' he ventured.

'Sorry.'

'No, please, feel free, but just don't—ah, here's Anthea.'

She was a wonderful girl, she'd made a pot of Darjeeling as well. I could understand any man dallying with his PA if she was like Anthea. I had mine with three sugars. Anthea and Ian conferred sotto voce about some messages that had come through, and then she left.

Ian crossed his legs and ran his fingers up and down the crease of his trousers. 'All I really want to say in my clumsy way, Eve, is that nothing is your fault. It's not a conspiracy against you, or either of us. It will work itself out: messily no doubt, but no one's going to die as a result. You really mustn't take it all on yourself.'

'I'll do my best.'

'And of course I'll talk to the old boy. He's due to come up and see me soon, neutral ground is always best.'

'Yes.'

'You know, we've always been there for our two. But the real test isn't when something awful happens to your child, but when your child makes something awful happen. Don't you agree?'

I nodded.

'Speaking of which. Eve—' I looked soddenly at him—anything more was getting to be an effort. 'I really wouldn't be happy if you got back in the car.'

Damn. How could I have been so stupid? And why, when he was usually so maddeningly punctilious in these matters, had Ian failed to remind me? Because, some distant voice of conscience murmured, he couldn't face pouring petrol on the fire by curtailing my drinking.

'No, well I won't, of course.'

He looked relieved. 'Good. Take the train and we'll sort out getting the car back tomorrow.'

'I might spend the night in town,' I said defiantly. 'I'm not working tomorrow.'

'That's a good idea. You could do a show or something.'

'I could.'

'I tell you what.' He opened his desk drawer and took out a bunch of keys. 'Would you like to go to my place and put your feet up for a bit? Freshen up, make yourself at home, take a nap if you want to? It's only a couple of stops on the tube.' He removed one key from the ring and laid it on my side of the desk.

'You think about it while I splash my boots.'

I was tempted. Ian's flat would certainly be clean and tidy, and the notion of kicking my shoes off and collapsing on top of a neatly made bed was enormously seductive. I leaned forward to pick up the key and noticed the family photograph he still had on the desk—it dated from a few years ago and it was of all four of us on the last family holiday we'd spent together. The holiday, on Corsica, had not been an unmitigated success, but we were smiling like good 'uns for the co-operative waiter.

There was a smaller photo in front of this. Oh yes, there she was. I felt as if I recognised her. She was dark, rounded, pretty, a 'bonny Jean' kind of woman.

'Julia.' Ian was back in the room.

'Yes, I gathered.'

There was an awkward pause. He came over and sightly adjusted the position of both pictures, establishing his right (I knew him so well) to have both of them there.

'She won't be at the flat, you know.'

'OK.'

'She's in Bournemouth at the moment.'

'Right.'

I didn't know whether this meant that when not in Bournemouth she was at the flat, or whether the two remarks were unconnected. But Ian (he knew me so well) answered the unspoken question.

'I'm on my own there.'

'OK.' I picked up the key. 'Thanks.'

'My pleasure. And look—I'll order you a cab, company account.'

'Thanks.'

*   *   *

The flat was functional, only marginally more personal than the office. If I'd been hoping for a bit of a snoop I was disappointed. It was about half the size of mine at Cliff Mansions and the kitchen was just a slot. There were lots of microwave meals in the freezer, but there was salad in the fridge and a bowl of apples on the table in the living room. It was furnished and fitted in an unexceptionable, colour-co-ordinated way. I guessed everything had

264

been bought in a single afternoon.

I didn't pry in drawers, I didn't want to. And interestingly there were no photographs here. He obviously wasn't going to have us all beaming from the dressing table when he and Julia were on the job—and why would he need a picture of her when he was seeing her all the time?

The one thing I needed was bread—drink always brought on a compulsion to carbo-load, and Ian's Kensington creams felt as if they were bobbing about whole and undigested on my own personal wine lake ... I looked for a bread bin, but there was none. There was a garlic loaf in the freezer but defrosting that seemed a bit extreme. No bananas, either. However, he did have a large storage jar full of the knobbly mixed cereal that looked as though someone had smashed a couple of dozen flapjacks with a hammer. I ate several handfuls, and then went to lie down.

Lying down, like fresh air, is one of those things you think you need when you're drunk, but which serves to bring home the reality of your condition in the most unpleasant ways. As soon as my head hit Ian's well-laundered pillow I fell into something, but it wasn't sleep; more like a parallel universe of gross discomfort. I swooped, I spun, I looped the loop, with my stomach following half a turn behind. I felt hot, and my mouth was dry, but I couldn't clamber back into that state of full consciousness necessary to fetch a glass of water. My head teemed with fretful images of Ben, Sabine and Ian all doing strange things like riding horses and dancing the gavotte (there had recently been a Jane Austen adaptation on BBC1). The headache from hell rumbled like distant thunder in the background, ready to burst over me the moment I attempted anything rash, like taking my head off the pillow.

When I eventually did so, wakefulness gave me the mauling I so richly deserved. The headache, the nausea, the giddiness and the dehydration were worse than in my sick fancies, and my earlier depression returned with the force of a piano falling down stairs.

To make things worse, for a long moment I had no idea where I was, or even in which part of the country. It was almost dark, and until I fixed on the rattle of rain and the hiss of traffic on wet streets I thought it was the middle of the night. I peered at my watch: it was twenty to six, quite late enough. The thunder, I now discovered, had not been a figment of my imagination—it was right overhead, and the next clap—dear God!—sent darts of lightning right through my head.

Very slowly, creeping like a nonogenarian and holding the walls where possible, I made my way into the bathroom. I couldn't bear to turn on the light, so felt my way to the basin and leaned over the cold tap. I took a few gulps and splashed my face. I didn't bother fumbling for a towel, I liked the feel of the water and wanted to let it dry there. I couldn't see a medicine cabinet, but somewhere, surely, there must be Ian's store of everyday medication—aspirins and indigestion tablets, perhaps even those fizzy things for hangovers . . . I would go back and lie down again, propped up on the pillows this time, and gather enough strength for a proper, fully-lit foray in ten minutes or so . . .

So it was that I was creeping back in the semi-darkness, barefoot and with my waistband undone, my hair standing on end and water dripping from my face, when the door of the flat opened and there, silhouetted in a shaft of light that showed me up to full advantage, was Julia.

'Good Lord,' she said. 'I'm so sorry.'

*   *   *

Not half as sorry as I was.

She didn't put a foot wrong, of course. Just as I recognised her, so she at once recognised me, which was a little disheartening given the state I was in. She said this was only a pit stop, I said I was just going, and then she stood her wet umbrella outside the door and withdrew to the living room while I dragged myself together.

When I came back she was sitting with her coat still on, eating an apple and watching the *Six o'clock News*. A perfectly judged cocktail of messages—I am at home here, but I am only passing through, I am a fact but not a threat. She needn't have worried. Recent events had done her a great favour—in the space of a day she had moved several places down the anxiety listings, and at this moment I felt too ill for anything but flight.

'Right, I'm off.'

She put down her apple core and got up, dusting her hands. 'Do you have an umbrella?'

'No, but I'll get a cab.'

'You'll be lucky,' she said, 'in this. No, you just might on the corner here—they drop off at the hotel.'

'I'll be alright.'

I went to the front door, and she followed me. Then we both began to speak at the same time.

'I'm sorry I—'

'I do hope you—'

'Sorry.'

'I'm pleased we've met,' she said. 'It's been something I wanted but didn't know how to bring about. Perhaps this was the only way it was going to happen.'

'Yes.'

'Good-bye then. And all the best.'

'Thank you.'

I went out, and she closed the door quietly behind me.

*　　　*　　　*

I should have gone straight to Victoria and caught the next train home. The trouble was I didn't want to go back to my empty flat where the only company would be problems that I was in no state to solve.

A cab pulled up right next to me which put me on the spot. I was in its sheltering warmth before I'd even decided where I was going.

The driver assessed me in the rearview mirror. 'Round the block, then?'

'Um—no, hang on . . .' I clasped my brow. I could actually feel the throb of my head beating under my hand. To hell with it. Back there in Ian's flat I had just proved, hadn't I, that this was the perfect condition in which to negotiate delicate social situations.

'Do you know Troughtons Hotel in Vane Street?' I asked.

He clicked his teeth cheerily. 'Retreat of the rich and famous.'

It didn't look anything much, which convinced me he was probably right. The utter discretion of the outside of Troughtons didn't even run to declaring itself a hotel. Once I'd passed through the tall and solid outer door there was a small brass plate in the hushed lobby between that and the swing door, but even then the word 'Hotel' didn't appear. The foyer, from which polished oak stairs spiralled up into dimly-lit upper reaches contained only one gigantic carved chair and a highly polished table with a vase of lilies. However, a man in a black jacket and pinstripes appeared as if by magic and asked in a beautifully-modulated Scottish voice what he could do for me.

'I believe there's a Mr Charles McNally staying here? I wondered if he was in.'

'He is here, yes,' said the man. 'Is he expecting you?'

'He said to drop in. My name's Eve Piercy.'

'Fine, Mrs Piercy, he's in two-thirteen, the lift is round the corner. I'll tell him you're on your way.'

'Thank you.'

The upper storeys of hotels are always quiet, and a little dreamlike, but the second floor of Troughtons was positively eery. If I hadn't had someone else's word for it I'd have thought there was only me in the entire building.

I found number two thirteen, but as I raised my hand to knock the door opened.

Charles McNally was barefoot, in grey joggers and a frayed jumper. His hair was sticking up on one side as though he'd been lying on it. A black

269

and white film flickered on television in the middle distance.

'Eve, are you ever seeing nature in the raw . . . ! Come in, come in, sorry about the mess, come on . . .'

He walked ahead of me into the suite—it was vast—and zapped the television. There were clothes scattered everywhere, papers all over the table, a room service tray loaded with plates on the floor. From the pelmet of the smoke-grey ceiling-to-floor curtains hung a lifesize toy gibbon in fluffy banana yellow.

My host scratched the back of his head, grinning anxiously. 'This is the best surprise, Eve, but if you'd have rung I could have spared you all this.'

'It was a spur of the moment decision. And it doesn't matter.'

Now what? I wondered. I'd pictured ordered calm, a stately bout of verbal fencing, drinks in the bar (tomato juice for me), the flash of the gold Amex, the offer of dinner duly declined, and a lift to the station. A grown-up, self-affirming encounter that would send me back to Littelsea feeling rather less like Bagwoman and more able to adopt a sophisticated overview of my troubles.

'Sit down, please.'

'Thanks.'

Instead of which—I looked around me—it looked as if I'd linked up with my very own Bagman.

'Don't go away,' he exhorted, walking backwards and holding out his hand as if I were an apparition. 'I'll be right back.'

I sat there and waited, and wished I hadn't come. The suite had a distinctive smell, not

270

unpleasant but familiar and evocative. I sniffed. I knew who I was reminded of: Ben. Oh God, I thought, he's pigging it, I feel like death, this is the worst mistake of my life.

He came back in, having put on some Nikes, and a blue polo shirt instead of the jumper. He had also, I thought rather touchingly, put water on his hair but the measure had been only partially successful and the odd strand was continuing to stick straight up.

'I have to tell you,' he said ruefully, 'that you look great.'

'Really?' I couldn't even remember what I'd put on, the early morning when I'd done so was like another life. 'Oh, this.'

'It suits you, really. Now what would you like Eve? I'm afraid my body clock's shot to pieces, where've we got to? Afternoon tea or what?'

'Well,' I said cautiously, 'it's about quarter past seven, I'm really on my way home—'

'But you have to eat. Shall we do that?'

'No!' I said, rather too sharply. 'No, thanks, to be honest I'm feeling a little delicate today.'

'Right,' he said, 'I know what we both need. Brandy and soda, plenty of ice.'

'I'm not sure——'

'Trust me.'

He went to the mini-bar—it was behind panelling, and very far from mini—and produced whopping drinks in heavy cut-glass tumblers. I took an extremely tentative sip but to my surprise the ice-and-fire slipped down rather well, and I took another.

He sat down on the sofa and raised his glass. 'Cheers, Eve. This is so great.'

271

It wasn't, and we both knew it. If it was not what I'd had in mind in my befogged state outside Ian's building, how much less it must be what he'd been thinking of when he rang me.

'Cheers.'

'Let me get rid of this crap.' He got up again and went to put the tray outside the door. Without the big suit, the big car, the clouds of oil-man glory he seemed not just smaller, but younger. The balance of confidence was more evenly distributed in spite of my indisposition.

'I haven't been out of this place all day,' he told me, returning to the sofa, 'and I guess it shows.'

'Have you found anywhere to live yet?'

'I keep looking at places, but the thought of buying one frightens the shit out of me.'

'You've got somewhere in the States?'

He shook his head. 'A rented apartment. To be frank I wouldn't mind staying here. I love hotels. They're cosy. You can be alone but not lonely, I like that.'

'I hate them,' I said. 'Especially on my own. After one night they give me shortness of breath.'

'But you stayed with your daughter,' he reminded me.

'That was a holiday. And she was around.'

'I don't get out enough,' he said, 'I'm a bum. Who said travel broadens the mind? All I do when I travel is work and make an in-depth study of the local television.'

I thought how strange that Charles McNally, globetrotting bachelor and fearless troubleshooter should like hotels because they made him feel safe. I pictured him jetting into exotic places all over the world and rushing to his room to muss the bed, test the TV, check the towelling robe . . . It was bizarre.

'How are your family?' he asked. 'No actually I mean your son, because I do bump into your daughter from time to time.'

Go with that, I thought. 'Yes, she said.'

'She's a smart girl, Mel.'

'I've always thought so.' The fact that he so readily remembered her name made me think this wasn't just flannel.

'And your son?'

'He's fine. I don't see much of him.'

'New romance keeping him busy, huh?' I felt my stomach lurch, and he added: 'Our mutual friend Martin Drage said your boy was dating his daughter. I remember they looked good together at that party . . . we were watching from the terrace?'

'Oh, yes—yes.'

'Lucky kids.'

'Yes.'

Could I never get away from it? I felt absolutely dog-tired. Charles, too, seemed to have slipped into a reverie. The sleeping giant of good manners heaved beneath my exhaustion.

'What were you watching on telly?' I asked.

'*Whistle Down the Wind*, do you know it?'

'I remember it.'

'It's absolutely one of my all-time favourites, a classic. It's showing on the in-house channel. Those child actors were just so great.'

'Hayley Mills.'

'That's right. She could break your heart in that movie.'

I could hardly believe we were having this conversation, and that he was displaying this almost childish enthusiasm for an old, English, black and

273

white film.

I nodded at the screen. 'Don't let me stop you.'

'Oh for goodness' sake, Eve . . . You didn't come all this way to watch TV.'

And what exactly, I wondered, had I come all this way for?

I shrugged. 'Go on. I'd like to see a bit of it—it'd be nostalgic.'

'OK, if you say so.'

He switched it on. There was the windswept northern landscape, the children in their belted gabardine macs and wellies, Hayley's pale, big-eyed face as she talked to the convict in the barn, the man they believed to be Jesus . . . There was that haunting music . . .

*   *   *

I don't know which of us fell asleep first, but I was the first to wake up. The film had finished and the in-house listings were on the screen. I didn't move to turn it off because I didn't want to wake Charles McNally, who was dead to the world. He lay on his stomach on the sofa with one hand trailing on the carpet. He hadn't been lying down the last time I looked, so he must have watched me drift off and then made himself comfortable. Oh God, had my mouth dropped open? Had I snored? Shit— dribbled?

He sighed heavily and I thought he was going to wake up, but he only turned his head the other way. What a paradigm of middle-aged social interaction in the nineties we were—spark out in front of the box.

I looked around the suite and experienced a

momentary itch to tidy up. But this after all was a five-star hotel 'retreat to the rich and famous' as the taxi driver had said. Gingerly I picked up my bag off the floor, found a biro and a blank page at the back of my diary, and considered carefully what to write. No point in apologising too profusely for falling asleep, since he'd done the same; not much point either in thanking him fulsomely for allowing me to watch television amongst his dirty washing.

In the end I put: 'Nice to see you, take care of yourself, Yours, Eve.'

He didn't move a muscle as I placed the note beneath the remote control on the arm of the sofa, and the door made no sound as I closed it behind me.

*   *   *

I bought a first-class ticket back to Littelsea, so I could sit on my own and in comfort. I wondered how on earth I was going to get the car back. Since calling Ben was out of the question, even if I'd had Nozz's number, I'd have to get a taxi the other end as well. When I got there there were no cabs waiting and I had to call for one. The driver was insinuating and the price was extortionate.

There were four messages on the answering machine. The first wasn't for me: 'This is a message for Ben, from Sophie. Where are you? Not that long till I go, so give us a ring—OK? Bye for now.'

The next two were both from Sabine, at first cool. 'Eve, it's Sabine. It would be nice to see you.' The second was almost peremptory. 'This is Sabine for Eve. Give me a ring when you get in.'

The fourth message was no more than a short

silence—I guessed Sabine again, losing patience. Well let her sweat, I thought, and left the machine on. The phone rang twice more, once as I was taking my make-up off and again just before I plunged into sleep, but on neither occasion did I hear a voice other than my son's.

*   *   *

I didn't sleep late next morning—habit I suppose—but I did lie in bed for ages, unable to face another round of crisis management. The voice of common sense told me that I should get back into work and re-impose a structure on my life, but it might as well have recommended an assault on K2.

I finally broke cover at ten. I had a bath and put on jeans and a T-shirt, which felt weird on a weekday morning. The latter of the two calls had been from a London number that I didn't recognise. It was a sunny morning and I went out on to the balcony. Brave and calm, I thought—but when the doorbell rang it made me jump so much that I slopped coffee on myself.

'Hello?'

'Mrs Eve Piercy?'

'Yes.'

'Interflora for you.'

It was very nearly the whole of Interflora for me. The little man from our local branch looked like a floribunda Burnham Wood.

'Hope you've got enough vases.'

There were four dozen yellow roses, I counted as I put them in the bath. Then I took the card back on to the balcony.

'These can't possibly say how sorry I am, but I

hope they're pretty. I'll call when I feel less like a jerk and an idiot. Charles.'

Like an idiot, I cried.

CHAPTER FOURTEEN

Later that morning I forced myself to go into Ben's room. It was like World War Three as usual and, also as usual, the door was open. Compared with the obsessive secrecy of his teenage years I usually found this openness touching, but today it seemed bitterly ironic. I opened the bottom of the sash window as far as it would go and went at the room like a thing possessed. I was going to bring it back under my control. This room was part of my flat, dammit, and as such it was my right to have it decent.

I picked up all the clothes and hurled them on to the landing. I'd wash the lot but by God I wasn't going to be too fussy about looking at labels. Then I stripped the bed and threw the sheets on the pile as well, Algy with them. I fetched a binbag and filled it in record time: I didn't waste time on the decision-making process, anything that wasn't instantly recognisable as something else I designated rubbish. Everything that was something else I stuffed in the drawers or the wardrobe. I draped the duvet and the bedside rug out of the window. I hoovered and wiped and polished and went round the edges of the window frame with an old toothbrush. I replaced the rug and put clean sheets on the bed. For a simple domestic operation it felt amazingly like vandalism.

On second thoughts I rescued Algy from the tangle of dirty sheets and submerged him in a tepid solution of handwash in the kitchen sink. His beady eyes stared up at me through the scummy foam like Glenn Close at the end of *Fatal Attraction*.

I found some vases and put the roses on every available surface. I wondered what the significance of yellow was. Ribbons I knew, but roses ...? Perhaps it was just an avoidance of red, or pink, the colours of romance. It was a very long time since I'd received flowers from anyone but my husband, and I wished I could have taken more pleasure from them. But it had been such a strange, unsatisfactory meeting, and now that I was back, with the enormity of Ben's actions hanging over me, I could see how impossible it was for Charles McNally to understand the smallest thing about my life. We were on separate planets, and only red wine and jealousy had prompted me so unwisely to visit his.

I was just stuffing the cut-off ends of the roses in the swingbin when the doorbell rang again.

'Mrs Piercy—it's Anthea.'

'Who?'

'Anthea—from Mr Piercy's office?'

'Anthea!'

I buzzed the door open and went down to meet her. We caught up with one another on the second landing, where she was taking a breather.

'Golly, you are high up ...!'

'I'm sorry. Come and have a coffee.'

'No, marvellous, really, you must be so fit ...! Look—I don't want to disturb you, I wasn't really expecting you to be in, I was going to put a note through the door, but then I thought I might as well—oh my goodness!'

'What are you doing down here?'

'I brought your car back.'

I was mortified. 'Anthea, you didn't! But it's miles, I feel so awful!'

She waved a hand, too breathless to speak as we went in. 'No . . . honestly . . .'

'How did you start it? I've got the key.'

'Luckily Mr Piercy's still got one on his keyring. I've got it here to give back to you . . .' She handed it to me.

'This really is very kind of you, I don't know what to say.'

'Please, I enjoy driving, and I was going the opposite way to all the traffic. Mr Piercy said you'd be lost without it, and I'm being thoroughly compensated, he's given me the day off.'

'Heavens, I should hope so.'

As I filled the kettle, she asked: 'Do you mind if I call a cab to take me back to the station?'

'I'll give you a lift, it's the least I can do.'

'It's on the company, Mr Piercy was most insistent.'

'Well if you're sure . . . The phone's in the sitting room—there's a taxi number on the pad.'

In a couple of minutes she came back in and I handed her her coffee.

'Thanks, no sugar thanks. He'll be here in about ten minutes. What absolutely gorgeous roses everywhere.'

'Aren't they?' We leaned back on the worktops. 'They just arrived this morning.'

'So lovely—from an admirer?'

The charming candour of this question probably influenced my answer.

'Yes,' I said, 'I think they may be.'
'Lovely,' said Anthea again. 'Lucky you.'

*   *   *

What I needed was someone from my own planet to dump on. My glimpse of the Chatsworths lunching *en famille* at The Esplanade made me think that their early return from holiday might have something to do with the boys. It wouldn't—couldn't—be in the same league as our situation, but there was much to be said for a trouble shared, and as the mother of sons Ronnie would at least be entirely sympathetic.

The strangeness of being around the flat on a weekday morning reminded me that if I was going to take any more time I was going to have to get a doctor's note. I rang the surgery and made an appointment with Dr Edworth, the only woman in the practice, for early afternoon, after which I resolved to go and call on Ronnie. On both these counts I was enormously grateful to have the car back, and I called Ian to say so.

'My pleasure,' he said. 'I knew Anthea wouldn't mind, she'd much rather be buzzing about the place than stuck here with me.'

In one of those odd coincidences I passed Dennis driving out of the health centre car park as I drove in. He was in his business suit, and looking preoccupied: he didn't see me. Or at least I hoped he didn't, and that he wasn't just cutting me—so jumpy was I that I expected hourly to be stoned in the street. In the waiting room, staring at long-obsolete pictures of a footballer's wedding, I assured myself that I was definitely not in the best

280

of health. I was stressed, and that combined with my time of life—well, I did need a few days off.

Dr Edworth was anyway a famously soft touch, who tended to accept patients' own diagnosis.

'No other problems?' she asked, having recommended rest and a course of Vitamin B Complex. 'No new aches or pains?'

'No . . .' I was tempted, but restrained myself. Perhaps she'd heard anyway. 'No.'

She glanced at my notes. 'It's about time you came along to the well-woman clinic for a checkup, do you think you could manage that?'

'Yes, of course.'

She scribbled the dates of the next few clinics on a card and gave it to me. 'I advise a few days of fresh air and fun.'

My smile must have looked like a gargoyle's grimace.

*   *   *

Somewhat to my surprise, Philip answered the door.

'Yes, she is—hang on.' He went to the foot of the stairs and called up: 'Mum! It's Eve!'

'Coming . . .'

'Come on in,' said Philip. We hung about in the hall.

'I thought you were in Turkey,' I said.

'I was, but cash was running out, and Mum wasn't well . . .'

'Did you have a good time?'

'Oh, I tell you . . .' He brightened up. 'Brilliant. I want to go back.'

'I've never been.'

'You should, really. I thought everyone did in the

281

sixties.'

'I've led a very sheltered life,' I said, not joking, and he didn't smile.

'How's Ben? Haven't seen him in ages.'

My heart hammered. 'Haven't you?'

'No—must be oh, I dunno. Ages.'

'He's been around.'

'But around the Drages, yeah? That Sophie's got a lot to answer for.' My relief was echoed by his as Ronnie came down the stairs. 'Here she is. See you.'

'Ronnie,' I said, 'you look wonderful.'

She was slim and luminous in jeans and a loose aquamarine velvet shirt. 'You like? I don't think of myself as a jeans kind of person but I decided to break out, and Dennis bought me the shirt in France.'

'I just saw Dennis at the surgery, but he didn't see me.'

'He was picking up a prescription. You're not ill are you?'

'Not really—but not malingering either.'

We went and sat in the drawing room. Philip put his head in: 'Kettle's on.'

'Eve?'

'No thanks.'

The moment he'd gone I had to unburden myself. I think what I most dreaded was that she might already know or, worse, have heard something and not believed it. But her reaction of shock and dismay was the first to echo my own and so bring me real comfort.

'Oh, Eve—that's terrible, I am so, so sorry. You poor thing, what must you have been going through?'

'Hell. Absolute hell.'

'What on earth was Sabine thinking of?'

I shrugged. 'There aren't any excuses, Ronnie. She didn't even pretend to make any. I know it sounds old-fashioned, but the only word for it is brazen.'

Ronnie shook her head. 'It is extraordinary. Poor Martin—do you think he knows?'

'I've no idea. I dread meeting him, Ronnie. I dread meeting anyone—I feel the whole town is talking about it.'

'No, I'm sure they're not,' she said firmly. 'This is the first I've heard of it, unless the boys are being quite uncharacteristically discreet—what's Ben saying?'

'Not much. He's incredibly hostile and defiant. When I confronted him he treated me as though I were the person who'd done something wrong.'

'Poor Eve. You don't need it.' Ronnie leaned forward and held out her hand to me. I took it. Hers was very smooth, and cool as she gave mine a quick squeeze. Her kindness, her voice, her touch, all did for me.

'He's left,' I gasped, before breaking into wracking sobs. 'He just walked out ... Oh God, Ronnie, what am I going to do ...?'

To her eternal credit she didn't answer that question. All she did was to come and sit on the arm of the chair and put her arm round my shoulders and stroke my hair. Dimly, through the maelstrom of sobs, I heard Philip's voice and felt her wave him away. I was making a spectacle of myself but I couldn't stop and Ronnie didn't suggest that I should. All she did when I began to run out of steam was to get up and fetch us both a brimming schooner of Amontillado.

'Best thing at this time of day,' she said, returning to her chair.

'Thank you Ronnie,' I sniffed. 'You're a pal.'

'I should certainly hope so.'

'What must Philip think?'

'That you're upset. Don't worry, he's very used to emotional scenes. Look,' she pondered her rings for a moment, 'what's the worst that can happen?'

I knew, because she had already shown me, that she understood my feelings, otherwise I might have suspected her of making light of them. As it was I gave the question serious consideration.

'I don't know. At the moment I feel this is it.'

'Yes, of course. But truthfully, Eve, it isn't. What is it you're deep down afraid of?'

'I suppose . . . I suppose I'm afraid of losing Ben. I've already lost Sabine as a friend, and I may lose others, but for Ben to do this and then to go off, hating me . . . It's more than I can bear. It's as if the whole of my life's exploded in front of my eyes.'

'Well,' Ronnie got up to fetch the decanter. 'If it's Ben hating you you're afraid of, my humble opinion is that it's not going to happen.'

I watched as she topped up my glass. 'It already has.'

'Nonsense.' She filled hers and sat down again with the decanter on the table next to her. 'Eve, you *know* that's not true. If ever a son loved his mother it's your Ben, it's plain for all to see.'

'But he was so cold—he stormed out—you should have heard the things he said.'

'Yes, but he's young and you know what they say about the best form of defence. Have you seen him since then?'

'No. And there hasn't been a phone call, a message—nothing.'

'Do you know where he is?'

'I know who he's with, but not the address or number.'

'I'm sure we can find out. Shall we? Then you could contact him.'

She had stopped me in my tracks as surely as if I'd walked into a lamp post.

'Isn't it up to him to contact me?'

'Probably, but do they ever? And I suppose his life is upside down, too. Climbing down's a bit of a bugger at the best of times, and they have further to climb from at that age, don't they?'

'Maybe I will,' I muttered.

Ronnie leaned forward again, her glass cradled in her hands. 'Eve, you probably don't want to hear this at this precise moment, but I really must say it.'

I looked at her warily. 'Go on.'

'It's just that Ben is such a lovely chap. You're very lucky. He may have done something very, very stupid and rash, but that doesn't make him wicked. He's still a kind, affectionate, thoroughly nice boy—'

'Adorable, Sabine says.'

'Well . . .' Ronnie smiled ruefully, 'she's right.'

'I'm not going to make excuses for them.'

'Nor me. Nor me. But keep on thinking the best of Ben—he does you so much credit, Eve. This isn't true colours, it's a lapse.'

'Christ! If this is a lapse I hope I don't live to see the full-blown fall from grace!'

'You probably will, of course you will. I rather envy you.' She sounded not smug, but slightly wistful. I realised I had talked about nothing but

285

myself since arriving three quarters of an hour ago.

'I'm sorry, Ronnie. How was the holiday? I got your postcard but I think you'd already got back. It looked lovely.'

'It was, as far as it went.'

'And then you were ill?'

'Yes—I liked that lovely virus so much I asked it to stay. To be honest I didn't feel too bad, but it's awfully inconvenient to be running all the time, and the stuff the French doctor prescribed gave me a reaction, so when my head wasn't over the basin, my bottom was over the loo . . . !'

'That really is dire,' I agreed, but she was so droll that I had to laugh with her. 'What rotten luck.'

'It was, but it couldn't be helped. Anyway, I expect we'll get away later in the year.'

'And you've shaken it off now.'

'Oh yes—I've got to have a few tests and whatnot, which means no tennis but I'm perfectly optimistic.'

'Tests?'

She sighed and grimaced. 'You know what medicos are like about the runs, especially the foreign sort—it's into the Lublijanka forthwith to have telescopes inserted where no telescope should ever go.'

I had to admit I didn't know, but we were at least both laughing as we went into the hall. By the front door Ronnie put her hands on my shoulders.

'You see,' she said, kissing me on both cheeks. 'There is life after scandal.'

*   *   *

Trying not to think too hard about what I was

286

doing I went back through town. I told myself that if I saw a parking space in the street I would use it. If not, then it wasn't meant to be. I think that subconsciously I was relying on the fact that there were never any non-carpark spaces in town.

Today, of course, there were. It was late afternoon, the lull between the day shoppers and the after-work crowd. I told myself I'd missed the first one, but the next was in a side road between the Royal Mail sorting office and the mall containing HMV. Not just one either, but quite a little block of spaces, a direct challenge to my excuse-making abilities.

I left the car and approached HMV cautiously. I wanted to see Ben before he saw me, to try and gauge his mood and manner. But he must have been in the stock room, or taking a break, there was no sign of him.

I went in, and approached Nozz, who was on the till.

'Afternoon, madam,' he said. 'Latest from Boyzone?

'Is he about?'

'Don't tell me he didn't tell you.' Nozz shook his head with heavily ironic disbelief.

'Tell me what?'

'Sorry to be the harbinger of bad tidings.'

'Nozz—what?'

'He's left—more precisely he was asked to leave.'

'He got the sack?' I felt not so much dismay as a leaden acceptance of the inevitable.

Nozz assumed a sympathetic expression. ' 'Fraid so. It was a really bum rap, because he could sell anything, but there've been a few times recently when he hasn't showed—' Nozz shrugged—'it was one too many.'

'And the long lunch hours . . .' I murmured, more or less to myself.

'How did you know about those?'

'You told me.'

'Right . . .'

'OK,' I said, 'thanks Nozz. I don't suppose you know where he is, do you? I would like to speak to him.'

'You could try my place.'

'Thanks.'

'Do you know where I am?'

'I don't actually.'

Without the slightest hesitation Nozz wrote his address and phone number on the back of a receipt slip, and handed it to me. I took heart from this—friends had clearly not been sworn to silence, nor been told to treat me like a leper. But there was something I still didn't know.

'Nozz . . . You don't have any idea why he was failing to turn up, do you?'

'Not a clue.'

I chose my words carefully. 'It doesn't have anything to do with his new relationship does it?'

Nozz shrugged. 'I seriously doubt it. I mean you know Ben, that's not his style.'

'No, I suppose not.'

'And Sophie never struck me as the type—not always up for it, like Pearl. She was out all day checking cows for the first signs of madness. No, if you ask me he just got bored with this place.'

In recent days I'd become super-sensitive to evasions and equivocation. I was a human lie-detector, but I could discern nothing in Nozz's

288

voice or look to indicate that he was being anything but honest.

'Oh well,' I said. 'Never mind. It was never exactly brain surgery, was it?'

'If it was, I wouldn't be doing it.' He put up a hand to dismiss my apology. 'It's alright, I know what you're saying.'

*　　　*　　　*

I located Nozz's flat quite easily—it was the ground floor of a red-brick Edwardian semi near the station—but having found it my resolve deserted me. The restraints of the workplace would have prevented us having a scene. Here there would be no such restraints. By turning up on the doorstep of his retreat I would be wrongfooting him, albeit unintentionally, and to the turmoil of his private life would now be added the humiliation of the sack. As I sat in the car and stared at the front of the house, and the small bay window, partly obscured by laurel, the door opened and Ben came out.

He looked perfectly normal and composed. I don't know what I'd expected—after all, I too was in emotional uproar, but my appearance was much the same as usual. He walked a few yards and then paused, felt in his pocket, and took out his keys. Now I spotted the VW, parked on his side, but facing me. He was going to get in and drive away, right past me. If he spotted me and I hadn't made myself known it would look as if I'd been sitting here spying on him.

I got out and called his name. He was in the process of unlocking the door, and though he

289

didn't look up I sensed that he had heard me. I began to cross the road.

'Ben!'

He got into the driver's seat and slammed the door. I began walking—almost running—up the pavement towards him.

'Ben . . . ?'

There was now no doubt that he was ignoring me, his eyes focused quite unnecessarily on the key as he turned it in the ignition. I reached the car and knocked frantically on the window. The car's small engine thrummed into noisy life.

'Ben, please!'

He turned away from me, checking the street behind over his shoulder as he pulled out. I was left standing on the kerb with tears of pain and anger running down my face.

No more, I told myself as I rushed back to the car to hide my humiliation . . . No more, as I wiped my cheeks and blew my nose . . . No more! It was intolerable. I remembered something about the sharp tooth of a child's ingratitude. Let him come to me when he ran out of cash, when Martin punched him on the nose, when Sabine, for God's sake, dumped him, as she surely would—let him just come crawling to me and we'd see who the grown-up was!

*   *   *

Clive rang up just as I was going to bed—he wasn't late, but I was early.

'Eve—I hope I'm not disturbing you.'

'Not at all, I'm standing here in my Wincyette trying to decide between tea and cocoa.'

290

'Ah, hah ...' he laughed nervously, not sure whether I was joking, or serious, or irritated. 'Well look, I won't keep you—'

'I've sat down now.'

'This is a longshot, but I wonder if you'd care to come to a concert at the Melrose Hall on Friday.'

I only hesitated for a split second, but he jumped in. 'I'm not much of a concert-goer myself, but I've been given these tickets by a colleague whose cousin is singing in it, and it's a charity do, so I ought to show willing. I really would like some congenial company, someone who knows me well enough to give me a poke in the ribs if I fall asleep.'

He was trying in his donnish way to reassure me that this wasn't a date. 'Thank you,' I said, 'I'd like to.'

'Oh good, that is a relief. It's snippets of this and that as far as I can make out. My friend's cousin is a kind of middle-rank soprano—we haven't heard of her but she gets plenty of work I gather.'

'Clive, I haven't heard of anyone anyway.'

'Shall I see you at the Melrose Hall at about seven, then?'

'I'll be there.'

I plumped for the cocoa, and looked in on Ben's room on my way to bed. Its awful neatness stabbed my heart. On the smooth, plump pillow sat Algy in all his handwashed, tumble-dried glory, his stubby arms and legs outstretched in an empty embrace.

*　　　*　　　*

The next day, Thursday, I bit the bullet and returned Sabine's call. To my horror—it was ten a.m.—the phone was answered by Martin. At the

291

sound of his voice I went hot and cold, and it didn't get any better.

'Eve—can't stop I'm on my way out. Which one do you want?'

'I'm sorry?'

'Who do you want—my wife or your son?'

All the breath went out of me for a moment, snatched away by this dizzying switchback of relief and shock.

'Eve?'

'I didn't know Ben was there.'

'Parents know nothing, I've learnt that—hang on, here's Sabine.'

The receiver the other end was stifled for a moment and then Sabine's voice said 'Hello Eve.'

'I'm returning your call, but this is obviously a bad moment,' I said with icy sarcasm.

'Yes, why don't we have lunch or something?'

'I can't believe Ben's actually there, as we speak, what the hell is going on?'

'I tell you what, shall I come down and meet you outside your office at twelve?'

'I'm not at the office. Come to the flat.'

'I shall. *A tout à l'heure.*'

*　　　*　　　*

She arrived on the dot, and ran up the stairs with light, quick steps. She wore cream jeans and a pink sweatshirt and her hair had been cut spectacularly, statement-making short.

I marched ahead of her into the sitting room and faced her with my arms folded.

'What was Ben doing there?'

'He came to see Sophie.' My expression must

have told her what I thought of that, for she added: 'He's going up north with her for a few days.'

That hurt so much I had to turn away. With my back to her I said: 'You know he lost his job.'

'Yes, that was unfortunate, but he'll get another, better one. He's a bright boy.'

She was unbelievable.

'And what about Martin? He obviously doesn't know anything yet.'

'No,' she said, 'and what he does not know will not hurt him.' There was a warning note in her voice.

'I'm not going to say anything.'

'Good heavens, I never dreamed that you would, Eve. You are far too sophisticated to do anything so stupid.'

'No I'm not!' I snapped. 'And there would be nothing stupid about telling Martin. It simply isn't my place to do it.'

'Precisely.' She looked around. 'May I sit down?'

'If you want.'

She sat on the sofa. I continued to stand there, looking down at her, but instead of feeling superior I felt like an adolescent miscreant up before the beak.

'Don't worry,' she said, 'I didn't mean all that about lunch.'

'Of course not, you only said it because Martin was there.'

She let this pass. Her slim hands rested on her knees, fingers loosely linked, wrists together as though caught in handcuffs.

'The reason I rang,' she said, 'is because I want you to know that we are trying to work things out.'

'That's simple,' I said bitterly. 'Stop.'

293

'It's not simple, it is complicated,' she went on as though I hadn't spoken. 'And we are doing our best. Ben will be away for a little while and Martin and I will have some time together. We shall see.'

'What about me?' I asked. 'What role do you see for your boyfriend's mother in all of this?'

She looked up at me steadily. 'It's not my business to tell you what your role should be, Eve.'

'But you want me to keep quiet about it.'

'I don't see the need to cause unnecessary pain.'

This was too much. 'Sabine, if you could only hear yourself! The hypocrisy of it! The only person you're trying to protect is yourself!'

'Not the only one. But I am frightened.'

'Good. You should be.'

'I'll go.' She got up. 'You have some beautiful flowers.'

I didn't answer. With her hand on the front door latch she said: 'Charles McNally may be coming down for the weekend. He mentioned he especially wanted to see you.'

'He has my telephone number.'

'Then I'm sure you'll be hearing from him.'

When I closed the door after her I was shaking. Ben had gone 'up north' and I was the last to know. The notion that she had any power to influence my relationship—if it could be called that—with Charles McNally sickened me. As did her composure, her restraint, her queenly refusal to apologise—I felt that until that moment I'd never known what it was to hate someone.

*   *   *

On Friday I decided I couldn't face sitting through

294

a concert with Clive. I even got as far as picking up the phone, but he didn't answer, and the bleeps for 'Call Waiting' made me replace the receiver—it might be Ben.

But it was Desma, asking about tennis.

'I know Ronnie can't,' she said. 'She goes in for those tests on Sunday. But what about Sabine?'

'She can't either.'

'So shall we have another singles—I really enjoyed it.'

'Oh Desma, I don't know, I've been a bit down myself this week—'

'It might be just what you need, then.'

'I don't know . . .'

'Look, let's say we'll do usual time and place and if you really can't face it give me a buzz, OK?'

Placed in an opt-out position I knew that I would probably go. The last thing I felt like was playing tennis, I felt drained and exhausted, but if Charles McNally was going to be around at the weekend I wished to appear to have at least some semblance of a life. Falling asleep in front of the TV in a hotel room could in his case be attributed to a high-octane job—I had no such excuse.

For the same reason I did not, in the end, cry off the concert with Clive. A Friday night in on my own, feeling wretched about Ben, was not a recipe for self-esteem. And if Charles were to arrive tonight I wanted Sabine to find out that I was not as available as she might imagine.

*   *   *

As it turned out, neither concert nor tennis was quite the simple time-filler I'd anticipated. Clive

295

was in ebullient form and looking, if not unrecognisable, then very definitely a new man. He told me he'd lost half a stone, but it looked more because of a marked redistribution; he'd had his trademark whispy hair cut short which made him appear less bald; and his grappling with the bugbear exercise had given him an increased air of confidence. He showed not the slightest sign of falling asleep in the concert, which was accessibly tuneful, and he was cheerful and amusing over interval drinks.

'This is so jolly, Eve—we should do it more often.'

'We should.'

'After all, you and I are in a similarly semi-detached state. Except, of course,' he added hastily, 'I realise that you are moving towards full detachment, whereas I am pulled in the opposite direction—still, you know what I mean.'

I remembered what Helen had told me at our last meeting, about the distant train.

'Have you and Helen spoken at all recently?'

'No, but I'm mustering my forces.'

'I can see that!'

'Dear Eve . . .' He blushed, he was such a nice man. 'No, since getting more of a grip of myself I have realised that there is nothing, absolutely nothing less alluring than self-pity. All that whining, dear Lord . . .!' He shuddered. 'I was without doubt what the students call a sad bastard.'

We laughed. 'If you were, it was with some justification.'

'Never mind, enough is enough. The next time I see Helen I shall, I hope, be rather better company.'

I had no doubt of it. In spite of everything, it was a happy evening and I slept better than I had in several days.

*   *   *

I woke up feeling that tennis might not be completely out of the question, but Desma was at her most indefatigable, covering the court like a gnat in a paper bag. She demolished me in straight sets, and even lifted the best-of-five which we tacked on the end.

In the Cutter I said: 'Sorry not to have given you a better game.'

'Not at all. I was having a good day,' she added honestly. 'It happens like that sometimes, doesn't it?'

We were sharing a large helping of chips with mayonnaise and she was getting through them at an impressive rate.

'How's everything?' I asked. 'Any more on the Rick front?'

She shook her head. 'But he knows where I stand. I told him that as far as I was concerned playing away was not an option—for either of us. I said it wasn't what we got married for and he might as well know that if I ever found that he'd been fooling around I'd pack my bag, and Bryony's, and we'd be home to mother before you could say decree nisi.'

'He can never accuse you of equivocation,' I said. 'What pretext did you find for all that?'

'There was a documentary on TV—what makes marriage work, sort of thing. It opened up the debate a treat.'

'And did Rick—debate?'

'Not so's you'd notice. He agreed with every word I said.'

'You still think there's something going on?'

Desma licked mayonnaise off her fingers. 'I'm sure there has been. I don't know what stage it's at now, but I have a feeling it may not last. Rick will be scared shitless.'

'He doesn't want to lose you,' I agreed.

'Maybe.' She scrunched up her napkin. 'But he *definitely* doesn't want to lose Bryony, and I'm afraid I'm not above using our daughter as a human shield.'

'You're very brave,' I said.

'Correction,' said Desma. 'I'm not brave, and I'm not beautiful and I'm not particularly bright. But I'm very, very practical.'

*   *   *

I considered the merits of practicality as I drove home. But on my return nothing could have been further from my mind as I listened to Charles McNally's recorded message.

'Hello Eve. It's twelve noon, and I just checked in at the hotel overlooking the sea here. The—er—' I could hear him checking the notepaper— 'Esplanade. Sabine invited me to stay but it was you I came to see this time so it didn't seem right to treat their place like a flophouse. If you have any time this weekend I'd really appreciate the chance to make up for behaving like such a slob in town. I'll call again later. Bye now.'

How strange, I thought, that he and I had been in the same building for an hour or more—he had probably been recording that message in his room as Desma and I sat in the Cutter Bar.

He was not staying with the Drages. He had not asked me to call him. He had come to see me. My heart had been heavy for days, but now it showed that it had not forgotten how to beat faster.

CHAPTER FIFTEEN

He called again when I was in the shower. I'd left the machine on, and it was strange to hear first Ben's voice, then his—the two people who were most in my thoughts, talking to each other, as it were, through me.

I grabbed a towel and stumbled through to pick up the receiver.

'Charles?'

'Is that Eve at last?'

'I was in the—I'd only just got in and hadn't turned this thing off.'

'Look, it's so great to be by the sea, would you like to go for a walk?'

'Yes.'

'Come on over then, I'm out here already.'

I trailed the phone closer to the balcony door and sure enough there he was, standing leaning on the promenade rail with his ankles crossed, talking into a mobile.

'I'll just get changed.'

Five minutes later I crossed the road. He was facing the other way now, watching the people on the beach, but he turned round as I approached.

'Eve—hi there.'

'Hello.'

I sensed for a moment his uncertainty about how to greet me—a kiss, a handshake, both—but in the end he took my hand and enfolded it briefly in both of his. He was wearing a denim shirt, navy fleece waistcoat, cords and desert boots: the upmarket American version of what to wear for a walk by the sea, more suited to the panoramic rocks and surf of Big Sur than the grumbling shingle of Littelsea—but I liked it.

'I'm in your hands. Which way shall we go?'

That wasn't difficult. The nicest walk was up the cliff path, but the associations of that particular route were still too fresh and too painful.

'Let's go along to the Martello Tower,' I said. 'It dates from the Napoleonic Wars, and there's a little museum inside.'

'Sounds good to me.'

We began walking. He said nothing, and I remembered from before that he wouldn't speak simply to fill a silence. But silences made me anxious.

'The roses are amazing,' I said accordingly. 'Thank you.'

'Were they pretty? I hope so.'

'And so many—I hardly knew where to put them all.'

He smiled apologetically. 'They had a big job to do.'

'Not really,' I assured him. 'After all, I fell fast asleep too.'

'You're kidding.'

Either he was being polite or he hadn't watched my head lolling as I dropped off. 'We were both spark out. I just happened to wake up first.'

300

'So I can stop feeling like an asshole, at least on that count.'

'Definitely.'

'That's a relief.'

There ensued another short silence, which again I broke. 'Did you have a good drive down?'

'We did. Or should I say it looked good from where I was sitting. I don't have to drive.'

'Even at a weekend?'

'Especially on a weekend. Un-American, I know, but I hate to drive.'

'I find that so surprising . . .'

He gave a droll shrug. 'Only reason I got to the top, Eve, so I could get someone like Marian to run me about.'

'You have a woman driver?' I recalled the dark-suited figure at the wheel, after the Drages' party.

'Weird, huh?'

'I don't mean that. But you must admit it's not very usual.'

'She's terrific. I don't know I'm moving. That's the thing about not driving oneself, you totally trust whoever's in charge.'

'And I suppose—in your work—everyone else has to trust you,' I said, venturing into an area we had never touched on.

'They absolutely do.'

I waited for him to add something, some colourful example or anecdotal evidence. None was forthcoming, but I did not, as I might have done before, feel that I was being rebuffed—more that he did not wish to weigh down this pleasant occasion with talk of work. I was beginning to relax with him.

Our expedition was, as the soccer pundits might

have said, a game of two halves. We walked quite briskly for the mile and a half to the Martello Tower, making intermittent small talk. I told him about Littelsea—what there was to tell—and he prompted me with supplementary questions and kindly comments along this-is-so-typically-English lines. For Littelsea he traded his own home town of Denver. From the unfocused edges of what he told me I formed a picture of a preppy upbringing with private school, horses, skiing and a black-tie social life more strictly stratified than anything I'd encountered in supposedly classbound Britain.

That was the first half. We reached the Martello Tower and went round the museum at that slightly dutiful strolling pace one feels bound to adopt when doing such things with another person. Seeing it through Charles's eyes I was a little dismayed: the building was cold and musty, the conversion into a museum not especially imaginative or sympathetic, and the display itself modest. I'd seen it all before anyway—it was a regular jaunt with visitors—and was surprised at his interest in everything. I kept finding that I'd left him behind as he pored over old maps and letters, or stood admiring the handiwork of Huguenot prisoners. At one point he began talking to the museum guide, a retired naval officer employed by the National Trust, and I thought we'd never get away, especially as there was only a handful of visitors in the building and the guide was dying to air his knowledge. But it was impossible to feel impatient—Charles was so personable and such a good listener, I could see that it was (as the guide said when they shook hands) a pleasure to do business with him.

302

The way out took us past the tea room. 'Shall we?' he asked.

'If you like.'

In answer, he went over to the counter. The place was empty and the two ladies behind the urn made a fuss of us. We had tea for two and Charles had a slice of carrot cake. The metal-and-formica table wobbled dangerously if you leaned on it, but after a first mouthful he tapped the cake appreciatively with his fork.

'That is terrific.'

'It looks good. I believe it's all home-made.'

'You want some?'

'No thanks.'

He addressed the ladies, over his shoulder: 'Did you make this cake?'

'I'm afraid not,' replied their spokesperson. 'Another of our helpers did, she bakes three times a week.'

'Tell her it's worth it.'

They beamed girlishly. 'We will, thank you!'

'You've made their day,' I confided in him.

He looked at me. 'You're making mine.'

In the little shop—another lady, another smile— he bought a selection of maps and leaflets and a large expensive book about the Cinque Ports of which they probably only sold one a year. I was outside the door before I realised that yet again he wasn't with me. When he emerged he was carrying an additional small National Trust gift carrier, which he held out to me.

'You probably have a house full of this stuff,' he explained, 'so let's just say I can't think who else to give it to.'

It was a bone china mug decorated with part of

one of the old naval letters from the museum, and on the other side a crest with the motto 'Fortitudine'. It was a nice piece, but I knew it would have been horribly overpriced.

'I haven't got anything like it,' I said, 'and thank you—it's lovely.'

'Here,' he said, opening his carrier bag to take my present. 'Let me. Can we walk back along the beach?'

'Yes, of course. It's pretty heavy going on the shingle, but if you don't mind that . . .'

'Let's go.'

We went down the precipitous steps and he led the way almost to the water's edge before striking back towards home.

This was when another sea change took place. It could have been for any number of reasons: our slower and less even pace on the stones; the heave and sigh of the waves at our side; the westering sun ahead of us; the indefinably different feel of a homeward journey . . . But whatever it was, it freed us up as though we'd just downed a bottle of wine instead of a pot of Tetley's, and we began to talk about ourselves.

It turned out he hadn't been the *summa cum laude* ivy league graduate of my supposition, but the only boy in a family of four who had struggled unsuccessfully to do justice to an expensive education and to reach a par with his three over-achieving older sisters. He'd had a happy and privileged boyhood, and the indulgent love of his mother and sisters had protected him from any sense of disappointment until he was in his late teens. Consistently poor grades across the board had led to one of those more-in-sorrow-than-in-

304

anger talks with his father, and he had gone direct from high school onto the ground floor of Ankatex, where a certain bloody-mindedness had set in.

'I couldn't beat 'em,' he explained, speaking of the other management trainees, 'so I sure as hell wasn't going to join 'em. I'd been trying to do that with the girls for my whole life up to that point, and I just reckoned "Enough". If I couldn't find the cure for the common cold or win the Pulitzer then I was going to have to be a tough guy—the toughest. I was going to get out of a suit and into overalls.'

'And now you're back in a suit.'

He shrugged, accepting the analysis. 'Some of the time. I got too good at it.'

I stumbled and lost my balance for a second, and he said 'Whoa—' and put his free arm round my shoulders to steady me. As we walked on he simply allowed his arm to slip down to my waist. It was a gesture chivalrous rather than flirtatious, but the underlying assumption was that I would not object. Object? Kansas in August had nothing on me. I kept my own hands in my pockets but I was suddenly, devastatingly aware of how nice it was to feel a man's arm about me, and not just any man's, but Charles McNally's . . .

. . . who was now asking me about myself.

I told him, without labouring the point, about my separation from Ian. About the difference between our married life in the barn-like rectory, and our respective reincarnations as flat-dwellers. About our continuing amity which had been shaken in my case by the arrival of Julia. And about our children—up to a point. About Ben's transgressions I felt not only that it would be disloyal to Ben and unfair to Charles to discuss

305

them so soon, but that I didn't want anything to smudge this bright interlude of self-absorption.

'Eve,' he said admiringly, 'you are such a calm person.'

I had to laugh. 'I beg your pardon? *Calm?*'

'Your whole life has changed, and yet you're so together, you have such a positive attitude.'

God forgive me, I thought. 'Not always.'

'I know women who spend a fortune on counselling just trying to get to where you are. You believe in God or something?'

'Not really.'

'Not really? You do or you don't.'

'I suppose I'd like to, but I don't. Do you?'

'No.'

'I'd have thought that in disaster-management, it would practically have been a prerequisite.'

'Quite the opposite,' he said, suddenly stopping—and so halting us both—to look out to sea. 'If I thought I was up against some divine power I'd never get out of bed in the morning.'

'But if you believed in the divine power you'd reckon it was on your side.'

'Good point.'

As he said this he smiled, and made some small, appreciative movement with the hand that rested on my waist. I was glad we were outside with the sea breeze in our faces so that my blush wouldn't be noticed.

He released me, put down the bag and picked up a stone, which he sent skimming expertly over the surface of the water, leaping half a dozen times like a flying fish.

'You've done that before,' I observed admiringly.

'You bet—' he threw another—'and I can't tell

you what an asset it is at cocktail parties.'

We walked on, laughing.

*   *   *

When we reached Cliff Mansions we went back up on to the prom. It had clouded over and the breeze had become a chilly, nibbling wind.

'Would you like to come in?' I asked. I glanced at my watch. 'Another cup of tea or something?'

'I'd like to see where you live.'

'Come on then.'

He made light of the stairs, I noticed, but as I unlocked the door of the flat he commented: 'That explains the great legs.'

'Sorry?'

He jerked a thumb over his shoulder as he came in. 'No elevator. Hey this is really nice . . .'

He put the National Trust bag on the hall table and went into the living room and straight to the balcony. 'What a view. No wonder so many people want to end their lives by the sea.'

'That wasn't necessarily what I had in mind.'

He laughed. 'Of course not, I didn't mean you. But all that space . . . it's like the desert, it puts things in perspective.'

'And it's constant, but always changing.'

'*Plus ça change, plus c'est la même chose,*' he agreed. 'You lucked out with this, Eve—you must be happy here.'

'I am.' I indicated the three vases of roses. 'See how lovely they are, they did you proud.'

In reply he gently touched one of the roses nearest him, and the touch made me shiver, as though it had been for me.

'So what else do you have here?' he asked. 'Do I get the tour?'

'It's nothing special. There isn't much to see.'

'Yes but I'm looking for an apartment right now, I have this sudden interest in bathrooms and closets.'

'All right—but I reserve the right to keep the door closed where there's a mess.'

'Eve!' he came up to my shoulder as I led the way. 'You have a short memory. You owe me a mess. In fact, I demand one if I'm ever going to feel at ease in your company again.'

I conceded this, and dutifully opened doors and pointed out the obvious, as one does with prospective buyers. He seemed genuinely interested, and tactfully confined his questions to structural matters. I couldn't help feeling self-conscious—seeing my home through his eyes made me feel vulnerable, not because of untidiness but because, with Ben gone, it presented an almost spinsterly neatness. Also, a vase of the yellow roses stood on my dressing table amid an intimate womanly cluster of bottles and jars. Happily he made no comment on this, though he did exclaim over Ben's room.

'Your son sleeps in here? What is he, a monk?'

'Hardly. He's away at the moment so I took the opportunity to spring clean.'

'I wonder will he appreciate that . . .' He was walking across to the bed as he spoke, and picked up Algy. 'Your son's?'

'Yes. He's one thing I'd never throw away.'

Charles pulled at the bear's ears before replacing him carefully on the pillow. 'They all go sometime.'

308

When we were back in the hall, he handed me my present. 'Don't forget this. Would you come and have dinner with me tonight, at the hotel?'

'I'd love to.'

'Is the food all right there? I guess you'd know more about that than me—you must be honest. We could go somewhere else, Marian hasn't found herself a date as far as I know.'

'No, the Esplanade's fine. And it's comfortable.'

'Which is a real consideration at our age.' I couldn't tell if he was joking or not. 'What, about seven in the lobby?'

*   *   *

As I closed the front door I looked at my watch—it was five o'clock. I prided myself on my ability to get ready in ten minutes flat, but suddenly two hours seemed like no time at all to effect the transformation I had in mind. It was terribly important that I surprise him, show him an aspect of myself that he had not seen and might not have suspected. If I had stopped to analyse it I'd have admitted that the effect I sought was sexy. Instead, as I got into a dressing gown, turned on the taps and rummaged through the wardrobe I registered only annoyance that I had taken my shorter skirts to the Oxfam shop. There were one or two of Mel's in the spare room, but they were a size ten. It was cooler now, especially in the evening, so the blue shift I'd worn to have dinner with Ian was no longer appropriate.

I had to abandon the search because the bath was almost overflowing. Up to my neck in hot water (an expression with a disturbing double

309

meaning for me at that moment) I continued to grapple with the clothes question. It was a cliché— a full wardrobe and not a thing to wear. I realised that under normal circumstances I might have rung Sabine for advice on the issue. The realisation brought home to me just how much I had lost, and still stood to lose, because of what had happened. Even Ronnie's reassuring remarks about Ben couldn't alter the fact that he and Sabine were guilty of playing fast and loose not only with each other, but with the trust which ought to be taken for granted between family and friends.

As I sat in front of the mirror with my hair in a towel, a handful of yellow rose petals scattered over the dressing-table glass like little boats on a lake, I thought wistfully that here was a black hole in my friendship with Charles. How could a committed bachelor, accustomed to defining himself through his work (he had, after all, admitted as much) sympathise with the sulphurous complications of my life? I could neither consult nor confide in him about it, but in not doing so I felt I was being less than honest.

I spent ages putting on make-up in order to look natural, and then blew dry and tonged my hair. I emptied the old supermarket carrier containing my tights on to the bed and spent further crucial minutes establishing, with many oaths and imprecations, that I did not have a pair that was unladdered. But this entirely predictable turn of events did at least solve the skirt problem—I'd have to wear trousers. And I did have a nice pair of claret velvet jeans that I'd bought in the sales in February, which I was now slim enough to wear and which I could team with an old but favourite

310

cream silk shirt. Dangly Navajo earrings which Mel had brought back from holiday last summer completed a look which I fancied was casually elegant and—I undid another button—feminine.

I arrived at the Esplanade fifteen minutes late and saw him sitting to the right of the door, talking on his mobile phone. I was the tiniest bit put out by this—was he the sort who had to fill every spare minute with work?—but the moment he saw me he switched it off and got to his feet. He had arrived at pretty much the same conclusion as me on the what-to-wear issue—he'd put on a nice sage-green jacket with a pale blue shirt and navy trousers. Stylish, comfortable—we'd acknowledged the importance of that—but not too smart.

'Sorry about the phone,' he said, tucking it in his breast pocket, 'I have to leave it switched on.'

'Like a doctor, I suppose—in case of emergencies.'

'Exactly.'

Beguilingly, he said this in a way which implied he knew his work was not of the calibre of a doctor's. I found it very easy to forgive him.

'Let's have a drink,' he said, waiting for me to sit down. 'What are you having?'

When the waiter had gone, he remarked: 'You look lovely.'

This time there was no offshore breeze to come to my rescue: I blushed, and it must have showed.

'Thanks,' I said. 'I didn't know what to wear.'

He lifted a shoulder. 'Who does?'

Oh God, I thought, oh dear God, it can't be true—he's so *nice*. He uses words like 'lovely', he seems to know what I'm thinking, it's as though I've known him all my life—Kansas again: and this time the corn was at least as high as an elephant's eye ...

' ... one of the few advantages to being a man,' he was saying. 'There are fewer options. But I really like clothes. Being raised in a houseful of women taught me a proper sense of their importance. Getting ready to go out was like an indoor sport in our house, I must have spent hours as a kid watching my sisters empty closets and turn out drawers and fall prey to the vapours just so they could go out and break some guy's heart in what they were wearing in the first place.'

I wasn't going to admit how accurate a picture this was. We talked fashion for a bit, and he commented, apropos of this, on Mel.

'She's what my mother would have called a bandbox. Smart as paint.'

'Yes, that's Mel—never a hair out of place.'

'You know, I admire that. It takes spirit to make that amount of effort every day of your life.'

It seemed only polite (and I hoped disarming) to concede the difference. 'It's not something I've ever been able to do.'

'You don't need to, Eve. You have a terrific daughter there, but she doesn't have what you have.'

He did not look at me as he said this. Luckily for me, the menus arrived.

*   *   *

Over dinner I asked him to tell me more about his work. No doubt in deference to my ignorance he confined himself to broad brushstrokes.

'It's addictive,' he said. 'I can't deny that when

312

my time's up in the New Year I'm going to be in deep withdrawal.'

'So what is it you're addicted to,' I asked. 'Danger?'

'Does that seem pretentious?'

'No.'

'It's the danger, it's the unpredictability—the having to get in there and do something with no time to think. It's the Ah! factor.' He exhaled on the 'Ah!' so that it came out as a gasp.

'What's that?'

'The power of the elements ...?' He made it sound partly a question, as if he didn't want to sound pompous. 'You have the ocean right there, you know all about that. I get off on the desert, on fire and oil, those great natural tantrums that show us just how little we know. And if I'm honest—' he paused as the waiter charged our glasses—'if I'm honest, it stops me becoming introspective. Helps me stay a moving target.'

This struck me as a curious choice of words. 'Target? Who's after you?'

'Life.' He gave a self-deprecating chuckle. 'Adulthood.'

'You seem pretty grown-up to me.'

'It's all done with mirrors, believe me.'

Emboldened by the best part of a bottle of wine, this was my cue to ask the question which had been waiting in the wings all day.

'Have you never been married?'

'No, never have.'

'Any particular reason?'

He laughed, and then said 'We-ell ...' as if assembling a whole catalogue of reasons. 'No.'

'Oh.' I wondered if I'd overstepped the mark.

313

'All the usual ones I'm afraid. Never in the same place long enough, never met the right woman, never had the guts—'

'Oh come on!'

'True, though. Give me a firestorm over attrition any day.'

'It doesn't have to be attrition.'

'I believe you, but I never wanted to find out.'

Still, I thought, all those years . . . I couldn't even imagine a life at no stage marked out by the domestic rights of passage—marriage, babies, children growing up . . . Separation and divorce, even.

I said, with a flippancy I didn't feel: 'So you love 'em and leave 'em, do you?'

He shook his head. 'I should be so lucky. In every case but one they've left me. You're looking at the developed world's most experienced dumpee.'

'What about the one?'

For an awful moment I thought he was going to say that she'd died.

'Case in point,' he said. 'We were in serious danger of becoming a long-term prospect. I got shortness of breath.'

'I thought you were addicted to danger.'

'Yes.' He didn't smile, but he did look into my eyes. 'But only with the Ah! factor.'

*   *   *

At eleven o'clock he walked me back to Cliff Mansions.

'Where's Marian staying?' I asked.

'At the hotel. She'll have had her feet up in front

314

of the TV, she's the biggest fan of that hospital series on a Saturday night.'

'It must be a funny life for her. Is she married?'

'Divorced. It's not usual for her to work weekends. And she is extremely well paid.'

'She'd need to be.'

We reached the door. 'Thank you for this evening,' I said. 'I have enjoyed it.'

'And me. More than I can say. Will I see you at Sabine's tomorrow?'

I flashed hot and cold. 'I don't think so.'

'Really? I don't believe it—they asked me up for Sunday lunch, I assumed you'd be there.'

'No.'

'Why not?'

I wished he'd let it go. 'Because I wasn't invited.'

He frowned. 'I don't get it, when Sabine knew that I came down to see you.'

I could see I was going to have to tell the truth, if not the whole of it. 'Look, Charles, it sounds silly I know but Sabine and I have fallen out.'

'I'm sorry to hear that.'

'Quite badly. Something private. Shaking hands and letting bygones be bygones is simply not an option. Even Martin doesn't know, so I'd be grateful if you didn't mention it.'

'I wouldn't dream of it. But it makes me wish I wasn't going myself.'

Being excised from the Drages' guest list was a small price to pay to hear him say that. 'You'll have a wonderful time.'

'I have to go back to London in the afternoon . . . I'll call you, if I may.'

'Do. And thank you again for a lovely evening.'

Boldly and decisively, I held out my hand. But he

315

gently moved it aside, and with it my boldness, and instead touched my face. It was that same touch—gentle and appreciative—that he had given the roses in my flat.

'Thank you, Eve. 'Night.'

I didn't watch him walk away. But neither could I remember going up the stairs. I must have positively flown, because when I reached the flat I was out of breath. In the hall I let out one huge gasp: Ah!

CHAPTER SIXTEEN

That was a bitter-sweet Sunday. There was still no word from Ben, and it wasn't till later that I found Charles had rung me from his car.

He'd called at Cliff Mansions twice, apparently, but found me out—I'd driven over to Brighton to stop myself thinking about lunch at the Drages. Wild horses wouldn't have dragged me there even with an invitation, but I couldn't escape a writhing resentment that Charles would be at Sabine's groaning board, complimenting her on her hospitality, joking with Martin and getting pleasantly tanked—as who wouldn't with a handsomely-paid Marian to drive them home? I thought how nice it would have been if he'd simply bucked the engagement for me. But that was unreasonable, for the Drages were his friends and had done nothing, as far as he was concerned, to jeopardise the friendship. Also, he was a nice man with good manners and all the right instincts. If he had skipped lunch at the last moment and for no good reason, I might in my heart of hearts (a place I was becoming acquainted with) have thought less of him.

In Brighton I called Clive and we went to a pub, after which I carted him round the Lanes. Like Helen, he had not the least interest in shopping, or in making those small but crucial consumer choices which I found so much fun. You could never have accused either of them of having bad taste, because they had no idea what taste was in the first place.

Still, he was patience itself with me. In one shop I pored for ages over a wonderful wooden box full of old jewellery. It was junk, really, or the watchful young man in black would never have allowed allcomers to rummage through it, but Bouvier's had taught me there were treasures to be found in these job lots. Clive first wandered round the shop, then stood by my side, looking over my shoulder. He wasn't interested in my search, but I didn't feel guilty for keeping him hanging about: I knew he was perfectly happy to keep me company.

I came across a little brooch in brass and leather, fashioned like a billycock hat resting on a cane.

I held it up. 'What do you think?'

'You mustn't ask me, Eve, what do I know?'

I nudged him affectionately. 'I didn't ask what you knew, I asked what you thought.'

I offered it to him, but instead of taking it he peered from a safe distance as though the brooch were a poisonous spider.

'Well?'

'It's an amusing notion.'

'That's what I thought.'

'Where would one put it?'

'On a lapel or a collar—on a hat, even. I'm going

317

to get it.'

When I'd paid for the brooch, there was Clive, leaning over the box with one hand behind his back, picking gingerly at the jewellery with the other.

'See anything you like?'

'No, no!' He sounded quite alarmed, as if I were trying to trap him. I remembered something.

'Helen likes rings, doesn't she?'

'Yes, but um—I don't know if I've ever given her one. Except for a wedding ring, of course, which is hardly a complex business . . . And anyway just at the moment . . .'

'Surprise her.' I took his sleeve and pulled him further along the counter, where there was a tray of heavy rings tailormade for Helen's long, Bloomsburyish hands.

'I don't have any immediate plans—'

'No, but when you do.'

'I can't help feeling,' he said, with an anxious furrowing of the brow, 'that she might find such a present laughable . . .'

'Why ever would she do that?'

'Well—out of character.'

'Clive!' I exchanged an exasperated look with the young man in black. 'You've already proved what Catherine said—it doesn't have to be like this. Everything can change. If you want Helen back, give it a go! Turn up in all your altered glory and woo her.'

'I go along with that,' said the young man. Clive blushed fiercely but did not, to his credit, tell him to mind his own business.

'May we have a closer look?' I asked.

'Of course you may.' The young man took the

318

tray out and put it on top of the counter. Tactfully, without comment, he pointed at one or two of the rings. There was one on his own finger, a big oval reddish stone engraved with a gryphon.

To cover Clive's embarrassed dithering, I said: 'The one you're wearing's nice.'

He held out his hand. 'This is for sale too.'

The extended hand, the ring—it was all a bit much for Clive, who in spite of being surrounded by students most of the time managed to lead a very sheltered life.

'It's a personal letter seal,' explained the young man, removing it and laying it on the counter. 'A signet ring with attitude, really—I should be wearing it on my little finger but it's too big.'

'Gorgeous, isn't it?' I held it up in front of me.

'Um . . .'

'Does your friend have a large hand?' asked our helper.

'Yes,' I said.

Clive murmured: 'She's my wife, actually.'

'Oh well then—you know what she likes. Most of these look wonderful on the right person, but they do need a large, long-fingered hand to carry them off successfully.'

Quite suddenly, and to my great satisfaction, Clive was on his mettle.

'Helen has very beautiful hands,' he said.

The young man's face softened. 'Lucky lady. It's something I always look at, the hands. Eyes and hands.'

Clive nodded at the red ring. 'I think that's a bit ornate.'

'Absolutely.'

'Could you show me this shiny black one . . . ?'

Ten minutes later we left the shop, me wearing my brooch and Clive with a little box containing the jet ring. I wondered why I'd been so pushy with him. I didn't use to intervene in my friends' relationships—but if Clive was in the proccess of reinventing himself I wanted him to do it properly. And I also wanted happy endings.

'You will go and see her, won't you?' I asked over tea and scones.

'I do want to.'

'But will you?'

'Yes—yes I will. Catherine thinks, I don't know if she's right, that I should invite her out rather than go to her house.'

There seemed to be a lot of us taking an interest. 'That's a good idea. Neutral ground.'

He sighed. 'I'm not good at dinners.'

'You're good at concerts,' I reminded him. 'We had a lovely evening.'

'We did, didn't we? Well, maybe that . . .'

'It doesn't really matter what it is, so long as it's something you both enjoy. After all I don't suppose she goes out much with—' I checked myself. 'I don't suppose she goes out much at the moment.'

'No, perhaps not.'

'You and she had a different sort of life together from the one she leads now,' I said, 'and I'm sure she misses it.'

He looked at me doubtfully. 'Do you?'

'Clive—' I put my hand on his shoulder—'I do.'

*   *   *

It was my own confused feelings which had made me so determined to influence Clive, but the very same feelings ensured that I forgot all about him the moment I got home.

'Eve—it's Charles. I called at your house a couple of times, but you were out—and you still are, so I hope you're having a nice day. Sabine gives good lunch, as you know, but I thought she and Martin were a little on edge, so maybe they have a bad conscience. I find it so hard to imagine anyone falling out with you. I'll call soon from town and perhaps you'll come up and let me convert you to jazz. I want to talk to you again anyhow. Bye now . . . Bye.'

His reference to Martin and Sabine caused me another frisson of doubt—no wonder he couldn't imagine us falling out, the whole bad business was outside his frame of reference. I wondered if the Drages' edginess meant that Martin now knew, and if so whether that meant the end of my protected status. In spite of our long acquaintance I didn't know Martin all that well. He was just Martin—big, bluff, genial, and expansive. And above all, successful. It was almost impossible to imagine how he might react to something which he would surely see as a failure. Like many jovial extroverts, he might well have a volcanic temper. If he chose to teach Ben a lesson he could inflict terrible damage, both physical and emotional—and how could Ben possibly defend himself? He had effectively betrayed Martin on two counts—with his daughter and his wife. The enormity of the whole thing—and my isolation within it—swept over me again, and I sank down on the sofa with my head between my hands.

Mel rang up when she got back to the hotel—Sunday was a normal working day for her, and wasted no time in coming to the point.

'What in God's name has that little toe-rag been up to?'

My heart sank. 'You obviously know.'

'Yes, but what was he thinking of, Mother?' Her voice rose furiously, hurting my ears.

I winced. 'Darling, please. How did you find out?'

'I spoke to Dad.'

This knocked me sideways. 'I haven't even discussed it with your father.'

'No, but Ben has. He's there, staying with them.'

There seemed to be no end to the shocks I had to sustain. 'I see.'

'You weren't aware of that?'

'I thought he was with Sophie in Yorkshire.'

'Mother—is that likely?'

I took a couple of deep breaths. 'I've long since stopped deciding what is or isn't likely. A few weeks ago this whole thing would have been about as recognisable as the dark side of the moon.'

'Shall I come over?'

'No!' I realised I'd sounded a bit sharp, and added. 'It's a very kind thought but there isn't a thing you can do.'

'Except get tough.' Her voice was sharp with disdain. 'I bet no one has.'

'You're wrong there—'

'Has anyone actually told him *he's* wrong, in no uncertain terms?'

'Yes.'

'He's behaved atrociously. Call me old-fashioned but what he needs is for Martin to find out and give him a bloody good hiding!'

Coming as it did so close to my own worst fears

322

this touched a nerve.

'Mel, shut up for two minutes!' She did. 'I can't speak for Ian, but there's no question of my being soft on Ben. I was simply appalled, and furious. But he couldn't seem to accept he'd done anything wrong—' I heard her snort of disgust—'and he left home the same day. I've only seen him once since, and we haven't spoken at all. So please don't take that tone, I'm the one who's been here, coping with it, and it's been no bed of roses I can assure you!'

I knew she wouldn't apologise, but she came close. 'All right. I accept that. I'm just so angry.'

'Me too. What did your father say about it?'

'He said Ben was there—'

'With both of them?'

'He said "us" so I suppose so. He said Ben was there, and gave a brief outline of the goings-on.'

A brief outline—that sounded like Ian. Calm, businesslike, not jumping to any conclusions. But the thought of Julia sitting in on this family crisis made me clench my teeth.

'Mother?'

'I do think he might have told me Ben was there.'

'To be fair I think he'd only just arrived, and from what I gather it was unexpected—so come to think of it he could have been with Sophie before that.'

'It's nice to know I was right about something.'

'Oh, poor Mother ...' for the first time Mel sounded sympathetic, but not for long—her energies were directed elsewhere. 'He's so lucky I'm out here—if I got my hands on him I'd wring his selfish little neck!'

It took me an hour to calm down after she'd

rung off. I wasn't so obtuse that I couldn't see the irony of it. Mel was the first person I'd discussed it with who was, without a doubt, angrier than me, and the exchange had left me in tatters. My own anger, it seemed, was Janus-faced.

During the evening a fierce offshore wind blew up and the draughts to which Cliff Mansions was a martyr whined through every window frame and door. I drew all the curtains, but they still swelled in the breeze. In these conditions the flat became a restless place—I could imagine the Victorian foundations tottering unsteadily as the shingle sucked back and forth. The next day the windows on the seaward side would be frosted with salt and the rust would have bitten a bit deeper into the balcony furniture.

At about ten o'clock I called Ian. The times were certainly out of joint because Julia answered, something she had never done before.

'It's Eve—please may I speak to Ian?' Only some very faint and distant scruple prevented me from saying 'my husband'. I could hear piano music in the background, something wistful and highbrow, a Chopin étude perhaps. My, but how the Blondie fan had come up in the world . . .

'Of course, hang on.'

To her credit she didn't cover the receiver but simply said, 'Ian, it's Eve'. I heard him say 'Oh, right . . .' and then there was a short interval, during which the music was turned down, before he picked up the receiver.

'Hello, I was going to ring you.'

'Hello—I gather Ben's there.'

'He is, yes.'

'You didn't tell me.'

324

'I was about to, that's why I was going to call. He just turned up last night.'

'Can I speak to him?'

'Well—actually he's asleep in his room. He was shot to pieces when he got here and we were up most of last night.'

'And what conclusions did you all reach?' I was unable to keep the sarcasm out of my voice.

'None whatever. Julia went to bed, but he needed to offload so I listened.'

'Where's he been? I haven't seen him for days.'

'He was at Sophie's mother's I believe—but naturally that's over now.'

I very nearly made a tasteless crack about Sophie's mother but that vestigial scruple did its stuff again.

'He's very low,' said Ian. 'I was quite shocked.'

'So's Mel,' I said. 'She was on the phone earlier, going thermonuclear. She wants to come over and wring his neck.'

'I hope you dissuaded her.'

'I did, just about. What's he going to do?'

'I've no idea and I don't think he has either.'

I asked sarcastically: 'No plans to come home, I suppose? To see his mother who's been worried sick about him?'

'The trouble with home,' replied Ian, 'is that it's Littelsea.'

'He has to face the music some time.'

There was a pause during which I could picture Ian pursing his lips thoughtfully before saying: 'Look, Eve, why don't you come up here and see him? It might be easier for all of us to put a bit of distance between ourselves and the seat of the infection.'

As if to reinforce his point there was a tremendous gust of wind which rattled the balcony door, and I heard one of the chairs outside fall, with a clank.

'All right,' I said. 'Tomorrow after work.'

'That would be fine,' he said in a tone of voice which implied reservations, 'but Wednesday would be even better.'

'Wednesday?' I was outraged. 'He could be battening on someone else by then!'

'He won't, believe me. And we'll have the place to ourselves—you can spend the night.'

'Why?' I asked rudely. 'Where will Julia be?'

'In Scotland with her parents.'

'I see. I might come home again anyway.'

'That's up to you.'

'All right, I'll see you then.' I almost let him go and then, at the last minute, almost shouted, 'Ian!'

'What?'

'Will you tell Ben I called?'

'Of course.'

'And—give him my love.'

'Of course.'

'Thanks. Goodnight then.'

'Goodnight.'

It wasn't a good one. I was seriously wound up, and Cliff Mansions shivered and moaned around me like a whole coachload of souls in torment. When two or three storm-tossed hours had crawled by I gave up, put on my dressing gown and the lights and went back into the living room with a cup of tea. It was twenty to one. The wind showed no sign of abating, and when I parted the curtains I could see the sea bucking and rearing like a herd of wild mustang threatening to burst through the

326

fragile rails of the promenade. I shivered and let the curtain drop. The rose petals were hanging by the merest thread now, and every now and then the draught would shake one loose to drift to the ground.

It may have been the dying roses, or the wild sea, or just the small-hours blues, but I had no compunction in dialling Troughtons. They were civility itself, but told me that Mr McNally's line was busy.

'Are you sure?' I asked stupidly.

'I'm afraid so. May we give him a message?'

'No, it's all right . . .'

For some reason I was more embarrassed at this discovery than I would have been at waking him up. Apparently this wasn't late at all to him, he was still hard at it, doing what oilmen did.

I turned on the television and let Peter Cushing and Vincent Price do their diabolical damnedest until I fell asleep.

*   *   *

It was no surprise, having spent half the night awake and the other half dozing on the sofa with a cricked neck, that my return to work next day was not a shining exemplar of renewed energy and resolve.

'Good grief 'n stuff,' said Jo in her pointblank way. 'You look shot at, are you sure you should be back?'

'Quite sure, I just didn't sleep well.'

'You may be able to snatch forty winks here if you play your cards right, we're not exactly rushed off our feet.' She saw me glance apprehensively at

327

my desk. 'No, don't worry, I've fielded most things.'

'Jo, you are a brick.'

'Call me Wonderwall.'

In fact I found it surprisingly soothing to be back in the old routine, and the morning, held together by a modest amount of paperwork and a few phone calls, passed painlessly. It was a relief to be in a place where the barbed-wire entanglements of my domestic life could not touch me.

But I was not, it turned out, safe from other people's. At one-fifteen, just as I was about to go out for a sandwich, the receptionist buzzed me and said there was a visitor for me. When I went out, there was Helen, in a big beige bouclé coat, looking like a rather washed-out grizzly bear.

'I don't need feeding,' she said, scratching the back of her left hand, which I noticed was already dry and sore.

'Fine, but I do. Come and keep me company.'

She strode alongside me to Roots, and waited at a table, eyes staring, hands thrust into her hair, as I collected coffee and three rounds of bean salad on brown—I was properly sceptical of her pronouncement about food. On the same basis I got the extra large coffee: I knew if I got her a cup of her own she'd push it disdainfully aside, but if I had a large one in front of me she'd help herself quite freely in the belief that this somehow didn't count.

She said nothing till I'd got my teeth into the first large, well-earned chunk, and then announced, staring at my plate: 'Well, he's gone.'

I chewed frantically, eyes watering, trying to clear my mouth enough to respond, but she was too glum to need me.

'Yesterday afternoon. He had a go at a speech. He said he wasn't good enough for me, which struck me as quite sweet until round about three this morning when I realised he meant the opposite.'

I swallowed at last. 'He may have meant the opposite,' I said stoutly, 'but he spoke the plain truth.'

'Hm.' She picked up a sandwich and took a huge, absent-minded bite.

'I am so sorry, Helen. It's hellish for you. But at least you were expecting it.'

'Oh I was, I was . . . I'm very fortunate really . . .'

There was no escaping the sarcasm, or the fact that she had a point. 'So what else did he say?'

She steepled her hands, musing. 'Umm . . . He said he couldn't go on using me like this. He couldn't leave his wife and children—not that I ever asked him to—and that I deserved better. Then we had sex. Then came the not-good-enough-for-me bit.'

I was shocked. 'You went to bed with him?'

'Why not? It won't be happening again.'

'It just seems so—I don't know . . .' She continued to dispose of the sandwich without signs of relish. 'He got what he wanted even then.'

'Mm—I wanted it too.'

'You must be devastated.'

She dusted her palms. 'I feel numb.'

'You'll probably hit an awful downer. Do you want to come and stay?' I heard myself extend this invitation with a sort of horrified detachment. What was I saying? But in her case I was completely safe.

'Out of the question. I make an apalling guest at

the best of times, of which this is not one.'

I gave the plate a nudge and she took another sandwich. 'Will you be all right?'

'I doubt it, but neither shall I be sticking my head in the oven.'

She ate, and I drank some coffee. 'Do you know what I honestly dread the most?'

'What?'

'The boredom. I've had ecstasy—what the devil do I do now?'

As she polished off my lunch, I realised I had no answer. The jet ring had a big job to do.

*   *   *

That night I slept the sleep of the utterly shattered. There were no messages, no calls, and no storms. When I woke up it was to soggy, still weather. A passenger ship in the bay was like a painted ship upon a painted ocean. All the roses were finally dead and I had to collect them up in swathes of newspaper and take them down to the outside bin. I decided that tomorrow, rather than stay at Ian's, I'd book into a hotel. This would at least give me the opportunity of calling Charles again, maybe even of seeing him. I warned the people at work that I might be late in on Thursday and tried not to catch Jo's quizzical eye

During the day I had to go and visit a nice young couple who wanted to flog some hideous inherited Jacobean furniture. They obviously felt rather guilty about it, and I tried to reassure them.

'It seems awful I know,' the girl said when I'd presented them with the preliminary quote, 'but we desperately need the cash.'

330

'That's not awful,' I told her. 'After all you didn't go out and choose these pieces, they just came your way. Whoever buys them will buy them because they're exactly to their taste.' This analysis ignored the probability of the pieces being acquired by a dealer, but it seemed to cheer them up.

My meeting with them brought Mrs Rymer to mind and after work I drove out to Whitegates to see her. At only six-fifteen the residents were still having supper, but I waited in something called the music room, and at six-thirty a nurse accompanied her in and asked if we'd like coffee.

'My friend from the real world would probably prefer a drink,' said Mrs Rymer. 'What would you like? They have most things.'

I asked for white wine and the nurse brought something sweetish, but well chilled, along with a small cafetière and two cups.

'I hope you don't mind my turning up like this,' I said, 'without letting you know.'

She closed her eyes. 'My dear, you have no idea . . . Anything, but anything, unscheduled is like manna from heaven to we inmates. Is that all right?'

'It's fine. Hitting the spot.'

'Have you come straight from your work? You know I was astonished at the size of the cheque.'

'Good. Yes, all your things did very well.'

'And did they go to good homes, do you know?'

'I'm afraid I don't.' I recalled my conversation with the young couple, but I knew she wouldn't be so easily fobbed off. 'Some of them will have been bought by dealers.'

'Of course,' she agreed. 'To make their way in the world. And how are you?' I must have hesitated

331

fractionally, for she added: 'Did you resolve your dilemma?'

This simple question, which had so dominated our last meeting, made me realise how much had happened in a short time. I had to collect my thoughts before answering, and she prompted me again: 'Your gentleman friend?'

'Yes—he's fine. I got in touch with him and we've seen each other a couple of times since then.'

Mrs Rymer's eyes were on my face. 'And would it be indelicate to ask if the friendship is likely to blossom as the rose?'

Her choice of words must have been completely fortuitous, but it was uncanny how in tune she was—she had all her buttons on and no mistake.

'I think it might. It's hard to say.'

'But you would like it to.'

'Yes.' I admitted. 'Yes, I would.'

'Well, cheers!' She raised her coffee cup and held it towards my glass. 'Good luck to you. You don't know how I envy you.'

We clinked. A little wary of opening myself up further, I asked how her family were.

'They're avoiding me,' she replied.

'Oh—surely not.'

'Don't misunderstand me. They come here, separately and severally, they take me out, they ring me up, they're models of devotion, I cannot fault them. But—' She took a sip of her coffee, making me wait, trouper that she was, for the punchline. 'But they don't want to hear what I might have to say.'

I didn't prompt her, because it was clear she was in the mood for bean-spilling.

'They're having a rocky time—my son and

daughter-in-law,' she said. 'they think I don't know because I'm in here out of harm's way. What they fail to take into account is that when a person is cooped up they learn to extract every ounce of value from visits. And because I'm in the same place all the time I see them under laboratory conditions—I've always been observant, and now I notice every little shade and nuance, every alteration no matter how minute—and in the case of my son and daughter-in-law the changes are glaringly obvious.'

I said cautiously: 'Long-term marriage is a hard row to hoe these days.'

She shot me a bright, caustic look. 'Any marriage to my son would be.'

'Oh, really?' Not for the first time I was taken aback by her alarming candour. 'So, what, he . . . ?'

'He has other women. It's nothing new, he's an old-fashioned philanderer. Or a newfangled one if you prefer. He's been at it since a few months after they married.'

'How do you know?'

She put her cup down slowly and deliberately. 'I know. One does. His father was exactly the same.'

'That must have been very hard for you.'

'Not really. But it is hard for my daughter-in-law. She doesn't have the temperament for it.'

'I wonder who does?'

'A woman in that position has three choices, I think,' she said. 'She can leave. She can stay and do likewise. Or she can turn a blind eye.'

'And which do you recommend?'

'Any one, so long as she can hang on to her *amour propre*—that really is the main thing, don't you agree, to be able to hold one's head up and

333

enjoy one's life. What else is there after all? I'm of no fixed religion, but I simply can't believe there's a place in heaven for martyrs to marriage. It would be like an eternal dentist's waiting room, the most soulless and depressing place imaginable.'

I wanted to laugh, but there was a spectre at the feast. 'What about your daughter-in-law? What's she chosen?'

'I suppose you'd say she's turning a blind eye, but it's nearly killing her. All she ever wanted was to preside over hearth and home and enjoy the security that went with it. Now she's effectively being left on her own and she's finding more and more things to do. I worry that she'll go into a flat spin and disappear altogether, poor Jane.'

She couldn't keep the note of impatience out of her voice. I felt a pang of empathy with her— nothing was less comfortable than divided loyalties.

'It must be very awkward for you.'

She shrugged. 'Not really. It's they who have to live with it. But that doesn't mean I have to. I don't intend to drop off the perch this year, or even next, but even the most optimistic prognosis wouldn't give me more than another five. And the great thing about being on the home straight is that there's no possible advantage in remaining silent. Any day now I shall give him what for, and I shall tell her to pull herself together.' She suddenly smiled broadly. 'And they'll both take offence— who knows? It may bind them together in adversity.'

I stayed another twenty minutes or so, during which we talked about books we were reading and programmes we'd watched on television—she was a sports fanatic and Whitegates had Sky, so she was

334

able to bring me up to date on the more far-flung tennis and golf tournaments.

When I got up to go, there was still something I was dying to know.

'I hope you don't mind my asking—but what did you do?'

'About the philandering? We parted company.'

I frowned. 'But I thought you said that you and your husband—'

'No, no . . .' She struggled to her feet, chuckling, and took my arm. 'No, no, my husband wasn't Julian's father. Gerhardt was.'

CHAPTER SEVENTEEN

I was still turning over these contradictory impressions in my mind as I travelled up to London on the train the following evening. There was something both invigorating and daunting about Mrs Rymer's pragmatism, with the emphasis placed so firmly on individual responsibility. In spite of her age, hers was a surprisingly contemporary creed, which set less store by doing the right thing than by doing oneself justice. And yet I sensed in her a strong, idiosyncratic morality, and didn't envy the hapless Julian when she decided to say her piece.

I arrived at Ian's flat at seven-thirty, and Ben answered the door. He looked dreadfully thin and his hair, so often the barometer not just of fashion but of his state of mind, was cut penitentially short.

'Mum.'

My fierce, high-minded speech died in my throat. 'Hello darling.'

We kissed warily. From some point off, Ian called: 'Come on in and grab a drink, I'm at a ticklish stage!'

'What can he be doing?' I asked.

'Cooking supper. What would you like?'

'White wine would be lovely.'

The bottle stood ready opened on the table, along with Evian water, two cans of Pils and assorted glasses. Chrysanths were in a glass vase, piano music sounded softly from the CD player. The whole thing reeked of careful stage management, but I couldn't blame them for that. On the contrary, they—or more particularly Ian—had been at pains to create an environment in which it would seem churlish to behave badly.

Ben handed me my drink and poured himself an orange juice with water. I didn't comment on this abstemiousness. Ian came in from the kitchen. He was wearing a dark blue shirt similar to the one from Bath—maybe they'd bought them both at the same time.

'I hope you're hungry,' he said, kissing my cheek, 'because I've done fish pie.'

'It smells good.'

'Your recipe, Mum,' said Ben.

'Well, it's fairly bombproof.'

Ian poured himself a drink. 'It may well be, but I've got veg to synchronise so I'll leave you to it for a few minutes.'

He withdrew tactfully. Ben sat down. I studied a painting on the wall. The trouble was that deprived of my righteous anger I had nowhere to go.

'How are you?' I asked.

'Pretty shattered. I don't seem to be able to sleep. I go out like a light when I get into bed and

336

then two hours later I'm staring at the ceiling.'

'That's awful. The best thing is not to fight it. Force yourself to stay up late. If you do wake up turn the light on and read, or watch TV . . .'

'Yes, I know.' He'd obviously been told this a hundred times. 'I'll give it a go.'

I bit the bullet. 'You went to stay with Sophie?'

'For a couple of days. We were never anything but mates, you know, although no one would believe it.'

He lit a cigarette. I twiddled my glass. We were skirting round the big one.

'How much does she know?'

'All of it.'

'God . . .' I put my hand to my eyes. The bad feelings stirred inside me. I could almost taste them in my mouth. 'What must she think?'

He didn't reply. When I looked at him he was gazing at the carpet between his knees, but one heel was jiggling restlessly.

'What does she say about it?'

'She realises it's a bugger.' He rubbed his face impatiently. 'Look, can we *not* discuss this in terms of bringing shame and disgrace on the family name and what the neighbours will say?'

'I wasn't doing that!'

'You may not have said it but it's there, Mum, in your whole attitude.'

I smarted in silence. Ian came to the door. 'Not long now, everyone OK?' Neither of us replied so he had the good sense to retire.

Ben said: 'If I actually tell you what happened, will you listen?'

'Yes.'

'And will you believe me?'

337

'Of course!'

'You'll let me finish, yeah? And not keep telling me how it looks to you, or how it's going to look to everyone else?'

'All right.'

He began to crumble the blackened dead matches in the ashtray. 'You do realise you've never once asked me to tell you about it.'

'I thought I did little else! You walked out on me, remember?'

'No you didn't!' His face got whiter the more heated he became. 'I walked out because all you wanted me to do was eat shit.'

'Ben—!'

'It's true. You just stood there sounding off about how it was the end of the world and the worst thing that had ever happened—you were so bloody sorry for yourself!'

The fact that this was true didn't help. I was incensed.

'And *you* weren't prepared even for a single second to admit you'd done anything wrong. And you're still not!'

Ian entered, carrying the fish pie.

'Someone fetch the beans . . . ?' he said.

*   *   *

Supper was awful. Not the food—as Ian pointed out, he was perfectly capable of following a recipe, and the rest was common sense—but the atmosphere. Bizarrely, we steered clear of the most pressing topic while we ate. Ian, sitting behind the fish pie, tried to keep the ball of conversation in the air. Almost single-handed he covered the final

Test (he'd found a taker for Ben's ticket), news from Mel, what we might do at Christmas and whether global warming would turn Littlesea into San Tropez. It took a lot to put me off my food but tonight I couldn't do much more than push it around. Ben did a little better, but as one who was used to watching him eat I could tell it might as well have been gall and wormwood.

Thank goodness Ian had been to no further trouble. It was cheese and biscuits and fruit for afters. I declined, he said he'd have some in a minute and Ben went to fetch another cigarette and sat on the edge of the sofa with his head hanging.

Ian avoided my eye. Neutrality, it seemed, was to be his watchword. Which was fine, commendable even, so why did it get on my nerves so badly? I decided that it was because he seemed to have placed himself in the position of arbiter and referee instead of full participant.

Chiefly because I couldn't stand the thought of him bringing his chairpersonly skills to bear on our exchanges I opened the batting with Ben before his father returned from the kitchen.

'All right, I'm asking you now. I'm listening. Please tell me the whole story.'

'It's not that long. Couple of months? Nothing happened till after that party when I met Sofe. We just got on so well, and she's so bright—I can't think of a girl I ever liked that much. We liked being with each other. And suddenly her parents— well, Martin, and Sabine, seemed like regular people. You know I always had him down for a fat cat and her for an airhead, but with Sophie there they seemed all right. They were funny, their door

339

was always open, they really seemed pleased that we were friends.'

At this point, the minutes would have shown, Ian joined us with the coffee.

'I didn't always know when Sofe would be back, so I was quite often there with Sabine. We talked. And she's no airhead—well, you know that. She's really sharp and witty. Plus, she's beautiful. What can I say? She looks great, she smells wicked ... she has that walk. I began to fancy her so much it hurt. I used to get a stiffy just walking up to the house.'

Here Ian gave a small cough as he handed me my cup.

'I felt bad about it. Sort of funny and bad. I told Sofe and we laughed like drains—after all, Sabine's not her mother, there's a certain distance there. It seemed like a bit of a joke, our little secret, something perfectly containable. And it was until Sabine began to show an interest.' He stubbed out his cigarette. 'I was there one evening and Sofe and Martin went to bed early because they were going to some farmfest next day. Sabine offered me a coffee. She was looking—amazing. I was having a real problem with the whole thing, but I didn't want it to end, either. When it came time for me to go, she kissed me. Not a social kiss, on the lips. That was it: we had sex, the most incredible ...'

Ian and I sat there like a couple of Chinese fire dogs, staring at him. Though Ian, of course, must have heard all this before. My flesh crawled. The silence seemed interminable, but was probably only fifteen seconds.

'I couldn't stop then, neither of us could. It was every time I went up there, and we got less and less careful. Sophie was scared shitless in case Martin found out, and worried about him, too. But she's a very, very cool customer. She said if her dad ever suspected anything and asked her directly, I needn't expect her to lie, and I wouldn't have done. The crap thing is, I like Martin, he's a nice bloke.' He shook his head. 'Anyway, it was mad. Completely mad. I couldn't think about anything else. I still can't. And she's the same.'

I cleared my throat, but still my voice sounded husky. 'You were infatuated. You did the right thing in getting away.'

He gave a short laugh. 'I'll have to go a lot further than Yorkshire to get over this one. And I'm going to.'

'Oh?' He didn't answer, he seemed to have fallen into a reverie. I looked at Ian.

'I've found something for him with our lot in Denmark,' he said.

It took an effort after what I'd just heard, but I went and sat next to Ben and put my arm round him. 'It will be for the best, darling.'

He didn't look at me. His shoulders felt hard and hot, rigid as metal. 'Will it?'

'I know it sounds trite, but time and space are great healers. Given both you will get over it.'

'I don't want to get over it.'

'No, but—'

'I'm in love with her.'

I glanced at Ian again, who gave a don't-ask-me shrug: he'd heard all this—now it was my turn.

I played for time: 'Are you sure?'

'Yes.' His voice was almost a whisper.

'Because no one would blame you for being infatuated. She's much older than you and as you

341

say very attractive—'

'She loves me, too.'

I felt a surge of pure bile. 'She made a play for you, Ben, that's not—'

'Don't use that expression!' He glared at me. 'It's disgusting. There was no *play*, as you put it. It wasn't a game. I love Sabine and she loves me. And why do you say infatuated as if you know something that I don't? I don't know what the difference is—do you?' He turned to look at Ian. 'Do you?'

Ian pursed his lips reflectively. 'I think what we mean by infatuation is feelings that are overwhelming and obsessive, but which for all kinds of reasons don't include a real sense of partnership. Maybe they're more about gratification than giving. But I'm not making much of a fist of it . . . And of course only you know what your feelings really are. We aren't trying to hijack them.'

I thought that if I'd sounded pompous Ian—with the best of intentions—had left me for dead. But at least he'd had a go, and I was grateful for his use of 'we'—he hadn't needed to do that, and to align himself with my poorly chosen words.

'I see,' said Ben. 'Well thanks.' He didn't need to pile on the irony, we were only too well aware of it.

'What does Sabine say?' I asked.

'That she loves me.'

I don't know why, but every time he said the word 'love' it tore at me so that I had to catch my breath.

'What does she want?' asked Ian. 'I mean, how does she plan to handle this?'

'She'd like us to be together. We both would.'

'So does she plan to leave Martin?' I had to hand it to Ian—it was a necessarily brutal question, asked gently.

I thought Ben shook his head—the smallest movement imaginable but Ian asked again: 'Do you think she'll leave him?'

'No!' Ben stood up abruptly. He seemed surrounded by a shimmer of pure energy like heat haze. 'I don't know, and I bet that makes your fucking day, doesn't it?'

I tried to catch hold of his hand but he evaded me with the swift, fierce fear of a wild animal. Ian and I sat there with downcast eyes, rebuked. All three of us were completely still, but it wasn't the stillness of peace, or even of reflection. It was as if the room were full of thorns and by not moving we were avoiding pain. But the barbs were inside us too—I now knew what it meant to feel one's heart was bleeding.

Ben moved towards the door. His neck below the new haircut was thin and boyish. It was Ian who found a voice to speak for both of us.

'Ben—please don't go.'

He stopped, with his back still turned to us.

'Please,' I said. 'We love you.'

His head dropped and he made a choking sound. Clenched his fists and held them to the sides of his head. It was awful. All his typical style, grace and confidence had deserted him. He was on the rack. I found myself actually praying that he wouldn't walk out as he must feel he had every right to do—and yet to turn back would need unimaginable courage.

But that was what he did. There was even a kind of defiant pride in the way he didn't bother to hide his tears, and in deference to that pride I didn't

343

attempt to touch or comfort him as he collapsed on to a chair.

He just sat there and cried for a minute or two, big sobs, from the gut, that shook him all over. His tears splashed on to his jeans, and on to the carpet. Ian—the only man in London still to carry such a thing for practical purposes—produced a clean handkerchief and leaned forward to lay it on the sofa next to his son. And yet in spite of that dreadful weeping the thorns seemed to have retreated. I was conscious of my own breathing, and my heartbeat, as though both had been in suspension and were now resumed.

After that long couple of minutes, Ben picked up the handkerchief, mopped his eyes and blew his nose. We waited. He had come back. He was going to talk to us.

'Look,' he said, 'you're entitled to your opinion. I can't ask you to get inside my head, any more than I can get inside Sabine's. But when she told me she loved me, I believed her. I don't just want to, I do believe her.' He addressed me: 'Don't take this the wrong way, but I think I know her better than you do.'

I stifled the impulse to disagree with him, up to a point. 'Differently, anyhow.'

'No Mum—better. More completely. You don't have to list all her faults for my benefit, I know what they are, and she knows mine. The thing was we seemed to be nicer, kinder people when we were with each other. More honest, even, although I know you'll find that hard to take. We didn't have any secrets.'

'Except,' said Ian gently, 'from the rest of us. You can see that.'

'Yes. But what were we supposed to do? OK, I know, you said it before—stop. But when something feels that good, it's not so easy. When you're so happy you keep thinking there must be a way through which will make other people happy too—or at least not unhappy. So you hang on and play for time and hope for the best. And then it was taken out of our hands.'

'By me,' I said.

'Yes, but it could have been anyone. It was going to happen.'

He lit yet another cigarette. It was a measure of Ian's forbearance that he had not just allowed Ben to smoke, but even refrained from leaping up to empty the ashtray. We were walking on eggshells.

'So what now?' I asked.

'I'm going to fucking Denmark.' His tone wasn't aggressive, but weary.

I caught Ian's eye. 'It was Ben's idea,' he explained.

'But you said you didn't want to go—that you didn't want to get over it,' I said.

'I don't. But I can't ask Sabine just to walk out on Martin, either. And she wouldn't do it. We can't go on, and we can't stop. We sure as hell can't go backwards. So I'm going, and she's staying . . .'

'For how long?'

He seemed not to have heard me, but Ian replied for him: 'The initial contract's six months.'

'I think it's very brave of you,' I said.

'It's not *brave*.' He was scornful. 'We *love* each other. We want to give ourselves at least a chance of doing the right thing. Contrary to what you two seem to think it's not our intention to spread blood all over the walls.'

'I'm sorry.'

He shook his head, eyes closed. 'No—no, it's me, I'm sorry.'

'And when the six months is up?'

'She's going to write to me. She knows what I want, but if it's not going to happen she'll write and tell me.'

'And you'll accept that.'

'I doubt it.' He may have felt my quiver of apprehension, for he added, 'But I'll abide by it. If Sabine's found a way of being happy with Martin, then I'll butt out.'

I could say nothing, I was choked.

'What we don't yet know,' said Ian after a pause. 'is where Martin stands on all this, or if he even knows.'

'There's no reason why he should,' said Ben, 'unless someone's gone out of their way to tell him. As far as I'm aware it's only you two and Sophie who know about it.'

'And we certainly wouldn't have said anything,' I declared a little over-emphatically, remembering how strongly I'd been tempted.

'Then it's up to Sabine whether he finds out or not.'

I remembered something else—that I'd confided in Ronnie Chatsworth. But Ronnie, of all people, was the sort who would carry a secret to her grave.

*   *   *

I stayed about another half an hour, but after the emotional switchback we'd been on all three of us were suddenly exhausted. Conversation dried up. The Test highlights were mentioned, and that was

346

my cue.

This time when I kissed Ben goodbye, he put his arms round me as he always used to do. He knew how I felt, and he gave my back a little rub, comforting me.

'So long Mum . . . Take it easy.'

'When are you off?'

'Next week. But I'll have to come down and pick up some stuff.'

'I'll see you then.'

'Definitely.'

Ian came down with me while I found a cab. In the lift, he said: 'It was good you came. It brought things to a head.'

'I seem to have done just about everything wrong.'

'Not at all. He was always more natural with you. More himself. I think we got somewhere this evening, don't you?'

'Somewhere . . . I don't know where.'

The lift opened and we crossed the hall. Out on the pavement I spotted a cab more or less right away. The driver sat patiently as we made our farewells.

'In my opinion,' said Ian, 'for what it's worth, we must have done something right. Given the situation as is, I think Ben's behaving with astonishing maturity. He was wonderful in there.'

'Yes, he was.'

'After all, as he would say, stuff happens. That's life. But how you deal with it—that's character.'

*   *   *

I didn't go to my hotel, but to Troughtons. It was

only nine-thirty, and I was going to get the receptionist to put me through to Charles's room. I was then going to suggest we go out for a drink. I was already teetering on that dangerous emotional cusp between elation and despair, or I should never have been so daring. I was almost in a mood to cast caution to the winds. I no longer saw Charles's ignorance of my problems as a difficulty, but a blessed relief. I wanted to recapture that sweet, specific pleasure that had nothing to do with anyone else, and feel again that focus and that light touch which was for me alone and not my family, no matter how honourably they'd behaved.

I was quite light-headed with anticipation by the time I got there and made the cabbie's day by overtipping monstrously.

'Well thank *you* sweetheart,' he exclaimed with amiable chauvinism.

'Just don't expect it every time,' I replied feistily.

There was no one about in the foyer, and this time I spotted a brass bell on the table, which I tinkled cautiously. At once the pinstriped gentleman appeared, apologising profusely for not having known I was there (by telepathy, I suppose) and come sooner.

'I wonder,' I said, 'if I could speak to Mr McNally?'

'I'm very sorry madam, Mr McNally's no longer with us.'

I smiled anxiously, there was something in his turn of phrase. 'How do you mean?'

'He checked out last night.'

I felt as though I'd been doused with cold water. 'Oh. Did he say where he was going?'

'The Emirates, I believe.'

348

'I see.'

'How long for?'

'I'm afraid I have no idea.'

'Oh.' I realised I must be starting to look like some sad and desperate jiltee, but it was a little late for pride now. 'I don't suppose he left any messages . . . for anyone?'

'Not that I know of, but I shall go and check. It's Mrs Piercy, isn't it?'

'That's right.' Even this feat of memory couldn't cheer me.

'I won't keep you a moment.'

I stood rooted to the spot in the richly-carpeted hush of the hall. As before, no other people, either guests or staff, were to be seen. I was completely alone with my devastating disappointment.

Pinstripes reappeared with a quietly sympathetic expression. 'I'm sorry to have kept you waiting. No, Mrs Piercy—I'm afraid there were no messages.'

Outside in the street, for the first and last time in twenty-seven years I took off my wedding ring and put it in my bag.

*   *   *

The hotel I'd booked into was not like Troughtons. It was bright, bustling, competitively priced and handy for the southeastern railway termini. My room could have been in any similar chain in any city just about anywhere in the world. I could not, in other words, have chosen a place better calculated to deepen my sense of abandonment.

Automaton-like I went through all those little rituals intended to make oneself feel more at home. I drew the curtains, turned on the bedside

349

lamps, the television and the kettle, pulled down the bedspread, kicked off my shoes and collapsed on the bed with the prepacked Golden Oaties for company.

I finished the biscuits, but they might as well have been sawdust. The exhaustion which excitement about seeing Charles had temporarily dispelled, swept back over me, but a mangling depression wouldn't allow me to sleep. I couldn't believe that he had simply returned to the UAE without a word, when he had been so keen to see me again, when he must have known I might be in touch. There again, had I been colossally naïve? Was turning up late in the evening at the hotel of a man I barely knew really the behaviour of a mature, sensible woman? He might have been anywhere—restaurant, club, friends, the bloody *jazz* on which he was so keen—and the result would have been the same. But no, it wouldn't have been quite the same: leaving the country required decisions and forward planning, and meant an absence of several days, at least, rather than a few hours. How could he just have gone without a word? What did he think had passed between us last weekend? Had I got it quite so disastrously wrong? Hadn't he pursued me, rather than the other way round? And—and this was worst of all— was all that thoughtfulness and interest simply a front, so much well-honed American flim-flam, all in a day's work for the middle-aged bachelor with a woman in every major city? Maybe Charles McNally was, after all, just another of the poolside sharks and I merely small fry swimming foolishly into his gently smiling jaws . . .

I remembered, oh, how I remembered, that little

350

gesture of his—the way he had touched the roses, and later, my cheek. In the past few days the mere memory of that touch had been enough to light me up. It was not too much to say that it had kept me going. But now, with mauling masochism, I could picture him practising that gesture in front of a mirror . . .

At midnight I took the half-bottle of champagne from the minibar and drank it, accompanied by a packet of cashew nuts, thus ensuring that I didn't go to sleep for another two hours. This was, I reflected, the second recent occasion that I had spent in a hotel room, overwrought and the worse for drink. And on neither occasion had Charles McNally been available. Perhaps it was time I learnt something from the experience.

*   *   *

I woke again at three-thirty, dehydrated and with a throbbing head. I fetched water from the bathroom and crept back beneath the duvet.

As I stumbled back down the shallow slope into uncomfortable sleep I was vouchsafed one of those unexpected, unconnected thunderclaps of understanding. Suddenly, I knew why the word 'love' on my son's lips, had so disturbed me.

With talk of love, Ben's boyhood was finally over.

351

CHAPTER EIGHTEEN

The message on my machine was from Marian, his driver. She had a brisk, classless voice.

'Mrs Piercy, this is a message from Mr McNally. He's been called away to an emergency in the Gulf, so he'll be gone for quite a few days. He sends his best, and he'll be in touch when things are back under control.'

Like a doctor—it was me who'd said it. But surely—*surely*—he could have called himself? I didn't like the idea of being part of the conversational currency between him and Marian. I'd been relegated to something on his man-in-a-hurry list. The message simply completed my humiliation.

*　　　*　　　*

Desma called into the office mid-morning to ask about tennis on Saturday.

'Sabine can't,' she said, 'because Martin's whisking her off somewhere luxurious for the weekend, lucky for some. But Ronnie's back in circulation, and she says she'd like to play, as long as we make allowances.'

'Last time she said that and we did as she asked that she practically annihilated us,' I reminded her.

'Then we'll carry on as usual—but it'll be American anyway so it'll even out. Can you make it?'

'Yes.'

There seemed no point, now, in doing anything

352

but resuming the status quo. I had been on a white-water ride, with thrilling glimpses of passion—my own and other people's—appalling dangers, life-threatening plunges and moments of pure, breathtaking exhilaration. But now, I told myself dully, I'd returned to the safe backwater where I truly belonged.

At the door of Bouvier's, as I showed Desma out I recollected myself sufficiently to ask how Ronnie's tests had gone.

'She said they found something, but it's quite treatable apparently.'

'Found something? You mean—what did they find?'

Desma shrugged. 'That's all Ronnie said. But she sounded quite relaxed about it, and I think one has to take people at face value on these things.'

'I suppose so.'

'By the way—' Desma, with her back to the street, gave a small backward jerk of the head—'look behind me.'

The Shaws' Clio was parked, engine idling, at the kerb, with Rick at the wheel. He caught my eye and waved, giving me his shy, sweet smile. Of Bryony in the back there was no sign.

Desma widened her eyes, grinning. 'I'm being taken out to lunch at the Mill. And Bryony's at my mother's until six, so the afternoon stretches ahead.'

Her delight was infectious, and I gave her a hug that was only slightly envious. 'Have a wonderful time.'

'Don't you worry.' She looked at Rick then back, briefly, at me. 'Ain't life grand?'

353

Saturday wasn't awfully good tennis weather. It was grey and blustery with occasional brief, tetchy showers—exactly the conditions in which technical soundness came into its own. Our threesome evolved into a battle between Ronnie's accuracy, and Desma's tireless energy in retrieving it. When they were both on the same side of the net I did not much more than serve and watch the returns whistle past. I tried to be grown-up and not to keep apologising, but when we had played thirteen games and I was firmly established as the kiss of death, it began to rain more steadily and I used that as my excuse.

'Look, is it just me or is it getting rather unpleasant out here?'

'It's not and it is,' said Desma. 'Cutter without more ado? I'll go and get the car, we don't want to walk in this.'

'You are a so and so,' I told Ronnie as we zipped up rackets and jackets at the bench. 'What does it take to mar your game?'

She laughed. 'Well not a growth in the nethers, that's for sure.'

I was knocked back by this cheery admission. 'Oh Ronnie, I am sorry.'

'No, I'm only spitting it out because it's easier to do that and get it out of the way. There's every chance they can zap it. I certainly don't want it ruling my life and everyone else's.'

We began walking towards the road. 'Well, if your tennis is anything to go by . . .'

'Plenty of room for improvement. I'm going to take some coaching while the going's good.'

Every phrase made me jump. 'How do you mean?'

She nudged me. 'I mean before I start treatment in earnest and turn into a black and midnight hag incapable of tiddlywinks, never mind tennis.'

'I see.'

'Want to join me?'

'Sure, why not?' I was only too willing to be carried along by her breezy optimism. It was an entirely selfish response: Ronnie was the sane one, the sporty one, the happy, well-adjusted, settled one—she was my touchstone, and I needed her to stay that way. Anything less than a full and complete recovery was unthinkable.

At the Cutter Bar—well, it was only a matter of time—Desma all unwittingly jumped in with both feet.

'Maybe next week our style correspondent will deign to be with us once more.'

Lucky for me Ronnie was quick on her feet. 'I think now they've got that smart new set-up at Headlands she's not going to find the public courts quite so appealing. We'd probably be well advised to cast round for a Saturday morning replacement.'

'But Sabine's irreplaceable!'

'No one's that,' said Ronnie firmly. 'And anyway, we're all going to be invited up there. So we shan't be losing a player, we'll be gaining a venue.'

I looked at her gratefully. 'How well you put it.'

'It's true. Now Desma, Eve and I are going to start coaching, are you on for that?'

*   *   *

At two o'clock Dennis arrived at the Cutter, to

collect Ronnie.

'Ah, my chauffeur,' she said, taking his hand as he stood next to her. 'Are you going to join us for a drink?'

Rather to my surprise, Dennis agreed. He ordered a low alcohol beer and pulled over a chair from a neighbouring table.

'It's turned horrible out there,' he said. 'Did you manage to play at all?'

'Sort of,' replied Ronnie. 'Coarse tennis, but it was fun.'

'Where's Sabine, couldn't she make it?'

'No ...' Ronnie tapped the back of his hand. 'I told you, she and Martin have taken off for somewhere baronial in the Lakes this weekend.'

'Hell's teeth,' commented Dennis cheerfully, 'if it's anything like this up there she'll be eating the curtains by teatime.'

I wondered—unworthily, I knew—if Ronnie had passed on anything of what I'd told her, and his next remark went straight for the nerve.

'What's Ben doing with himself these days? I haven't seen him for ages.'

'You just don't go to the right clubs, Dennis,' said Desma. He laughed but he wasn't to be deflected.

'No, he usually comes round ... Still working in that shop?'

'As a matter of fact he's off to Denmark soon, to work in one of Ian's outfits for a few months.'

'That sounds like an excellent idea. He's such a personable young man, he always seems to me to be rather—what's the word—under-achieving.'

'Dennis!' said Ronnie. 'That didn't sound terribly polite.'

'I'm sorry, Eve—it was meant to be a compliment.'

'I realise that.'

Ronnie sighed reflectively. 'Much as I love them I sometimes wish our two would take off and work abroad for a bit.'

'No you don't,' said Dennis. 'Not really. You'd suffer from silent-washing-machine syndrome in no time.'

'Wanna bet?'

'And anyway—' he rose and extended his hand to her—'they're hardly like to disappear just at the moment, are they?'

When they'd left, Desma went out to the Ladies. I watched Ronnie and Dennis cross the carpark and get into their midnight blue Rover. Dennis held the passenger door open for his wife, and ducked his head inside for a moment when she was seated. I had always thought of Ronnie as the larger and more colourful of the two. Dennis was quiet, dependable, an awfully nice man but not a barrel of laughs. Today, for the first time, I noticed that he had a slow, wry smile; and in fact was taller than her.

*   *   *

With it being so overcast, and early October, it got dark early. I very soon exhausted my reduced domestic duties around the flat and saw a long evening of stir-craziness stretching ahead of me. It was hard to remember those not-so-long-ago days when this flat was my nest, the symbol of my cosy, protected independence, my retreat from the messy world of embattled relationships. Now I rattled restlessly from room to room, like the heroine of some latterday fairytale, immured in a tower of my own making. The tidy cushions seemed to resist my weight, the uncluttered kitchen had developed a slight echo. I felt alone, but watched. I couldn't settle.

In shameless desperation I called Helen.

'Well no,' she said, 'I can't, actually. Bugger.'

This was so unlike her usual weary acquiescence, that I commented on it.

'What are you doing?'

'You sound astonished.'

'No, no, not at all, it's just that—'

'It's all right, you have every right to be. My diary doesn't make exciting reading at the best of times. As a matter of fact Clive is coming round here to take me out.'

'Really?' So there was a God. I was surprised by how chuffed I was.

'I can't imagine why I agreed to it. A more pointless exercise would be hard to imagine. But he was uncharacteristically insistent.'

Without thinking I asked: 'Did you tell him about John?'

'Hardly. Come on Eve.'

'No, I suppose you wouldn't.'

'Kerridge has become a non-person, don't let's talk about him.'

'I'm sorry. So why—excuse me for asking—but why is going out with Clive so pointless?'

'Oh, I don't know ...' Her voice tailed away into something between a mumble and a sigh. ' ... I suppose I feel somewhat sheepish.'

'Why on earth should you?' I asked, though of course the question was rhetorical, for we both knew exactly why. It was just the first time that Helen had conceded it.

'Hmm ... anyway ...' She gave a small, distant cough. 'What about tomorrow?'

'Yes, that'd be nice—do you want to come for lunch?'

'If you like ... but don't go to any trouble.'

'I won't.'

In fact, the moment I put the phone down I began to wonder what I could provide for Sunday lunch which would be acceptable but appear to have cooked itself. Not that Helen, having issued her token admonition, would give another thought to how much effort had been expended. I went into the kitchen which yielded chocolate digestives, bran flakes, a pint and a half of milk and an awful lot of the sort of dry ingredients whose chief property is to be used once and then sail stolidly past their sell-by date. Given that the cupboard was bare I was going to have to go to the supermarket anyway. It was a sad admission, but I didn't mind—it would give me something to do. I would go now, this minute—the local superstore had recently turned twenty-four-hour, and I pictured a whole different nocturnal clientele, cruising the aisles for malt whisky, Mates and Marlboros before a night on the town.

In reality, there seemed to be no difference between the ten a.m. and ten p.m. crowds, even down to a surprising number of insomniac toddlers. It was a sign, I told myself, of crusty old age to find this irritating. The one person who did accord with my pre-conceptions turned out not to be a customer at all but a member of staff. For who should be officiating on the one-basket express check-out but Pearl, her breasts threatening to burst out of her aqua gingham-checked overall like a couple of leaping dolphins.

'How's Ben?' she asked as she pinged my bar-codes.

'Off to work in Denmark for a while.'

'Oh? Why's that then?' Her intuition was sound—she didn't for a moment believe he was going because he wanted to.

'He was bored with HMV,' I said, 'and this vacancy came up in his father's company.'

'Has he still got the same girlfriend?'

'She's gone back up north to go to college, so that may have something to do with it.'

She nodded. I looked for a gleam of *schadenfreude* but none was detectable. 'Give him my love.'

'I will . . .' I presented her with my loyalty card. 'And how are you?'

She swiped. 'I'm expecting a baby, end of March.'

'Pearl, that's lovely. Who—' I was about to say 'Whose is it?' but there were three people behind me in the queue. 'You look very well.'

'It's Nozz,' she said, answering the question I hadn't asked.

'He must be pleased.'

'Yeah, he's well made up about it.'

'Well many, many congratulations to both of you.' I took my change. 'I'll tell Ben when next I see him.'

'Yeah.' She began on the next batch. 'Don't forget to give him my love.'

'I won't. Bye Pearl.'

'See you.'

I digested this information on the way home. A few months, no, a few weeks ago, the idea of Pearl as parent would have seemed ludicrous. Now I had no difficulty with it whatsoever. On the contrary, seeing her sitting there, ripely content in her overall, she seemed the epitome of the fecund mother-to-be. I could easily picture her and Nozz proudly pushing their buggy along the prom outside my window.

The times, undoubtedly, were a-changing—I only wished I was changing with them.

*   *   *

I cooked a seafood lasagne for Helen and me, with a big salad, and some wicked cheese and crusty bread for afters. It had to be something good tempered, because she was notoriously unpunctual and on this occasion we hadn't set a time, so ETA could have been anything from eleven a.m. to three in the afternoon.

She turned up at one-forty-five, managing to look rather wonderful in a spinach-green tweed suit which went well with her faded auburn hair and was just unfashionable enough to be stylish. To my amazement she had also brought a bottle of wine, and a box of Black Magic.

'Bless you,' I said, putting the wine on the table and handing her a shot from the winebox, 'but you shouldn't have done.'

Not bothering to take issue with this, she took her glass to the balcony window. 'It's quite nice to be by the sea.'

'I like it,' I agreed. Having her there, knowing how unhomely her own surroundings were, rekindled some of my fondness for my own. 'Now that I'm used to it I think I might feel claustrophobic anywhere else.'

'Can we go over there afterwards?' she asked, like a child.

'Of course. When the weather's fine this is the best time of year, with the people gone.'

'"The people",' she gave a dry, staccato laugh. 'When we say the people in that way, we're always referring to everybody but us.'

'You know what I mean.'

'I know exactly what you mean.'

'Come and eat.'

We sat down at the table. As I dished out the lasagne she leaned on the table, chin in her hands, watching me with her rather vacant stare. I noticed that she was wearing the jet ring on the third finger of her right hand. I knew she wouldn't volunteer anything about her meeting with Clive, but I took the ring as a good sign.

We were on the cheese when I put myself out of my misery, and asked: 'So how did it go last night?'

'Oh . . . Yes, it was fine.'

'How was Clive?'

'He seemed very well. Very bright-eyed and fresh-faced, put me to shame.'

'He's been on this health and fitness regime.'

She grimaced. 'He didn't mention that.'

No, I thought he wouldn't—he knows his subject. 'But you had a nice evening?'

'We did. He took me to a concert in Brighton and then we went and had dinner at some eastern place, God knows what it all must have cost.'

'I'm sure that wasn't a consideration, Helen. What sort of concert was it?'

'Not classical—two clever young men and a piano, very witty and polished.'

'Sweet and Sour?'

'That was it. They were right up my alley. I actually laughed out loud on several occasions.'

She sounded mildly astonished. The evening had obviously been a big success.

'So will you see Clive again, do you think?'

'Probably. Since we live within a few miles of one another it is on the cards.'

'Good!'

She stretched out a hand to take more Port Salut. 'He gave me this ring.'

'Oh, isn't that . . .' I leaned forward to admire it. 'That really is handsome.'

'I must say I found it all rather alarming.'

'Alarming? Why?'

'He's bought me books and bath salts for so long I simply cannot imagine him in a jeweller's shop, choosing a ring.'

'Well there you are,' I said, trying unsuccessfully to keep the note of triumph out of my voice, 'he still has the power to surprise you.'

She licked her finger to pick up crumbs. 'Hmmm . . .'

*   *   *

Clive wasn't the only one with the power to surprise, as I soon found out. After we'd cleared lunch away we left Cliff Mansions and crossed the prom on to the beach. We sat about halfway down with our backs to the windbreak, and then I changed places so that Helen, who was smoking, was downwind.

'This is the sort of beach I remember from my childhood,' she remarked, eyes narrowed.

'A very British beach,' I suggested.

'And none the worse for that. I had a black woolly bathing costume that got easily waterlogged, and some canvas pumps to help cope with the stones.'

'I had some of those. But they tended to float off your feet when you were swimming.'

'They did. And a bathing hat. White rubber with a press stud.'

'Tell me about it, only mine was blue. Getting it off your head was agony, like pulling sticking plaster off the hair on your arm.'

'You know,' she said reflectively, 'my parents never swam. I don't even know whether they could or not. My brother and I learnt with the school at the local baths. And yet Mother and Father would sit there, reading and doing the crossword while we bobbed about in the waves, in all weathers, miles out of our depth . . .'

So that's where she got it from, I thought, her massive, trusting vagueness.

'Do you ever go in?' she asked suddenly.

'Yes, in the summer. Early or late in the day, when the beach isn't too crowded.'

'I wouldn't mind, some time.'

'Then you must. It's a date.'

She was in the most expansive form I'd seen her in for ages, and I dared to hope I knew the reason why. But then she said, as if she'd read my mind:

'Clive asked me to go back.'

'Oh, did he?'

'Would I think about going back, those were his exact words.'

364

'And will you?'

'I don't need to think about it.'

At long last we were getting there. I didn't prompt her. We sat side by side looking at the sea until, after a few seconds, she pushed her cigarette end into the pebbles, and said: 'It's out of the question.'

It was no surprise, I'd expected some sort of objection, even if nothing quite as emphatic. 'Why's that?'

'Because Eve it *is* ...' She began lighting up another. 'The moment is past.'

This struck me as a bit rich. 'How can you say that? Kerridge has buggered off exactly as you predicted he would, and Clive on your own admission is a new man.'

She jabbed at me two fingers clamping a cigarette. 'Exactly.'

'What?'

'He's over me, just as I'm over him.'

'I honestly don't—'

'He may not even know it yet, but it's plain as the nose on his face. He only came after me last night out of habit. He doesn't need me any more. On the contrary, it would be a retrograde step.'

I shook my head in disbelief. 'Whence all this selflessness? What do *you* want?'

'I've no idea. But not Clive. If we were to go back to each other now it would be just that—going backwards. I won't say I learned anything from Kerridge, but I have changed. And so, it turns out, has my husband.'

'But isn't that a good thing? Could you—not go back, exactly, but start afresh?'

'I think not.'

'Did you say all this to him?'

'I did.'

It had become like pulling teeth again. 'And?'

'After a little token protest, he agreed.'

'He agreed with your analysis.'

'That's what he said.'

'I see.'

I don't know why I was so disappointed, because I knew she was talking sense. I suppose I had become attached to my happy-ending scenario, and this was all so bleakly realistic. It also displayed an obduracy in Helen's character of which I'd never really taken account.

She coughed. 'Anyway, the new Clive isn't for me. He's for the lovely Catherine.'

She sounded quite matter-of-fact, but I still jumped in without thinking: 'I assure you that's not what he said—' I stopped, hideously embarrassed. But all she did, without looking at me, was raise an eyebrow. 'Helen, I'm sorry.'

'For what?'

'What will you—do you have any plans?'

'No. I'll carry on as I am for the time being. Though I could do with getting out of that bloody village.' She flashed me a sudden, lively grin. 'Maybe I'll move to the seaside.'

*   *   *

That evening Ben called and said he'd be down the following night to pick up his things.

'Is it OK if I spend the night?'

'What a question—of course it's OK.'

'Thought I'd better check. After last time.'

'But this is still your home, darling.' I thought a

366

little guiltily of the blitz I'd imposed on his room. 'Some daft bust-up doesn't change that.'

'I don't know about daft. Still, it's high time I was out of there. You need your space.'

How little he knew, I thought. My space as he called it had become a kind of solitary confinement. I was going to have to brace myself for this, the big departure.

I was sorting through the Sunday paper, weeding out the sections I wasn't interested in before taking the rest to bed with me, when I saw Ankatex mentioned in a small paragraph on the front page of the business section. Trouble at mill, apparently, was causing Ankatex shares to wobble. But the oil fire outside Karnesh in the Emirates was now being brought under control. Ankatex troubleshooter Charles McNally, within weeks of retiring from the front line, was quoted as saying it had been a tough one but not, he was happy to say, too tough. In italics at the bottom of the paragraph the paper's man in the UAE advised Ankatex investors to hold their nerve—McNally's was a famously safe pair of hands.

So he was doing what he liked best, facing the firestorm. I put the paper down and stared out at the sea. On this quiet night it was no more than a denser area of darkness between the streetlamps and the stars. If I listened really hard I could hear the faint hiss of the incoming waves as they dragged the stones beneath them on their crawl up the beach. It was strange to think that my furthest horizon marked out only a minute fraction of the distance which separated me from Charles McNally.

*   *   *

Ben was already there when I got home on Monday night at six. He called from his room as I closed the front door.

'Hi, I'm in here.'

His rucksack was in the middle of the floor, and most of his clothes were on the bed.

'Decision-making process,' he explained.

'Can you find everything?'

'Sure—it's leaving things out that's the problem.'

I came into the room and sat down on the chair. I felt shy. It was hard to recollect the easy come-and-go of our previous life together. We hadn't even exchanged a kiss.

'When do you actually leave?'

'Wednesday—afternoon flight from Heathrow.'

'Have you sorted out somewhere to live?'

'All taken care of, I'm lodging with some bloke Dad knows—low rent plus a bit of babysitting.'

That reminded me of something. 'I saw Pearl the other night, she's working in the supermarket.'

'Oh yes?' He gave me a flash of the old grin. 'How is the Pearly Put-Out?'

'She's a pregnant pearly put-out.'

He sat down on the bed. I had his complete attention, for possibly the first time in weeks. 'You're joking.'

'Not at all. And guess whose it is.'

He shook his head slowly, eyes on my face. 'I give up.'

'Nozz.'

'Nozz, the jammy bastard . . .' he breathed. 'He didn't waste much time.'

'He's very pleased, according to her.'

368

'Going to make an honest woman of her?'

'I've no idea. You'll have to ask him.'

He began picking up clothes and stuffing them into the rucksack. 'How was she, then?'

'Looking wonderful. Blooming, as you're supposed to do.'

'Happy?'

'Absolutely. But she was very insistent I give you her love.'

He gave a short laugh, and shook his head again, but there was an expression of real tenderness on his face. 'She never gives up.'

We tried to have a completely normal evening. Bacon and eggs in the kitchen, enjoyable rubbish on the TV ... But it wasn't normal and we both knew it. Cravenly, I longed to go to bed, simply to shorten this period of dread. After the *Nine o'clock News* I switched off and yawned.

'I think I might—'

'Mum, have you seen Sabine at all?'

'No.'

'Do you know how she is?'

'No, I don't. I really don't have any contact with her at all these days.'

'I just wondered if you'd heard anything.'

'No. Or at least I know they went away this weekend, to somewhere in the Lakes.'

His head was turned away. 'They both went.'

'Yes.'

'I wish I knew ...' His voice wavered, he paused, and took a breath. 'I just wish I knew how she was ... what she's feeling.'

'I can't help.'

'I realise that. But it seems mad, me sitting down here and her up there, not speaking, or touching—

or anything. Mad and fucking *wrong*.'

'It's what you decided to do,' I reminded him, trying to sound calm over rising panic. 'Space and time for her to make her decision, remember?'

There was a long silence. His leg, triggered by that jumping nerve, quivered uncontrollably.

'Yeah,' he said at last. 'I know.'

I stayed up a little longer, ostensibly clearing up the kitchen, but actually keeping an eye on him. To my relief the moment seemed to pass. He switched the TV back on and I even heard him grunt with laughter at something.

'All right,' I said, 'I'm going to bed. Don't forget to turn everything off.'

I leaned over and kissed him, and he reached his head up to kiss me back, and laid his hand on my arm for a second.

' 'Night Mum.'

I was just about to get into bed when he called from the hall: 'I'm going for a bit of a walk, shan't be long.'

'Right—oh, Ben?' I was too late, the front door closed firmly behind him.

I actually turned my bedroom light off and looked out of the window, but he failed to appear on the prom. I lay in bed in a state of red alert, my brain whirring. He hadn't gone for a walk at all, of course—he'd driven up to Headlands to lay siege to Sabine and get a beating from Martin ... or worse still they had arranged to meet in advance, they might even now be—oh God ... or worst of all, they were heading for the night ferry, and I'd never see him again—

After no more than fifteen minutes the front door opened and closed and he went into his room,

370

walking quietly so as not to wake me, as I lay there bathed in a sweat of relief and shame.

*   *   *

I'd already decided that the next morning I'd leave for work at the same time he left. That way our last farewells would be outside in the road where I'd stand less chance of disgracing myself and embarrassing him. Until that moment we kept busy, doing the usual morning things, not talking much—I kept the radio on in my bedroom and the kitchen, the familiar authoritative voices covering our tense silences.

He didn't comment on the fact that I was leaving three quarters of an hour earlier than usual. Looking at his backpack as he went down the stairs reminded me of something inconsequential.

'Won't you need a suit?'

'Might do. I'll get one over there—Dad subbed me.'

'Oh.'

The day was fine and cold. The gulls clustered on the roofs and chimney pots glittered in the sun, but it was chilly in the early morning shadow of Cliff Mansions. He loaded the backpack into the back seat of the VW and then there was nothing left to do.

'Now you take care, darling,' I said, 'and give me a ring, even if it's only to—'

'Mum ...' He enfolded me in a huge, hungry hug, his face buried in my shoulder. All I could think of was that I must try to keep my own face under control so that I didn't go to pieces completely when he let me go. But when at last he

371

did, he didn't even look at me again. He got quickly into the Beetle, twisted round to reverse, and drove off.

*   *   *

I needed some of the extra time to compose myself, so I drove east out of Littelsea on the Brighton Road and turned off to one of the clifftop vantage points. When I reached the parking area I left the car and walked past the collection of picnic tables and along the broad track to the edge of the cliff. The ground fell away slightly where the track petered out, so I didn't see the car until the last moment. It was strictly illegal to bring a vehicle this close to the cliff edge, and I was astonished to see that it was the Chatsworths' Rover. As I drew closer I could hear music swelling from it, and recognised Elgar's *Dream of Gerontius*, one of Ian's favourites.

It was as well the music was loud, and that I was on foot, otherwise Dennis might have seen me, when it was obviously his express intention to be alone. He was sitting very upright in the driver's seat, his hands resting side by side on the bottom of the steering wheel. He wore his dark three-piece suit—like me, he must have been on his way to work. But also like me his mind was elsewhere. Never had I been so conscious of a person being in a world of their own. His face was set, and pale. His eyes stared at something that only he could see. And his cheeks were wet with tears.

CHAPTER NINETEEN

In trying to escape my own unhappiness it seemed I'd stumbled on a far greater one. All day I was haunted by the memory of Dennis's face. Until that moment I'd been content to shelter beneath the wide, warm wings of Ronnie's gallantry—we all had. But Dennis was living every minute with the unremitting truth which I too could no longer escape. She was going to die.

It was quiet in the office and Jo and I went to the pub for lunch. She was one of those naturally talkative people with whom one didn't have to make an effort, but even she noticed something was amiss.

'All right Mrs Piercy—spit it out.'

'What?'

'Tell Auntie Jo all about it.'

'I'm sorry, have I been that bad?'

'You haven't been bad at all but there's obviously something on your mind.'

'Too much, really—I don't want to bore you with it.'

'And I don't want to pry—but you won't bore me.'

She was a good person to unburden to, because work was the only place we met, and all we had in common, so she had the advantage of objectivity, and I the comfort of knowing I wasn't betraying any confidences. Even so I didn't mention Ben—I wouldn't have trusted myself.

'The fact is,' I told her, 'I thought I had problems, but I've just found out that a friend of mine is going to die.'

'It's the only sure thing in life,' she said, quite seriously.

'Yes, but soon, within the foreseeable future. I've just seen her husband, and it was awful.'

'Poor lady.'

'To look at her you wouldn't know she was ill, she's one of those people who literally bounce with life—I play tennis with her.'

'People do get over the big C, you know. If it's caught early enough, and if she's a fighter, she may see it off.'

'I know, but I think in this case—I believe she hasn't got long.'

'Tricky,' said Jo in her practical way. 'Because she can be wonderfully brave, but you can only be sad.'

She had put her finger on it exactly. 'Right. It's so hard to know how to behave. I feel I've been a pretty lousy friend, completely wrapped up in my own troubles.'

Jo leaned forward. 'I bet she's glad of that. She won't want you round there with homemade cakes every five minutes.'

I had to laugh. 'Too true, any cake I made would only hasten the end.'

'On the other hand,' said Jo, 'perhaps she would like to talk about it. I mean it's one thing being brave, but it's another feeling you mustn't dump on your friends because it's not manners.'

'But how on earth—I can't imagine how to provide the opening.'

Jo opened a hand, tilted her head. 'Ask a few questions?'

'You're pointing out the obvious.'

374

'Best never to ignore it. And anyway I'm not a very subtle operator, the obvious is the only thing I see.'

'Thanks,' I said, 'I'll give it a go.'

'Let's have another.'

When she got back with two more glasses, she said: 'So that's your friend. Now what about you?'

'Oh, it's nothing, not in the same league.'

'Cheers. It may not be life and death, but if it's getting you down . . . Man trouble?'

I considered this. Was I suffering from man trouble? The phrase implied an habituation with the opposite sex that I simply did not have.

'Not really. The man in question hasn't been any trouble, exactly. Unless you count disappearing at a moment's notice.'

'Doesn't sound very convenient.'

'It's not.'

'So what's his explanation?'

'He's an oil company troubleshooter—he's in charge of putting out a fire in the Gulf.'

'I've got to say that as explanations go,' said Jo, 'that sounds like a pretty good one.'

She was right of course. Once again she'd pointed out the obvious: it was a good explanation. Charles McNally had an important job, and he'd had to go and do it, and the sensible thing for me to do was to get on with my life and wait, with a good grace.

'Thanks Jo,' I said, when it came to going-home time, 'for being the voice of commonsense.'

'Forget it,' she said, 'I'm basically a bit thick, but sometimes that helps to cut down the options.'

*　　　*　　　*

375

On the way back I went into a petrol station to top the car up. After I'd moved to the side of the forecourt to fill the screenwash I saw the Drages' Mercedes pull up. I watched in shameful fascination as Martin, in black tie, got out and stood for what seemed like ages filling up their vast tank. I could see Sabine, her face framed by a big fur collar, sitting in the passenger seat.

When he'd finished he said something to her, and went into the shop. I started to get back into the car but I wasn't quite quick enough—she'd seen me and was getting out.

I could, of course, have simply pretended not to see her, and driven away. I could have been out of there, and out of harm's way, in seconds. But for some reason I didn't. As she began to walk towards me I closed the car door and waited. She looked absolutely beautiful, like an art nouveau nymph in her narrow, pale grey furtrimmed coat and sleek short hair—beautiful and very, very thin. Fragility was not a word I had ever associated with Sabine, but tonight she looked fragile.

'Eve.'

'Hello Sabine.'

'How are you?'

'Not so bad.'

She came closer, to my side of the car, and I could smell her scent—the same one I'd smelt on Ben, a zillion years ago.

She said: 'Isn't it awful about Ronnie?'

'Yes. Hard to believe.'

'And Dennis . . . and those poor boys.' Her voice trembled, there was no doubting her sincerity.

'She wants to play tennis again,' I said. 'Just until

she starts her chemotherapy. Will you be able to join us?'

'I should like that, very much.'

There was the tiniest emphasis on the first word which prompted me to reply: 'I should, too.'

I held out my right hand, and she took it with her left. She wore silk gloves and her hand felt insubstantial and boneless, like a child's. We stood there like schoolgirls, holding hands, too full of feeling to speak.

Martin emerged from the shop, slipping his wallet into his inside breast pocket. When he found his wife wasn't in the car he looked around and spotted us.

'Eve—greetings stranger!'

He advanced on us with his big, rolling stride, beaming all over his face. We let go hands and he came between us and kissed me heartily on both cheeks. He doesn't know, I thought, and felt relief wash through me.

'It's been far too long, where've you been hiding?'

'Life's been very busy.'

'Isn't it ghastly news about Ronnie?'

'We were talking about it.'

He put his arm around Sabine. She was like a slender fern in the shelter of a great oak: he both overshadowed and protected her. She smiled out at me from his embrace but her eyes were dark.

'Sophie's started at college,' said Martin. 'Having a whale of a time. There was a moment back there in the summer when I thought you girls would be buying new hats, but the young are so damn fickle!'

'The best time for it, though,' I said.

He chuckled, jingling his keys in his pocket.

'That's right, plenty of wild oats, and when you settle down you're too exhausted for anything but fidelity, isn't that right cherry?'

'Absolutely.' She smiled. 'We'll be in touch, Eve.'

'Better hit the road.' He began steering her away.

'Are you going somewhere nice?' I asked, suddenly not wanting to let them go. 'You both look wonderfully elegant.'

'London,' said Martin. 'Boring as hell, gotta be done. Bye now!'

She looked over his guiding arm at me as they moved away—those sad eyes, a little *moue* of farewell ... I climbed into my car, but stayed to watch them go. They were talking together in the front of the Range Rover. Martin, turning the key, was laughing. Sabine raised her hands in a gesture of not-serious exasperation, then patted his cheek, directed a kiss at him. She missed, but it was still a kiss.

As they drove away my heart contracted for Ben, in his self-imposed exile. His would be a long, lonely wait. Sabine was going to do the right thing.

*   *   *

Still heartsore I went into his room when I got back. It was as he'd left it, the duvet slewed off and discarded clothes scattered about. I tidied it up, but this time it only took a moment. As I turned the light off I had the feeling something was missing. It wasn't until I was pouring myself a drink in the kitchen that I realised he'd taken Algy with him.

*   *   *

Mel rang at nine o'clock. After our last exchange the sound of her voice made my skin prickle, but this time she wasn't angry. In fact she sounded, for her, quite mellow.

'I thought you might be feeling bereft,' she said.

'Why?' I asked warily.

'Well ... the brown-eyed broth of a boy has gone, hasn't he?'

'Yes.'

'It's all right Mother, I've calmed down. He does seem to be making the right moves, even if it is a bit late in the day. Damage limitation's better than nothing.'

'Did you speak to him then?'

'He called from Dad's place. Dad probably put him up to it. I was pretty furious, as you know, I spoke my mind. But he took it like a man.'

'Yes,' I agreed. 'Dad and I feel that on balance, given all that's happened, Ben's emerged from it rather well.'

'Oh,' said Mel, 'you think he's emerged, do you? My understanding is that this sojourn *outre mer* could turn out to be only a hiatus.'

'In theory, yes. But in fact, I think it's the end of it.'

'I see. What about her?'

'Sabine? She seems to be making the best of it.'

'I'm sure she is. Struggling along with her heated pool and her domestics and her Mercedes sports. My heart bleeds.'

'Mel . . . come on.'

'Hush my mouth. What's the point anyway? I didn't ring to rake over all this stuff. I wondered if you'd looked at your newspaper lately.'

379

'You mean about the fire? Yes, I saw it by accident in the business section.'

'So you know Charles McNally's out here?'

'Yes.'

There was a pause, she seemed to be waiting for me to add something. When I didn't, she said: 'He's the hero of the hour. McNally's last stand, that kind of thing.'

'I can imagine.'

'You can imagine, but you're not really interested.'

My daughter had, as usual, succeeded in needling me where I least wished to be needled. 'No, I am interested. But I don't think he is, so I've decided as they say to let it go.'

'Why?'

I breathed deeply. 'Mel, love, I'm sure you have my welfare at heart but you force me to say this—it really is none of your business.'

'Mother dear—that's true.'

'And anyway I already told you why.'

'Because you think he's not interested?'

'He's very charming, and very kind and he paid me a gratifying amount of attention for a little while. But the fact remains that I hardly know him, and I stupidly mistook charm and kindness for something else. He'll be back in London some time and we may well run into one another, in which case—'

'You're quite wrong,' she cut in sharply. 'Or at least you're wrong now. You were right in the first place. There's a spark there for you, Mother, take it from one who knows.'

'But you don't know him that well either. Surely,' I added, because I hadn't meant it to sound

380

unkind.

'I observe these things. I keep my ear to the ground. Plus, I care about you and I wouldn't tell you something that wasn't true.'

'Oh, Mel . . .' I was remorseful.

She sighed humorously. 'Honesty—it is my cross! Now listen, while we're into plain speaking, I've a suggestion to make.'

I steeled myself for the thinly veiled order to follow. 'Go on.'

'McNally's due back here on Saturday. There'll be some kind of celebration. Why don't you get your backside out here and be part of it.'

I groaned. 'Darling, don't be *ridiculous!*'

'I'm perfectly serious. Surprise him. And yourself.'

'I couldn't.'

'Of course you could. Buy a ticket, jump on a plane, Bob's your uncle. If you're worried about the expense I can help with that.'

'Heavens, I wouldn't dream of it, but that's not the point. What I meant—'

'Oh, I know what you meant!' She was scornful. 'You mean you're chicken.'

'I mean it would be inappropriate!' I shouted. 'What on earth would he think?'

'That you like him!' she shouted back. If you upped the ante with Mel you got it back with interest. 'That you've been thinking about him! That you're not some dull, tight-arsed provincial lady but a sentient being who's not afraid to give in to a wild impulse!'

Bootless to point out that the impulse was all hers—but I did so anyhow.

'OK,' she said in a normal tone of voice, 'so I

suggested it. But this is your turn to be honest—wouldn't you like to do it?'

I was so thoroughly wound up I found it hard to know what I would like. There were still plenty of reasons for not doing it (which was not the same thing I realised) and these I began to catalogue.

'We have absolutely nothing in common, Mel. He thinks I'm this tranquil mother-earth figure which you and I know is risible, and as far as I can see he's a work-obsessed commitment-phobe who—'

'You've been watching too much *Oprah*.'

'—who likes to keep on the move, to present a moving target, to use his own words.'

'So he's not perfect. Neither on your own admission are you. So?'

'So it would never work, so I'm not going to do it, so that's that!'

When I'd put the phone down I was shaking with anger and frustration and my eyes were stinging with tears. Why did she have to be like this, my daughter whom I loved and admired, whom I spoke of so highly to other people? Why did she feel compelled, so regularly and so unerringly, to place her finger on a jumping nerve? Yet again, safe in her luxury hotel, she'd overstepped the mark—she'd lit the blue touch paper and retired, content to leave me in this sorry state: battered, bothered and bewildered.

I knew it should have been bewitched, but I wasn't admitting to that.

*   *   *

The next day was another long one. Jo was in the

Brighton office for the day, so there was no one to talk to. I was pleased when Ian called me in the afternoon to say Ben had got off safely, and to give me the address and telephone number of the family he'd be lodging with.

'Are they nice?' I asked.

'Of course they're nice! They'll probably spoil him rotten. One thing's for sure, he'll put weight on, the Danes are among the biggest eaters in Europe.'

'I miss him, Ian.'

'I know, and I also know he's not that brilliant about keeping in touch, that's why I thought you'd like the address, so you can contact him.'

'I appreciate it.'

'I spoke to Mel yesterday,' he said, in a lighter tone which at once aroused my suspicions.

'Me too.'

'She said she's invited you out there again for a break.'

Oh she said that, did she? Invite, was it? 'I'm not sure it was quite as clear cut as that.'

He ignored this. 'Are you going to? After all that's been going on it sounds like a jolly good idea. The weather will be a lot kinder than on your last visit, and it might be just what you need, a bit of sympathetic company.'

Sometimes I wondered if he knew Mel at all. 'I couldn't possibly justify the time off, or the cost.'

'You're entitled to another week, surely? And you shouldn't have any qualms about accepting her offer, she's doing well over there and I'm sure she'd like to do it. Remember we used to dream of the time when our children could support us? Well this is it!'

383

*   *   *

It was no accident, Mel talking about me to Ian. She knew how to organise a pincer movement. If I was too timid to adopt her plan, then Ian's more humdrum scenario might persuade me to do what she believed I secretly wanted. She was so transparent.

The annoying thing was that there was a picture forming in my mind, a picture I could neither banish nor ignore—a picture of what it would be like to feel around me, hot from the firestorm, the arms of Charles McNally, hero of the hour . . .

*   *   *

I pushed it aside, of course. I got home determined to reintroduce a sense of purpose into my evenings. When I'd eaten I sat down at my desk to write some letters. I needed to debrief, and regroup. On the way back I'd bought a funny, tasteless good luck card which I sent to Ben with what I hoped was a sufficiently un-heavy note inside. Rummaging for stamps, I found my first letter to Sabine—six sides of densely-scrawled lined paper, written at the height of my fury—stuffed into one of the desk's cubbyholes. It took a considerable effort of will not to reread it, but I managed it and even, for safety's sake, tore it into small pieces before dropping it in the waste paper basket. Now, I considered, was the time to write to Sabine again. I made a start, but was brought up short by the awful possibility that Martin might see the letter. I had another, better idea. I'd send a note to both of them, inviting them for supper. That way Martin would feel included, and Sabine would draw the more personal inference.

I asked them for a Saturday night in four weeks' time, and wrote an invitation to the Chatsworths as well.

*   *   *

I then turned my attention to Mrs Rymer. She'd said at my last visit how much she liked receiving things in the post. I suspected she was probably a shrewd judge of letters so I didn't try to conceal the fact that I'd been a bit down, while expressing appreciation for her making me so welcome. I would have asked her to dinner with the Drages, but she'd never have made it up Cliff Mansions' very own South Col. I said I hoped her son and daughter-in-law would resolve their problems to everyone's satisfaction, and told her I looked forward to an update when we next saw one another.

By this time I'd got the bit between my teeth. The urge to communicate was strong upon me, and yet the communication was mainly with myself. I dropped an elegant Bouvier's postcard to Clive, asking if there were any more concerts in the offing and then, in the interests of balance, wrote one to Helen as well saying that of course she'd done the right thing, and that she and I must make a point of seeing a lot more of one another.

Finally, I grasped the nettle and wrote to Mel. But whereas all the other missives had flowed, this one never found its stride. The note I wanted to strike was humble but not apologetic, affectionate but not craven—in other words, mature. I wished to explain myself, more in sorrow than in anger, and to point out how very unwise it would be to tear halfway across the world to see a man I scarcely knew on the slenderest and most fanciful of pretexts . . .

It was no good. I abandoned the letter to Mel, but left it on the desk in case genius burned any brighter the next day. The others I stamped and took into the hall.

A storm was brewing, I could hear thunder rumbling round the horizon, and a couple of seconds later the sea was lit by the pale glare of lightning. One of those second-nature domestic promptings told me it was rubbish-collection in the morning and if I didn't want to get soaked I'd better take my current batch down now.

I hauled the liner out of the swing bin and carted it into first the sitting room, then the bedroom, to empty the waste paper baskets. The thunder boomed ominously. There was a small hole in the bottom of the black bag, where the corner of a rogue orange juice carton had pierced it, but I couldn't be bothered to battle with a second one. All I had to do was get this lot down the stairs.

As I staggered down, holding the top of the bag with one hand and trying to take the strain at the bottom with the other, I reflected on the truth of the platitude 'Life goes on'. Your heart might be in shreds, your past a patchwork of make-do-and-mend and your future a howling desert, but household rubbish went on for ever.

The first handfuls of cold autumn rain were spattering down as I emerged on to the pavement. The wheelie-bins for Cliff Mansions were in a covered bay, down a ramp to the left of the front steps, an area known without affection as the Black Hole. Resting the binbag on my instep I switched on the single dusty lightbulb and hobbled to my appointed bin. With a single heave I'd be free—and I was, except that the bag finally gave up the unequal struggle and spewed forth its contents in a malodorous cascade.

Fortunately most of it landed in the bin, and by sneakily dropping the bag on top of it I could give the impression that the accident had happened in situ. A few bits and pieces were scattered at my feet and I started to collect them up, wishing I had a pair of gloves; bacon rinds, eggshells, used tissues, soggy teabags, one or two unopened wodges of junk mail, soggy with juice—and something else.

In the shadow of the bin my squeamishly questing hand struck something solid and hirsute. For a split second I thought it might be a rat, and jumped back with a little shriek. But the creature didn't move, and now I could see its bright, unfocused eyes, and its squat inanimate limbs reaching upward, not waving but drowning.

For a long moment Algy and I stared at one another. Then, without a qualm I picked up the old toy, and dropped it in the bin.

*   *   *

As I scuttled out of the Black Hole the wind got up in earnest, and hurled stinging whips of rain against the front door as it banged shut behind me. I ran all the way up the stairs. In the flat, I turned the light off in the hall, and in the living room—I wanted to see the sea.

But seeing it wasn't enough, tonight. I wanted to feel it too. Recklessly I opened the balcony doors. Even with an onshore wind the result was dramatic. A great swirling torrent of salty air poured in. The curtains billowed like sails, the room seemed small and insubstantial, a little crow's-nest of a home perched precariously on its rigging of bricks and mortar. The reverberating crash of the waves was split by a synchronised snarl of thunder and lightning.

My letter to Mel, lying abandoned on the desk, was snatched up and tossed into a corner. I didn't care—I was going to see her.

CHAPTER TWENTY

There had been several occasions in the past few months when I'd felt the spectral nudge of unfinished business, but none more so than on that flight back to the UAE. So much had happened since my last visit, it was as though that intervening period was the foreign country, and this a return, a closing of the circle. To add to this impression the plane on which I managed to get a seat on Friday afternoon was coincidentally the same Lufthansa flight on which I'd travelled before.

As we took off in drizzle from Heathrow I was strung out with tiredness. I knew I shouldn't drink, but I ordered a large gin and tonic anyway, and felt the warm buzz of the alcohol translate tension into torpor.

The jet's rise to cruising level was like a long awaited exhalation. I was on my way.

Once I'd made the decision—or had it made for me—it had been simplicity itself to put it into practice. Bouvier's were perfectly accommodating, because it was to be no more than a long weekend. Jo, with clenched fist, told me to go for it.

Sorting out my handbag I found Mrs Rymer's key zipped into the inside pocket. I opened the envelope I'd written to her and enclosed the key and letter in a jiffy bag, adding a PS. 'Why not give this to your daughter-in-law? She may know what it's for.'

After I'd posted my letters there were only three other people I contacted. One was Ian, who was far too generous to suggest I was taking his advice.

'I'm so glad—but why just a few days? You'll scarcely be over the jetlag.'

'That's all I need, a jolt to the system.'

'It'll be that all right! Mel probably won't let you leave that soon.'

'Oh—she will. If Ben calls, give him my love and say I'll be back on Tuesday if he wants to reverse the charges.'

'I'll tell him your movements. As to calls, if he wants to make them he's going to have to bankroll them.'

Good old Ian, getting the balance right.

I faxed Mel at the Miramar to say I was coming and to give her the flight number. This was dealing with her on her own businesslike terms. I had neither expected nor received any response, but I anticipated she'd be there at the gate to meet me.

Thirdly, and with a choking sense of occasion, I

had called on Ronnie.

Beginning with the safe stuff, I told her I couldn't make tennis, and why, but added that Sabine was available.

'You've spoken to her yourself?'

'I can't take any credit for that—I bumped into them at a petrol station.'

'And what—you made it up, right there by the self-service pumps?'

'By the air and water, actually.'

We were sitting on the windowseat in the conservatory with a glass of wine, and she patted me on the back. 'Well done you. It can't have been easy for either of you.'

There followed a silence—the first uncomfortable silence I'd ever experienced in Ronnie's company. She didn't seem to find it so: she was looking extremely pretty, with make-up on and hair newly done, a brilliant green-and-blue silk scarf. But now I saw that under the soft folds of the scarf her neck and shoulders were parlously thin, and that the make-up and hairdo were concealment. The old in-the-pink Ronnie hadn't cared a fig because she hadn't needed to.

'Actually,' I said, 'we owed our moment of truth to you.'

'Me? How for goodness' sake?'

'We were saying how sorry we were about you being ill.'

'Oh ...' She gave an appreciative, self-deprecating laugh. 'You mean there's always someone worse off than yourself.'

'That's right.'

'So it's an ill wind, then—to pile cliché on cliché.'

'How's it going?' I asked.

'God, Eve, you don't really want to know—' She looked me straight in the eye and I could see in her own a shockingly untypical fear. 'Do you?'

'I wouldn't have asked otherwise.'

'Well, since you ask—it's the boys. Oh dear ... it's the boys.' Her mouth contorted, and she covered it with one hand, her brows drawn together.

'I'm so sorry.'

What could I say? But she got a grip, and went on as though I hadn't spoken. 'Dennis too, of course, but somehow one feels—I feel—that he will be all right. He knows the score, he's coming to terms with it ... But they're so determined that I'm going to get better, and if I don't then it's some sort of communal failure. Simon's angry and rude, and Philip's in danger of becoming a martyr to helpfulness. They're embarrassed, really.' She gave a rueful little laugh. 'They don't want or need this obligation to feel unhappy. They want to get on with their lives without feeling guilty about it. Like me, they want this bloody illness to get off their case.'

'But they love you,' I said, 'and you can't protect them from their sadness.'

'I know.' She shook her head. 'I know that. I just wish it could be a year ago, Eve, when they could be obnoxious and I could tear them off a strip without questions in the House.'

'But you think Dennis is coping?'

'More than that.' Her face softened into what could only be described as an expression of pure love. 'He's being a complete star. It's not easy—I'm not easy—and it's going to get worse, but he never

391

puts a foot wrong. It sounds an awful thing to say, but I never knew he had it in him.'

'Good for him,' I said. I remembered the car on the cliff, the music, the look on Dennis's face ... He had it in him all right, it was growing in him just as it was in her. Only his pain wouldn't end with her death.

'At the risk of sounding saccharine,' said Ronnie, 'all this has taught me to appreciate what I've got.'

'I'm sure.'

She began to weep. 'In the unlikely event that they discover a cure in the next six months, I shall never, ever again, take my husband for granted.'

*   *   *

So we had talked, and it had been a relief for both of us. It seemed that a little of the responsibility for courage had been passed to me, and a little of the need for mourning passed to her. Dennis got home just as I was leaving and I'd been able to offer help with lifts to and from the hospital. I couldn't have said that this particular trouble shared was halved—how could it be?—but at least Ronnie had allowed me to stand alongside her for a moment and stare it squarely in the face, and neither of us had gone to pieces.

*   *   *

There had been one more thing. As I made a final check of the kitchen before leaving I took the A A Milne postcard from the noticeboard and put it in my bag. Somewhere over Austria I took it out, tore it into several pieces and stuffed it deep in the pocket of the seat in front for the cabin staff to deal with.

*   *   *

Considering how poorly I'd been sleeping lately the last thing I expected was to drop off in the cramped conditions of an international flight. But when the supper trays had been removed and we were droning miles up over southern Europe I did sleep, deep and sound, like a child.

At Bahrain, only an hour from our destination, we refuelled, and we were allowed to stretch our legs in the transit lounge. In the minute chink of air between the aircraft and the terminal's air conditioning I felt the thumping body blow of desert heat for which nothing—even past experience—could quite prepare you. I went to the cloakroom to wash and smarten myself up. I wanted to greet Mel firing on all cylinders, a woman who'd made her own decision for her own reasons.

On the last leg of the flight the man sitting next to me, who had been mercifully quiet so far, asked me politely about my journey. I told him I was going to visit my daughter.

'Is she with one of the oil companies?'

'Ankatex.'

'Ankatex, really? They've been having a somewhat torrid time recently,' he remarked. 'But I gather they're back from the brink.'

As I watched the first thin strands of man-made light threading the interminable darkness below I thought: and the brink is where I'm heading.

393

Mel was in pole position at the barrier, the first person I saw as I came through. She looked trim and cool in a white sleeveless shirt, khaki shorts and spotless white deck shoes. I noticed she'd grown her hair and was wearing it in a French plait.

As expected she never mentioned our fight on the phone.

'Hi,' she said, 'good old Lufthansa, bang on time.'

We exchanged our usual collected kiss, and she took charge of my trolley. As we went out into the carpark I instinctively fanned my face with my hand and she gave me a mischievous look.

'Better than last time, surely?'

'You forget. It's autumn back home.'

She had the use of one of the Ankatex cars, a white Japanese jeep which she drove with go-to-hell competence. As we roared down the tree-lined fast lane into the city, men with gold jewellery in gas-gobbling Cadillacs and black-swathed ladies at the wheels of BMW convertibles moved aside for her, and I didn't blame them. Only occasionally did she lift a single arrogant finger in acknowledgement.

When the city limits had reduced our speed a little I asked:

'What time does Charles arrive?'

'Tomorrow, early morning. I've arranged for you to meet him.'

'You've arranged . . . ?' My stomach turned over. 'Is that such a good idea?'

'I think it's inspired, but then I would wouldn't I.'

'How early?'

'Mm—seven a.m.'

I'd somehow imagined it would be the evening, a chance to get my head together, to look my best, to prepare.

'So what time do we need to leave?'

'You'll need to be on the road by six-fifteen.'

I realised I'd made an idiotic assumption. 'Where will you be?'

'In bed I hope. We're going wadi-bashing later on. Tomorrow's my only day off.'

My head was spinning, but I did my best to carry on regardless. 'So I should order a cab—or something—tonight?'

Her eyes on the road, she laid a cool hand on my forearm. 'Panic not. It's all taken care of. You can go in with Charles's driver.'

'Marian?'

'Who's she?'

'Nothing.'

'His name's Yussif. He's like Omar Sharif on speed and without the funny teeth.' She slid me a wicked look. 'Who knows? You may forget all about Charles McNally and never be seen again.'

*   *   *

The cool, marbled hall of the Miramar, with its palms, mirrors and splashy fountain was as I remembered. The girls on the reception desk greeted me like the second coming, but Mel was brisk.

'No playtime for my mother tonight,' she told them, heading for the lift. 'She's got an early start.'

'You're in with me this time,' she told me on the

way up. She had moved to a higher floor since I was there last, but the room was identical. It was immaculately tidy, except for Mel's work clothes sprawled on one of the twin beds.

'Carry on and use the bathroom,' she said. 'I'm just going to have a last one with the others in the American Bar. Don't forget to book a wake-up call—Yussif'll be at the front door from six.'

Beyond the huge plate glass windows a complex three-dimensional spider web of lights fanned out, and I recognised the constellations of tankers out beyond the breakwater. Here, too, I overlooked the sea, but it was a very different element from the fretful waves of Sussex. This sea was hot, motionless, thickly saline, glistening like a pool of oil in the moonlight.

I unpacked, had a bath and put out my clothes for the morning. Then I got into bed, leaving Mel's bedside lamp on so she'd be able to see to get undressed. I wished now that I hadn't slept for so long on the plane. My watch, adjusted to local time, told me that I had not much more than five hours before I had to get up again, but my body, still marching to a different drum, couldn't relax.

I was still awake when Mel got back. I listened to her cleaning her teeth, having a pee, removing her make-up. Then she turned off the bathroom light, undressed and slipped into the other bed. She must have been reading, for the lamp remained on, and suddenly she asked:

'Are you awake?'

'I'm afraid so.' I turned over. 'I'm still in a different zone.'

'And nervous?'

'Terrified.' At this time in the morning, with

both of us in our shiny, bare-eyed night-time faces, there seemed no point in maintaining my bold front. She'd undone the French plait and her hair was pulled back in a scrunchy. She looked exactly as she had at twelve years old. Without make-up the old looked older but the young, unfairly, younger.

She put her book on the bedside table and lay down on her side, facing me. There was an intimacy in her attitude, a willingness to share confidences, like two schoolgirls on a sleep-over.

'I'm proud of you,' she said.

'I hope it's going to be all right.'

'It will be.'

'He's not going to think it's the most diabolical liberty—turning up in his car?'

She shook with laughter. 'It's a diabolical liberty turning up at all. That's the whole point. You might as well be hung for a sheep.'

'I suppose so.'

We stared at each other in silence, then she said: 'You're mad about him aren't you?'

'I'm certainly mad ... And he's at least partly responsible.'

'You have good taste, Mother. He's the business.'

'Is he? It's not just me?'

'Oh no ...' She reached behind her to switch off the light. 'Don't worry. It's not just you.'

As I lay in the dark, listening to my dear daughter go to sleep I tried unsuccessfully to banish from my mind what I'd seen in her face, just before the light went out.

You could protect your children, it seemed, from everything but yourself.

I was awake before the alarm call came through, and mindful of Mel's lie-in stifled it on the first ring. She lay flat on her back with her arms above her head. I remembered the position from childhood—she was surely the only person who could fall asleep like that without her mouth dropping open.

She didn't stir as I washed, dressed and put my make-up on. But as I opened the door to leave, she murmured: 'Good luck.'

*   *   *

Yussif was waiting for me in the foyer. He wore an elegant pearl-grey suit, soft black shoes, a shirt so white it was almost blue, and a burgundy silk tie. He was leaning on the reception desk talking to the girls but the moment I stepped out of the lift he straightened up and fixed me with a hooded gaze which managed to be both respectful and haughty.

'Mrs Piercy?'

'Yes.'

'Please come this way.'

I followed as he stalked to the door and held it open for me. He wasn't much taller than me, but his bearing and his hawkish features made him seem immense. I was glad I was wearing my long blue dress, and that I'd wrapped my silk throw round my shoulders against the cool of early morning: it made me feel more dignified, a little less foolishly western.

A white Rolls-Royce waited outside. As I got into the back seat, I wondered what on earth Yussif made of the unorthodox arrangement which had been foisted on him by my daughter.

We glided down the ramp from the hotel entrance and out on to the highway. There was a stream of traffic coming the other way, but heading out of town we were able to pick up speed. I thought we might perhaps have been doing seventy, but when I leaned forward for a glimpse of the speedometer we were brushing a hundred: a parallel universe.

As we began to leave the city behind, Yussif said: 'Mrs Piercy, is the temperature comfortable for you?'

'Perfect, thank you.'

'Please let me know if you wish any adjustments.'

'I will—thank you.'

He glanced at me in the driving mirror. 'Would you care for some music?'

I remembered the dire janglings and moanings of what Mel and her friends referred to as wadi-pop. But any assertiveness wilted before Yussif's magnificent dignity.

'I don't mind.'

He pressed a button, raised a long, brown finger to his lips. 'I play soft.'

The car filled with Mozart.

It may have been the wonderful car, the music, Yussif himself, or my own light-headed sense of adventure, but it was another fifteen minutes before I realised we were heading not back along the coast road to the airport, but into the desert. The road surface had deteriorated and even the Rolls bounced a little through the sandy potholes. A dense red sun with edges sharp as a coin was crawling up the sky and on either side stretched a sea of crested and rippled dunes, pale gold shot with pink and interleaved with dense black shadows.

I leaned forward, and at once the music was turned down.

'No, I like it—I just wondered, we're not going to the airport?'

He shook his head. 'Ankatex airstrip. Not far now.'

'Oh.' I sat back. After a moment's silence in deference to anything I might want to add, Mozart returned.

A few minutes later we turned off the bumpy road on to an even worse one. The outlook on my side was now marred by a cluster of ugly low-rise buildings, but from the other window the view, lit by the rising sun, was breathtaking. The far off towers of the city shimmered on the horizon like the rigging of a ghostly armada on this rolling desert sea.

The Rolls purred to a halt. We'd circumnavigated the ugly buildings so that they were now behind and to the left of us. In front, a landing strip cut straight as an arrow into the dunes to the east. Already the air above the ground was beginning to tremble in the heat. Tendrils of fine sand curled and pirouetted across the tarmac.

In the far north west a plume of dark cloud stained the early morning sky. Now that we had stopped I could see a sprinkling of minute carbonised particles, like black snow, on the windscreen of the car.

I laid my hand on the door, but Yussif turned, raising an admonitory finger.

'Mrs Piercy—too hot. Please wait in the car.'

He must have noticed my disappointment, for his expression softened slightly, and he ducked his head forward, pointing upward. 'Look, you can see.'

I leaned between the two seats. A small plane with the red and blue Ankatex logo was making its descent from due north, its wings rocking slightly on the thermals as it came down. As we watched the undercarriage came down like the legs of a stooping hawk. The sky was so bright that my eyes watered. Yussif turned off the music and now I could hear, through the car's air conditioning, the sharp drone of the aircraft engine, and see the sand swirl as it came into land.

'Now, Mrs Piercy—get out if you would like.'

*   *   *

I wasn't the only person there, but I might as well have been. I know there was a man in overalls running to the cockpit of the plane, and two more at the entrance to the building. There was the pilot. There was Yussif, waiting by the car.

But I was alone. And when he came down the small flight of steps, so was he. He didn't look as I'd naïvely expected—blackened, stooped, battle-weary—but cool and urbane in a short-sleeved shirt and tie. I remembered his remark about it taking spirit to look good ... He carried, of all things, a briefcase in one hand, his flight bag and jacket slung over his shoulder.

He saw me, and recognised me, at once. I knew it just from the angle of his head as he paused at the foot of the steps. The heat, growing more intense by the moment, seemed to hold and protect us in its fierce grasp. The distance between us made light of the differences of my imagination.

401

The miles of desert gave us privacy.

Slowly, he put down his bags, and dropped his jacket on top of them. It slid to the ground but he didn't notice. As he began to walk towards me he stretched out his hand, palm uppermost.

I took a step, and reached the brink—
Another, and I took the plunge—
Ah—!